A WORLD OF FICTION

TWENTY TIMELESS SHORT STORIES

Sybil Marcus
English Language Program
University of California,
Berkeley Extension

Longman

A World of Fiction: Twenty Timeless Short Stories

Text and photo credits: Credits appear on pages 285–287.

A publication of World Language Division
Editorial director: Joanne Dresner
Acquisitions editor: Allen Ascher
Development editor: Françoise Leffler
Production editor: Liza Pleva
Text design: The Wheetley Company, Inc.
Text design adaptation: Circa 86
Cover design: Curt Belshe
Cover art: Marc Chagall, *Paris Through the Window (Paris par la fenêtre),* 1913, Solomon R.
Guggenheim Museum, New York, Gift, Solomon R. Guggenheim, 1937, Photograph by
David Heald © The Solomon R. Guggenheim Foundation, New York.

Library of Congress Cataloging in Publication Data

Marcus, Sybil.
    A world of fiction : 20 timeless short stories / by Sybil Marcus.
        p.   cm.
    ISBN 0-201-82520-1 (pbk.)
    1. English language--Textbooks for foreign speakers.   2. Manners
and customs--Fiction.   3. Short stories.   I. Title.
PE1128.M3365   1995
428.6'4--dc20
                                                                94-31206
                                                                CIP

7 8 9 10–CRS–00

To my Mother, who believed in me,
and
to Ron and Daniel, whose loving support made it all possible.

CONTENTS

Loneliness and Alienation

Social Change and Injustice

PREFACE

This book arises from the conviction that close scrutiny of a fine literary text is in itself a richly satisfying and fruitful endeavor as the story's embedded meanings yield to an ever deeper probing by the reader. To facilitate the in-depth discussion that flows from any profound story, I encourage my students to think of themselves as archaeologists, whose aim is to dig out the buried meanings in the text. In the process, I believe advanced students of language will also sharpen their reading, comprehension, oral, grammar, and writing skills in an integrated, sophisticated, and enjoyable manner. Even the shyest and most tongue-tied students quickly grasp that since there are few absolute rights or wrongs when it comes to analyzing a layered story, they may speak out without embarrassment and share their interpretations with the class. In addition, the ensuing discussion can enhance intercultural sensitivity and awareness that there are universal truths and sentiments that bind us all.

A World of Fiction presents twenty unabridged short stories, many of which are recognized masterpieces in the genre, and all of which were originally written in English. The stories embrace a variety of themes, literary and linguistic styles, and time frames. They are rich in vocabulary, idioms, and imagery, and their subjects stimulate student exchange and debate. Above all, they embody for me the essence of great short stories in which the authors, to quote Nobel Prize Laureate, Nadine Gordimer, successfully manage to "express from a situation in the exterior and interior world the life-giving drop—sweat, tear, semen, saliva—that will spread intensity on the page."

The stories in this anthology are divided loosely into four thematic categories: Husbands, Wives, and Lovers; Parent and Child; Loneliness and Alienation; and Social Change and Injustice. These divisions are inevitably arbitrary since most stories easily straddle more than one category. Each story is classified, therefore, according to its dominant theme. I have graded the stories, starting each section with an accessible piece by virtue of its length or content, and working up to stories of greater thematic and/or stylistic complexity. In three of the sections humorous stories help lighten the overall seriousness. Over the years I have successfully used this method, as well as these particular short stories, with my advanced students from multiple cultures.

An underlying premise of my approach both in the classroom and in this book is that students must read each story twice at home, making full use of the glossary as they familiarize themselves with the plot and theme(s). After the first reading they are equipped to discuss the intricacies of the plot, while after the second reading they are poised to discover the interior thematic connections in the story. Once they have explored the issues of plot and theme, they move on to an examination of the particular stylistic elements that distinguish the story. After this, their work as literary critics is done, and they are free to express their judgments on the characters and their actions, as well as to ponder the larger issues through their individual cultural prisms.

Following this analytical process, the transition to the study of grammatical structures and vocabulary items inherent in the story is a smooth one since students generally find it easier to absorb and implement grammatical and lexical items that they are familiar with in context. Finally, as a result of their immersion in literature and language, students are ready to write essays in which they integrate what they have learned.

HOW TO USE THIS BOOK

Each chapter in this anthology is based on a complete short story and is divided into four sections that call upon the diverse language and literary skills of the student.

PART 1: FIRST READING

A. Thinking about the Story

At this point students are encouraged to express their visceral responses to the story. The aim is to stimulate an immediate and personal reaction in which the student can relate to a character or situation.

B. Understanding the Plot

Questions in this section lead students through the story in chronological order, eliciting their understanding of its characters, action, setting, and time frame. Students who experience any difficulties with the story during their first reading may find it helpful to turn to the plot questions in midreading to aid their comprehension. This section may be completed either orally or in writing, depending on the needs of the class.

PART 2: SECOND READING

The questions in Part 2 should be answered orally since students benefit from sharing their thoughts and perspectives in a spirited interchange. In some cases small group discussions may be more apt, while at other times the fertilizing effects of a cross-cultural class discussion can generate excitement and insights.

A. Exploring Themes

Before embarking on a second reading of the story, students are given guidelines regarding key aspects of language and theme to look for, so that by the end of this reading they are ready to tackle the more demanding and substantive questions on theme and style.

B. Analyzing the Author's Style

This section concentrates on the more specialized stylistic elements of the story, such as metaphor, simile, symbol, personification, and alliteration. Students are required to analyze the way in which the author manipulates language to underscore themes and create linguistic richness. Before tackling the questions in this section, students should familiarize themselves with the definitions contained in the Explanation of Literary Terms that begin on page 273, which has illustrative examples culled from the stories in this anthology.

C. Judging for Yourself

The questions in this section enable students to adopt a more flexible approach to the text and to move beyond the limits of the story. Students may be encouraged to conjecture on events that have not been spelled out or to judge the wisdom of a character's actions. Sometimes they are asked to reflect on possible solutions to problems raised in the story or to propose resolutions of crises.

D. Making Connections

This is an opportunity to exploit the cross-cultural, multiethnic components of a class as students are asked to share their views on the controversial actions or standpoints raised in the story, using their own cultural and societal values as a touchstone.

E. Debate

A debate culminates the oral section. By this stage students should have acquired the necessary vocabulary and command of English to enable them to present their oral arguments cogently and confidently.

HOW TO CONDUCT A DEBATE

A debate is conducted around a proposal of a controversial nature. There are two teams made up of two to three people per side. One side will argue as strongly as it can for the proposal, while the other side will try to present equally compelling arguments against it. The goal of each side is to persuade the audience (the rest of the class) of the superiority of its arguments. It is helpful to have a moderator to ensure that the debate progresses in an orderly fashion. Debates follow a special order: The first member of the team supporting the proposal opens the debate. Then he or she is followed by the first member of the opposing side. Team members continue to alternate until everybody has had a chance to speak. Then it is the audience's turn. Members of the audience should offer their own comments on what they have heard. When everyone has finished speaking, the final summing up begins. This is done by the opening debater on each side, who tries to incorporate the points that favor the team's arguments. Finally, the audience votes to see which team has won by virtue of its stronger presentation.

PART 3: FOCUS ON LANGUAGE

In most chapters this section offers students a chance to review and practice a particular grammatical aspect that is well illustrated in the story. Structures covered include gerunds, present participles, main and subordinate clauses, tenses, prepositions, prefixes, and suffixes. In addition to the grammar areas, every chapter has a Building Vocabulary Skills section to help students expand their vocabulary. The accompanying exercises have been varied as much as possible to engage the students and discourage any element of rote.

PART 4: WRITING ACTIVITIES

By the time students arrive at this section, they have carefully considered the story and its related topics and have also acquired a more complete vocabulary and concentrated on some grammar. They are now equipped to tackle the writing assignments, which range from paragraphs to complete essays. Guidelines help them structure their writing. Wherever feasible, one question encourages students to incorporate the language skills they have just practiced, thus reinforcing their learning in a different way. Another question is designed to get students to explore a literary work, movie, painting, or even an opera that they are familiar with and that in some way duplicates the theme of the story under discussion. Finally, students are sometimes asked to make connections between stories in the anthology, offering them a chance to refine further their practice in comparison and contrast.

ACKNOWLEDGMENTS

I am deeply grateful to the following people whose help has been invaluable to me while writing this book.

Ellen Rosenfield, who some years ago agreed to my request to teach an intensive literature class for advanced students and who has constantly offered me support, constructive criticism, and encouragement in my teaching and writing endeavors.

Elizabeth Schulz, my typist, without whom this book would not have been completed, and whose skill, cheerful companionship, and prudent editing suggestions were a source of much needed strength to me.

Nancy Perry, whose scrupulously minute editing of my manuscript forced me to face squarely its weaknesses and try to make it better.

Francoise Leffler, who oversaw the production of the book with unfailing competence and calm.

Ruth Finnerty, whose eagle eye scoured the manuscript at the last minute and who devoted time and energy beyond the call of duty to this task.

My colleagues, Kathleen Berry, Nick Crump, Steve Hayes-Pollard, Jim Seger, and Mertis Shekeloff, who generously gave of their time to review my manuscript and whose incisive comments and suggestions were enormously helpful to me.

Nyla Marnay and Sile Convery, who as academic coordinators in the English Language Program at the University of California, Berkeley Extension, smoothed my path administratively in every possible way.

My students, who never fail to excite me with their enthusiasm and insights.

My husband Ron Berman and my son Daniel, who took over the thankless task of taking dictation when my arms failed me.

My sister-in-law, Ellen Berman, whose generosity in providing my family with a computer at a critical moment, helped save the day.

My editor, Allen Ascher, to whom above all I owe a debt of gratitude for taking my inchoate proposal and helping me mold it into a book, and for seeing me through every stage of this project with warmth, good humor, and wise counsel.

HUSBANDS, WIVES, AND LOVERS

◆◆◆◆◆◆◆◆◆◆◆◆◆◆◆◆◆◆◆◆◆◆◆◆◆

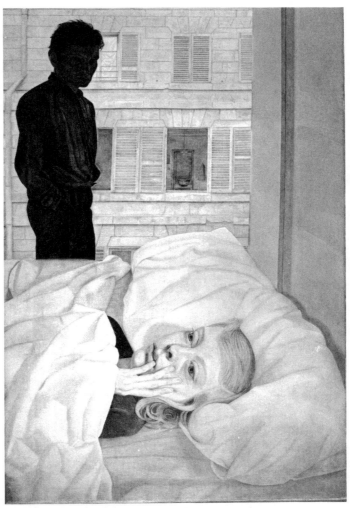

Lucian Freud, *Hotel Bedroom*, 1954

◆◆◆◆◆◆◆◆◆◆◆◆◆◆◆◆◆◆◆◆◆◆◆◆

Can-Can

ARTURO VIVANTE *(b. 1923)*

◆◆◆

BORN IN ITALY, Arturo Vivante studied medicine in Rome and practiced there for eight years. He now lives in the United States where he has been a full-time writer for over thirty years. He has published two novels, *A Goodly Babe* (1951) and *Doctor Giovanni* (1969), as well as several volumes of short stories, such as *The French Girls of Killini* (1967) and *Run to the Waterfall* (1979), an autobiographical account of a half-Jewish family in Italy before and after World War II. Other works include *Writing Fiction* (1979), *Essays on Art and Ontology* (1980), and *Tales of Arturo Vivante* (1990). He has also translated into English the poems of Giacomo Leopardi, Italy's famous nineteenth-century lyric poet. Vivante is quoted as saying, "I write to know the mystery that even a small matter holds."

CAN-CAN

A husband arranges a secret meeting with a woman and is surprised by the outcome.

I'm going to go for a drive," he said to his wife. "I'll be back in an hour or two."

He didn't often leave the house for more than the few minutes it took him to go to the post office or to a store, but spent his time hanging around,[1] doing odds jobs—Mr. Fix-it, his wife called him—and also, though not nearly enough of it, painting—which he made his living[2] from.

"All right," his wife said brightly, as though he were doing her a favor. As a matter of fact, she didn't really like him to leave; she felt safer with him at home, and he helped look after the children, especially the baby.

"You're glad to be rid of[3] me, aren't you?" he said.

"Uh-huh," she said with a smile that suddenly made her look very pretty—someone to be missed.

She didn't ask him where he was going for his drive. She wasn't the least bit inquisitive, though jealous she was in silent, subtle[4] ways.

As he put his coat on, he watched her. She was in the living room with their elder daughter. "Do the can-can, mother," the child said, at which she held up her skirt and did the can-can, kicking her legs up high in his direction.

He wasn't simply going out for a drive, as he had said, but going to a café, to meet Sarah, whom his wife knew but did not suspect, and with her go to a house on a lake his wife knew nothing about—a summer cottage to which he had the key.

"Well, goodbye," he said.

"Bye," she called back, still dancing.

This wasn't the way a husband expected his wife—whom he was about to leave at home to go to another woman—to behave at all, he thought. He expected her to be sewing or washing, not doing the can-can, for God's sake. Yes, doing something uninteresting and unattractive, like darning[5] children's clothes. She had no stockings on, no shoes, and her legs looked very white and smooth, secret, as though he had never touched them or come near them. Her feet, swinging up and down high in the air, seemed to be nodding to him. She held her skirt bunched up,[6] attractively. Why was she doing that of all times *now?* He lingered.[7] Her eyes had mockery[8] in

---

1. **hanging around** not having anything specific to do	5. **darning** sewing a tear in material
2. **made his living** earned enough money to live on	6. **bunched up** gathered into folds
3. **be rid of** be free of	7. **lingered** stayed behind
4. **subtle** not obvious	8. **mockery** making fun of (negatively)

Margin line numbers: 5, 10, 15, 20, 25, 30

them, and she laughed. The child laughed with her as she danced. She was still dancing as he left the house.

He thought of the difficulties he had had arranging this *rendezvous*[9]— going out to a call box; phoning Sarah at her office (she was married, too); her being out; his calling her again; the busy signal; the coin falling out of sight, his opening the door of the phone box in order to retrieve it; at last getting her on the line; her asking him to call again next week, finally setting a date.

Waiting for her at the café, he surprised himself hoping that she wouldn't come. The appointment was at three. It was now ten past. Well, she was often late. He looked at the clock, and at the picture window for her car. A car like hers, and yet not hers—no luggage rack on it. The smooth hardtop gave him a peculiar pleasure. Why? It was 3:15 now. Perhaps she wouldn't come. No, if she was going to come at all, this was the most likely time for her to arrive. Twenty past. Ah, now there was some hope. Hope? How strange he should be hoping for her absence. Why had he made the appointment if he was hoping she would miss it? He didn't know why, but simpler, simpler if she didn't come. Because all he wanted now was to smoke that cigarette, drink that cup of coffee for the sake of them, and not to give himself something to do. And he wished he could go for a drive, free and easy,[10] as he had said he would. But he waited, and at 3:30 she arrived. "I had almost given up hope," he said.

They drove to the house on the lake. As he held her in his arms he couldn't think of her; for the life of him[11] he couldn't.

"What are you thinking about?" she said afterwards, sensing his detachment.[12]

For a moment he didn't answer, then he said, "You really want to know what I was thinking of?"

"Yes," she said, a little anxiously.

He suppressed[13] a laugh, as though what he was going to tell her was too absurd or silly. "I was thinking of someone doing the can-can."

"Oh," she said, reassured. "For a moment I was afraid you were thinking of your wife."◆

---

9. **rendezvous** meeting at a special time and place
10. **free and easy** with a clear conscience
11. **for the life of him** as if his life depended on it
12. **detachment** indifference, uninvolvement
13. **suppressed** restrained, held back

PART ◆1◆ **FIRST READING**

A. Thinking about the Story

Now that you've read "Can-Can," consider how you would feel if your spouse cheated on you. Do you sympathize with any of the characters—the husband, the wife, or the mistress?

B. Understanding the Plot

1. What is the can-can?
2. What does the husband do for a living?
3. Is he a hard worker?
4. Whom is the husband going to meet?
5. Does the wife suspect her husband of adultery?
6. Why was it so difficult for the husband and Sarah to arrange a meeting?
7. What is the husband's state of mind as he sits waiting for his lover?
8. What happened when the husband and his lover reached their rendezvous?
9. What was the husband's lover concerned about?
10. Is she reassured by his answer to her question?

PART ◆2◆ **SECOND READING**

A. Exploring Themes

You are now ready to reread "Can-Can." Try to understand why the characters act as they do and what thoughts about life Arturo Vivante is attempting to convey in the story. Look carefully at the way he uses language to express his ideas.

1. What is the significance of the can-can in the story?
2. Does the wife do the can-can for her child or her husband? Explain your answer.
3. What effect does the dance have on her husband?
4. What do the couple expect from each other in marriage? Does each fulfill the other's expectations?

B. Analyzing the Author's Style

Before you begin to work on this section, turn to the detailed explanation of irony (page 280) and symbol (page 283).

IRONY

Irony is embedded in "Can-Can," with respect both to the situations in which the characters find themselves and to their comments and thoughts. For example, Vivante writes of the husband as he sits waiting for his lover's car:

> *A car like hers, and yet not like hers—no luggage rack on it. The smooth hardtop gave him a peculiar pleasure.* (lines 45–46)

Here we have an ironic contrast between the husband's earlier excited anticipation of the meeting and his surprising feeling of relief that it is not his lover's car arriving.

Pick out and explain several other examples of irony in the story.

SYMBOL

Vivante uses the can-can as a central **symbol** to illustrate a deeper meaning in the story. To unearth the richness of the can-can as a symbol, first explore the various associations you have with the dance. Then answer the following questions.

1. What does the can-can symbolize in the story?
2. In the scene where the wife does the can-can, how does the language reinforce the symbol?
3. What theme in the story is highlighted by the symbolic dance?

C. Judging for Yourself

Express yourself as personally as you like in your answers to the following questions:

1. Do you think the expectations the couple have of each other are reasonable?
2. Do you think the husband will continue the affair?
3. Should the husband have left the restaurant when he had the opportunity?
4. Have the husband and wife learned anything from the episode?
5. What do you imagine their marriage will be like in the future?

D. Making Connections

1. How is adultery viewed in your culture?

2. Does the couple's marriage in "Can-Can" reflect the kind of marriage common in your culture?

3. In your country would politicians or other public figures be denied or forced to leave office if they committed adultery? What do you think should happen to them?

E. Debate

Debate the proposal: Adultery is a crime and should be punished by law.

P A R T ◆3◆ **FOCUS ON LANGUAGE**

A. Gerunds and Present Participles

"Can-Can" contains several examples of gerunds and present participles. Although **gerunds** and **present participles** both share an *-ing* ending, in other words, the same form, their function is quite different.

The **gerund** is a type of verbal, which is a part of speech that is related to verbs but acts as another part of speech. There are three kinds of verbals: gerunds, participles (present, past, and perfective), and infinitives. The gerund acts as a verbal noun and is used in the same way as a noun. Being a noun, the gerund or gerund phrase can be the subject of a sentence or the object of a verb or preposition. For example:

> ***Arranging this rendezvous*** *was very difficult for him.*

The gerund phrase *arranging this rendezvous* is the subject of the verb *was.*

> *He couldn't imagine **arranging this rendezvous.***

The gerund phase *arranging this rendezvous* is the object of the verb *could imagine.*

> *He expected her to be . . . doing something uninteresting and unattractive, like **darning children's clothes.*** (lines 26–29)

The gerund phrase *darning children's clothes* is the object of the preposition *like.*

The **present participle** is another type of verbal. It can act as part of a verb in the progressive tense or as an adjective. As an adjective the present participle or the present participial phrase must modify a noun or pronoun. For example:

> Her feet, **swinging up and down high in the air**, seemed to be nodding to him. (lines 31–32)

The participial phrase *swinging up and down high in the air* modifies the noun *feet.*

Note: Because participles come from verbs, they share with verbs the elements of transitivity and time.

When used as part of a verb in the **progressive tense,** the participle shows that an action is in progress. For example:

> Why **was** she **doing** that of all times now? (lines 32–33)

1. Find the paragraph in "Can-Can" that is composed mainly of gerunds and underline them.

2. In the sentences that follow, decide if the italicized word is a gerund, present participle, or part of a verb in the progressive tense, and write your choice on the line provided.

    a. "I'm *going* for a drive," he said to his wife. _____

    b. She hated *sewing* for the family. _____

    c. She held up her skirt and did the can-can, *kicking* her legs up high in his direction. _____

    d. He objected to *seeing* her in this new role. _____

    e. *Waiting* so long for his lover at the cafe made him feel nervous.

    _____

    f. He looked at his watch, *hoping* she wouldn't come. _____

    g. How strange he should be *wishing* for her absence. _____

    h. *Smoking* a cigarette helped steady his nerves. _____

    i. "What are you *thinking* about?" she said, *sensing* his detachment.

    _____ _____

    j. *Suppressing* a laugh, he answered her honestly. _____

3. Write three sentences using the verb *get rid of* as a gerund, as a present participle, and as a verb in the progressive tense. Do the same with the verb *linger.*

B. Building Vocabulary Skills

Many common expressions consist of two nouns, adjectives, or adverbs separated by *and*. For example:

> And he wished he could go for a drive, ***free and easy***, as he had said he would. (lines 53–54)

Use a dictionary to help you with the following expressions. Then write sentences that show you understand them.

free and easy	cut-and-dried
up and down	hit-and-run
pepper-and-salt	open-and-shut
black-and-white	spic-and-span
to and fro	far and away

Can you think of any more such expressions? Ask a native speaker or your teacher to help you.

P A R T ◆ 4 ◆ **W R I T I N G   A C T I V I T I E S**

1. Imagine a scene in which the wife in "Can-Can" is waiting for her husband to return. Write about her thoughts and feelings as the hours go by. Try to use gerunds and present participles in your writing.

2. Write a letter offering advice to a close friend who has confided in you that he or she is in love with a married person.

3. *The Scarlet Letter* by Nathaniel Hawthorne and *Anna Karenina* by Leo Tolstoy are two famous novels that deal with adultery. In an essay of two to three pages, discuss any well-known work in your language that involves that subject. Outline the plot, explaining what drives the character to adultery. Are the characters treated sympathetically?

4. In an essay of one to two pages, compare "Can-Can" with "The Kugelmass Episode" by Woody Allen (page 42). What similarities do you see in the two stories? Which story do you prefer? Why?

Story of an Hour

KATE CHOPIN *(1851–1904)*

◆◆◆

BORN IN ST. LOUIS, Missouri, Kate Chopin came of
French-Creole parentage on her mother's side and Irish immigrants
on her father's side. She grew up in a household dominated by
generations of women, and it was from her great-grandmother that
she heard the tales of the early French settlers to St. Louis that were
later to influence many of her short stories with their colorful
descriptions of Creole and Acadian life.

Much of Chopin's writing deals with women searching for
freedom from male domination, and she is considered to be an
early feminist writer. She wrote over a hundred short stories, many
of which were published in two collections: *Bayou Folk* (1894)
and *A Night in Acadia* (1897). Her two novels, *At Fault* (1890) and
The Awakening (1899), deal with the controversial themes of
divorce and adultery, respectively. Denounced as immoral, *The
Awakening* caused a public uproar, which left Chopin deeply
depressed and discouraged. As a result, she wrote very little in the
last five years of her life.

STORY OF AN HOUR

A wife has a startling reaction to the news of her husband's death.

Knowing that Mrs. Mallard was afflicted with[1] a heart trouble, great care was taken to break to her as gently as possible the news of her husband's death.

It was her sister Josephine who told her, in broken sentences, veiled hints[2] that revealed in half concealing. Her husband's friend Richards was there, too, near her. It was he who had been in the newspaper office when intelligence[3] of the railroad disaster was received, with Brently Mallard's name leading the list of "killed." He had only taken the time to assure himself of its truth by a second telegram, and had hastened to forestall[4] any less careful, less tender friend in bearing the sad message.

She did not hear the story as many women have heard the same, with a paralyzed[5] inability to accept its significance. She wept at once, with sudden, wild abandonment,[6] in her sister's arms. When the storm of grief[7] had spent itself she went away to her room alone. She would have no one follow her.

There stood, facing the open window, a comfortable, roomy armchair. Into this she sank, pressed down by a physical exhaustion that haunted[8] her body and seemed to reach into her soul.

She could see in the open square before her house the tops of trees that were all aquiver[9] with the new spring life. The delicious breath of rain was in the air. In the street below a peddler[10] was crying his wares.[11] The notes of a distant song which someone was singing reached her faintly, and countless sparrows[12] were twittering[13] in the eaves.[14]

There were patches of blue sky showing here and there through the clouds that had met and piled above the other in the west facing her window.

She sat with her head thrown back upon the cushion of the chair quite motionless, except when a sob came up into her throat and shook her, as a child who has cried itself to sleep continues to sob in its dreams.

She was young, with a fair, calm face, whose lines bespoke[15] repression[16] and even a certain strength. But now there was a dull stare in her eyes, whose

---

1. **afflicted with**   troubled with
2. **veiled hints**   indirect suggestions
3. **intelligence**   news
4. **forestall**   prevent
5. **paralyzed**   helpless (literally, unable to move)
6. **abandonment**   unrestrained emotion
7. **grief**   intense sadness
8. **haunted**   spread throughout (as a ghost's presence)
9. **aquiver**   shaking
10. **peddler**   one who sells goods in the street
11. **crying his wares**   shouting out what he has to sell
12. **sparrows**   small birds
13. **twittering**   making short, rapid bird sounds
14. **eaves**   the parts of a roof where birds nest
15. **bespoke**   indicated
16. **repression**   holding in one's feelings

gaze was fixed away off yonder on one of those patches of blue sky. It was not a glance of reflection, but rather indicated a suspension of intelligent thought.

There was something coming to her and she was waiting for it, fearfully. What was it? She did not know; it was too subtle[17] and elusive[18] to name. But she felt it, creeping out of the sky, reaching toward her through the sounds, the scents, the color that filled the air.

Now her bosom rose and fell tumultuously.[19] She was beginning to recognize this thing that was approaching to possess her, and she was striving[20] to beat it back with her will—as powerless as her two white slender hands would have been.

When she abandoned herself a little whispered word escaped her slightly parted lips. She said it over and over under her breath: "Free, free, free!" The vacant stare and the look of terror that had followed it went from her eyes. They stayed keen[21] and bright. Her pulses beat fast, and the coursing blood warmed and relaxed every inch of her body.

She did not stop to ask if it were not a monstrous joy that held her. A clear and exalted[22] perception enabled her to dismiss the suggestion as trivial.

She knew that she would weep again when she saw the kind, tender hands folded in death; the face that had never looked save[23] with love upon her, fixed and gray and dead. But she saw beyond that bitter moment a long procession of years to come that would belong to her absolutely. And she opened and spread her arms out to them in welcome.

There would be no one to live for during those coming years; she would live for herself. There would be no powerful will bending her in that blind persistence with which men and women believe they have a right to impose a private will upon a fellow-creature. A kind intention or a cruel intention made the act seem no less a crime as she looked upon it in that brief moment of illumination.

And yet she had loved him—sometimes. Often she had not. What did it matter! What could love, the unsolved mystery, count for in face of this possession of self-assertion[24] which she suddenly recognized as the strongest impulse of her being!

"Free! Body and soul free!" she kept whispering.

Josephine was kneeling before the closed door with her lips to the keyhole, imploring for admission. "Louise, open the door! I beg; open the door—you will make yourself ill. What are you doing, Louise? For heaven's sake open the door."

"Go away. I am not making myself ill." No; she was drinking in a very elixir of life[25] through that open window.

---

17. **subtle**   indirect, not obvious
18. **elusive**   hard to catch
19. **tumultuously**   with violent emotion
20. **striving**   trying very hard
21. **keen**   sharp

22. **exalted**   raised
23. **save**   except
24. **self-assertion**   insistence on her own worth
25. **elixir of life**   substance capable of prolonging life

Her fancy[26] was running riot[27] along those days ahead of her. Spring days, and summer days, and all sorts of days that would be her own. She breathed a quick prayer that life might be long. It was only yesterday she had thought with a shudder[28] that life might be long.

She arose at length and opened the door to her sister's importunities.[29]   75
There was a feverish triumph in her eyes, and she carried herself unwittingly[30] like a goddess of Victory. She clasped her sister's waist, and together they descended the stairs. Richards stood waiting for them at the bottom.

Some one was opening the front door with a latchkey. It was Brently Mallard who entered, a little travel-stained, composedly carrying his grip-   80
sack[31] and umbrella. He had been far from the scene of accident, and did not even know there had been one. He stood amazed at Josephine's piercing cry; at Richards' quick motion to screen him from the view of his wife.

But Richards was too late.

When the doctors came they said she had died of heart disease—of joy   85
that kills. ◆

---

26. **fancy**   imagination
27. **running riot**   going out of control
28. **shudder**   uncontrollable shake

29. **importunities**   continued begging
30. **unwittingly**   unknowingly
31. **grip-sack**   traveling bag

PART  **1**   **FIRST READING**

A. Thinking about the Story

Were you able to feel and sympathize with Mrs. Mallard's intense frustration with her life as a conventionally married woman?

B. Understanding the Plot

1. How does Josephine break the news of Brently Mallard's death to his wife?

2. Why does she do it in this way?

3. How was Brently Mallard supposed to have died?

4. Why did Richards want to be the one to bring the bad news?

5. What is unusual about Mrs. Mallard's first reaction to the news?

6. In what season does the story take place?

7. What do the descriptions of the people, animals, and nature that Mrs. Mallard sees and hears from her window have in common? (lines 19–25)

8. About how old do you think Mrs. Mallard is? Justify your answer.

9. What word most accurately describes how Mrs. Mallard feels when she gets over the first shock of hearing her husband is dead?

10. Why was Mrs. Mallard so unhappy in her marriage?

11. What is the effect of the dash in the sentence: "And yet she had loved him—sometimes"? (line 60)

12. What does the comparison in lines 76–77 suggest about Mrs. Mallard's feelings?

PART **2** **SECOND READING**

A. Exploring Themes

You are now ready to reread "Story of an Hour." Think carefully about why Mrs. Mallard was so unhappy in her marriage. Remember that the story was written in 1894, when women had far less freedom and fewer choices than today.

1. What is the thematic importance of the season in "Story of an Hour"?

2. Are Mrs. Mallard's feelings toward her husband totally negative? Justify your answer.

3. How would you describe the state of Mrs. Mallard's mental health up until the time she heard the news of her husband's death?

4. What does Mrs. Mallard's struggle to repress her feelings of joy on hearing about her widowhood tell you about her state of mind at that moment?

5. How is the ending ironic?

B. Analyzing the Author's Style

Before you begin to work on this section, turn to the detailed explanation of epiphany (page 278), metaphor (page 280), simile (page 282), and personification (page 280).

EPIPHANY

"Story of an Hour" builds up to the moment when Mrs. Mallard experiences her **epiphany** (an unexpected moment of profound enlightenment) and utters the words, "Free, free, free!" (lines 42–43), thus expressing her intuitive and shocked understanding that her husband's death has released her to fulfill herself as an individual, something she had never dared to think about openly until then.

1. In "Story of an Hour" Mrs. Mallard has another such moment of lightning intuition. What is it? Explain its implications.

2. If you have read "The Boarding House" (page 98), look at the following question: Toward the end of the story Mr. Doran has a similar moment of illumination, which helps him make up his mind about whether to marry Polly. What is it? How does it affect his actions?

METAPHOR AND SIMILE

There are a number of **metaphors** (implied comparisons) and **similes** (explicit comparisons in which *like* or *as* is used to join the two elements) in the story. An example of metaphor is contained in the sentence: *Mrs. Mallard lit up when she realized she was free at last.* Here her feeling of joy is compared with the effect a light has when it is turned on. Similarly, an example of simile is contained in the sentence: *Mrs. Mallard's eyes shone like polished gems when she realized she was free at last.* In this instance, the comparison between her eyes and shining jewels is clearly asserted.

Look at the following expressions from the story and say whether they are metaphors or similes. Explain the separate elements of the comparison in each expression.

veiled hints	(lines 4–5)
storm of grief	(line 13)
her will [was] as powerless as her two white slender hands would have been	(lines 39–40)
she was drinking in a very elixir of life	(lines 69–70)
she carried herself . . . like a goddess of Victory	(lines 76–77)

PERSONIFICATION

Personification (the giving of human characteristics to nonhuman things) features prominently in "Story of an Hour." One example is when Mrs. Mallard becomes aware of the "delicious breath of rain" outside her window (line 20). Rain is not something living that can breathe, and yet she feels as if the rain is breathing on her. In fact, the complexity of this image is increased still further by the word *delicious,* since this adds a metaphorical element of rain that can also be eaten like some tasty food.

Find three more examples of personification in the text and explain them. Say how they heighten the effect of the writing.

C. Judging for Yourself

Express yourself as personally as you like in your answers to the following questions:

1. In your view was Mrs. Mallard at all unreasonable regarding her husband?
2. What do you imagine a regular day in Mrs. Mallard's life was like?
3. Should Mrs. Mallard have asked for a divorce?
4. Do you think Brently Mallard had any idea about what his wife was feeling?
5. Do you think Mrs. Mallard was doomed to die young? Why?

D. Making Connections

1. Do many women in your country feel that marriage is to some extent imprisoning?
2. If you had to choose between marriage and a career, which would you choose?
3. Do you think women are more likely to suffer from depression than men? Explain your answer.
4. How easy is it to obtain a divorce in your country? Is there a stigma attached to divorce?

E. Debate

Debate the proposal: Marriage is a bad bargain for women.

P A R T  **FOCUS ON LANGUAGE**

A. Suffixes

Suffixes are additions at the end of a word that are used to form nouns, verbs, adjectives (including participial adjectives), and adverbs. For example, **nouns** can be formed by the addition of the suffix *-ment* as in *abandonment* (line 13), *-ion* as in *repression* (line 29), and *-ence* as in *persistence* (line 56); **verbs** can be formed by the addition of *-en* as in *hasten* (line 9); **adjectives** can be formed by the addition of *-ed* as in *afflicted* (line 1), *-able* as in *comfortable* (line 16), *-less* as in *motionless* (line 27), *-ive* as in *elusive* (line 34), *-ing* as in *creeping* (line 35), *-ous* as in *monstrous* (line 46), *-ful* as in *powerful* (line 55), and *-ish* as in *feverish* (line 76); and **adverbs** can be formed by the addition of *-ly* as in *gently* (line 2).

Look at the following words from the story, and with the aid of your dictionary write the correct form of the word in the blank spaces. If more than one choice is possible, select one answer.

NOUN	VERB	ADJECTIVE	ADVERB
_____	_____	amazed	_____
_____	assure	_____	_____
_____	breathe	_____	_____
_____	_____	bright	_____
_____	_____	comfortable	_____
_____	_____	_____	composedly
dream	_____	_____	_____
exhaustion	_____	_____	_____
_____	_____	_____	faintly
_____	_____	_____	fearfully
_____	hasten	_____	_____
illumination	_____	_____	_____
_____	_____	paralyzed	_____
persistence	_____	_____	_____
_____	possess	_____	_____
_____	reveal	_____	_____
significance	_____	_____	_____
strength	_____	_____	_____
terror	_____	_____	_____
thought	_____	_____	_____

B. Building Vocabulary Skills

Complete the sentences with the correct preposition. All the expressions used appear in the story.

1. Mrs. Mallard was afflicted _____ heart disease.

2. In the face _____ her sister's importunities, she opened the door.

3. She felt this terrible emotion creep out _____ her inner self.

4. Mr. Mallard might have been surprised to hear that he imposed his will _____ his wife.

5. She couldn't wait _____ the moment when she would be free.

6. The scene outside was aquiver _____ spring life.

7. Richards tried to assure himself _____ the truth of his friend's death.

8. During Mrs. Mallard's married life she suffered from a suspension _____ hope.

9. The clouds were piled _____ the eaves of the roof where the twittering birds nested.

10. At first she looked _____ her elation as a monstrous joy.

P A R T **W R I T I N G   A C T I V I T I E S**

1. In an essay of one to two pages, outline your views on what it takes to have an ideal marriage. Consider factors like the value of having similar or opposite temperaments; of one partner being more willing to compromise; of sharing the same religious, educational, social, and economic background, and so on. Say whether you believe such a union is attainable.

2. Write a short story on marriage in which one of the characters has a moment of epiphany.

3. *The Age of Innocence* by Edith Wharton is a story of a nineteenth-century couple trapped by the conventions of their day in an unhappy marriage. The book has been made into a movie starring Daniel Day-Lewis and Michelle Pfeiffer. Imagine you are a book or movie critic and write a review of a book or movie dealing with a similar theme.

4. Both Mrs. Mallard and the central character in "Disappearing" (page 168) are trapped in unhappy marriages. Write a comparison of the two women, and discuss the respective endings to their stories.

ANN BEATTIE *(b. 1947)*

◆◆◆

BORN IN WASHINGTON, D.C., to middle-class parents, Ann Beattie grew up and was educated there, receiving a degree in English literature from the American University. She has taught at Harvard and the University of Virginia.

In her novels and short stories she has come to be identified with the counterculture of the 1960s and 1970s. Her writing, with its spare style, leans heavily toward minimalism. The tone is deeply pessimistic. Her characters come mainly from the middle and upper-middle classes and for the most part are unhappy and frustrated in love, work, and family.

Her short fiction includes the following anthologies: *Distortions* (1976), in which the characters experiment with drugs and sexual freedom, *Secrets* (1978), *The Burning House* (1982), and *Where You'll Find Me & Other Stories* (1986). She has also written several novels: *Chilly Scenes of Winter* (1976), *Falling in Place* (1980), *Love Always* (1985), and *Picturing Will* (1989).

SNOW

A lover looks back on an affair and reflects on what went wrong.

I remember the cold night you brought in a pile of logs and a chipmunk[1] jumped off as you lowered your arms. "What do you think *you're* doing in here?" you said, as it ran through the living room. It went through the library and stopped at the front door as though it knew the house well. This would be difficult for anyone to believe, except perhaps as the subject of a poem. 5
Our first week in the house was spent scraping,[2] finding some of the house's secrets, like wallpaper underneath wallpaper. In the kitchen, a pattern of white-gold trellises[3] supported purple grapes as big and round as Ping-Pong balls. When we painted the walls yellow, I thought of the bits of grape that remained underneath and imagined the vine popping through,[4] 10
the way some plants can tenaciously[5] push through anything. The day of the big snow, when you had to shovel the walk[6] and couldn't find your cap and asked me how to wind a towel so that it would stay on your head— you, in the white towel turban, like a crazy king of snow. People liked the idea of our being together, leaving the city for the country. So many people 15
visited, and the fireplace made all of them want to tell amazing stories: the child who happened to be standing on the right corner when the door of the ice-cream truck came open and hundreds of Popsicles[7] crashed out;[8] the man standing on the beach, sand sparkling in the sun, one bit glinting[9] more than the rest, stooping to find a diamond ring. Did they talk about 20
amazing things because they thought we'd turn into one of them? Now I think they probably guessed it wouldn't work. It was as hopeless as giving a child a matched cup and saucer. Remember the night, out on the lawn, knee-deep in snow, chins pointed at the sky as the wind whirled down all that whiteness? It seemed that the world had been turned upside down, and 25
we were looking into an enormous field of Queen Anne's lace.[10] Later, headlights off, our car was the first to ride through the newly fallen snow. The world outside the car looked solarized.[11]
You remember it differently. You remember that the cold settled in stages, that a small curve of light was shaved[12] from the moon night after 30
night, until you were no longer surprised the sky was black, that the

---

1. **chipmunk** a small striped squirrel-like animal
2. **scraping** removing something by scratching it off
3. **trellises** wooden framework used to support climbing plants
4. **popping through** pushing through suddenly
5. **tenaciously** persistently, by not giving up
6. **shovel the walk** remove snow from the path

7. **Popsicles** flavored frozen water
8. **crashed out** fell out noisily
9. **glinting** shining
10. **Queen Anne's lace** plant with small delicate white flowers
11. **solarized** exposed to sunlight
12. **shaved** removed bit by bit

chipmunk ran to hide in the dark, not simply to a door that led to its escape. Our visitors told the same stories people always tell. One night, giving me a lesson in storytelling, you said, "Any life will seem dramatic if you omit mention of[13] most of it." 35

This, then, for drama: I drove back to that house not long ago. It was April, and Allen had died. In spite of all the visitors, Allen, next door, had been the good friend in bad times. I sat with his wife in their living room, looking out the glass doors to the backyard, and there was Allen's pool, still covered with black plastic that had been stretched across it for winter. It had 40 rained, and as the rain fell, the cover collected more and more water until it finally spilled onto the concrete. When I left that day, I drove past what had been our house. Three or four crocuses[14] were blooming in the front—just a few dots of white, no field of snow. I felt embarrassed for them. They couldn't compete. 45

This is a story, told the way you say stories should be told: Somebody grew up, fell in love, and spent a winter with her lover in the country. This, of course, is the barest outline, and futile[15] to discuss. It's as pointless as throwing birdseed on the ground while snow still falls fast. Who expects small things to survive when even the largest get lost? People forget years 50 and remember moments. Seconds and symbols are left to sum things up: the black shroud[16] over the pool. Love, in its shortest form, becomes a word. What I remember about all that time is one winter. The snow. Even now, saying "snow," my lips move so that they kiss the air.

No mention has been made of the snowplow that seemed always to be 55 there, scraping snow off our narrow road—an artery[17] cleared, though neither of us could have said where the heart was. ◆

---

13. **omit mention of**   don't say anything about
14. **crocuses**   flowers that appear in early spring
15. **futile**   useless

16. **shroud**   a cover, commonly a burial sheet
17. **artery**   a blood vessel; also refers to a river or highway

PART ◆1 **FIRST READING**

A. Thinking about the Story

Did you find yourself hoping the lovers would get together again? Were your responses to the story influenced by any love affairs you have had?

B. Understanding the Plot

1. Who is the narrator of the story?
2. Whom is the narrator addressing?

3. Why is the narrator telling the story?

4. What did the couple first do on moving into the house?

5. What did the friends' fireside stories have in common? How do the two lovers react to the stories?

6. Explain the sentence: "Now I think they probably guessed it wouldn't work." (lines 21–22) How does the comparison that follows that statement help to illustrate what the narrator is saying?

7. What does the man mean when he says: "Any life will seem dramatic if you omit mention of most of it"? (lines 34–35) What does this statement tell you about him?

8. Who is Allen? How did his friendship differ from the other friends who visited that winter?

9. In what seasons does the story take place? What important event in the narrator's life occurs in each season?

10. Think about what you have learned about the lovers. Make a list of adjectives to describe each person.

P A R T ◆2◆ **S E C O N D   R E A D I N G**

A. Exploring Themes

You are now ready to reread "Snow." Look at how Beattie has created a kind of prose poem. The story is rich in atmosphere and imagery that help create the narrator's mood.

1. What is the importance of the chipmunk to the story?

2. What do the activities of scraping off the wallpaper in lines 6–9 and scraping off the snow in lines 55–57 have in common? How do these two activities relate to the central theme of the story?

3. What two elements are compared in the metaphor in lines 55–57? Explain the metaphor as fully as possible.

4. With what is the vine in line 10 linked later in the story? What do you think is the thematic point of the comparison?

5. What image does the black plastic covering Allen's pool evoke? How does this image reflect a theme of the story?

6. What part does memory play in the story?

7. Think of all the associations you have with the word *snow*, as well as the particular ways the author uses snow as metaphor and symbol. Explain as fully as possible the role of snow in the story.

B. Analyzing the Author's Style

Before you begin to work on this section, turn to the detailed explanation of point of view (page 281) and alliteration (page 273).

POINT OF VIEW: FIRST-PERSON NARRATION

"Snow" is narrated in the **first person,** which means that the story is told by a narrator using the pronoun *I.* The first-person narrator's point of view is necessarily *partial*, or incomplete.

1. How limited is the narrator's point of view in "Snow"?
2. Does the fact that the point of view is partial mean that you do not trust this narrator? Justify your answer.
3. How is the structure and language of the story affected by the person the narrator is addressing?
4. What is the tone of the narrator? Give examples to support your answer. Note: For information on tone, see page 284.

ALLITERATION

The vocabulary in "Snow" is highly poetic, and Beattie uses **alliterative** language (the repetition of a consonant) throughout the story. For example, the head of the lover is described as being wrapped *in the white towel turban, like a crazy king of snow.* (line 14) Notice the double alliteration: **t**owel/**t**urban and **c**razy/**k**ing. There is also a weaker alliterative allusion in **wh**ite/to**w**el. The use of the unvoiced consonants (**t**, **k**, and **wh**) helps reinforce the softness of the mood.

1. Find as many other examples of alliteration as you can in the story. Write them down and underline the repeated consonant. Say what the effect of the repetition is when read aloud.
2. What other elements in the story make you think of a poem?

C. Judging for Yourself

Express yourself as personally as you like in your answers to the following questions:

1. Which partner do you think broke up the affair?
2. Does it seem to you that there is any chance of the lovers getting together again?
3. Whom do you relate to more—the man or the woman? Say why.
4. Did the absence of a clear-cut plot bother you? Say why or why not.

D. Making Connections

1. In your culture is it acceptable for people to live together before marriage?

2. Do you think it is true to say that opposites attract? In your view do people with very different outlooks have a better or worse chance of making the relationship work?

3. When people fall in love in your country, how is their courtship conducted?

4. Do men and women have trouble communicating with each other in your culture? For example, do men have more difficulty than women expressing what they feel? Do men and women tend to interpret the same event differently?

E. Debate

Debate the proposition: It is unnatural to expect to remain in love with one person for a lifetime.

P A R T ◆3◆ **FOCUS ON LANGUAGE**

A. Alliteration

Look at the following list of alliterative expressions.

cold and calculating	spic-and-span
fast and furious	sugar and spice
flip-flop	tried and true
hotheaded	wild and woolly
life and limb	world-weariness

With the aid of a dictionary, your teacher, or a native speaker, replace the italicized words in the exercise below with an appropriate expression from the list. Use each expression once only.

1. This is a *well-tested* recipe. My mother has made it many times.

2. I'm tired of your *unruly* behavior. You need to calm down.

3. According to the well-known nursery rhyme, little girls are made of *sweet ingredients* and all things nice.

4. Politicians frequently *reverse themselves* when they want to back out of promises made during an election campaign.

5. Our neighbor finds that nothing pleases her anymore. She is suffering from *extreme boredom.*

6. When I was younger, I frequently risked *my physical safety* without thinking about it.

7. If you weren't so *reckless*, you wouldn't always be getting into trouble.

8. Although our room looked *spotless*, it was still not good enough to pass the sergeant's inspection.

9. I love movies that have *thrilling* car chases.

10. What a *scheming* person she is. I believe she planned the murder all along.

B. Building Vocabulary Skills

Look at the following list of verbs, all of which appear in the text, although not necessarily in the same form as in the list. Complete the sentences with the correct verb from the list. You may need to change the tense or form of the verb.

scrape (line 6)	glint (line 19)
support (line 8)	stoop (line 20)
pop through (line 10)	whirl (line 24)
shovel (line 12)	omit (line 34)
wind (line 13)	sum up (line 51)

1. At last we saw the crocus as it _____ the snow at the end of a dreadfully hard winter.

2. It is sometimes necessary for lovers _____ some details of their past if they want to keep their partners happy.

3. That winter we _____ snow for days after each blizzard.

4. If you could _____ the best moments of our affair, what would they be?

5. When you _____ the material around your body, you looked like an Indian princess.

6. I am sure we will uncover all the past of the house if we _____ off all the layers of paint.

7. Although the storm _____ outside, we felt so cozy indoors that we hardly noticed it.

8. We didn't know whether the walls that _____ the roof would hold up after a month of heavy snowfalls.

9. If the key _____ in the snow, I would have found it easily.

10. As I _____ to put a log on the fire, a chipmunk scampered past.

PART ◆4◆ **WRITING ACTIVITIES**

1. Write a memory piece on someone very close to you. Include a description of the person, the setting that you most associate with him or her, and at least one event that involved both of you. Narrate your essay in the first person, and try to make some use of alliteration in your descriptions.

2. Alfred Tennyson, the British Victorian poet, wrote:

   > *'Tis better to have loved and lost*
   > *Than never to have loved at all.*

   Write a two-page essay commenting on the idea expressed in the above couplet. Say whether you agree or disagree with its sentiment. Give reasons for your answer. In your essay include references to well-known real-life or fictional love affairs that have gone wrong. In your conclusion say how personal experience has influenced your answer.

3. Literature and the movies are full of stories of passionate love affairs that failed to work out. Gustave Flaubert's *Madame Bovary* and D. H. Lawrence's *The Rainbow* are two outstanding literary examples, and *Casablanca*, with Humphrey Bogart and Ingrid Bergman, has become a movie classic. Choose a novel, play, poem, or movie centering on a star-crossed love affair that moved you deeply. In a two-page essay briefly recount the plot and explain why you were so affected.

The Legacy

VIRGINIA WOOLF (1882–1941)

◆◆◆

BORN IN LONDON, Virginia Woolf is recognized as one of the most important novelists of this century. Influenced by James Joyce and Marcel Proust, she attempted to create a new form for the novel by experimenting with stream of consciousness writing, in which she disrupted time in an effort to capture the inner thought processes of her characters.

Woolf wrote novels, short stories, essays, literary criticism, and biographies. Her novels include *Mrs. Dalloway* (1925), *To the Lighthouse* (1927), and *The Waves* (1931). Among her short story collections are *Kew Gardens* (1919) and *A Haunted House and Other Short Stories* (1943). Her book *A Room of One's Own* (1929), in which she deals with the problems of being a woman writer, is recognized as an important example of early feminist literature. In 1941, deeply depressed by the two world wars she had experienced, as well as by her increasing inability to deal with severe chronic depression, Woolf drowned herself.

THE LEGACY

*When a well-known politician's wife dies, her husband finds
that she has left him an unusual legacy.*

inscription

"For Sissy Miller." Gilbert Clandon, taking up the pearl brooch[1] that lay
among a litter[2] of rings and brooches on a little table in his wife's drawing-
room, read the inscription: "For Sissy Miller, with my love."

It was like Angela to have remembered even Sissy Miller, her secretary.
Yet how strange it was, Gilbert Clandon thought once more, that she had   5
left everything in such order—a little gift of some sort for every one of her
friends. It was as if she had foreseen her death. Yet she had been in perfect
health when she left the house that morning, six weeks ago; when she
stepped off the kerb[3] in Piccadilly and the car had killed her.

He was waiting for Sissy Miller. He had asked her to come; he owed   10
her, he felt, after all the years she had been with them, this token of
consideration.[4] Yes, he went on, as he sat there waiting, it was strange that
Angela had left everything in such order. Every friend had been left some
little token of her affection. Every ring, every necklace, every little Chinese
box—she had a passion for little boxes—had a name on it. And each had   15
some memory for him. This he had given her; this—the enamel dolphin
with the ruby eyes—she had pounced upon[5] one day in a back street in
Venice. He could remember her little cry of delight. To him, of course, she
had left nothing in particular, unless it were her diary. Fifteen little
volumes, bound in green leather, stood behind him on her writing table.   20
Ever since they were married, she had kept a diary. Some of their very
few—he could not call them quarrels, say tiffs[6]—had been about that diary.
When he came in and found her writing, she always shut it or put her hand
over it. "No, no, no," he could hear her say. "After I'm dead—perhaps." So
she had left it him, as her legacy.[7] It was the only thing they had not shared   25
when she was alive. But he had always taken it for granted[8] that she would
outlive him. If only she had stopped one moment, and had thought what
she was doing, she would be alive now. But she had stepped straight off
the kerb, the driver of the car had said at the inquest.[9] She had given him
no chance to pull up. . . . Here the sound of voices in the hall interrupted   30
him.

"Miss Miller, Sir," said the maid.

---

1. **brooch**   a piece of jewelry that fastens with a pin
2. **litter**   untidy arrangement
3. **kerb**   British spelling of *curb* (edge of a sidewalk)
4. **token of consideration**   small sign of regard
5. **pounced upon**   suddenly grabbed
6. **tiffs**   small disagreements
7. **legacy**   what is left to someone after death, inheritance
8. **taken for granted**   assumed
9. **inquest**   official inquiry into cause of death

She came in. He had never seen her alone in his life, nor, of course, in tears. She was terribly distressed,[10] and no wonder.[11] Angela had been much more to her than an employer. She had been a friend. To himself, he thought, as he pushed a chair for her and asked her to sit down, she was scarcely distinguishable from any other woman of her kind. There were thousands of Sissy Millers—drab[12] little women in black carrying attaché cases.[13] But Angela, with her genius for sympathy, had discovered all sorts of qualities in Sissy Miller. She was the soul of discretion;[14] so silent; so trustworthy, one could tell her anything, and so on.

Miss Miller could not speak at first. She sat there dabbing[15] her eyes with her pocket handkerchief. Then she made an effort.

"Pardon me, Mr. Clandon," she said.

He murmured. Of course he understood. It was only natural. He could guess what his wife had meant to her.

"I've been so happy here," she said, looking round. Her eyes rested on the writing table behind him. It was here they had worked—she and Angela. For Angela had her share of the duties that fall to the lot of a prominent[16] politician's wife. She had been the greatest help to him in his career. He had often seen her and Sissy sitting at that table—Sissy at the typewriter, taking down letters from her dictation. No doubt Miss Miller was thinking of that, too. Now all he had to do was to give her the brooch his wife had left her. A rather incongruous[17] gift it seemed. It might have been better to have left her a sum of money, or even the typewriter. But there it was—"For Sissy Miller, with my love." And, taking the brooch, he gave it her with the little speech that he had prepared. He knew, he said, that she would value it. His wife had often worn it. . . . And she replied, as she took it almost as if she too had prepared a speech, that it would always be a treasured possession. . . . She had, he supposed, other clothes upon which a pearl brooch would not look quite so incongruous. She was wearing the little black coat and skirt that seemed the uniform of her profession. Then he remembered—she was in mourning,[18] of course. She, too, had had her tragedy—a brother, to whom she was devoted, had died only a week or two before Angela. In some accident was it? He could not remember—only Angela telling him. Angela, with her genius for sympathy, had been terribly upset. Meanwhile Sissy Miller had risen. She was putting on her gloves. Evidently she felt that she ought not to intrude. But he could not let her go without saying something about her future. What were her plans? Was there any way in which he could help her?

---

10. **distressed**   deeply upset
11. **no wonder**   not surprisingly
12. **drab**   dull
13. **attaché cases**   small leather cases for carrying papers
14. **soul of discretion**   a perfect example of trustworthiness
15. **dabbing**   lightly patting
16. **prominent**   well known
17. **incongruous**   unsuitable
18. **in mourning**   in a state of grief for someone who has died

She was gazing at the table, where she had sat at her typewriter, where the diary lay. And, lost in her memories of Angela, she did not at once answer his suggestion that he should help her. She seemed for a moment not to understand. So he repeated:

"What are your plans, Miss Miller?"   75

"My plans? Oh, that's all right, Mr. Clandon," she exclaimed. "Please don't bother yourself about me."

He took her to mean that[19] she was in no need of financial assistance. It would be better, he realized, to make any suggestion of that kind in a letter. All he could do now was to say as he pressed her hand, "Remember, Miss   80
Miller, if there's any way in which I can help you, it will be a pleasure. . . ." Then he opened the door. For a moment, on the _threshold_, as if a sudden thought had struck her, she stopped.

"Mr. Clandon," she said, looking straight at him for the first time, and for the first time he was struck by the expression, sympathetic yet searching, in   85
her eyes. "If at any time," she continued, "there's anything I can do to help you, remember, I shall feel it, for your wife's sake, a pleasure. . . ."

With that she was gone. Her words and the look that went with them were unexpected. It was almost as if she believed, or hoped, that he would need her. A curious, perhaps a fantastic idea occurred to him as he returned   90
to his chair. Could it be, that during all those years when he had scarcely noticed her, she, as the novelists say, had entertained a passion for him? He caught his own reflection in the glass as he passed. He was over fifty; but he could not help admitting that he was still, as the looking-glass showed him, a very distinguished-looking[20] man.   95

"Poor Sissy Miller!" he said, half laughing. How he would have liked to share that joke with his wife! He turned instinctively to her diary. "Gilbert," he read, opening it at random,[21] "looked so wonderful. . . ." It was as if she had answered his question. Of course, she seemed to say, you're very attractive to women. Of course Sissy Miller felt that too. He read on. "How   100
proud I am to be his wife!" And he had always been very proud to be her husband. How often, when they _dined_ out somewhere, he had looked at her across the table and said to himself, "She is the loveliest woman here!" He read on. That first year he had been standing for Parliament.[22] They had toured his constituency.[23] "When Gilbert sat down the _applause_ was terrific.   105
The whole audience rose and sang: 'For he's a jolly good fellow.' I was quite overcome." He remembered that, too. She had been sitting on the platform beside him. He could still see the glance she cast at him, and how she had tears in her eyes. And then? He turned the pages. They had gone to Venice. He recalled that happy holiday after the election. "We had ices at Florians."   110
He smiled—she was still such a child; she loved ices. "Gilbert gave me a

---

19. **He took her to mean that**   He assumed that
20. **distinguished-looking**   appearing important
21. **at random**   without any plan

22. **standing for Parliament**   running for election to the British legislature
23. **constituency**   area he would represent in Parliament

most interesting account of the history of Venice. He told me that the Doges[24]. . .” she had written it all out in her schoolgirl hand. One of the delights of travelling with Angela had been that she was so eager to learn. She was so terribly ignorant, she used to say, as if that were not one of her charms. And then—he opened the next volume—they had come back to London. “I was so anxious to make a good impression. I wore my wedding dress.” He could see her now sitting next to old Sir Edward; and making a conquest of that formidable[25] old man, his chief. He read on rapidly, filling in scene after scene from her scrappy fragments.[26] “Dined at the House of Commons. . . . To an evening party at the Lovegroves’. Did I realize my responsibility, Lady L. asked me, as Gilbert’s wife?” Then, as the years passed—he took another volume from the writing table—he had become more and more absorbed in his work. And she, of course, was more often home. . . . It had been a great grief to her, apparently, that they had had no children. “How I wish,” one entry read, “that Gilbert had a son!” Oddly enough he had never much regretted that himself. Life had been so full, so rich as it was. That year he had been given a minor post in the government. A minor post only, but her comment was: “I am quite certain now that he will be Prime Minister!” Well, if things had gone differently, it might have been so. He paused here to speculate upon what might have been. Politics was a gamble, he reflected; but the game wasn’t over yet. Not at fifty. He cast his eyes rapidly over more pages, full of the little trifles,[27] the insignificant, happy, daily trifles that had made up her life.

    He took up another volume and opened it at random. “What a coward I am! I let the chance slip again. But it seemed selfish to bother him with my own affairs, when he had so much to think about. And we so seldom have an evening alone.” What was the meaning of that? Oh, here was the explanation—it referred to her work in the East End.[28] “I plucked up courage and talked to Gilbert at last. He was so kind, so good. He made no objection.” He remembered that conversation. She had told him that she felt so idle, so useless. She wished to have some work of her own. She wanted to do something—she had blushed so prettily, he remembered, as she said it, sitting in that very chair—to help others. He had bantered[29] her a little. Hadn’t she enough to do looking after him, after her home? Still, if it amused her, of course he had no objection. What was it? Some district? Some committee? Only she must promise not to make herself ill. So it seemed that every Wednesday she went to Whitechapel.[30] He remembered how he hated the clothes she wore on those occasions. But she had taken it very seriously, it seemed. The diary was full of references like this: “Saw Mrs. Jones. . . . She has ten children. . . . Husband lost his arm in an accident. . . . Did my best to find a job for Lily.” He skipped on. His own name occurred less frequently.

---

24. **the Doges**   chief officials in the republics of Venice and Genoa
25. **formidable**   frightening
26. **scrappy fragments**   very incomplete diary entries
27. **trifles**   unimportant events
28. **the East End**   traditionally poor area of London
29. **bantered**   teased
30. **Whitechapel**   an area in the East End of London

His interest slackened.[31] Some of the entries conveyed nothing to him. For example: "Had a heated argument about socialism with B. M." Who was B. M.? He could not fill in the initials; some woman, he supposed, that she had met on one of her committees. "B. M. made a violent attack upon the upper classes. . . . I walked back after the meeting with B. M. and tried to convince him. But he is so narrow-minded." So B. M. was a man—no doubt one of those "intellectuals," as they call themselves, who are so violent, as Angela said, and so narrow-minded. She had invited him to come and see her apparently. "B. M. came to dinner. He shook hands with Minnie!" That note of exclamation gave another twist to his mental picture. B. M., it seemed, wasn't used to parlourmaids; he had shaken hands with Minnie. Presumably he was one of those tame working men who air their views in ladies' drawing-rooms. Gilbert knew the type, and had no liking for this particular specimen, whoever B. M. might be. Here he was again. "Went with B. M. to the Tower of London. . . . He said revolution is bound to[32] come. . . . He said we live in a Fool's Paradise." That was just the kind of thing B. M. would say—Gilbert could hear him. He could also see him quite distinctly—a stubby[33] little man, with a rough beard, red tie, dressed as they always did in tweeds,[34] who had never done an honest day's work in his life. Surely Angela had the sense to see through him? He read on. "B. M. said some very disagreeable things about —." The name was carefully scratched out. "I told him I would not listen to any more abuse of —" Again the name was obliterated. Could it have been his own name? Was that why Angela covered the page so quickly when he came in? The thought added to his growing dislike of B. M. He had had the impertinence to discuss him in this very room. Why had Angela never told him? It was very unlike her to conceal anything; she had been the soul of candour.[35] He turned the pages, picking out every reference to B. M. "B. M. told me the story of his childhood. His mother went out charring.[36]. . . When I think of it, I can hardly bear to go on living in such luxury. . . . Three guineas[37] for one hat!" If only she had discussed the matter with him, instead of puzzling her poor little head about questions that were much too difficult for her to understand! He had lent her books. *Karl Marx, The Coming Revolution.* The initials B. M., B. M., B. M., recurred repeatedly. But why never the full name? There was an informality, an intimacy in the use of initials that was very unlike Angela. Had she called him B. M. to his face? He read on. "B. M. came unexpectedly after dinner. Luckily, I was alone." That was only a year ago. "Luckily"—why luckily?—"I was alone." Where had he been that night? He checked the date in his engagement book. It had been the night of the Mansion House dinner. And B. M. and Angela had spent the evening alone! He tried to recall that

(margin annotations: Parlourmaid / presumably; obliterated; Impertinence; conceal / candour)

155
160
165
170
175
180
185
190

---

31. **slackened** lessened
32. **is bound to** is certain to
33. **stubby** short and broad
34. **in tweeds** clothes made from a rough woolen material

35. **soul of candour** a perfect example of honesty
36. **charring** housecleaning
37. **three guineas** three pounds and three shillings (old British currency)

evening. Was she waiting up for him when he came back? Had the room looked just as usual? Were there glasses on the table? Were the chairs drawn close together? He could remember nothing—nothing whatever, nothing except his own speech at the Mansion House dinner. It became more and more inexplicable to him—the whole situation: his wife receiving an unknown man alone. Perhaps the next volume would explain. Hastily he reached for the last of the diaries—the one she had left unfinished when she died. There, on the very first page, was that cursed[38] fellow again. "Dined alone with B. M. . . . He became very agitated. He said it was time we understood each other. . . . I tried to make him listen. But he would not. He threatened that if I did not . . ." the rest of the page was scored over.[39] She had written "Egypt. Egypt. Egypt," over the whole page. He could not make out a single word; but there could be only one interpretation: the scoundrel[40] had asked her to become his mistress. Alone in his room! The blood rushed to Gilbert Clandon's face. He turned the pages rapidly. What had been her answer? Initials had ceased. It was simply "he" now. "He came again. I told him I could not come to any decision. . . . I implored[41] him to leave me." He had forced himself upon her in this very house. But why hadn't she told him? How could she have hesitated for an instant? Then: "I wrote him a letter." Then pages were left blank. Then there was this: "No answer to my letter." Then more blank pages; and then this: "He has done what he threatened." After that—what came after that? He turned page after page. All were blank. But there, on the very day before her death, was this entry: "Have I the courage to do it too?" That was the end.

Gilbert Clandon let the book slide to the floor. He could see her in front of him. She was standing on the kerb in Piccadilly. Her eyes stared; her fists were clenched. Here came the car. . . .

He could not bear it. He must know the truth. He strode to the telephone.

"Miss Miller!" There was silence. Then he heard someone moving in the room.

"Sissy Miller speaking"—her voice at last answered him.

"Who," he thundered, "is B. M.?"

He could hear the cheap clock ticking on her mantel-piece; then a long drawn sigh. Then at last she said:

"He was my brother."

He *was* her brother; her brother who had killed himself. "Is there," he heard Sissy Miller asking, "anything that I can explain?"

"Nothing!" he cried. "Nothing!"

He had received his legacy. She had told him the truth. She had stepped off the kerb to rejoin her lover. She had stepped off the kerb to escape from him.◆

---

38. **cursed**   beastly
39. **the page was scored over**   the words were blocked out by writing over them
40. **scoundrel**   worthless person
41. **implored**   begged

P A R T ◆1◆ **FIRST READING**

A. Thinking about the Story

At what point in the story did you grasp the full significance of Gilbert Clandon's legacy? Were you quicker than Gilbert to understand what had happened? What earlier clues did you perhaps miss?

B. Understanding the Plot

1. What puzzles Gilbert Clandon about the circumstances surrounding his wife's death?

2. What does Gilbert assume caused her death?

3. How does Gilbert initially account for Sissy Miller's extreme distress when she enters the room? What does he later remember about her?

4. Why does Gilbert feel the gift of a brooch to Sissy Miller is a "rather incongruous gift"? (line 54)

5. Why does Sissy Miller extend an offer to help Gilbert?

6. What does "that first year" (line 104) refer to? What was Gilbert trying to achieve then? Was he successful?

7. Why did Gilbert particularly enjoy traveling with his wife, Angela?

8. What are Gilbert's career ambitions at age fifty?

9. Why did Angela Clandon want to do volunteer work in the East End of London? What was Gilbert's response to her request?

10. What two political ideologies are contrasted in the story?

11. Why was Angela so amazed when B. M. shook hands with Minnie?

12. What does Gilbert assume B. M. wanted Angela to do? What do you think B. M. asked Angela to do?

P A R T ◆2◆ **SECOND READING**

A. Exploring Themes

You are now ready to reread "The Legacy." This time around, consider how Gilbert Clandon, as a result of his egotism, persistently misinterprets his wife's actions.

1. How does Gilbert Clandon expect his wife to behave throughout their married life?

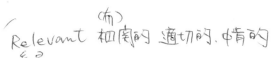

2. How does Angela Clandon change during the course of their marriage?

3. What is the relevance to the theme of the story of the details Gilbert can and cannot remember concerning the night of the Mansion House dinner? (lines 190–196)

4. What is Gilbert Clandon's attitude toward the working class? Explain your answer with examples from the text.

5. What is the role of B. M. in the story?

B. Analyzing the Author's Style

Before you begin to work on this section, turn to the detailed explanation of point of view (page 281).

POINT OF VIEW

In "The Legacy" the **point of view** of the story is filtered through the eyes of Gilbert Clandon, whose figurative blindness is crucial to its theme and plot. For example, when Clandon reflects on Angela's regret that they'd had no children, he thinks complacently, *Oddly enough he had never much regretted that himself. Life had been so full, so rich as it was.* (lines 126–128) He has no conception that as full and rich as his life was, so his wife's had been correspondingly empty and poor.

1. How does Gilbert Clandon's limited point of view influence his perception of his wife, B. M., and Sissy Miller? Give as many examples as possible.

2. How much does Gilbert's understanding of the events change by the end of the story?

3. Why is it ironic that Gilbert thinks of Sissy Miller as "the soul of discretion; so silent; so trustworthy, one could tell her anything, and so on." (lines 40–41) What other examples of irony can you find that arise out of Gilbert's limited perceptions?
Note: For information on irony, see page 280.

C. Judging for Yourself

Express yourself as personally as you like in your answers to the following questions:

1. Do you feel at all sympathetic toward Gilbert Clandon? Explain your answer.

2. In your view should Angela Clandon have confessed to what was going on while she was still alive?

3. What do you think a typical day in Angela's life was like before she began her volunteer work? Contrast this with a typical day in Gilbert's life.

4. Why do you suppose Angela was so attracted to B. M.?

5. Do you think learning the truth about Angela and B. M. will affect Gilbert's future plans? Explain your answer.

D. Making Connections

1. Is suicide considered morally wrong in your religion or society? Is it more prevalent among certain groups or ages in your country?

2. How is adultery viewed in your country? Are there moral or legal constraints against it?

3. What political ideologies compete for the public vote in your country? Are any political beliefs outlawed?

4. Is it customary to keep a diary back home? If so, what kinds of people tend to do it? If not, explain why.

E. Debate

Debate the proposal: Suicide is the coward's way out of solving problems.

PART  **FOCUS ON LANGUAGE**

A. Building Vocabulary Skills

The following descriptions are used by Gilbert Clandon when thinking about himself, his wife, Sissy Miller, and B. M.

childlike	narrow-minded
distinguished-looking	prominent
distressed	soul of candour
drab	soul of discretion
impertinent	stubby
lovely-looking	trustworthy

Without looking back at the story, place each of these descriptions under the appropriate character from "The Legacy" in the columns below.

GILBERT CLANDON	ANGELA CLANDON	SISSY MILLER	B. M.

The following adjectives do not appear in the text, but they could apply to the characters given above. Decide which adjectives refer to which character and place them in the corresponding column.

arrogant   patronizing

loyal   bitter

modest   deceitful

vain   compassionate

lonely   argumentative

radical   hard-working

Make up three more fitting descriptions for each character. Add these to the appropriate columns above.

PART ◆4◆ **WRITING ACTIVITIES**

1. Choose two of the four main characters featured in "The Legacy."
    Create an imaginary dialogue between them, using some of the
    adjectives you used in the language exercise in Part 3. Your dialogue
    should be about a page long.

2. Imagine you find Angela Clandon unconscious after her suicide
    attempt. Would you try to save her? In a two-page essay consider the
    pros and cons of allowing her to kill herself. Would the prevailing
    attitude toward suicide in your country affect your reasoning?

3. Luis Buñuel's film *Belle de Jour* starred Catherine Deneuve as a
    wealthy surgeon's wife who finds release from the frustrations of her
    daily routine by secretly working as a prostitute in a brothel during
    the afternoon. Write an essay on a book or movie you are familiar
    with that revolves around a wife or husband who lives a hidden life
    unknown to the spouse. Analyze what drives the person to such
    deception. Say which partner you sympathize with more, and why.

The Kugelmass Episode

WOODY ALLEN *(b. 1935)*

◆◆◆

BORN IN BROOKLYN, New York, to a lower-middle-class Jewish family, Woody Allen (formerly Allen Stewart Konigsberg) grew up shy and withdrawn. However, he quickly demonstrated a flair for writing and performing comedy. After writing the script for the movie *What's New Pussycat?* in 1965, he moved into the triple role of screenwriter, actor, and director of his own movie *Take the Money and Run* (1969), positions he has occupied with increasing international fame and stature for over twenty-five years.

Allen's major movies include *Annie Hall* (1979), *Hannah and Her Sisters* (1986), and *Husbands and Wives* (1992). In addition to his many screenplays, he has written six plays, and three collections of essays and short stories: *Getting Even* (1971), *Without Feathers* (1975), and *Side Effects* (1980). His stories, most of which originally appeared in *The New Yorker* magazine, are for the most part satires and parodies of modern life with all its attendant neuroses, and make use of his zany humor, surrealistic visions, and talent for writing gag lines.

THE KUGELMASS EPISODE

*A New York professor has his deepest wish granted, after
which his life takes an unexpected turn.*

➤ "The Kugelmass Episode" is a parody, or humorous imitation, of Gustave
Flaubert's classic nineteenth-century novel *Madame Bovary*. To appreciate the story, it is
necessary to know the broad outline of the original novel: Emma Rouault attempts to
escape from her boring existence on her father's farm by marrying a rural doctor, Charles
Bovary. Emma quickly tires of her adoring husband's country ways and seeks excitement
in two love affairs—with Leon, a young law student, and Rodolphe, a wealthy
landowner. By the end of the book Emma has squandered all her husband's savings, is
rejected by her two lovers, and commits suicide, appreciating only at the last minute
Charles's faithful devotion to her.

Kugelmass, a professor of humanities at City College, was unhappily
married for the second time. Daphne Kugelmass was an oaf.[1] He also had
two dull sons by his first wife, Flo, and was up to his neck in alimony[2] and
child support.

"Did I know it would turn out so badly?" Kugelmass whined to his   5
analyst one day. "Daphne had promise.[3] Who suspected she'd let herself go
and swell up like a beach ball? Plus she had a few bucks, which is not in
itself a healthy reason to marry a person, but it doesn't hurt, with the kind of
operating nut[4] I have. You see my point?"

Kugelmass was bald and as hairy as a bear, but he had soul.   10

"I need to meet a new woman," he went on. "I need to have an affair. I
may not look the part, but I'm a man who needs romance. I need softness, I
need flirtation. I'm not getting younger, so before it's too late I want to make
love in Venice, trade quips[5] at '21,'[6] and exchange coy glances over red
wine and candlelight. You see what I'm saying?"   15

Dr. Mandel shifted in his chair and said, "An affair will solve nothing.
You're so unrealistic. Your problems run much deeper."

"And also this affair must be discreet," Kugelmass continued. "I can't
afford a second divorce. Daphne would really sock it to[7] me."

"Mr. Kugelmass—"   20

"But it can't be anyone at City College, because Daphne also works
there. Not that anyone on the faculty at C.C.N.Y. is any great shakes, but
some of those coeds[8]. . ."

---

1. **oaf** stupid person
2. **alimony** money paid to a spouse after a divorce
3. **had promise** could become someone special
4. **operating nut** brain, way of thinking
5. **trade quips** exchange witty remarks
6. **"21"** fancy New York restaurant
7. **sock it to** strongly attack
8. **coeds** female students

"Mr. Kugelmass—"

"Help me. I had a dream last night. I was skipping through a meadow holding a picnic basket and the basket was marked 'Options.' And then I saw there was a hole in the basket."

"Mr. Kugelmass, the worst thing you could do is act out. You must simply express your feelings here, and together we'll analyze them. You have been in treatment long enough to know there is no overnight cure. After all, I'm an analyst,[9] not a magician."

"Then perhaps what I need is a magician," Kugelmass said, rising from his chair. And with that he terminated his therapy.

A couple of weeks later, while Kugelmass and Daphne were moping around[10] in their apartment one night like two pieces of old furniture, the phone rang.

"I'll get it," Kugelmass said. "Hello."

"Kugelmass?" a voice said. "Kugelmass, this is Persky."

"Who?"

"Persky. Or should I say The Great Persky?"

"Pardon me?"

"I hear you're looking all over town for a magician to bring a little exotica[11] into your life? Yes or no?"

"Sh-h-h," Kugelmass whispered. "Don't hang up. Where are you calling from, Persky?"

Early the following afternoon, Kugelmass climbed three flights of stairs in a broken-down apartment house in the Bushwick section of Brooklyn. Peering through the darkness of the hall, he found the door he was looking for and pressed the bell. I'm going to regret this, he thought to himself.

Seconds later, he was greeted by a short, thin, waxy-looking man.

"You're Persky the Great?" Kugelmass said.

"The Great Persky. You want a tea?"

"No, I want romance. I want music. I want love and beauty."

"But not tea, eh? Amazing. O.K., sit down."

Persky went to the back room, and Kugelmass heard the sounds of boxes and furniture being moved around. Persky reappeared, pushing before him a large object on squeaky roller-skate wheels. He removed some old silk handkerchiefs that were lying on its top and blew away a bit of dust. It was a cheap-looking Chinese cabinet, badly lacquered.[12]

"Persky," Kugelmass said, "what's your scam?"[13]

"Pay attention," Persky said. "This is some beautiful effect. I developed it for a Knights of Pythias[14] date last year, but the booking fell through. Get into the cabinet."

---

9. **analyst**   psychoanalyst
10. **moping around**   doing nothing, in a depressed fashion
11. **exotica**   exciting, unusual things
12. **lacquered**   polished, coated with a shiny paint
13. **scam**   dishonest scheme
14. **Knights of Pythias**   group of men involved in charity work

"Why, so you can stick it full of swords or something?"

"You see any swords?"

Kugelmass made a face and, grunting, climbed into the cabinet. He couldn't help noticing a couple of ugly rhinestones[15] glued onto the raw plywood just in front of his face. "If this is a joke," he said.

"Some joke. Now, here's the point. If I throw any novel into this cabinet with you, shut the doors, and tap it three times, you will find yourself projected into that book."

Kugelmass made a grimace of disbelief.

"It's the *emess*,"[16] Persky said. "My hand to God. Not just a novel, either. A short story, a play, a poem. You can meet any of the women created by the world's best writers. Whoever you dreamed of. You could carry on[17] all you like with a real winner. Then when you've had enough you give a yell, and I'll see you're back here in a split second."

"Persky, are you some kind of outpatient?"[18]

"I'm telling you it's on the level," Persky said.

Kugelmass remained skeptical. "What are you telling me—that this cheesy[19] homemade box can take me on a ride like you're describing?"

"For a double sawbuck."[20]

Kugelmass reached for his wallet. "I'll believe this when I see it," he said.

Persky tucked the bills in his pants pocket and turned toward his bookcase. "So who do you want to meet? Sister Carrie? Hester Prynne? Ophelia? Maybe someone by Saul Bellow? Hey, what about Temple Drake?[21] Although for a man your age she'd be a workout."

"French. I want to have an affair with a French lover."

"Nana?"[22]

"I don't want to have to pay for it."

"What about Natasha in 'War and Peace'?"

"I said French. I know! What about Emma Bovary? That sounds to me perfect."

"You got it, Kugelmass. Give me a holler[23] when you've had enough." Persky tossed in a paperback copy of Flaubert's novel.

"You sure this is safe!" Kugelmass asked as Persky began shutting the cabinet doors.

"Safe. Is anything safe in this crazy world?" Persky rapped three times on the cabinet and then flung open the doors.

Kugelmass was gone. At the same moment, he appeared in the bedroom of Charles and Emma Bovary's house at Yonville. Before him was a beautiful woman, standing alone with her back turned to him as she

---

15. **rhinestones** cheap imitation gems
16. *emess* truth (Yiddish)
17. **carry on** have a love affair with
18. **outpatient** mentally disturbed person (slang)
19. **cheesy** poorly made, tasteless (slang)
20. **sawbuck** ten dollars
21. **Sister Carrie, Hester Prynne, Ophelia, and Temple Drake** beautiful troubled heroines in works by Theodore Dreiser, Nathaniel Hawthorne, William Shakespeare, and William Faulkner, respectively
22. **Nana** prostitute in Emile Zola's novel *Nana*
23. **Give me a holler** Shout to me

folded some linen. I can't believe this, thought Kugelmass, staring at the doctor's ravishing[24] wife. This is uncanny. I'm here. It's her.   105

Emma turned in surprise. "Goodness, you startled me," she said. "Who are you?" She spoke in the same fine English translation as the paperback.

It's simply devastating, he thought. Then, realizing that it was he whom she had addressed, he said, "Excuse me. I'm Sidney Kugelmass. I'm from City College. A professor of humanities. C.C.N.Y.? Uptown. I—oh, boy!"   110

Emma Bovary smiled flirtatiously and said, "Would you like a drink? A glass of wine, perhaps?"

She is beautiful, Kugelmass thought. What a contrast with the troglodyte[25] who shared his bed! He felt a sudden impulse to take this vision into his arms and tell her she was the kind of woman he had dreamed   115 of all his life.

"Yes, some wine," he said hoarsely. "White. No, red. No, white. Make it white."

"Charles is out for the day," Emma said, her voice full of playful implication.   120

After the wine, they went for a stroll in the lovely French countryside. "I've always dreamed that some mysterious stranger would appear and rescue me from the monotony of this crass[26] rural existence," Emma said, clasping his hand. They passed a small church. "I love what you have on," she murmured. "I've never seen anything like it around here. It's so . . . so   125 modern."

"It's called a leisure suit,"[27] he said romantically. "It was marked down."[28] Suddenly he kissed her. For the next hour they reclined under a tree and whispered together and told each other deeply meaningful things with their eyes. Then Kugelmass sat up. He had just remembered he had to   130 meet Daphne at Bloomingdale's.[29] "I must go," he told her. "But don't worry, I'll be back."

"I hope so," Emma said.

He embraced her passionately, and the two walked back to the house. He held Emma's face cupped in his palms, kissed her again, and yelled,   135 "O.K., Persky! I got to be at Bloomingdale's by three-thirty."

There was an audible pop, and Kugelmass was back in Brooklyn.

"So? Did I lie?" Persky asked triumphantly.

"Look, Persky, I'm right now late to meet the ball and chain[30] at Lexington Avenue, but when can I go again? Tomorrow?"   140

"My pleasure. Just bring a twenty. And don't mention this to anybody."

"Yeah. I'm going to call Rupert Murdoch."[31]

Kugelmass hailed a cab and sped off to the city. His heart danced on point. I am in love, he thought, I am the possessor of a wonderful secret.

---

24. **ravishing** unusually attractive
25. **troglodyte** early cave dweller
26. **crass** vulgar, insensitive
27. **leisure suit** unfashionable polyester suit
28. **marked down** put on sale
29. **Bloomingdale's** famous New York department store
30. **the ball and chain** insulting term for a wife, referring to shackles worn by prisoners
31. **Rupert Murdoch** internationally known media owner

What he didn't realize was that at this very moment students in various   145
classrooms across the country were saying to their teachers, "Who is this
character on page 100? A bald Jew is kissing Madame Bovary?" A teacher in
Sioux Falls, South Dakota, sighed and thought, Jesus, these kids, with their
pot and acid.[32] What goes through their minds!

Daphne Kugelmass was in the bathroom-accessories department at   150
Bloomingdale's when Kugelmass arrived breathlessly. "Where've you been?"
she snapped. "It's four-thirty."

"I got held up in traffic," Kugelmass said.

Kugelmass visited Persky the next day, and in a few minutes was again
passed magically to Yonville. Emma couldn't hide her excitement at seeing   155
him. The two spent hours together, laughing and talking about their
different backgrounds. Before Kugelmass left, they made love. "My God, I'm
doing it with Madame Bovary!" Kugelmass whispered to himself. "Me, who
failed freshman English."

As the months passed, Kugelmass saw Persky many times and   160
developed a close and passionate relationship with Emma Bovary. "Make
sure and always get me into the book before page 120," Kugelmass said to
the magician one day. "I always have to meet her before she hooks up with
this Rodolphe character."

"Why?" Persky asked. "You can't beat his time?"[33]   165

"Beat his time. He's landed gentry. Those guys have nothing better to do
than flirt and ride horses. To me, he's one of those faces you see in the
pages of *Women's Wear Daily*. With the Helmut Berger[34] hairdo. But to her
he's hot stuff."

"And her husband suspects nothing?"   170

"He's out of his depth. He's a lacklustre little paramedic[35] who's thrown
in his lot with a jitterbug.[36] He's ready to go to sleep by ten, and she's
putting on her dancing shoes. Oh, well . . . See you later."

And once again Kugelmass entered the cabinet and passed instantly to
the Bovary estate at Yonville. "How you doing, cupcake?" he said to Emma.   175

"Oh, Kugelmass," Emma sighed. "What I have to put up with. Last night
at dinner, Mr. Personality dropped off to sleep in the middle of the dessert
course. I'm pouring my heart out about Maxim's[37] and the ballet, and out of
the blue[38] I hear snoring."

"It's O.K., darling. I'm here now," Kugelmass said, embracing her. I've   180
earned this, he thought, smelling Emma's French perfume and burying his
nose in her hair. I've suffered enough. I've paid enough analysts. I've

---

32. **pot and acid**   marijuana and LSD
33. **beat his time**   win out over a rival (slang)
34. **Helmut Berger**   handsome Austrian actor
35. **lacklustre little paramedic**   insulting reference
    implying that Charles is stupid and unqualified as a
    doctor

36. **jitterbug**   someone who loves to dance to
    hot-rhythm music
37. **Maxim's**   famous restaurant in Paris
38. **out of the blue**   completely unexpectedly

searched till I'm weary. She's young and nubile,[39] and I'm here a few pages after Léon and just before Rodolphe. By showing up during the correct chapters, I've got the situation knocked.[40]

Emma, to be sure, was just as happy as Kugelmass. She had been starved for excitement, and his tales of Broadway night life, of fast cars and Hollywood and TV stars, enthralled the young French beauty.

"Tell me again about O. J. Simpson,"[41] she implored that evening, as she and Kugelmass strolled past Abbé Bournisien's church.

"What can I say? The man is great. He sets all kinds of rushing[42] records. Such moves. They can't touch him."

"And the Academy Awards?" Emma said wistfully. "I'd give anything to win one."

"First you've got to be nominated."

"I know. You explained it. But I'm convinced I can act. Of course, I'd want to take a class or two. With Strasberg[43] maybe. Then, if I had the right agent—"

"We'll see, we'll see. I'll speak to Persky."

That night, safely returned to Persky's flat, Kugelmass brought up the idea of having Emma visit him in the big city.

"Let me think about it," Persky said. "Maybe I could work it. Stranger things have happened." Of course, neither of them could think of one.

"Where the hell do you go all the time?" Daphne Kugelmass barked at her husband as he returned home late that evening. "You got a chippie[44] stashed[45] somewhere?"

"Yeah, sure, I'm just the type," Kugelmass said wearily. "I was with Leonard Popkin. We were discussing Socialist agriculture in Poland. You know Popkin. He's a freak on the subject."

"Well, you've been very odd lately," Daphne said. "Distant. Just don't forget about my father's birthday. On Saturday?"

"Oh, sure, sure," Kugelmass said, heading for the bathroom.

"My whole family will be there. We can see the twins. And Cousin Hamish. You should be more polite to Cousin Hamish—he likes you."

"Right, the twins," Kugelmass said, closing the bathroom door and shutting out the sound of his wife's voice. He leaned against it and took a deep breath. In a few hours, he told himself, he would be back in Yonville again, back with his beloved. And this time, if all went well, he would bring Emma back with him.

At three-fifteen the following afternoon, Persky worked his wizardry again. Kugelmass appeared before Emma, smiling and eager. The two spent a few hours at Yonville with Binet and then remounted the Bovary Carriage.

---

39. **nubile**   sexy (usually refers to women of marriageable age)
40. **I've got the situation knocked**   I'm sure to win (slang)
41. **O. J. Simpson**   American football star

42. **rushing**   rapid move in football
43. **Strasberg**   a famous acting teacher
44. **chippie**   immoral woman
45. **stashed**   hidden away

Following Persky's instructions, they held each other tightly, closed their eyes, and counted to ten. When they opened them, the carriage was just drawing up at the side door of the Plaza Hotel, where Kugelmass had optimistically reserved a suite earlier in the day.

"I love it! It's everything I dreamed it would be," Emma said as she swirled joyously around the bedroom, surveying the city from their window. "There's F.A.O. Schwarz.[46] And there's Central Park, and the Sherry[47] is which one? Oh, there—I see. It's too divine."

On the bed there were boxes from Halston and Saint Laurent.[48] Emma unwrapped a package and held up a pair of black velvet pants against her perfect body.

"The slacks suit is by Ralph Lauren," Kugelmass said. "You'll look like a million bucks in it. Come on, sugar, give us a kiss."

"I've never been so happy!" Emma squealed as she stood before the mirror. "Let's go out on the town.[49] I want to see 'Chorus Line' and the Guggenheim and this Jack Nicholson character you always talk about. Are any of his flicks[50] showing?"

"I cannot get my mind around[51] this," a Stanford professor said. "First a strange character named Kugelmass, and now she's gone from the book. Well, I guess the mark of a classic is that you can reread it a thousand times and always find something new."

The lovers passed a blissful weekend. Kugelmass had told Daphne he would be away at a symposium in Boston and would return Monday. Savoring each moment, he and Emma went to the movies, had dinner in Chinatown, passed two hours at a discothèque, and went to bed with a TV movie. They slept till noon on Sunday, visited SoHo, and ogled[52] celebrities at Elaine's.[53] They had caviar and champagne in their suite on Sunday night and talked until dawn. That morning, in the cab taking them to Persky's apartment, Kugelmass thought, It was hectic,[54] but worth it. I can't bring her here too often, but now and then it will be a charming contrast with Yonville.

At Persky's, Emma climbed into the cabinet, arranged her new boxes of clothes neatly around her, and kissed Kugelmass fondly. "My place next time," she said with a wink. Persky rapped three times on the cabinet. Nothing happened.

"Hmm," Persky said, scratching his head. He rapped again, but still no magic. "Something must be wrong," he mumbled.

"Persky, you're joking!" Kugelmass cried. "How can it not work?"

"Relax, relax. Are you still in the box, Emma?"

"Yes."

---

46. **F. A. O. Schwarz**   large toy store
47. **the Sherry**   exclusive New York hotel (The Sherry Netherland Hotel)
48. **Halston and Saint Laurent**   fashion designers
49. **go out on the town**   go out and enjoy oneself
50. **flicks**   movies
51. **get my mind around**   understand
52. **ogled**   stared rudely at
53. **Elaine's**   New York restaurant frequented by celebrities
54. **hectic**   rushed and confused

Persky rapped again—harder this time.

"I'm still here, Persky."

"I know, darling. Sit tight."

"Persky, we *have* to get her back," Kugelmass whispered. "I'm a married   265
man, and I have a class in three hours. I'm not prepared for anything more
than a cautious affair at this point."

"I can't understand it," Persky muttered. "It's such a reliable little trick."

But he could do nothing. "It's going to take a little while," he said to
Kugelmass. "I'm going to have to strip it down.55 I'll call you later."   270

Kugelmass bundled Emma into a cab and took her back to the Plaza. He
barely made it to his class on time. He was on the phone all day, to Persky
and to his mistress. The magician told him it might be several days before he
got to the bottom of the trouble.

"How was the symposium?" Daphne asked him that night.   275

"Fine, fine," he said, lighting the filter end of a cigarette.

"What's wrong? You're as tense as a cat."

"Me? Ha, that's a laugh. I'm as calm as a summer night. I'm just going
to take a walk." He eased out the door, hailed a cab, and flew to the Plaza.

"This is no good," Emma said. "Charles will miss me."   280

"Bear with me, sugar,"56 Kugelmass said. He was pale and sweaty. He
kissed her again, raced to the elevators, yelled at Persky over a pay phone in
the Plaza lobby, and just made it home before midnight.

"According to Popkin, barley prices in Kraków have not been this stable
since 1971," he said to Daphne, and smiled wanly as he climbed into bed.   285

The whole week went by like that. On Friday night, Kugelmass told
Daphne there was another symposium he had to catch, this one in Syracuse.
He hurried back to the Plaza, but the second weekend there was nothing
like the first. "Get me back into the novel or marry me," Emma told
Kugelmass. "Meanwhile, I want to get a job or go to class, because watching   290
TV all day is the pits."57

"Fine. We can use the money," Kugelmass said. "You consume twice
your weight in room service."

"I met an off-Broadway producer in Central Park yesterday, and he said
I might be right for a project he's doing," Emma said.   295

"Who is this clown?" Kugelmass asked.

"He's not a clown. He's sensitive and kind and cute. His name's Jeff
Something-or-Other, and he's up for a Tony."58

Later that afternoon, Kugelmass showed up at Persky's drunk.

"Relax," Persky told him. "You'll get a coronary."   300

"Relax. The man says relax. I've got a fictional character stashed in a
hotel room, and I think my wife is having me tailed by a private shamus."59

---

55. **strip it down**   take it apart
56. **Bear with me, Sugar**   Be patient with me, darling
57. **the pits**   the worst situation imaginable (slang)

58. **he's up for a Tony**   he's been nominated for a
    Broadway theater award
59. **shamus**   detective (Yiddish slang)

"O.K., O.K. We know there's a problem." Persky crawled under the cabinet and started banging on something with a large wrench.

"I'm like a wild animal," Kugelmass went on. "I'm sneaking around town, and Emma and I have had it up to here[60] with each other. Not to mention a hotel tab that reads like the defense budget."

"So what should I do? This is the world of magic," Persky said. "It's all nuance."[61]

"Nuance, my foot.[62] I'm pouring Dom Pérignon and black eggs into this little mouse, plus her wardrobe, plus she's enrolled at the Neighborhood Playhouse and suddenly needs professional photos. Also, Persky, Professor Fivish Kopkind, who teaches Comp Lit[63] and who has always been jealous of me, has identified me as the sporadically appearing character in the Flaubert book. He's threatened to go to Daphne. I see ruin and alimony, jail. For adultery with Madame Bovary, my wife will reduce me to beggary."

"What do you want me to say? I'm working on it night and day. As far as your personal anxiety goes, that I can't help you with. I'm a magician, not an analyst."

By Sunday afternoon, Emma had locked herself in the bathroom and refused to respond to Kugelmass's entreaties. Kugelmass stared out the window at the Wollman Rink and contemplated suicide. Too bad this is a low floor, he thought, or I'd do it right now. Maybe if I ran away to Europe and started life over . . . Maybe I could sell the *International Herald Tribune,* like those young girls used to.

The phone rang. Kugelmass lifted it to his ear mechanically.

"Bring her over," Persky said. "I think I got the bugs[64] out of it."

Kugelmass's heart leaped. "You're serious?" he said. "You got it licked?"[65]

"It was something in the transmission. Go figure."[66]

"Persky, you're a genius. We'll be there in a minute. Less than a minute."

Again the lovers hurried to the magician's apartment, and again Emma Bovary climbed into the cabinet with her boxes. This time there was no kiss. Persky shut the doors, took a deep breath, and tapped the box three times. There was the reassuring popping noise, and when Persky peered inside, the box was empty. Madame Bovary was back in her novel. Kugelmass heaved a great sigh of relief and pumped the magician's hand.

"It's over," he said. "I learned my lesson. I'll never cheat again, I swear it." He pumped Persky's hand again and made a mental note to send him a necktie.

Three weeks later, at the end of a beautiful spring afternoon, Persky answered his doorbell. It was Kugelmass, with a sheepish expression on his face.

---

60. **have had it up to here**   are sick of
61. **nuance**   hint, shade
62. **my foot**   expression of disagreement (slang)
63. **Comp Lit**   Comparative Literature
64. **the bugs**   errors, problems (slang)
65. **You got it licked?**   You've solved it? (slang)
66. **Go figure**   Can you believe it? (slang)

"O.K., Kugelmass," the magician said. "Where to this time?"

"It's just this once," Kugelmass said. "The weather is so lovely, and I'm not getting any younger. Listen, you've read 'Portnoy's Complaint'?[67] Remember The Monkey?"[68]

"The price is now twenty-five dollars, because the cost of living is up, but I'll start you off with one freebie, due to all the trouble I caused you."

"You're good people," Kugelmass said, combing his few remaining hairs as he climbed into the cabinet again. "This'll work all right?"

"I hope. But I haven't tried it much since all that unpleasantness."

"Sex and romance," Kugelmass said from inside the box. "What we go through for a pretty face."

Persky tossed in a copy of "Portnoy's Complaint" and rapped three times on the box. This time, instead of a popping noise there was a dull explosion, followed by a series of crackling noises and a shower of sparks. Persky leaped back, was seized by a heart attack, and dropped dead. The cabinet burst into flames, and eventually the entire house burned down.

Kugelmass, unaware of this catastrophe, had his own problems. He had not been thrust into "Portnoy's Complaint," or into any other novel, for that matter. He had been projected into an old textbook, "Remedial Spanish,"[69] and was running for his life over a barren, rocky terrain as the word "*tener*" ("to have")—a large and hairy irregular verb—raced after him on its spindly[70] legs. ◆

---

67. **Portnoy's Complaint**   erotic novel by Philip Roth
68. **The Monkey**   female character in *Portnoy's Complaint*, skillful at fulfilling Portnoy's sexual fantasies
69. **Remedial Spanish**   Spanish for slow learners
70. **spindly**   thin

PART ◆1◆ **FIRST READING**

A. Thinking about the Story

Were you able to suspend your disbelief regarding the impossible setup and respond to the comedy of the situation and the one-line jokes?

B. Understanding the Plot

1. Why did Kugelmass marry Daphne? Why won't he divorce her?
2. Why is Kugelmass's analyst against his having an affair?
3. What does Kugelmass's dream mean?
4. What are the disadvantages of Temple Drake and Nana as potential lovers of Kugelmass?

5. Why does Kugelmass fear his "rival" Rodolphe?

6. What does Kugelmass think of Emma's husband, Charles?

7. What is Emma's main complaint against Charles?

8. What does Kugelmass criticize Emma for during her prolonged stay in the Plaza Hotel?

9. What are Emma's ambitions for herself during her New York visit?

10. Does Kugelmass's wife suspect that he is having an affair? Explain your answer.

11. What is different about Emma's last leave-taking from Kugelmass?

12. What happens to Kugelmass at the end?

P A R T ◆2◆ **SECOND READING**

A. Exploring Themes

You are now ready to reread "The Kugelmass Episode." Look at how Woody Allen exposes his characters' weaknesses through a dialogue peppered with jokes.

1. How is Kugelmass's relationship with his wife Daphne presented? Illustrate your answer with details.

2. What attitudes toward women are reflected in the story?

3. What are Emma's values? Explain your answer.

4. How does the story make fun of literature teachers and their students?

5. What is ironic about the ending of the story?

B. Analyzing the Author's Style

Before you begin to work on this section, turn to the detailed explanation of dialogue (page 277), characterization (page 275), and anachronism (page 274).

DIALOGUE

"The Kugelmass Episode" is composed almost entirely of **dialogue**, with virtually no descriptive writing. The dialogue is informal, slangy, and unmistakably from the New York of the 1970s. The short, snappy lines serve as a showcase for Woody Allen's famous one-line jokes.

The following dialogue from the story is representative of Allen's style:

"Did I know it would turn out so badly?" Kugelmass whined to his analyst one day. "Daphne had promise. Who suspected she'd let herself go and swell up like a beach ball? Plus she had a few bucks, which is not in itself a healthy reason to marry a person, but it doesn't hurt, with the kind of operating nut I have. You see my point?" (lines 5–9)

1. What is the effect of using dialogue in this fashion?
2. Which verbal jokes in the story appealed to you? Why?
3. How do you imagine a professor of humanities should speak? Does Kugelmass come up to your expectations or not? Explain your answer.
4. Can you tell the characters apart from the way they speak? If you can, how? If not, does that disturb you?

CHARACTERIZATION: ROUND AND FLAT CHARACTERS

Woody Allen employs a very distinctive method of **characterization,** which adds to the humor of his writing. Like all authors he makes choices about whether to create the characters in a **round** (multidimensional or complex) fashion or a **flat** (one-dimensional or predictable) fashion.

1. Are the characters in "The Kugelmass Episode" round or flat? Explain your answer.
2. How does the way the characters are presented affect your involvement with their predicament? Does this increase the humor of the situation for you?
3. Does the absence of descriptive writing affect the way the characters are presented? Explain your answer.
4. Choose a round character from another story in this anthology. Say what gives the character its multidimensional aspect.

ANACHRONISM AND HUMOR

In "The Kugelmass Episode" both Kugelmass and Emma are transported into a different century and country from their own. The many **anachronisms** that arise from this are an additional source of humor in the story as the reader is presented with the resulting inconsistencies in time and place. For example, when Emma and Kugelmass are strolling past the church in Yonville and she implores him to tell her more about the American football star O. J. Simpson, she is referring to a person not yet born and a game not yet played in the United States. Similarly, when Emma comments about an off-Broadway producer that "He's up for a Tony" (line 298), her use of twentieth-century slang about a contemporary American theatrical award she could not possibly know about in her nineteenth-century French life is humorously incongruous.

1. Give several examples of what Emma sees, does, and says that do not fit in with her nineteenth-century experience and language.
2. What elements of Kugelmass's conversations with Emma in Yonville reflect his twentieth-century orientation?

C. Judging for Yourself

Express yourself as personally as you like in your answers to the following questions:

1. Do you think Kugelmass deserved his fate at the end of the story? Justify your answer.
2. In your opinion might further analysis have helped Kugelmass?
3. Do you sympathize with Daphne Kugelmass? Why? Why not?
4. If it were possible, would you be interested in meeting Emma Bovary? Explain your answer.

D. Making Connections

1. Is divorce common in your culture? When a couple splits up, is it customary to award alimony?
2. Are Woody Allen's movies shown in your country? Which ones have you seen? Do you find his comedies funny? Why? Why not?
3. In your culture is it common to seek help for personal problems from an analyst, psychologist, or counselor? If not, whom do people usually turn to for help in these matters?
4. Are people like movie stars or pop singers the object of popular fantasies in your country? If yes, give examples. If no, explain why not.

E. Debate

Debate the proposition: Psychiatrists do more harm than good.

P A R T ◆3◆ **F O C U S   O N   L A N G U A G E**

A. Verbs that Introduce Dialogue

Since "The Kugelmass Episode" is composed mainly of dialogue, Woody Allen employs a variety of verbs to introduce the speakers.

Look at the following list of verbs that appear in the story:

whined (line 5)	sighed (line 176)
whispered (line 44)	implored (line 189)
yelled (line 135)	squealed (line 236)
snapped (line 152)	mumbled (line 258)

Complete the following dialogue with the most appropriate verb from the list. Use the simple past tense each time.

1. "Please, please can't I go to the party on Saturday night?" _____ the teenager.

2. "Where are you?" _____ the mountaineer, peering anxiously down the slope.

3. "Don't bother me now. I'm far too busy," _____ the boss to his employee.

4. "Pass me your opera glasses, please," the wife _____ to her husband during the performance.

5. The judge requested the witness to speak more clearly after she _____, "I'm not sure I can positively identify that man."

6. "I wish I could afford to go with you to Greece this summer," _____ my friend.

7. "You're always picking on me!" _____ the student to his teacher. "It's not my fault."

8. "Oh, good! Our favorite chocolate dessert!" _____ the children in delight.

B. Building Vocabulary Skills

In the following list the left-hand column contains idioms from the text. Make sure you understand their meaning in the context of the story. The right-hand column contains situations appropriate to each idiom.

Match each idiom to its situation. The first one is done for you.

IDIOMS	SITUATIONS
_d_ 1. up to his neck (line 3)	a. at mental arithmetic
____ 2. let herself go (line 6)	b. the tour group in Japan
____ 3. not be any great shakes (line 22)	c. the mystery
____ 4. act out (line 28)	d. in debt
____ 5. on the level (line 79)	e. by a long meeting
____ 6. held up (line 153)	f. after childbirth
____ 7. hooks up with (line 163)	g. to a sympathetic listener
____ 8. hot stuff (line 169)	h. in business dealings
____ 9. put up with (line 176)	i. a long illness
____ 10. pouring my heart out (line 178)	j. one's fantasies
____ 11. got to the bottom of (line 274)	k. because of an Oscar nomination

Write sentences using both the idiom and its corresponding situation. For example: He was up to his neck in debt, so he declared bankruptcy.

PART ◆4◆ **WRITING ACTIVITIES**

1. In an essay of two to five pages, consider this question: If you had the opportunity to go back in time, what aspects of late twentieth-century life would you willingly leave behind and which would you most like to take with you? Explain the reasons for your decisions.

2. Using "The Kugelmass Episode" as a model, create an extended dialogue of about two pages between one of the following: an unhappily married couple, a patient and his or her analyst, or you and your favorite movie star. Keep the dialogue naturally conversational. You may include some explanatory sentences, but keep them to a minimum. In your writing incorporate some of the new idioms and slang you have learned from the story.

3. Many books, movies, and artworks center on fantasy and magic. Fantasy is crucial to Gabriel García Márquez's *One Hundred Years of Solitude,* and almost all of Salvador Dali's paintings are rooted in the fantastic imagination. Write a one- or two-page essay describing the fantasy elements of a book, movie, or painting you are familiar with. Say how the work integrates the fantastic with the real. Conclude your piece with a paragraph on your personal response to fantasy and magic.

PARENT AND CHILD

◆ ◆ ◆ ◆ ◆ ◆ ◆ ◆ ◆ ◆ ◆ ◆ ◆ ◆ ◆ ◆ ◆ ◆ ◆

Mary Cassatt, *Mother and Child*, c. 1890

◆ ◆ ◆ ◆ ◆ ◆ ◆ ◆ ◆ ◆ ◆ ◆ ◆ ◆ ◆ ◆ ◆ ◆ ◆

A Short Digest of a Long Novel

BUDD SCHULBERG *(b. 1914)*

◆◆◆

BORN IN NEW YORK CITY, Budd Schulberg moved at the age of five to Hollywood, where his father became head of Paramount Studios. Schulberg has enjoyed a varied career as novelist, short story writer, playwright, travel writer, boxing editor, and writer of screenplays. Frequently employing the first-person narrative, Schulberg's novels explore how rapid success affects the moral fiber of his characters. He has said, "I believe that the seasons of success and failure are more violent in America than anywhere else on earth."

Schulberg's first novel, *What Makes Sammy Run?* (1941), a satire on Hollywood, catapulted him to fame. Other novels include *The Disenchanted* (1950), modeled on F. Scott Fitzgerald, whom he knew; *Sanctuary V* (1969), and *Everything That Moves* (1980). He has also published two collections of short stories: *Some Faces in the Crowd* (1953) and *Love, Action, Laughter, and Other Sad Tales* (1989).

A SHORT DIGEST[1] OF A LONG NOVEL

A father watches helplessly as his young daughter learns about betrayal.

Her legs were shapely and firm and when she crossed them and smiled with the self-assurance that always delighted him, he thought she was the only person he knew in the world who was unblemished.[2] Not lifelike but an improvement on life, as a work of art, her delicate features were chiseled[3] from a solid block. The wood-sculpture image came easy to him because her particular shade of blonde always suggested maple[4] polished to a golden grain.[5] As it had been from the moment he stood in awe and amazement in front of the glass window where she was first exhibited, the sight of her made him philosophical. Some of us appear in beautiful colors, too, or with beautiful grains, but we develop imperfections. Inspect us very closely and you find we're damaged by the elements.[6] Sometimes we're only nicked[7] with cynicism.[8] Sometimes we're cracked with disillusionment.[9] Or we're split with fear.

When she began to speak, he leaned forward, eager for the words that were like good music, profundity[10] expressed in terms that pleased the ear while challenging the mind.

"Everybody likes me," she said. "Absolutely everybody."

It was not that she was conceited. It was simply that she was only three. No one had ever taken her[11] with sweet and whispered promises that turned into morning-after lies, ugly and cold as unwashed dishes from last night's dinner lying in the sink. She had never heard a dictator rock her country to sleep with peaceful lullabies[12] one day and rock it with bombs the next. She was undeceived. Her father ran his hands reverently[13] through her soft yellow hair. She is virgin,[14] he thought, for this is the true virginity, that brief moment in the time of your life before your mind or your body has been defiled[15] by acts of treachery.

It was just before Christmas and she was sitting on her little chair, her lips pressed together in concentration, writing a last-minute letter to Santa Claus. The words were written in some language of her own invention but she obligingly translated as she went along.

---

1. **digest** a shortened literary form
2. **unblemished** unmarked, perfect
3. **chiseled** carved
4. **maple** a light-colored wood
5. **grain** the markings or texture of wood
6. **the elements** atmospheric forces like wind or rain
7. **nicked** bearing a small cut
8. **cynicism** belief that humans behave only selfishly
9. **disillusionment** state of mind after our dreams are destroyed
10. **profundity** intellectual depth
11. **taken her** made love to her
12. **lullabies** songs sung to babies to help them sleep
13. **reverently** respectfully
14. **virgin** pure, untouched; sexually innocent
15. **defiled** made impure

Dear Santa, I am a very good girl and everybody likes me. So please   30
don't forget to bring me a set of dishes, a doll that goes to sleep and
wakes up again, and a washing machine. I need the washing
machine because Raggedy Ann's[16] dress is so dirty.

After she finished her letter, folded it, and asked him to address it, he
tossed her up in the air, caught her and tossed her again, to hear her   35
giggle.[17] "Higher, Daddy, higher," she instructed. His mind embraced her
sentimentally: She is a virgin island in a lewd[18] world. She is a winged seed
of innocence blown through the wasteland. If only she could root
somewhere. If only she could grow like this.

"Let me down, Daddy," she said when she had decided that she had   40
indulged him[19] long enough, "I have to mail my letter to Santa."

"But didn't you see him this afternoon?" he asked. "Didn't you ask for
everything you wanted? Mommy said she took you up to meet him and you
sat on his lap."

"I just wanted to remind him," she said. "There were so many other   45
children."

He fought down the impulse to laugh, because she was not something
to laugh at. And he was obsessed with the idea that to hurt her feelings with
laughter was to nick her, to blemish the perfection.

"Daddy can't catch me-ee," she sang out, and the old chase was on,   50
following the pattern that had become so familiar to them, the same wild
shrieks and the same scream of pretended anguish[20] at the inevitable result.
Two laps around the dining-room table[21] was the established course before
he caught her in the kitchen. He swung her up from the floor and set her
down on the kitchen table. She stood on the edge, poised confidently for   55
another of their games. But this was no panting, giggling game like tag or
hide-and-seek. This game was ceremonial. The table was several feet higher
than she was. "Jump, jump, and Daddy will catch you," he would challenge.
They would count together, *one, two,* and on *three* she would leap out into
the air. He would not even hold out his arms to her until the last possible   60
moment. But he would always catch her. They had played the game for
more than a year and the experience never failed to exhilarate[22] them. You
see, I am always here to catch you when you are falling, it said to them, and
each time she jumped, her confidence increased and their bond deepened.

They were going through the ceremony when the woman next door   65
came in with her five-year-old son, Billy. "Hello, Mr. Steevers," she said.
"Would you mind if I left Bill with you for an hour while I do my marketing?"

"No, of course not, glad to have him," he said and he mussed Billy's
hair[23] playfully. "How's the boy, Billy?"

---

16. **Raggedy Ann**   a popular rag doll
17. **giggle**   small laugh
18. **lewd**   coarse, vulgar
19. **indulged him**   let him do what he wanted
20. **anguish**   intense sorrow or pain
21. **two laps around the dining room table**   twice around the dining room table
22. **exhilarate**   greatly excite
23. **mussed Billy's hair**   ran his fingers through Billy's hair, making it untidy

But his heart wasn't in it. This was the only afternoon of the week with her and he resented the intrusion. And then too, he was convinced that Billy was going to grow up into the type of man for whom he had a particular resentment. A sturdy,[24] good-looking boy, big for his age, aggressively unchildlike, a malicious,[25] arrogant, insensitive extrovert.[26] I can just see him drunk and red-faced and pulling up girls' dresses at Legion Conventions, Mr. Steevers would think. And the worst of it was, his daughter seemed blind to Billy's faults. The moment she saw him she forgot about their game.

"Hello, Billy-Boy," she called and ran over to hug him.

"I want a cookie," said Billy.

"Oh, yes, a cookie; some animal crackers, Daddy."

She had her hostess face on and as he went into the pantry, he could hear the treble[27] of her musical laughter against the premature[28] baritone[29] of Billy's guffaws.[30]

He swung open the pantry door with the animal crackers in his hand just in time to see it. She was poised on the edge of the table. Billy was standing below her, as he had seen her father do. "Jump and I'll catch you," he was saying.

Smiling, confident and unblemished, she jumped. But no hands reached out to break her flight. With a cynical grin on his face, Billy stepped back and watched her fall.

Watching from the doorway, her father felt the horror that possessed him the time he saw a parachutist[31] smashed like a bug on a windshield when his chute failed to open. She was lying there, crying, not so much in pain as in disillusionment. He ran forward to pick her up and he would never forget the expression on her face, the *new* expression, unchildlike, unvirginal, embittered.

"I hate you, I hate you," she was screaming at Billy through hysterical sobs.

Well, now she knows, thought her father, the facts of life. Now she's one of us. Now she knows treachery and fear. Now she must learn to replace innocence with courage.

She was still bawling.[32] He knew these tears were as natural and as necessary as those she shed at birth, but that could not overcome entirely the heavy sadness that enveloped him. Finally, when he spoke, he said, a little more harshly than he had intended, "Now, now, stop crying. Stand up and act like a big girl. A little fall like that can't hurt you." ◆

Margin line numbers: 70, 75, 80, 85, 90, 95, 100, 105

---

24. **sturdy**   firmly built, strong
25. **malicious**   wanting to hurt someone
26. **extrovert**   an outgoing personality who expresses feelings easily
27. **treble**   high-pitched note (singing)
28. **premature**   early

29. **baritone**   low-pitched note (singing)
30. **guffaws**   loud laughter
31. **parachutist**   someone who jumps from an airplane with a safety device
32. **bawling**   crying loudly

P A R T ◆**1**◆ **FIRST READING**

A. Thinking about the Story

Did you feel that the father's evaluation of his little girl was realistic? Did his attitude toward Billy make you at all uneasy?

B. Understanding the Plot

1. What does the father compare his daughter's appearance to in paragraph 1?

2. What does "the glass window" in line 8 refer to?

3. In what ways is the daughter still "undeceived?" (line 22)

4. Why is the jumping game the father and daughter play different from games like tag and hide-and-seek that they may play on other occasions? What in particular describes the jumping game's importance?

5. Why is the father unhappy about Billy's arrival?

6. What are the father's main complaints against Billy?

7. What bothers the father about his daughter's reaction to Billy's arrival?

8. How does Billy betray the little girl?

9. What comparison is used to express the father's reaction on seeing his daughter fall?

10. How is the daughter changed by her fall?

11. Why does the father speak harshly to his daughter at the end?

P A R T ◆**2**◆ **SECOND READING**

A. Exploring Themes

You are now ready to reread "A Short Digest of a Long Novel." Be sensitive to the undercurrents of jealousy the father displays toward Billy and the reasons for them.

1. What do you think the title means? Relate your answer to a central theme in the story.

2. What does the father's description of his daughter in paragraph 1 reveal about his feelings toward her?

3. What is the role of the sexual imagery in the story?

4. What is the importance of the jumping game to the story? In your answer look at both occasions on which the game is played and show how the girl is affected each time.

5. What does Billy represent for the father?

B. Analyzing the Author's Style

Before you begin to work on this section, turn to the detailed explanation of imagery (page 279), simile (page 282), and metaphor (page 280).

IMAGERY: SIMILE AND METAPHOR

In "A Short Digest of a Long Novel" Budd Schulberg constantly surprises the reader with his unexpected **imagery**, particularly his deft use of **simile** (an explicit comparison using *like* or *as* to unite the two elements) and **metaphor** (an implied comparison). For example, he writes of the father's horror as he impotently watches his daughter fall:

> . . . *her father felt the horror that possessed him the time he saw a* **parachutist smashed like a bug on a windshield** *when his parachute failed to open.* (lines 92–94)

Here the two elements compared are the disintegrated parachutist and a crushed bug, which are in turn analogous to the father's emotions regarding his daughter's fall. The complex overall effect is to express the depth of the father's feelings as well as to act as a comment on the exaggeration of his response, for the one event is not by any stretch of the imagination really comparable to the other.

In an earlier example, a beautifully precise metaphor captures the father's fears about what lies ahead for his daughter when he worries about her as a *virgin island in a lewd world.* (line 37) In this instance, his innocent daughter is compared in his mind to an untouched island surrounded by a vulgar world ready to corrupt and overwhelm it/her.

1. The long opening paragraph of "A Short Digest of a Long Novel" contains a sustained metaphor that explains how the father sees his daughter. What is it? Explain how the metaphor is extended and reworked throughout the paragraph.

2. What simile does the father use to describe his daughter's speech? What are the implications of employing such a simile to describe a three-year-old child?

3. Later in the story this same simile is translated into a metaphor, applying to both Billy and the daughter. Write down the metaphor and explain its two components. What does the metaphor describing Billy's voice reveal about the father's feelings toward him?

4. Pick out the simile in lines 18–20. What two elements are being compared? How does this simile reflect the father's state of mind?

5. What new metaphors can you find in lines 37–39? How do they fit in with the way the father views his daughter?

6. The last paragraph contains a metaphor and a simile. Pick them out and explain them.

C. Judging for Yourself

Express yourself as personally as you like in your answers to the following questions:

1. Do you think that the father's jealousy is understandable?

2. Why do you suppose the mother plays such a small role in the story?

3. What effect might the father's protectiveness have on his daughter's development?

4. In your view did Billy's behavior justify the father's fears?

5. Do you feel the father's belief in his daughter's innocent perfection is unrealistic?

D. Making Connections

1. Do fathers tend to be very protective of their daughters in your culture? If so, how does this protectiveness manifest itself?

2. Are small children spoiled in your country? Who spoils them—mothers or fathers? Is one sex more spoiled than the other?

3. What are the traditional games parents play with small children in your country? Do you know whether any of these games are played elsewhere in the world?

4. Do you celebrate Christmas? If yes, describe a typical Christmas in your country. If not, describe a holiday custom that particularly excited you as a child.

E. Debate

Debate the proposal: It is never too early to teach a child a lesson in reality.

P A R T ◆3◆ **F O C U S O N L A N G U A G E**

A. Prefixes

Prefixes are placed at the beginning of words. Some examples of prefixes are *un-, im-, a-, ir-, in-, il-, dis-, mis-, pre-, re-, non-, mal-,* and *em-*. Adding prefixes to words changes their meaning. For example, the prefix *un-* when added to the word *popular* (well liked), changes the meaning to not well liked.

Look at the words in the following column. All of them appear in some form in the story. Add prefixes to these words and use each prefixed word in a sentence to illustrate its meaning. Your sentences should accurately reflect the content of the Schulberg story.

assure _____

bitter _____

illusion _____

likes _____

mature _____

perfect _____

reverently _____

sensitive _____

step _____

sturdy _____

B. Building Vocabulary Skills

In "A Short Digest of a Long Novel" Billy is described by the father as a boy likely to grow into "a *malicious, arrogant, insensitive* extrovert." (line 74) He is also imagined to be "*drunk* and *red-faced,* and *pulling up girls' dresses at Legion Conventions.*" (line 75) These strings of connected adjectives help us to picture the adult Billy through the intense imagination of the father, while at the same time serving as an ironic commentary on the father's jealousy of the boy.

Complete the following sentences with an apt adjective or adjectival phrase of your own. Relate your responses to the story.

1. The father lovingly regarded his baby daughter as virginal, untouched, and _____.

2. Her shapely, _____, _____ legs were neatly crossed as she sat waiting for her father.

3. His daughter's hair, blonde and finely polished and _____, hung over her face.

4. As we get older, it is easy to see ourselves as disillusioned, cynical, and _____.

5. The child's _____, _____, musical voice rang in his ears long after he had left her.

6. He couldn't bear that she be exposed to lies as ugly, _____, and cold as the unwashed dishes from last night's dinner lying in the sink.

7. As he chased her round the table, she ran _____, screaming, and _____ in her efforts to elude him.

8. The moment he saw Billy's sturdy, _____, and _____ body, he knew he wasn't going to like him.

9. With a smile as confident, _____, and powerful as a conqueror, she reached out her arms and jumped.

10. Filled with embittered, _____, and _____ feelings, she lay screaming on the floor.

PART ◆4◆ **WRITING ACTIVITIES**

1. Write an essay detailing an occasion in your life in which you experienced a profound change that affected you permanently. It could be related to an event like the death of a loved one, a meaningful religious ceremony, or the first time you left home. Be sure to convey when, why, and how you were so changed.

2. Write two or three paragraphs describing a child you know. Using the opening of the Schulberg story as a model, start your description without revealing the identity of your character, and slowly lead up to your revelation. Bring your child to life through fresh imagery appealing to the various senses, and try to sustain a metaphor through several lines of writing. Your metaphor might be based on your character's appearance, personality, or a particular nickname.

3. The movie *Father of the Bride*—the original with Spencer Tracy and Elizabeth Taylor and the remake with Steve Martin and Kimberly Williams—deals with the conflict a father has when his cherished only daughter announces she is getting married. Write an essay on any book, movie, or play you have read or seen that centers on the father-daughter relationship. In the essay analyze the nature of this bond, and say what aspects of the relationship you think are particular to the work you chose and which are more universal.

Mother

GRACE PALEY *(b. 1922)*

◆◆◆

BORN IN NEW YORK CITY to Russian Jewish immigrants, Grace Paley heard English, Russian, and Yiddish spoken at home in the Bronx. As a result, she developed an acute ear for reproducing dialect, and her stories are full of Jewish, Black, Irish, and other ethnic accents. Paley currently teaches in the English Department at Dartmouth College. In addition to her writing and academic career, she has also led a politically active life, taking a vocal position against the Vietnam War and fighting for women's rights and pacifism, among other social and political causes.

Paley's stories often employ first-person narrators and are peopled with vulnerable ordinary characters who endure the ups and downs in their lives with love, humor, and patience. She has published three collections of short stories: *The Little Disturbances of Man: Stories of Men and Women in Love* (1959), *Enormous Changes at the Last Minute* (1976), and *Later the Same Day* (1985). She has also published a volume of poetry, *Leaning Forward* (1986).

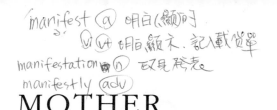

MOTHER

Years after her death a mother is remembered by her child.

One day I was listening to the AM radio. I heard a song: "Oh, I Long[1] to See My Mother in the Doorway." By God! I said, I understand that song. I have often longed to see my mother in the doorway. As a matter of fact, she did stand frequently in various doorways looking at me. She stood one day, just so, at the front door, the darkness of the hallway behind her. It was New Year's Day. She said sadly, If you come home at 4 A.M. when you're seventeen, what time will you come home when you're twenty? She asked this question without humor or meanness. She had begun her worried preparations for death. She would not be present, she thought, when I was twenty. So she wondered.

Another time she stood in the doorway of my room. I had just issued a political manifesto[2] attacking the family's position on the Soviet Union. She said, Go to sleep for godsakes, you damn fool, you and your Communist ideas. We saw them already, Papa and me, in 1905. We guessed it all.

At the door of the kitchen she said, You never finish your lunch. You run around senselessly. What will become of you?

Then she died.

Naturally for the rest of my life I longed to see her, not only in doorways, in a great number of places—in the dining room with my aunts, at the window looking up and down the block, in the country garden among zinnias and marigolds,[3] in the living room with my father.

They sat in comfortable leather chairs. They were listening to Mozart. They looked at one another amazed. It seemed to them that they'd just come over on the boat. They'd just learned the first English words. It seemed to them that he had just proudly handed in a 100 percent correct exam to the American anatomy[4] professor. It seemed as though she'd just quit the shop for the kitchen.

I wish I could see her in the doorway of the living room.

She stood there a minute. Then she sat beside him. They owned an expensive record player. They were listening to Bach. She said to him, Talk to me a little. We don't talk so much anymore.

I'm tired, he said. Can't you see? I saw maybe thirty people today. All sick, all talk talk talk talk. Listen to the music, he said. I believe you once had perfect pitch.[5] I'm tired, he said.

Then she died. ◆

5

10

15

20

25

30

35

---

1. **long**   want badly
2. **manifesto**   a declaration of intentions or principles
3. **zinnias and marigolds**   brightly colored summer flowers

4. **anatomy**   the study of the various parts of the body
5. **perfect pitch**   the ability to recognize and reproduce a musical note exactly

P A R T ◆1◆ **F I R S T R E A D I N G**

A. Thinking about the Story

Were you drawn into the universal aspects of the mother-child relationship depicted in the story?

B. Understanding the Plot

1. Through whose eyes is the story told?
2. What was the narrator's mother's major concern regarding her teenage child?
3. What country were the parents born in? How do we know?
4. What were the political beliefs of the narrator as a teenager?
5. What do you think the events of 1905 were that the narrator's mother referred to? Note: You may have to consult an encyclopedia to help answer this question.
6. What profession was the father studying for?
7. Why was the father particularly proud of his examination results?
8. Explain the expression: "She'd just quit the shop for the kitchen." (lines 26–27)
9. What was the father's attitude toward his work?
10. What leisure-time activity did the narrator's parents share? How does the mother's perfect pitch relate to this activity?

P A R T ◆2◆ **S E C O N D R E A D I N G**

A. Exploring Themes

You are now ready to reread "Mother." Look at how Paley has packed so much information and such a range of feeling and time into such a small space. This gives "Mother" the density of a poem.

1. How would you characterize the mother's relationship with her child?
2. How does the relationship between the parents change?
3. How did the economic circumstances of the family change? Give examples to illustrate your answer.
4. What does the narrator's mother imply happened to them in Russia in 1905?

5. In what ways have the adult narrator's feelings toward his or her mother altered?

6. What is the mood of the narrator?

7. What sentence is repeated in the story? Why?

B. Analyzing the Author's Style

Before you begin to work on this section, turn to the detailed explanation of flashback (page 278).

FLASHBACK

Most of the information essential to an understanding of "Mother" is conveyed through **flashbacks**, in which the narrator interrupts the present time and returns to the past. For example, at the start of the story the narrator-protagonist (the central character who also tells the story) is listening to the radio; then the next moment the reader is transported back to a much earlier event that occurred one New Year's Day when the narrator was seventeen.

1. How many flashbacks does "Mother" contain? Where does each flashback begin and end?

2. What word links several of the flashbacks? What is the thematic significance of the situation described by this word?

3. What is the effect of telling this story in a rapid series of flashbacks?

C. Judging for Yourself

Express yourself as personally as you like in your answers to the following questions:

1. Do you feel the mother was overprotective of her child?

2. What role do you think the father played in his child's upbringing?

3. In your view does the narrator have reason to regret his or her behavior toward the mother?

4. Do you think the narrator is male or female? Justify your answer.

5. About how old do you estimate the narrator to be at the start of the story? Give reasons for your answer.

D. Making Connections

1. Are male teenagers in your culture given more freedom than female teenagers by their parents?

2. Do teenagers in your country tend to be more politically radical than their parents?

3. Do teenagers feel a need to express their individuality in your country? If so, how? If not, why not?

4. Would you say that you had a closer relationship with your mother than with your father when you were a teenager? Explain why or why not.

E. Debate

Debate the proposal: The difficulties of being a parent of a teenager are vastly exaggerated.

PART ◆3◆ **FOCUS ON LANGUAGE**

A. Tenses Expressing and Referring to the Past

THE SIMPLE PAST

The **simple past** is used for something that began and ended at a certain time in the past. For example:

*She **stood** one day, just so, at the front door, the darkness of the hallway behind her.* (lines 4–5)

THE PAST PROGRESSIVE

The **past progressive** is used to show that an action was in progress when something else occurred. It takes the form of the past tense of *be* plus the *present participle*. For example:

*One day I **was listening** to the AM radio. I heard a song: "Oh, I Long to See My Mother in the Doorway."* (lines 1–2)

Note: The above sentence could also be written as

*One day I **was listening** to the AM radio when I heard a song: "Oh, I Long to See My Mother in the Doorway."*

THE PRESENT PERFECT

The **present perfect** can be used in several situations. It takes the form of the present tense of *have* plus the *past participle*.

A. It is used to indicate that an action has begun in the past and continues or recurs up to the present. For example:

*I **have** often **longed** to see my mother in the doorway.* (lines 2–3)

B. It is used to show that something has or has not occurred at an unspecified time in the past. For example:

*I **have seen** my mother in the doorway.*

C. It is used to suggest that an action has very recently been completed. For example:

*My mother is here. I **have** just **seen** her in the doorway.*

Note: In the present perfect tense we are more concerned with the effect of an action at the present moment and less interested in when the action started.

THE PRESENT PERFECT PROGRESSIVE

The **present perfect progressive** is used to suggest that an action that has been going on in the past is still continuing. It takes the form of *have/has been* plus the *present participle*. For example:

*I**'ve been longing** to see my mother in the doorway for months.*

THE PAST PERFECT

The **past perfect** is used to show that something had already been completed before another action began in the past. It takes the form of the past tense of *have* plus the *past participle*. For example:

*I **had** just **issued** a political manifesto attacking the family's position on the Soviet Union. She said, Go to sleep for godsakes, you damn fool. . . .* (lines 11–13)

Note: The above sentence could also be written as

*I **had** just **issued** a political manifesto attacking the family's position on the Soviet Union when she said, Go to sleep for godsakes, you damn fool.*

PAST PERFECT PROGRESSIVE

The **past perfect progressive** is used to show that something had been happening up until something else in the past interrupted the first action. It takes the form of *had been* plus the *present participle*. For example:

> I **had** just **been issuing** a political manifesto attacking the family's position on the Soviet Union, when she ordered me to go to sleep at once.

Note: In this example she interrupted me while I was talking, whereas in the past perfect example I had already finished talking.

PRACTICE WITH TENSES THAT REFER TO THE PAST

Complete the sentences with a correct tense of the verb in parentheses. The verb in parentheses applies to both sentences in a pair. Although it may be possible, do not use the same tense in each pair. The first one is done for you as an example.

1. (behave) When I was a teenager, I frequently____*behaved*____ badly toward my mother.
   I knew that I __*had been behaving*__ badly. I promised I would stop.

2. (achieve) It amazed my parents that they _____ so much in such a short time.
   "We _____ so much in such a short time," said my father in amazement to my mother.

3. (listen) My mother _____ to music when I came home from school.
   My mother _____ to music every day of my school life.

4. (talk) "I _____ to you for the past ten minutes and you haven't heard a word!" said my mother in exasperation.
   I _____ to you for at least ten minutes before I realized you hadn't heard a word.

5. (return) My parents _____ to Russia only once since they arrived in this country.
   My parents _____ to Russia for the first time last year.

6. (worry) Although my mother continually _____ about dying, she didn't express her fears to me.
   Although my mother _____ about dying for years, she only expressed her fears to me last week.

7. (hand in) You _____ your exam, so there is nothing we can do about it.
   You _____ your exam, so there was nothing we could do about it.

8. (run around) When I was younger, I _____ senselessly.
   I _____ senselessly for years before I was stopped by the death of my mother.

9. (quit) After my father graduated, my mother _____ working.
   "I didn't know you _____ working!" exclaimed my father to my mother.

10. (look for) I always _____ my mother in the garden.
    Although I _____ my mother in the garden for nearly ten minutes, I still hadn't found her by the time dinner was served.

11. (study) My father and mother _____ English soon after they arrived in the United States.
    My father and mother _____ English for the past three months.

B. Building Vocabulary Skills

Working with a partner, substitute the following italicized words or expressions with a synonym from the text. Try to do this exercise from memory, referring back to the text only if necessary.

1. I read your *declaration of principles* last night and have decided to vote for you.

2. Teenagers frequently act *thoughtlessly* and suffer the consequences.

3. To play the violin well a musician needs *a totally accurate ear*.

4. After immigrating to a new country, it is not uncommon to *yearn* for one's place of birth.

5. Any student who *submits* his essay late will be penalized.

6. I don't know where you get your *spite* from.

7. The government *gave out* a pamphlet explaining its policy toward immigration.

8. The lessons involving *the study of the body* were my father's favorite classes at university.

PART ◆4◆ **WRITING ACTIVITIES**

1. Write a memory piece of two or three pages, focusing on an event in your teenage years. As in "Mother," start in the present and use something unexpected like a sound, a smell, or a gesture to trigger your memory and send you back into the past. Think about using past and present tenses appropriately.

2. Write a two-page essay analyzing the roots of the teenage rebellion against parental and other authority. Begin your essay with a consideration of why adolescents traditionally feel the need to challenge the rules of adult society. Consider the positive and negative aspects of this confrontation, and say what steps you would advocate to improve the situation.

3. Marcel Proust's *Remembrance of Things Past* is one of the most famous works of fiction centering on memory. Write a book review for a newspaper or magazine on a book you have read in which a character looks back on events that occurred in the past. Briefly explain its contents and say why you recommend it.

4. "Mother" and "Snow" (page 22) are both told by narrator-protagonists using flashbacks. In an essay compare and contrast the use of flashbacks in both stories. Were the flashbacks more effective in one story than the other? Explain why.

The Rocking-Horse Winner

D. H. LAWRENCE *(1885–1930)*

◆◆◆

BORN IN NOTTINGHAMSHIRE, England, David Herbert Lawrence was the son of a coal-miner father and teacher mother. He was one of England's most versatile and controversial writers, producing a large body of work that includes novels, plays, poems, essays, travel pieces, and letters. Several of his novels—*The Rainbow* (1915), *Women in Love* (1920), and *Lady Chatterley's Lover* (1928)—were considered obscene and were initially banned in much of the world. His famous novel *Sons and Lovers* (1913) was heavily autobiographical and dealt with the themes of sex, class, and family that were to preoccupy him always.

In 1912, Lawrence eloped to Europe with Frieda von Richthofen Weekley, the wife of one of his university professors and mother of three children. They married in 1914. Frieda became the inspiration for many of his fictional heroines. After World War I, the Lawrences traveled extensively, living in the warmer climates of Italy, Mexico, New Mexico, and Australia, among other places, as he sought relief from the tuberculosis that was killing him.

THE ROCKING-HORSE WINNER

A young boy is determined to solve his mother's financial worries. The method he chooses defies human logic and is ultimately dangerous.

There was a woman who was beautiful, who started with all the advantages, yet she had no luck. She married for love, and the love turned to dust. She had bonny[1] children, yet she felt they had been thrust upon her, and she could not love them. They looked at her coldly, as if they were finding fault with her. And hurriedly she felt she must cover up some fault in herself. Yet what it was that she must cover up she never knew. Nevertheless, when her children were present, she always felt the centre of her heart go hard. This troubled her, and in her manner she was all the more gentle and anxious for her children, as if she loved them very much. Only she herself knew that at the centre of her heart was a hard little place that could not feel love, no, not for anybody. Everybody else said of her: "She is such a good mother. She adores her children." Only she herself, and her children themselves, know it was not so. They read it in each other's eyes.

There were a boy and two little girls. They lived in a pleasant house, with a garden, and they had discreet servants, and felt themselves superior to anyone in the neighbourhood.

Although they lived in style, they felt always an anxiety in the house. There was never enough money. The mother had a small income, and the father had a small income, but not nearly enough for the social position which they had to keep up. The father went into town to some office. But though he had good prospects,[2] these prospects never materialized. There was always the grinding sense of the shortage of money, though the style was always kept up.[3]

At last the mother said: "I will see if *I* can't make something." But she did not know where to begin. She racked her brains,[4] and tried this thing and the other, but could not find anything successful. The failure made deep lines come into her face. Her children were growing up, they would have to go to school. There must be more money, there must be more money. The father, who was always very handsome and expensive in his tastes, seemed as if he never *would* be able to do anything worth doing. And the mother, who had a great belief in herself, did not succeed any better, and her tastes were just as expensive.

And so the house came to be haunted by the unspoken phrase: *There must be more money! There must be more money!* The children could hear

1. **bonny**   healthy and attractive
2. **had good prospects**   anticipated a good future
3. **kept up**   maintained
4. **racked her brains**   thought as hard as she could

it all the time, though nobody said it aloud. They heard it at Christmas, when the expensive and splendid toys filled the nursery. Behind the shining modern rocking-horse, behind the smart doll's house, a voice would start whispering: "There *must* be more money! There *must* be more money!" And the children would stop playing, to listen for a moment. They would look into each other's eyes, to see if they had all heard. And each one saw in the eyes of the other two that they too had heard. "There *must* be more money! There *must* be more money!"

It came whispering from the springs of the still-swaying rocking-horse, and even the horse, bending his wooden, champing[5] head, heard it. The big doll, sitting so pink and smirking[6] in her new pram, could hear it quite plainly, and seemed to be smirking all the more self-consciously because of it. The foolish puppy, too, that took the place of the teddy-bear, he was looking so extraordinarily foolish for no other reason but that he heard the secret whisper all over the house: "There *must* be more money!"

Yet nobody ever said it aloud. The whisper was everywhere, and therefore no one spoke it. Just as no one ever says: "We are breathing!" in spite of the fact that breath is coming and going all the time.

"Mother," said the boy Paul one day, "why don't we keep a car of our own? Why do we always use uncle's, or else a taxi?"

"Because we're the poor members of the family," said the mother.

"But why *are* we, mother?"

"Well—I suppose," she said slowly and bitterly, "it's because your father had no luck."

The boy was silent for some time.

"Is luck money, mother?" he asked, rather timidly.

"No, Paul. Not quite. It's what causes you to have money."

"Oh!" said Paul vaguely. "I thought when Uncle Oscar said *filthy lucker,*[7] it meant money."

"*Filthy lucre* does mean money," said the mother. "But it's lucre, not luck."

"Oh!" said the boy. "Then what *is* luck, mother?"

"It's what causes you to have money. If you're lucky you have money. That's why it's better to be born lucky than rich. If you're rich, you may lose your money. But if you're lucky, you will always get more money."

"Oh! Will you? And is father not lucky?"

"Very unlucky, I should say," she said bitterly.

The boy watched her with unsure eyes.

"Why?" he asked.

"I don't know. Nobody ever knows why one person is lucky and another unlucky."

"Don't they? Nobody at all? Does *nobody* know?"

"Perhaps God. But He never tells."

---

5. **champing**   impatient
6. **smirking**   smiling in a silly, self-satisfied way

7. **filthy lucker**   should be written as *filthy lucre*, which is a negative term for money.

"He ought to, then. And aren't you lucky either, mother?"

"I can't be, if I married an unlucky husband."

"But by yourself, aren't you?" 80

"I used to think I was, before I married. Now I think I am very unlucky indeed."

"Why?"

"Well—never mind! Perhaps I'm not really," she said.

The child looked at her to see if she meant it. But he saw, by the lines of 85 her mouth, that she was only trying to hide something from him.

"Well, anyhow," he said stoutly, "I'm a lucky person."

"Why?" said his mother, with a sudden laugh.

He stared at her. He didn't even know why he had said it.

"God told me," he asserted, brazening it out.[8] 90

"I hope He did, dear!" she said, again with a laugh, but rather bitter.

"He did, mother!"

"Excellent!" said the mother, using one of her husband's exclamations.

The boy saw she did not believe him; or rather, that she paid no attention to his assertion. This angered him somewhere, and made him want 95 to compel her attention.

He went off by himself, vaguely, in a childish way, seeking for the clue to "luck." Absorbed, taking no heed of other people, he went about with a sort of stealth, seeking inwardly for luck. He wanted luck, he wanted it, he wanted it. When the two girls were playing dolls in the nursery, he would sit 100 on his big rocking-horse, charging madly into space, with a frenzy that made the little girls peer at him uneasily. Wildly the horse careered,[9] the waving dark hair of the boy tossed, his eyes had a strange glare in them. The little girls dared not speak to him.

When he had ridden to the end of his mad little journey, he climbed 105 down and stood in front of his rocking-horse, staring fixedly into its lowered face. Its red mouth was slightly open, its big eye was wide and glassy-bright.

"Now!" he would silently command the snorting steed.[10] "Now, take me to where there is luck! Now take me!"

And he would slash the horse on the neck with the little whip he had 110 asked Uncle Oscar for. He *knew* the horse could take him to where there was luck, if only he forced it. So he would mount again and start on his furious ride, hoping at last to get there. He knew he could get there.

"You'll break your horse, Paul!" said the nurse.

"He's always riding like that! I wish he'd leave off!" said his elder sister 115 Joan.

But he only glared down on them in silence. Nurse gave him up. She could make nothing of him. Anyhow, he was growing beyond her.

One day his mother and his Uncle Oscar came in when he was on one of his furious rides. He did not speak to them. 120

---

8. **brazening it out**   deliberately sounding confident, even though he might be wrong

9. **careered**   moved at top speed

10. **snorting steed**   noisy horse

"Hallo, you young jockey![11] Riding a winner?" said his uncle.

"Aren't you growing too big for a rocking-horse? You're not a very little boy any longer, you know," said his mother.

But Paul only gave a blue glare from his big, rather close-set eyes. He would speak to nobody when he was in full tilt.[12] His mother watched him with an anxious expression on her face.

At last he suddenly stopped forcing his horse into the mechanical gallop and slid down.

"Well, I got there!" he announced fiercely, his blue eyes still flaring, and his sturdy long legs straddling apart.

"Where did you get to?" asked his mother.

"Where I wanted to go," he flared back at her.

"That's right, son!" said Uncle Oscar. "Don't you stop till you get there. What's the horse's name?"

"He doesn't have a name," said the boy.

"Gets on without all right?" asked the uncle.

"Well, he has different names. He was called Sansovino last week."

"Sansovino, eh? Won the Ascot. How did you know this name?"

"He always talks about horse-races with Bassett," said Joan.

The uncle was delighted to find that his small nephew was posted with all the racing news.[13] Bassett, the young gardener, who had been wounded in the left foot in the war and had got his present job through Oscar Cresswell, whose batman[14] he had been, was a perfect blade of the "turf."[15] He lived in the racing events, and the small boy lived with him.

Oscar Cresswell got it all from Bassett.

"Master Paul comes and asks me, so I can't do more than tell him, sir," said Bassett, his face terribly serious, as if he were speaking of religious matters.

"And does he ever put anything on a horse he fancies?"[16]

"Well—I don't want to give him away— he's a young sport, a fine sport, sir. Would you mind asking him himself? He sort of takes a pleasure in it, and perhaps he'd feel I was giving him away, sir, if you don't mind."

Bassett was serious as a church.

The uncle went back to his nephew and took him off for a ride in the car.

"Say, Paul, old man, do you ever put anything on a horse?" the uncle asked.

The boy watched the handsome man closely.

"Why, do you think I oughtn't to ?" he parried.

"Not a bit of it! I thought perhaps you might give me a tip for the Lincoln."

The car sped on into the country, going down to Uncle Oscar's place in Hampshire.

---

11. **jockey**   professional who rides a horse in a race
12. **in full tilt**   moving at full speed
13. **was posted with all the racing news**   was fully informed about racing
14. **batman**   servant of an officer in the British army
15. **blade of the "turf"**   a lively follower of horse-racing
16. **put anything on a horse he fancies**   bet money on a horse he likes

"Honour bright?" said the nephew.

"Honour bright, son!" said the uncle.

"Well, then, Daffodil."   165

"Daffodil! I doubt it, sonny. What about Mirza?"

"I only know the winner," said the boy. "That's Daffodil."

"Daffodil, eh?"

There was a pause. Daffodil was an obscure[17] horse comparatively.

"Uncle!"   170

"Yes, Son?"

"You won't let it go any further,[18] will you? I promised Bassett."

"Bassett be damned, old man! What's he got to do with it?"

"We're partners. We've been partners from the first. Uncle, he lent me my first five shillings, which I lost. I promised him, honour bright, it was only   175 between me and him; only you gave me that ten-shilling note I started winning with, so I thought you were lucky. You won't let it go any further, will you?"

The boy gazed at his uncle from those big, hot, blue eyes, set rather close together. The uncle stirred and laughed uneasily.

"Right you are, son! I'll keep your tip[19] private. Daffodil, eh? How much   180 are you putting on him?"

"All except twenty pounds," said the boy. "I keep that in reserve."[20]

The uncle thought it a good joke.

"You keep twenty pounds in reserve, do you, you young romancer? What are you betting, then?"   185

"I'm betting three hundred," said the boy gravely. "But it's between you and me, Uncle Oscar! Honour bright?"

The uncle burst into a roar of laughter.

"It's between you and me all right, you young Nat Gould,"[21] he said, laughing. "But where's your three hundred?"   190

"Bassett keeps it for me. We're partners."

"You are, are you! And what is Bassett putting on Daffodil?"

"He won't go quite as high as I do, I expect. Perhaps he'll go a hundred and fifty."

"What, pennies?" laughed the uncle.   195

"Pounds," said the child, with a surprised look at his uncle. "Bassett keeps a bigger reserve than I do."

Between wonder and amusement Uncle Oscar was silent. He pursued the matter no further, but he determined to take his nephew with him to the Lincoln races.   200

"Now, son," he said, "I'm putting twenty on Mirza, and I'll put five on for you on any horse you fancy. What's your pick?"

"Daffodil, uncle."

"No, not the fiver on Daffodil!"

---

17. **obscure**   unknown

18. **You won't let it go any further**   You won't tell anybody

19. **tip**   special information

20. **keep that in reserve**   save it

21. **Nat Gould**   an English sportswriter who wrote 130 thrillers about horse-racing

"I should if it was my own fiver," said the child.

"Good! Good! Right you are! A fiver for me and a fiver for you on Daffodil."

The child had never been to a race-meeting before, and his eyes were blue fire. He pursed his mouth tight[22] and watched. A Frenchman just in front had put his money on Lancelot. Wild with excitement, he flayed his arms up and down, yelling *"Lancelot! Lancelot!"* in his French accent.

Daffodil came in first, Lancelot second, Mirza third. The child, flushed and with eyes blazing, was curiously serene. His uncle brought him four five-pound notes, four to one.

"What am I to do with these?" he cried, waving them before the boy's eyes.

"I suppose we'll talk to Bassett," said the boy. "I expect I have fifteen hundred now; and twenty in reserve; and this twenty."

His uncle studied him for some moments.

"Look here, son!" he said. "You're not serious about Bassett and that fifteen hundred, are you?"

"Yes, I am. But it's between you and me, uncle. Honour bright?"

"Honour bright all right, son! But I must talk to Bassett."

"If you'd like to be a partner, uncle, with Bassett and me, we could all be partners. Only, you'd have to promise, honour bright, uncle, not to let it go beyond us three. Bassett and I are lucky, and you must be lucky, because it was your ten shillings I started winning with . . ."

Uncle Oscar took both Bassett and Paul into Richmond Park for an afternoon, and there they talked.

"It's like this, you see, sir," Bassett said. "Master Paul would get me talking about racing events, spinning yarns,[23] you know, sir. And he was always keen on knowing if I'd made or if I'd lost. It's about a year since, now, that I put five shillings on Blush of Dawn for him: and we lost. Then the luck turned, with that ten shillings he had from you: that we put on Singhalese. And since that time, it's been pretty steady, all things considering.[24] What do you say, Master Paul?"

"We're all right when we're sure," said Paul. "it's when we're not quite sure that we go down."[25]

"Oh, but we're careful then," said Bassett.

"But when are you *sure?*" smiled Uncle Oscar.

"It's Master Paul, sir," said Bassett in a secret, religious voice. "It's as if he had it from heaven. Like Daffodil, now, for the Lincoln. That was as sure as eggs."[26]

"Did you put anything on Daffodil?" asked Oscar Cresswell.

"Yes, sir. I made my bit."

"And my nephew?"

---

22. **pursed his mouth tight**   drew his lips together in an expression of concentration
23. **spinning yarns**   telling long stories—not always true
24. **all things considering**   when everything is taken into account
25. **go down**   lose
26. **as sure as eggs**   absolutely certain

Bassett was obstinately silent, looking at Paul.

"I made twelve hundred, didn't I, Bassett? I told uncle I was putting three hundred on Daffodil."

"That's right," said Bassett, nodding.

"But where's the money?" asked the uncle. 250

"I keep it safe locked up, sir. Master Paul he can have it any minute he likes to ask for it."

"What, fifteen hundred pounds?"

"And twenty! And *forty,* that is, with the twenty he made on the course."

"It's amazing!" said the uncle. 255

"If Master Paul offers you to be partners, sir, I would, if I were you: if you'll excuse me," said Bassett.

Oscar Cresswell thought about it.

"I'll see the money," he said.

They drove home again, and, sure enough, Bassett came round to the 260 garden-house with fifteen hundred pounds in notes. The twenty pounds reserve was left with Joe Glee, in the Turf Commission deposit.

"You see, it's all right, uncle, when I'm *sure*! Then we go strong, for all we're worth. Don't we, Bassett?"

"We do that, Master Paul." 265

"And when are you sure?" said the uncle, laughing.

"Oh, well, sometimes I'm *absolutely* sure, like about Daffodil," said the boy; "and sometimes I have an idea; and sometimes I haven't even an idea, have I, Bassett? Then we're careful, because we mostly go down."

"You do, do you! And when you're sure, like about Daffodil, what 270 makes you sure, sonny?"

"Oh, well, I don't know," said the boy uneasily. "I'm sure, you know, uncle; that's all."

"It's as if he had it from heaven, sir," Bassett reiterated.

"I should say so!" said the uncle. 275

But he became a partner. And when the Leger was coming on Paul was "sure" about Lively Spark, which was a quite inconsiderable[27] horse. The boy insisted on putting a thousand on the horse, Bassett went for five hundred, and Oscar Cresswell two hundred. Lively Spark came in first, and the betting had been ten to one against him. Paul had made ten thousand. 280

"You see," he said, "I was absolutely sure of him."

Even Oscar Cresswell had cleared two thousand.

"Look here, son," he said, "this sort of thing makes me nervous."

"It needn't, uncle! Perhaps I shan't be sure again for a long time."

"But what are you going to do with your money?" asked the uncle. 285

"Of course," said the boy, "I started it for mother. She said she had no luck, because father is unlucky, so I thought if *I* was lucky, it might stop whispering."

"What might stop whispering?"

"Our house. I *hate* our house for whispering." 290

---

27. **inconsiderable**   unimportant

"What does it whisper?"

"Why—why"—the boy fidgeted[28]—"why, I don't know. But it's always short of money, you know, uncle."

"I know it, son, I know it."

"You know people send mother writs,[29] don't you, uncle?" 295

"I'm afraid I do," said the uncle.

"And then the house whispers, like people laughing at you behind your back. It's awful, that is! I thought if I was lucky—"

"You might stop it," added the uncle.

The boy watched him with big blue eyes, that had an uncanny[30] cold 300
fire in them, and he said never a word.

"Well, then!" said the uncle. "What are we doing?"

"I shouldn't like mother to know I was lucky," said the boy.

"Why not, son?"

"She'd stop me." 305

"I don't think she would."

"Oh!"—and the boy writhed[31] in an odd way—"I *don't* want her to know, uncle."

"All right, son! We'll manage it without her knowing."

They managed it very easily. Paul, at the other's suggestion, handed 310
over five thousand pounds to his uncle, who deposited it with the family lawyer, who was then to inform Paul's mother that a relative had put five thousand pounds into his hands, which sum was to be paid out a thousand pounds at a time, on the mother's birthday, for the next five years.

"So she'll have a birthday present of a thousand pounds for five 315
successive years," said Uncle Oscar. "I hope it won't make it all the harder for her later."

Paul's mother had her birthday in November. The house had been "whispering" worse than ever lately, and, even in spite of his luck, Paul could not bear up against it. He was very anxious to see the effect of the birthday 320
letter, telling his mother about the thousand pounds.

When there were no visitors, Paul now took his meals with his parents, as he was beyond the nursery control. His mother went into town nearly every day. She had discovered that she had an odd knack[32] of sketching furs and dress materials, so she worked secretly in the studio of a friend who was 325
the chief "artist" for the leading drapers. She drew the figures of ladies in furs and ladies in silk and sequins for the newspaper advertisements. This young woman artist earned several thousand pounds a year, but Paul's mother only made several hundreds, and she was again dissatisfied. She so wanted to be first in something, and she did not succeed, even in making sketches for 330
drapery advertisements.

She was down to breakfast on the morning of her birthday. Paul watched her face as she read her letters. He knew the lawyer's letter. As his

---

28. **fidgeted** moved uneasily
29. **writs** legal notices about debts
30. **uncanny** uncomfortably strange
31. **writhed** moved as if in pain
32. **knack** talent

mother read it, her face hardened and became more expressionless. Then a cold, determined look came on her mouth. She hid the letter under the pile of others, and said not a word about it.

"Didn't you have anything nice in the post for your birthday, mother?" said Paul.

"Quite moderately nice," she said, her voice cold and absent.

She went away to town without saying more.

But in the afternoon Uncle Oscar appeared. He said Paul's mother had had a long interview with the lawyer, asking if the whole five thousand could not be advanced at once, as she was in debt.

"What do you think, uncle?" said the boy.

"I leave it to you, son."

"Oh, let her have it, then! We can get some more with the other," said the boy.

"A bird in the hand is worth two in the bush, laddie!" said Uncle Oscar.

"But I'm sure to *know* for the Grand National; or the Lincolnshire; or else the Derby. I'm sure to know for *one* of them," said Paul.

So Uncle Oscar signed the agreement, and Paul's mother touched the whole five thousand. Then something very curious happened. The voices in the house suddenly went mad, like a chorus of frogs on a spring evening. There were certain new furnishings, and Paul had a tutor.[33] He was *really* going to Eton, his father's school, in the following autumn. There were flowers in the winter, and a blossoming of the luxury Paul's mother had been used to. And yet the voices in the house, behind the sprays of mimosa and almond-blossom, and from under the piles of iridescent[34] cushions, simply trilled and screamed in a sort of ecstasy: "There *must* be more money! Oh-h-h; there *must* be more money. Oh, now, now-w! Now-w-w— there *must* be more money! — more than ever! More than ever!"

It frightened Paul terribly. He studied away at his Latin and Greek with his tutor. But his intense hours were spent with Bassett. The Grand National had gone by; he had not "known," and had lost a hundred pounds. Summer was at hand. He was in agony for the Lincoln. But even for the Lincoln he didn't "know," and he lost fifty pounds. He became wild-eyed and strange, as if something were going to explode in him.

"Let it alone, son! Don't you bother about it!" urged Uncle Oscar. But it was as if the boy couldn't really hear what his uncle was saying.

"I've got to know for the Derby! I've got to know for the Derby!" the child reiterated, his big blue eyes blazing with a sort of madness.

His mother noticed how overwrought he was.

"You'd better go to the seaside. Wouldn't you like to go now to the seaside, instead of waiting? I think you'd better," she said, looking down at him anxiously, her heart curiously heavy because of him.

But the child lifted his uncanny blue eyes.

"I couldn't possibly go before the Derby, mother!" he said. "I couldn't possibly!"

---

33. **tutor** special home teacher   34. **iridescent** shining brightly

"Why not?" she said, her voice becoming heavy when she was opposed. "Why not? You can still go from the seaside to see the Derby with your Uncle Oscar, if that's what you wish. No need for you to wait here. Besides, I think you care too much about these races. It's a bad sign. My family has been a gambling family, and you won't know till you grow up how much damage it has done. But it has done damage. I shall have to send Bassett away, and ask Uncle Oscar not to talk racing to you, unless you promise to be reasonable about it: go away to the seaside and forget it. You're all nerves!"

"I'll do what you like, mother, so long as you don't send me away till after the Derby," the boy said.

"Send you away from where? Just from this house?"

"Yes," he said, gazing at her.

"Why, you curious child, what makes you care about this house so much, suddenly? I never knew you loved it."

He gazed at her without speaking. He had a secret within a secret, something he had not divulged, even to Bassett or to his Uncle Oscar.

But his mother, after standing undecided and a little bit sullen[35] for some moments, said:

"Very well, then! Don't go to the seaside till after the Derby, if you don't wish it. But promise me you won't let your nerves go to pieces.[36] Promise you won't think so much about horse-racing, and *events,* as you call them!"

"Oh no," said the boy casually. "I won't think much about them, mother. You needn't worry. I wouldn't worry, mother, if I were you."

"If you were me and I were you," said his mother, "I wonder what we *should* do!"

"But you know you needn't worry, mother, don't you?" the boy repeated.

"I should be awfully glad to know it," she said wearily.

"Oh, well, you *can,* you know. I mean, you *ought* to know you needn't worry," he insisted.

"Ought I? Then I'll see about it," she said.

Paul's secret of secrets was his wooden horse, that which had no name. Since he was emancipated from a nurse and a nursery-governess, he had had his rocking-horse removed to his own bedroom at the top of the house.

"Surely you're too big for a rocking-horse!" his mother had remonstrated.

"Well, you see, mother, till I can have a *real* horse, I like to have *some* sort of animal about," had been his quaint answer.

"Do you feel he keeps you company?" she laughed.

"Oh yes! He's very good, he always keeps me company, when I'm there," said Paul.

So the horse, rather shabby, stood in an arrested prance[37] in the boy's bedroom.

The Derby was drawing near, and the boy grew more and more tense. He hardly heard what was spoken to him, he was very frail, and his eyes

---

35. **sullen** unsmiling
36. **go to pieces** have a nervous breakdown

37. **stood in an arrested prance** looked as if it had suddenly stopped with its front hooves in the air

were really uncanny. His mother had sudden strange seizures of uneasiness about him. Sometimes, for half an hour, she would feel a sudden anxiety about him that was almost anguish. She wanted to rush to him at once, and know he was safe. 425

Two nights before the Derby, she was at a big party in town, when one of her rushes of anxiety about her boy, her first-born, gripped her heart till she could hardly speak. She fought with the feeling, might and main,[38] for she believed in common sense. But it was too strong. She had to leave the 430 dance and go downstairs to telephone to the country. The children's nursery-governess was terribly surprised and startled at being rung up in the night.

"Are the children all right, Miss Wilmot?"

"Oh yes, they are quite all right."

"Master Paul? Is he all right?" 435

"He went to bed as right as a trivet.[39] Shall I run up and look at him?"

"No," said Paul's mother reluctantly. "No! Don't trouble. It's all right. Don't sit up. We shall be home fairly soon." She did not want her son's privacy intruded upon.

"Very good," said the governess. 440

It was about one o'clock when Paul's mother and father drove up to their house. All was still. Paul's mother went to her room and slipped off her white fur cloak. She had told her maid not to wait up for her. She heard her husband downstairs, mixing a whisky and soda.

And then, because of the strange anxiety at her heart, she stole upstairs 445 to her son's room. Noiselessly she went along the upper corridor. Was there a faint noise? What was it?

She stood, with arrested muscles, outside his door, listening. There was a strange, heavy, and yet not loud noise. Her heart stood still. It was a soundless noise, yet rushing and powerful. Something huge, in violent, 450 hushed motion. What was it? What in God's name was it? She ought to know. She felt that she knew the noise. She knew what it was.

Yet she could not place it. She couldn't say what it was. And on and on it went, like a madness.

Softly, frozen with anxiety and fear, she turned the doorhandle. 455

The room was dark. Yet in the space near the window, she heard and saw something plunging to and fro.[40] She gazed in fear and amazement.

Then suddenly she switched on the light, and saw her son, in his green pyjamas, madly surging on the rocking-horse. The blaze of light suddenly lit him up, as he urged the wooden horse, and lit her up, as she stood, blonde, 460 in her dress of pale green and crystal, in the doorway.

"Paul!" she cried. "Whatever are you doing?"

"It's Malabar!" he screamed in a powerful, strange voice. "It's Malabar!"

His eyes blazed at her for one strange and senseless second, as he ceased urging his wooden horse. Then he fell with a crash to the ground, 465

---

38. **fought might and main** fought as hard as possible
39. **as right as a trivet** absolutely fine (a trivet is a three-footed stand or support)
40. **plunging to and fro** moving violently up and down

and she, all her tormented motherhood flooding upon her, rushed to gather him up.

But he was unconscious, and unconscious he remained, with some brain-fever. He talked and tossed, and his mother sat stonily by his side.

"Malabar! It's Malabar! Bassett, Bassett, I *know*! It's Malabar!" 470

So the child cried, trying to get up and urge the rocking-horse that gave him his inspiration.

"What does he mean by Malabar?" asked the heart-frozen mother.

"I don't know," said the father stonily.

"What does he mean by Malabar?" she asked her brother Oscar. 475

"It's one of the horses running for the Derby," was the answer.

And, in spite of himself, Oscar Cresswell spoke to Bassett, and himself put a thousand on Malabar: at fourteen to one.

The third day of the illness was critical: they were waiting for a change. The boy, with his rather long, curly hair, was tossing ceaselessly on the pillow. 480 He neither slept nor regained consciousness, and his eyes were like blue stones. His mother sat, feeling her heart had gone, turned actually into a stone.

In the evening, Oscar Cresswell did not come, but Bassett sent a message, saying could he come up for one moment, just one moment? Paul's mother was very angry at the intrusion, but on second thoughts she 485 agreed. The boy was the same. Perhaps Bassett might bring him to consciousness.

The gardener, a shortish fellow with a little brown moustache and sharp little brown eyes, tiptoed into the room, touched his imaginary cap to Paul's mother, and stole to the bedside, staring with glittering, smallish eyes at the 490 tossing, dying child.

"Master Paul!" he whispered. "Master Paul! Malabar came in first all right, a clean win. I did as you told me. You've made over seventy thousand pounds, you have; you've got over eighty thousand. Malabar came in all right, Master Paul."

"Malabar! Malabar! Did I say Malabar, mother? Did I say Malabar? Do you 495 think I'm lucky, mother? I knew Malabar, didn't I? Over eighty thousand pounds! I call that lucky, don't you, mother? Over eighty thousand pounds! I knew, didn't I know I knew? Malabar came in all right. If I ride my horse till I'm sure, then I tell you, Bassett, you can go as high as you like. Did you go for all you were worth, Bassett?" 500

"I went a thousand on it, Master Paul."

"I never told you, mother, that if I can ride my horse, and *get there,* then I'm absolutely sure – oh, absolutely! Mother, did I ever tell you? I *am* lucky!"

"No, you never did," said his mother.

But the boy died in the night. 505

And even as he lay dead, his mother heard her brother's voice saying to her: "My God, Hester, you're eighty-odd thousand to the good,[41] and a poor devil of a son to the bad. But, poor devil, poor devil, he's best gone out of a life where he rides his rocking-horse to find a winner." ◆

---

41. **eighty-odd thousand to the good**   a gain of
approximately eighty thousand pounds

P A R T ◆1◆ **F I R S T R E A D I N G**

A. Thinking about the Story

Could you feel the power of Paul's obsession? Were you able to respond to the supernatural element in the story?

B. Understanding the Plot

1. Why is there always a shortage of money in Paul's household? Is the family poor?

2. Whom does the mother blame for their financial difficulties? Is she correct?

3. Why does the mother think that luck is more important than wealth?

4. What does Uncle Oscar enjoy doing in his spare time?

5. Who is Bassett, and what is his connection to Uncle Oscar?

6. Why does Paul confide in Uncle Oscar?

7. At what point does Uncle Oscar start to take Paul seriously?

8. Why do people send Paul's mother writs? (line 295)

9. Why is the mother working *secretly* in a friend's studio? (line 325)

10. Does Paul's mother's birthday check solve her financial problems? Explain your answer.

11. What is the mother's attitude toward gambling?

12. Does Paul's mother show any love toward Paul? Explain your answer as fully as possible.

13. What killed Paul?

P A R T ◆2◆ **S E C O N D R E A D I N G**

A. Exploring Themes

You are now ready to reread "The Rocking-Horse Winner." Think carefully about why Paul is so driven to make money for his mother and about the role of those around him in encouraging this obsession.

1. What is the importance of the frequent references to "eyes" in the story?

2. What are the supernatural aspects of the story?

3. How important is social class to the story?

4. Who in your view is to blame for Paul's tragedy? You need not limit yourself to one person only.

5. What is the role of the father in the story?

B. Analyzing the Author's Style

Before you begin to work on this section, turn to the detailed explanation of symbol (page 283) and fable (page 278).

SYMBOL

D. H. Lawrence uses the rocking horse in the story as a powerful and complex **symbol** with several layers of meaning. The deeper you delve into the symbolism, the more it reveals about the wider personal and social issues Lawrence is concerned with.

1. What does the rocking horse symbolize? Give as many details as you can to support your answer.
2. What descriptions of the rocking horse scenes help reinforce the symbolism?
3. Why do you think Lawrence chose a rocking horse as the central symbol?
4. Money is used both literally and symbolically in the text. What is its symbolic importance?

FABLE

Lawrence's story of the child who rides a rocking horse in a desperate attempt to make money for his mother is written like a **fable**, which is a short story, often with animals in it, that is told to illustrate a moral.

1. What qualities does "The Rocking-Horse Winner" share with a fable?
2. How does the opening paragraph suggest a fable?
3. What is the moral of the story? Explain it in your own words.

C. Judging for Yourself

Express yourself as personally as you like in your answers to the following questions:

1. Do you think the mother is capable of loving anybody?
2. Do you think she learns her lesson at the end of the story?
3. Would you agree with her that it is important in life to be lucky?
4. Do you think that Bassett should be punished for his role in Paul's gambling?
5. In your view, could Paul's father have helped avert the tragedy?

D. Making Connections

1. What is the attitude toward gambling in your country?

2. Have you ever gambled? If so, in what way? Did you win or lose money?

3. Have you, or anybody you know, ever been obsessed by anything? If yes, explain the obsession.

4. Do you have superstitions in your country about what is lucky and unlucky? What are they?

5. Do you believe in the supernatural? Explain why or why not.

E. Debate

Debate the proposal: Gambling can bring more benefits than harm to a community.

P A R T ◆3◆ **FOCUS ON LANGUAGE**

A. Proverbs

A **proverb** is a short saying that expresses a common truth familiar to most people in a particular society. For example, in "The Rocking-Horse Winner" Uncle Oscar tells Paul, *A bird in the hand is worth two in the bush.* (line 348) This suggests that what we already have is more valuable than what we want but have not yet acquired. English (as are many languages) is rich in proverbs.

With a partner try to work out the meaning of the following proverbs:

A fool and his money are soon parted.

A rolling stone gathers no moss.

A stitch in time saves nine.

A watched pot never boils.

Better late than never.

Birds of a feather flock together.

Don't count your chickens before they hatch.

His bark is worse than his bite.

Look before you leap.

Make hay while the sun shines.

Money is the root of all evil.

Money talks.

Silence is golden.

Time is money.

Too many cooks spoil the broth.

Together work out a series of dialogues in which one of you says something that makes the other one respond with an appropriate proverb. The following dialogue is an example:

> **PARTNER A:** I've just been offered a part in a new play. However, since it's not the main role, I'm going to turn it down and wait for a better one.
>
> **PARTNER B:** I wouldn't do that. *A bird in the hand is worth two in the bush.*

Translate five proverbs from your language into English and share them with the class.

B. Building Vocabulary Skills

had good prospects	(line 21)
racked her brains	(line 25)
brazen it out	(line 90)
in full tilt	(line 125)
You won't let it go any further	(line 177)
pursed his mouth tight	(line 209)
go to pieces	(line 398)
fought might and main	(line 429)
eighty-odd thousand to the good	(line 507)

The following expressions are all explained in the glossary accompanying the story.

Make sure you understand the meaning of each expression. First give a situation in which the expression might appropriately be used. Then use it in a sentence, underlining the expression. The first one—*had good prospects*—is done for you as an example.

> **SITUATION:** The future looked promising for a young graduate.
>
> **SENTENCE:** In my first job I <u>had good prospects</u> and expected to be promoted in a few months.

PART ◆4◆ **WRITING ACTIVITIES**

1. Imagine you have won a million dollars from gambling. In a two-page essay, first consider how you would feel acquiring such a huge sum overnight. Next explain what you think you would do with the money, and give the reasons for your decisions. In your conclusion, say whether winning so much would be morally corrupting. Try to incorporate at least one proverb concerning money into your text.

2. Would you say your culture is particularly materialistic? After defining the term *materialistic,* examine this question in a two-page essay, giving as many reasons as possible to support your answer. In your conclusion, compare your country with what you know about the United States regarding attitudes toward money.

3. Henry James wrote a famous story, "The Turn of the Screw," in which the supernatural plays an extremely important part. The story was later made into a movie and an opera. Write an essay about a story, play, movie, or opera you have seen in which the supernatural is a dominant element. Briefly recount the plot. Then, using lines 33–49 of "The Rocking-Horse Winner" as a model, try to recreate the atmosphere of the work and say how you were affected.

The Boarding House

JAMES JOYCE *(1882–1941)*

◆◆◆

BORN IN DUBLIN, Ireland, James Joyce grew up to be
one of the most influential writers of the twentieth century. He was
a brilliant student, attending a famous Jesuit boarding school until
his father's bankruptcy forced him to leave. In 1904, he left the
Catholic church and departed from Ireland for good. Joyce married
and lived with his family in Trieste, Zurich, and Paris, where he
taught English and wrote the works that made him famous.

In 1914, Joyce published *Dubliners,* which he described as
representing "a chapter of the moral history" of Ireland. Then came
A Portrait of the Artist as a Young Man (1916), which fictionalized
Joyce's break with the Catholic church and his assumption of the
role of writer. His great novel *Ulysses* (1922), in which he
experimented with the technique of stream of consciousness, or
interior monologue, established Joyce as a major writer who
influenced the work of Virginia Woolf and William Faulkner,
among others.

THE BOARDING HOUSE

*A domineering mother watches her daughter flirt with a
young man and plots their future.*

Mrs Mooney was a butcher's daughter. She was a woman who was quite
able to keep things to herself:[1] a determined woman. She had married her
father's foreman, and opened a butcher's shop near Spring Gardens. But as
soon as his father-in-law was dead Mr Mooney began to go to the devil. He
drank, plundered the till,[2] ran headlong into debt. It was no use making him   5
take the pledge:[3] he was sure to break out again a few days after. By
fighting his wife in the presence of customers and by buying bad meat he
ruined his business. One night he went for[4] his wife with the cleaver, and
she had to sleep in a neighbour's house.

After that they lived apart. She went to the priest and got a separation   10
from him, with care of the children. She would give him neither money nor
food nor house-room; and so he was obliged to enlist himself as a sheriff's
man.[5] He was a shabby[6] stooped[7] little drunkard with a white face and a
white moustache and white eyebrows, pencilled above his little eyes, which
were pink-veined and raw; and all day long he sat in the bailiff's[8] room,   15
waiting to be put on a job. Mrs Mooney, who had taken what remained of
her money out of the butcher business and set up a boarding house in
Hardwicke Street, was a big imposing woman. Her house had a floating
population made up of tourists from Liverpool and the Isle of Man and,
occasionally, *artistes*[9] from the music halls. Its resident population was   20
made up of clerks from the city. She governed the house cunningly and
firmly, knew when to give credit,[10] when to be stern and when to let things
pass. All the resident young men spoke of her as *The Madam.*

Mrs Mooney's young men paid fifteen shillings a week for board and
lodgings (beer or stout at dinner excluded). They shared in common tastes   25
and occupations and for this reason they were very chummy[11] with one
another. They discussed with one another the chances of favourites and
outsiders.[12] Jack Mooney, the Madam's son, who was clerk to a commission
agent in Fleet Street, had the reputation of being a hard case. He was fond
of using soldiers' obscenities: usually he came home in the small hours.[13]   30

1. **keep things to herself**   keep a secret
2. **plundered the till**   stole money from the cash register
3. **take the pledge**   promise not to drink any alcohol
4. **went for**   attacked
5. **sheriff's man**   assistant to the official responsible for
   the safekeeping of prisoners
6. **shabby**   poorly dressed
7. **stooped**   bent over

8. **bailiff**   court official who arrests people and
   delivers formal court documents
9. **artistes**   French word for artists
10. **give credit**   allow someone to postpone payment
11. **chummy**   friendly
12. **favourites and outsiders**   horse-racing terms:
    likely winners and unlikely winners
13. **in the small hours**   very early in the morning

When he met his friends he had always a good one[14] to tell them, and he was always sure to be on to a good thing—that is to say, a likely horse or a likely *artiste*. He was also handy with the mits[15] and sang comic songs. On Sunday nights there would often be a reunion in Mrs. Mooney's front drawing-room. The music-hall *artistes* would oblige; and Sheridan played waltzes and polkas and vamped accompaniments. Polly Mooney, the Madam's daughter, would also sing. She sang:

> *I'm a . . . naughty girl*
> *You needn't sham:*[16]
> *You know I am.*

Polly was a slim girl of nineteen; she had light soft hair and a small full mouth. Her eyes, which were grey with a shade of green through them, had a habit of glancing upwards when she spoke with anyone, which made her look like a little perverse[17] madonna.[18] Mrs Mooney had first sent her daughter to be a typist in a corn-factor's office, but as a disreputable sheriff's man used to come every other day to the office, asking to be allowed to say a word to his daughter, she had taken her daughter home again and set her to do housework. As Polly was very lively, the intention was to give her the run of[19] the young men. Besides, young men like to feel that there is a young woman not very far away. Polly, of course, flirted with the young men, but Mrs Mooney, who was a shrewd judge, knew that the young men were only passing the time away:[20] none of them meant business. Things went on so for a long time, and Mrs Mooney began to think of sending Polly back to typewriting, when she noticed that something was going on between Polly and one of the young men. She watched the pair and kept her own counsel.[21]

Polly knew that she was being watched, but still her mother's persistent silence could not be misunderstood. There had been no open complicity[22] between mother and daughter, no open understanding, but though people in the house began to talk of the affair, still Mrs Mooney did not intervene.[23] Polly began to grow a little strange in her manner, and the young man was evidently perturbed. At last, when she judged it to be the right moment, Mrs Mooney intervened. She dealt with moral problems as a cleaver deals with meat: and in this case she had made up her mind.

It was a bright Sunday morning of early summer, promising heat, but with a fresh breeze blowing. All the windows of the boarding house were open and the lace curtains ballooned gently towards the street beneath the

---

14. **a good one** a good story
15. **handy with the mits** a good boxer
16. **sham** pretend
17. **perverse** contrary, improper
18. **madonna** the Virgin Mary
19. **give her the run of** allow her complete freedom

20. **passing the time away** waiting for something to happen
21. **kept her own counsel** didn't speak to anyone about the matter
22. **complicity** cooperation in a wrongful act
23. **intervene** interfere

raised sashes. The belfry[24] of George's Church sent out constant peals, and worshippers, singly or in groups, traversed the little circus before the church,[25] revealing their purpose by their self-contained demeanour[26] no less than by the little volumes in their gloved hands. Breakfast was over in the boarding house, and the table of the breakfast-room was covered with plates on which lay yellow streaks of eggs with morsels of bacon-fat and bacon-rind. Mrs Mooney sat in the straw arm-chair and watched the servant Mary remove the breakfast things. She made Mary collect the crusts and pieces of broken bread to help to make Tuesday's bread-pudding. When the table was cleared, the broken bread collected, the sugar and butter safe under lock and key,[27] she began to reconstruct the interview which she had had the night before with Polly. Things were as she had suspected: she had been frank[28] in her questions and Polly had been frank in her answers. Both had been somewhat awkward,[29] of course. She had been made awkward by her not wishing to receive the news in too cavalier[30] a fashion or to seem to have connived,[31] and Polly had been made awkward not merely because allusions of that kind always made her awkward, but also because she did not wish it to be thought that in her wise innocence she had divined[32] the intention behind her mother's tolerance.

Mrs Mooney glanced instinctively at the little gilt clock on the mantelpiece as soon as she had become aware through her reverie that the bells of George's Church had stopped ringing. It was seventeen minutes past eleven: she would have lots of time to have the matter out[33] with Mr Doran and then catch short twelve[34] at Marlborough Street. She was sure she would win. To begin with, she had all the weight of social opinion on her side: she was an outraged mother. She had allowed him to live beneath her roof, assuming that he was a man of honour, and he had simply abused her hospitality. He was thirty-four or thirty-five years of age, so that youth could not be pleaded as his excuse; nor could ignorance be his excuse, since he was a man who had seen something of the world. He had simply taken advantage of Polly's youth and inexperience: that was evident. The question was: What reparation[35] would he make?

There must be reparation made in such a case. It is all very well for the man: he can go his ways as if nothing had happened, having had his moment of pleasure, but the girl has to bear the brunt.[36] Some mothers would be content to patch up such an affair for a sum of money: she had known cases of it. But she would not do so. For her only one reparation could make up for the loss of her daughter's honour: marriage.

(line numbers: 70, 75, 80, 85, 90, 95, 100, 105)

---

24. **belfry**   bell tower
25. **traversed the little circus before the church**
      crossed the small circular area in front of the church
26. **demeanour**   outward behavior
27. **under lock and key**   locked away
28. **frank**   open and honest
29. **awkward**   embarrassed
30. **cavalier**   lighthearted
31. **connived**   plotted
32. **divined**   guessed
33. **have the matter out**   discuss the problem openly
34. **catch short twelve**   attend the midday service at church
35. **reparation**   payment for damage done
36. **bear the brunt**   assume the major part of the responsibility

She counted all her cards[37] again before sending Mary up to Mr Doran's room to say that she wished to speak with him. She felt sure she would win. He was a serious young man, not rakish[38] or loud-voiced like the others. If it had been Mr Sheridan or Mr Meade or Bantam Lyons, her task would have been much harder. She did not think he would face publicity. All the lodgers in the house knew something of the affair; details had been invented by some. Besides, he had been employed for thirteen years in a great Catholic wine-merchant's office, and publicity would mean for him, perhaps, the loss of his job. Whereas if he agreed all might be well. She knew he had a good screw[39] for one thing, and she suspected he had a bit of stuff put by.[40]

Nearly the half-hour! She stood up and surveyed herself in the pier-glass. The decisive expression of her great florid face satisfied her, and she thought of some mothers she knew who could not get their daughters off their hands.[41]

Mr Doran was very anxious indeed this Sunday morning. He had made two attempts to shave, but his hand had been so unsteady that he had been obliged to desist. Three days' reddish beard fringed his jaws, and every two or three minutes a mist gathered on his glasses so that he had to take them off and polish them with his pocket-handkerchief. The recollection of his confession of the night before was a cause of acute pain to him; the priest had drawn out every ridiculous detail of the affair, and in the end had so magnified his sin that he was almost thankful at being afforded[42] a loophole of reparation. The harm was done. What could he do now but marry her or run away? He could not brazen it out.[43] The affair would be sure to be talked of, and his employer would be certain to hear of it. Dublin is such a small city: everyone knows everyone else's business. He felt his heart leap warmly in his throat as he heard in his excited imagination old Mr Leonard calling out in his rasping voice: "Send Mr Doran here, please."

All his long years of service gone for nothing! All his industry and diligence thrown away! As a young man he had sown his wild oats,[44] of course; he had boasted of his free-thinking and denied the existence of God to his companions in public-houses. But that was all passed and done with . . . nearly. He still bought a copy of *Reynolds Newspaper* every week, but he attended to his religious duties, and for nine-tenths of the year lived a regular life. He had money enough to settle down[45] on; it was not that. But the family would look down on[46] her. First of all there was her disreputable[47] father, and then her mother's boarding house was beginning to get a certain fame. He had a notion that he was being had.[48] He could imagine his friends talking of the affair and laughing. She *was* a little

---

37. **counted all her cards**   went over her advantages
38. **rakish**   bold and wild
39. **screw**   salary
40. **he had a bit of stuff put by**   he had saved some money
41. **get their daughters off their hands**   get their daughters married
42. **afforded**   given
43. **brazen it out**   confront one's accuser confidently
44. **sown his wild oats**   behaved wildly in his youth
45. **settle down**   get married
46. **look down on**   feel superior to
47. **disreputable**   not regarded highly
48. **he was being had**   he was being tricked

vulgar; sometimes she said "I seen" and "If I had've known." But what would grammar matter if he really loved her? He could not make up his mind whether to like her or despise her for what she had done. Of course he had done it too. His instinct urged him to remain free, not to marry. Once you are married you are done for,[49] it said. ‹145›

While he was sitting helplessly on the side of the bed in shirt and trousers, she tapped lightly at his door and entered. She told him all, that she had made a clean breast of it[50] to her mother and that her mother would speak with him that morning. She cried and threw her arms around his neck, saying: ‹150›

"O Bob! Bob! What am I to do? What am I to do at all?"

She would put an end to herself, she said.

He comforted her feebly, telling her not to cry, that it would be all right, never fear. He felt against his shirt the agitation of her bosom. ‹155›

It was not altogether his fault that it had happened. He remembered well, with the curious patient memory of the celibate,[51] the first casual caresses her dress, her breath, her fingers had given him. Then late one night as he was undressing for bed she had tapped at his door, timidly. She wanted to relight her candle at his, for hers had been blown out by a gust. It was her bath night. She wore a loose open combing-jacket[52] of printed flannel. Her white instep shone in the opening of her furry slippers and the blood glowed warmly behind her perfumed skin. From her hands and wrists too as she lit and steadied her candle a faint perfume arose. ‹160›‹165›

On nights when he came in very late it was she who warmed up his dinner. He scarcely knew what he was eating, feeling her beside him alone, at night, in the sleeping house. And her thoughtfulness! If the night was anyway cold or wet or windy there was sure to be a little tumbler of punch ready for him. Perhaps they could be happy together . . . ‹170›

They used to go upstairs together on tiptoe, each with a candle, and on the third landing exchange reluctant good nights. They used to kiss. He remembered well her eyes, the touch of her hand and his delirium[53]. . .

But delirium passes. He echoed her phrase, applying it to himself: *"What am I to do?"* The instinct of the celibate warned him to hold back. But the sin was there; even his sense of honour told him that reparation must be made for such a sin. ‹175›

While he was sitting with her on the side of the bed Mary came to the door and said that the missus wanted to see him in the parlour. He stood up to put on his coat and waistcoat, more helpless than ever. When he was dressed he went over to her to comfort her. It would be all right, never fear. He left her crying on the bed and moaning softly: *"O my God!"* ‹180›

Going down the stairs his glasses became so dimmed with moisture that he had to take them off and polish them. He longed to ascend through the

---

49. **you are done for** you are destroyed
50. **she had made a clean breast of it** she had confessed everything
51. **the celibate** someone who does not have sex
52. **combing-jacket** loose jacket worn in the bedroom when brushing hair
53. **delirium** feverish excitement

roof and fly away to another country where he would never hear again of his   185
trouble, and yet a force pushed him downstairs step by step. The
implacable[54] faces of his employer and of the Madam stared upon his
discomfiture. On the last flight of stairs he passed Jack Mooney, who was
coming up from the pantry nursing[55] two bottles of *Bass*. They saluted
coldly; and the lover's eyes rested for a second or two on a thick bulldog face   190
and a pair of thick short arms. When he reached the foot of the staircase he
glanced up and saw Jack regarding him from the door of the return-room.

Suddenly he remembered the night when one of the music-hall *artistes,*
a little blond Londoner, had made a rather free allusion to Polly. The
reunion had been almost broken up on account of Jack's violence. Everyone   195
tried to quiet him. The music-hall *artiste,* a little paler than usual, kept
smiling and saying that there was no harm meant; but Jack kept shouting at
him that if any fellow tried that sort of game on with his sister he'd bloody
well put his teeth down his throat: so he would.

Polly sat for a little time on the side of the bed, crying. Then she dried   200
her eyes and went over to the looking-glass. She dipped the end of the towel
in the water-jug and refreshed her eyes with cool water. She looked at herself
in profile and readjusted a hairpin above her ear. Then she went back to the
bed again and sat at the foot. She regarded the pillows for a long time, and
the sight of them awakened in her mind secret, amiable memories. She   205
rested the nape of her neck against the cool iron bedrail and fell into a
reverie. There was no longer any perturbation[56] visible on her face.

She waited on patiently, almost cheerfully, without alarm, her memories
gradually giving place to hopes and visions of the future. Her hopes and
visions were so intricate that she no longer saw the white pillows on which   210
her gaze was fixed, or remembered that she was waiting for anything.

At last she heard her mother calling. She started to her feet and ran to
the banisters.

"Polly! Polly!"

"Yes, mamma?"   215

"Come down, dear. Mr Doran wants to speak to you."

Then she remembered what she had been waiting for. ◆

---

54. **implacable**   unable or unwilling to be pleased   56. **perturbation**   anxiety
55. **nursing**   carrying carefully

P A R T **1 FIRST READING**

A. Thinking about the Story

Did you object to Mrs. Mooney's attempt to influence the course of the
love affair between Polly and Mr. Doran?

B. Understanding the Plot

1. List all the reasons why Mrs. Mooney left her husband. Did they get a divorce?

2. What do the boarding house residents mean when they refer to Mrs. Mooney as "The Madam"? (line 23) Is the title accurate? Support your answer.

3. Explain what is meant by describing Jack Mooney as having "the reputation of being a hard case." (line 29) What details are given to support that description?

4. Why did Polly have to leave her job as a typist?

5. What did Mrs. Mooney hope would happen when she brought Polly home to the boarding house?

6. Explain the sentence, " . . . Mrs. Mooney . . . knew that the young men were only passing the time away: none of them meant business." (lines 51–52)

7. What is Mrs. Mooney determined to have Mr. Doran do? Is she confident of the outcome? Explain your answer.

8. Why do Polly and her mother not talk openly about what is happening in the house? When does the situation change? Does Polly understand what her mother is doing?

9. How does Mr. Doran view Polly as he sits waiting to see her mother? Draw up two columns representing her pros and cons in his eyes.

10. Who is Mr. Leonard? Why does Mr. Doran think of him that Sunday?

11. At what point does Mr. Doran finally decide what he will do? What is his decision and why does he come to it?

PART ◆2◆ **SECOND READING**

A. Exploring Themes

You are now ready to reread "The Boarding House." Look at how Joyce's carefully detailed descriptions of the characters and setting bring the story to life and contribute to both plot and themes.

1. What do we learn about the values of the Dublin society in which the characters live?

2. Show how the simile "she dealt with moral problems as a cleaver deals with meat" (lines 63–64) sums up Mrs. Mooney.

3. Whom do you consider to be a victim in this story? Why?

4. Show how the unspoken thoughts of the characters dominate the action and contribute to the themes. For example, Mrs. Mooney's assessment that Mr. Doran has saved quite a bit of money strengthens her determination to marry Polly off to him. (line 115)

5. If you had to give the story a new title that sums up a dominant theme, what would you rename it?

B. Analyzing the Author's Style

Before you begin to work on this section, turn to the detailed explanation of tone (page 284), humor (page 279), irony (page 280), and imagery (page 279).

TONE: IRONY AND HUMOR

"The Boarding House" has a richly **humorous** and **ironic tone.** The humor is expressed in the many descriptions that Joyce builds into the story as well as in the ironic contrast between the characters' actions and their thoughts or philosophies.

An example of a humorous description is the contrast between Mr. and Mrs. Mooney's appearance. When Joyce describes Polly's father as having *a white face and a white moustache and white eyebrows, pencilled above his little eyes, which were pink-veined and raw* (lines 13–15), he makes us think of a frightened little white mouse with pink eyes. He later contrasts Mr. Mooney's small, pale, nervous appearance with that of Mrs. Mooney, whose *decisive expression of her great florid face satisfied her.* (line 117)

An example of irony is contained in the scene that Sunday morning when Mrs. Mooney sits scheming in her breakfast room, determined to ensure the ultimate success of her plan regardless of the moral cost to Polly and Mr. Doran. It is clear that she is determined to end her meeting with Mr. Doran quickly so that she can go to the midday church service. The irony lies in her inability to see that her behavior has in fact violated the teachings of her church. (lines 65–99)

1. Why is it ironic that Mrs. Mooney should worry about Polly being in communication with her "disreputable" father? (line 45)

2. Explain the irony in the sentence, "She [Mrs. Mooney] dealt with moral problems as a cleaver deals with meat." (lines 63–64)

3. Why is it ironic for Mrs. Mooney to describe herself as "an outraged mother"? (line 93)

4. Why is Jack Mooney's outrage toward Mr. Doran ironic?

5. How does Joyce bring out the humor in the dilemma in which Mr. Doran finds himself? (lines 119–156)

6. What is comic about the scene in which Mr. Doran recalls how his affair with Polly developed? (lines 157–173)

7. Find one more example of both humor and irony in the story.

IMAGERY: ADJECTIVES

Colorful **imagery** may be found throughout "The Boarding House." In particular, the evocative **adjectives** Joyce uses both help us see the surface pictures more clearly and enable us to grasp the depth of the passions rocking the characters.

Look carefully at the way the adjectives work in the two extracts that follow.

> *Polly was a **slim** girl of nineteen; she had **light soft** hair and a **small full** mouth. Her eyes, which were **grey** with a shade of **green** through them, had a habit of glancing upwards when she spoke with anyone, which made her look like a **little perverse** madonna.* (lines 41–44)

What information can we deduce regarding the effect of Polly's appearance, her personality, and her behavior?

> *He remembered well . . . the first **casual** caresses her dress, her breath, her fingers had given him. . . . She wore a **loose open combing** -jacket of **printed** flannel. Her **white** instep shone in the opening of her **furry** slippers and the blood glowed warmly behind her **perfumed** skin.* (lines 157–164)

1. What atmosphere do the adjectives create?

2. What senses do the adjectives appeal to?

3. What does Mr. Doran feel as he watches Polly?

C. Judging for Yourself

Express yourself as personally as you like in your answers to the following questions:

1. What did you think Mr. Doran would do at the end? Do you agree with his decision?

2. In your view does the couple have a future together?

3. Do you think Mrs. Mooney is a good mother?

4. What kind of mother-in-law do you think Mrs. Mooney will be?

5. Do you approve of Mrs. Mooney's actions?

6. Would you like to have Mrs. Mooney as your landlady? Give reasons for your answer.

7. Do you feel sorry for any of the characters? Explain your answer.

D. Making Connections

1. What is the attitude toward sex before marriage in your culture?

2. How do young people meet each other in your country? What do you think of arranged marriages, computer dating, blind dates, or advertising as methods of meeting people for dating purposes?

3. Compare dating practices in your country with those in another culture. Which do you prefer and why?

4. Have you ever been forced into taking a major step you were uncertain about? Describe the incident and the outcome.

5. Who is the dominant parent in your family? In what ways does that parent dominate? Do you relate better to one parent than to the other?

E. Debate

Debate the proposal: Parents should have some influence over whom their children marry.

PART ◆3◆ **FOCUS ON LANGUAGE**

A. Oxymoron

An **oxymoron** is a figure of speech in which contradictory words are combined. Writers use it to heighten the effect of their texts.
  A well-known example of an oxymoron is:

*She felt like a **living death** at the height of her illness.*

Joyce writes of Polly:

*Her eyes . . . had a habit of glancing upwards . . . ,which made her look like a little **perverse madonna.*** (lines 42–44)

1. What contradictory facts do we learn about Polly from the description of her as a "perverse madonna"?

2. There is another example of an oxymoron in connection with Polly in lines 79–86. Say what it is and explain its meaning.

3. Use the following oxymorons in sentences to illustrate their meaning:

a cruel kindness   a sad celebration   fiercely peaceful
an honest thief   a loud hush

4. Make up five oxymorons of your own and share them with the class.

B. Adjectives

The following sentences come from the story. Circle the adjective that is closest in meaning to the highlighted adjective in the sentence.

1. *He was a **shabby** stooped little drunkard. . . .* (line 13)
   ragged, unhappy, dishonest

2. *Mrs. Mooney, who was a **shrewd** judge, knew that the young men were only passing the time away.* (lines 51–52)
   mean, experienced, clever

3. *Polly knew that she was being watched, but still her mother's **persistent** silence could not be misunderstood.* (lines 57–58)
   nagging, continued, irritating

4. *. . . she had been **frank** in her questions and Polly had been frank in her answers.* (lines 79–80)
   direct, tactful, calm

5. *She had been made awkward by not wishing to receive the news in too **cavalier** a fashion. . . .* (lines 81–82)
   lively, uncaring, angry

6. *The decisive expression of her great **florid** face satisfied her. . . .* (line 117)
   flowery, fat, red

7. *The recollection of his confession of the night before was a cause of **acute** pain to him. . . .* (lines 123–124)
   embarrassing, unpleasant, sharp

8. *From her hands and wrists . . . a **faint** perfume arose.* (lines 164–165)
   slight, sickly, cheap

9. *They used to go upstairs together on tiptoe . . . and on the third landing exchange **reluctant** good nights.* (lines 171–172)
   passionate, unwilling, long

10. *Her hopes and visions were so **intricate** that she no longer saw the white pillows on which her gaze was fixed. . . .* (lines 209–211)
    complex, confused, unrealistic

Make a list of the ten highlighted adjectives from the sentences above, and write an *antonym* (word of opposite meaning) next to each one.

C. Building Vocabulary Skills

Find the following ten idioms in the text. Then complete the sentences with the correct idiom. Use each idiom only once.

keep things to oneself (line 2)   go for (line 8)

have the run of (line 49)   pass the time away (line 52)

bear the brunt of (line 102)   make up for (line 105)

settle down (line 139)   look down on (line 140)

be had (line 142)   be done for (line 148)

1. Commuters often _____ by doing the crossword puzzle while riding the subway.

2. During one's teenage years it is common to _____ rather than confide in one's parents.

3. In many societies men are expected to _____ later than women.

4. It is a fact that women frequently have to _____ an unwanted pregnancy alone.

5. It is very arrogant to _____ other people.

6. Vicious dogs are known to _____ their victims' throats.

7. Nobody likes to _____ although it often occurs when one buys a second-hand car.

8. We assured our house guests that we wanted them to _____ our house while they were with us.

9. Nothing can _____ the death of my mother when I was seven.

10. When the stock market crashed, he felt he would soon _____.

PART ◆4◆ **WRITING ACTIVITIES**

1. Using lines 65–99 of "The Boarding House" as a model, create a scene of two to three paragraphs in which a character contemplates a course of action that may have far-reaching consequences. Concentrate on using adjectives to bring the surrounding environment to life as Joyce does in his extended description of the scene inside and outside the window. Situations your character might be thinking about could include whether to commit a crime, run away from home, or take revenge on someone.

2. Write an imaginary letter from Mr. Doran to a personal advice columnist (for example, "Dear Abby"), asking for help in his predicament. Include the columnist's reply to him.

3. "The Boarding House" comes from a collection of short stories called *Dubliners,* in which James Joyce uses Dublin as a physical and symbolic setting for the lives of people from many different walks of life. Write an essay of two pages about a book you have read or a movie you have seen in which a city plays a major role in the work. In your essay describe the aspects of the city that stand out and explain how the setting serves to influence the actions and lives of the characters.

10

Teenage Wasteland

ANNE TYLER *(b. 1941)*

◆◆◆

BORN IN MINNEAPOLIS, Minnesota, Anne Tyler spent her early childhood among rural Quaker communities. She moved with her family to Raleigh, North Carolina, where she attended high school. She went on to study at Duke University and came under the influence of novelist Reynolds Price. At the age of twenty-two, she published her first novel, *If Morning Ever Comes,* which attracted critical notice. The *New York Times Book Review* called it "a subtle and mature story." Her novel *Earthly Possessions* (1977) established her as an important writer. In 1988, she won the Pulitzer Prize for *Breathing Lessons,* and she is also well-known for *Dinner at the Homesick Restaurant* (1983) and *The Accidental Tourist* (1985), which was made into a movie. Her books and short stories examine minutely the complexities of family life.

TEENAGE WASTELAND

*A teenage boy withdraws from his family and comes under
the influence of an unconventional tutor whose methods
have questionable results.*

He used to have very blond hair—almost white—cut shorter than other children's so that on his crown a little cowlick[1] always stood up to catch the light. But this was when he was small. As he grew older, his hair grew darker, and he wore it longer—past his collar even. It hung in lank,[2] taffy-colored ropes around his face, which was still an endearing face, fine-featured, the eyes an unusual aqua blue. But his cheeks, of course, were no longer round, and a sharp new Adam's apple jogged in his throat when he talked.

In October, they called from the private school he attended to request a conference with his parents. Daisy went alone; her husband was at work. Clutching her purse, she sat on the principal's couch and learned that Donny was noisy, lazy, and disruptive;[3] always fooling around with his friends, and he wouldn't respond in class.

In the past, before her children were born, Daisy had been a fourth-grade teacher. It shamed her now to sit before this principal as a parent, a delinquent[4] parent, a parent who struck[5] Mr. Lanham, no doubt, as unseeing or uncaring. "It isn't that we're not concerned," she said. "Both of us are. And we've done what we could, whatever we could think of. We don't let him watch TV on school nights. We don't let him talk on the phone till he's finished his homework. But he tells us he doesn't *have* any homework or he did it all in study hall. How are we to know what to believe?"

From early October through November, at Mr. Lanham's suggestion, Daisy checked Donny's assignments every day. She sat next to him as he worked, trying to be encouraging, sagging[6] inwardly as she saw the poor quality of everything he did—the sloppy[7] mistakes in math, the illogical leaps in his English themes, the history questions left blank if they required any research.

Daisy was often late starting supper, and she couldn't give as much attention to Donny's younger sister. "You'll never guess what happened at . . ." Amanda would begin, and Daisy would have to tell her, "Not now, honey."

By the time her husband, Matt, came home, she'd be snappish.[8] She would recite the day's hardships—the fuzzy instructions in English, the

---

1. **cowlick** curl of hair growing in the wrong direction
2. **lank** hanging straight and thin
3. **disruptive** disturbing the order
4. **delinquent** not carrying out one's duties
5. **struck** affected, impressed
6. **sagging** drooping as if under a heavy weight
7. **sloppy** careless
8. **snappish** irritable

botched history map, the morass of unsolvable algebra equations. Matt would look surprised and confused, and Daisy would gradually wind down.[9] There was no way, really, to convey how exhausting all this was.

In December, the school called again. This time, they wanted Matt to come as well. She and Matt had to sit on Mr. Lanham's couch like two bad children and listen to the news: Donny had improved only slightly, raising a D in history to a C, and a C in algebra to a B-minus. What was worse, he had developed new problems. He had cut classes[10] on at least three occasions. Smoked in the furnace room. Helped Sonny Barnett break into a freshman's locker. And last week, during athletics, he and three friends had been seen off the school grounds; when they returned, the coach had smelled beer on their breath.

Daisy and Matt sat silent, shocked. Matt rubbed his forehead with his fingertips. Imagine, Daisy thought, how they must look to Mr. Lanham: an overweight housewife in a cotton dress and a too-tall, too-thin insurance agent in a baggy, frayed suit.[11] Failures, both of them—the kind of people who are always hurrying to catch up, missing the point of things that everyone else grasps at once. She wished she'd worn nylons instead of knee socks.

It was arranged that Donny would visit a psychologist for testing. Mr. Lanham knew just the person. He would set this boy straight,[12] he said.

When they stood to leave, Daisy held her stomach in and gave Mr. Lanham a firm, responsible handshake.

Donny said the psychologist was a jackass and the tests were really dumb; but he kept all three of his appointments, and when it was time for the follow-up conference with the psychologist and both parents, Donny combed his hair and seemed unusually sober and subdued. The psychologist said Donny had no serious emotional problems. He was merely going through a difficult period in his life. He required some academic help and a better sense of self-worth. For this reason, he was suggesting a man named Calvin Beadle, a tutor[13] with considerable psychological training.

In the car going home, Donny said he'd be damned if he'd let them drag him to some stupid fairy[14] tutor. His father told him to watch his language in front of his mother.

That night, Daisy lay awake pondering[15] the term "self-worth." She had always been free with her praise. She had always told Donny he had talent, was smart, was good with his hands. She had made a big to-do[16] over every little gift he gave her. In fact, maybe she had gone too far, although, Lord knows, she had meant every word. Was that his trouble?

---

9. **wind down** relax
10. **cut classes** deliberately missed classes
11. **a baggy frayed suit** a suit that is too large and is old and worn
12. **set this boy straight** help this boy to reform himself
13. **tutor** private teacher
14. **fairy** insulting reference to a male homosexual
15. **pondering** thinking deeply
16. **to-do** fuss

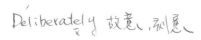

She remembered when Amanda was born. Donny had acted lost and bewildered. Daisy had been alert to that, of course, but still, a new baby keeps you so busy. Had she really done all she could have? She longed— she ached—for a time machine. Given one more chance, she'd do it perfectly—hug him more, praise him more, or perhaps praise him less. Oh, who can say . . .

The tutor told Donny to call him Cal. All his kids did, he said. Daisy thought for a second that he meant his own children, then realized her mistake. He seemed too young, anyhow, to be a family man. He wore a heavy brown handlebar mustache. His hair was as long and stringy as Donny's, and his jeans as faded. Wire-rimmed spectacles slid down his nose. He lounged[17] in a canvas director's chair with his fingers laced across his chest, and he casually, amiably questioned Donny, who sat upright and glaring in an armchair.

"So they're getting on your back[18] at school," said Cal. "Making a big deal about anything you do wrong."

"Right," said Donny.

"Any idea why that would be?"

"Oh, well, you know, stuff like homework and all," Donny said.

"You don't do your homework?"

"Oh, well, I might do it sometimes but not just exactly like they want it." Donny sat forward and said, "It's like a prison there, you know? You've got to go to every class, you can never step off the school grounds."

"You cut classes sometimes?"

"Sometimes," Donny said, with a glance at his parents.

Cal didn't seem perturbed. "Well," he said, "I'll tell you what. Let's you and me try working together three nights a week. Think you could handle that? We'll see if we can show that school of yours a thing or two. Give it a month; then if you don't like it, we'll stop. If *I* don't like it, we'll stop. I mean, sometimes people just don't get along,[19] right? What do you say to that?"

"Okay," Donny said. He seemed pleased.

"Make it seven o'clock till eight, Monday, Wednesday, and Friday," Cal told Matt and Daisy. They nodded. Cal shambled to his feet, gave them a little salute, and showed them to the door.

This was where he lived as well as worked, evidently. The interview had taken place in the dining room, which had been transformed into a kind of office. Passing the living room, Daisy winced[20] at the rock music she had been hearing, without registering it, ever since she had entered the house. She looked in and saw a boy about Donny's age lying on a sofa with a book. Another boy and a girl were playing Ping-Pong in front of the fireplace. "You have several here together?" Daisy asked Cal.

---

17. **lounged** sat in a relaxed fashion
18. **getting on your back** being a persistent nuisance (slang)

19. **get along** like one another, feel good together
20. **winced** moved one's body in response to pain

"Oh, sometimes they stay on after their sessions, just to rap.[21] They're a pretty sociable group, all in all. Plenty of goof-offs[22] like young Donny here."

He cuffed Donny's shoulder playfully. Donny flushed and grinned.

Climbing into the car, Daisy asked Donny, "Well? What did you think?"

But Donny had returned to his old evasive[23] self. He jerked his chin toward the garage. "Look," he said. "He's got a basketball net."

Now on Mondays, Wednesdays, and Fridays, they had supper early—the instant Matt came home. Sometimes, they had to leave before they were really finished. Amanda would still be eating her dessert. "Bye, honey. Sorry," Daisy would tell her.

Cal's first bill sent a flutter of panic through Daisy's chest, but it was worth it, of course. Just look at Donny's face when they picked him up: alight and full of interest. The principal telephoned Daisy to tell her how Donny had improved. "Of course, it hasn't shown up in his grades yet, but several of the teachers have noticed how his attitude's changed. Yes, sir, I think we're onto something[24] here."

At home, Donny didn't act much different. He still seemed to have a low opinion of his parents. But Daisy supposed that was unavoidable—part of being fifteen. He said his parents were too "controlling"—a word that made Daisy give him a sudden look. He said they acted like wardens. On weekends, they enforced a curfew.[25] And any time he went to a party, they always telephoned first to see if adults would be supervising. "For God's sake!" he said. "Don't you trust me?"

"It isn't a matter of trust, honey . . ." But there was no explaining to him.

His tutor called one afternoon. "I get the sense," he said, "that this kid's feeling . . . underestimated, you know? Like you folks expect the worst of him. I'm thinking we ought to give him more rope.[26]"

"But see, he's still so suggestible,"[27] Daisy said. "When his friends suggest some mischief—smoking or drinking or such—why, he just finds it hard not to go along[28] with them."

"Mrs. Coble," the tutor said, "I think this kid is hurting. You know? Here's a serious, sensitive kid, telling you he'd like to take on[29] some grown-up challenges, and you're giving him the message that he can't be trusted. Don't you understand how that hurts?"

"Oh," said Daisy.

"It undermines his self-esteem—don't you realize that?"

"Well, I guess you're right," said Daisy. She saw Donny suddenly from a whole new angle: his pathetically poor posture, that slouch so forlorn that

---

21. **rap** talk informally
22. **goof-offs** people who regularly avoid work (slang)
23. **evasive** secretive
24. **we're onto something** we're in the process of discovering something
25. **curfew** a strict time by which one has to be home or else be punished
26. **give him more rope** give him more freedom
27. **suggestible** easily influenced
28. **go along** accompany, approve of
29. **take on** assume

I would told Donney what I relized after have talked w/cal

his shoulders seemed about to meet his chin . . . oh, wasn't it awful being
young? She'd had a miserable adolescence herself and had always sworn no   155
child of hers would ever be that unhappy.

They let Donny stay out later, they didn't call ahead to see if the parties
were supervised, and they were careful not to grill[30] him about his evening.
The tutor had set down so many rules! They were not allowed any questions
at all about any aspect of school, nor were they to speak with his teachers. If   160
a teacher had some complaint, she should phone Cal. Only one teacher
disobeyed—the history teacher, Miss Evans. She called one morning in
February. "I'm a little concerned about Donny, Mrs. Coble."

"Oh, I'm sorry, Miss Evans, but Donny's tutor handles these things
now . . ."   165

"I always deal directly with the parents. You are the parent," Miss Evans
said, speaking very slowly and distinctly. "Now, here is the problem. Back
when you were helping Donny with his homework, his grades rose from a
D to a C, but now they've slipped back, and they're closer to an F."

"They are?"   170

"I think you should start overseeing his homework again."

"But Donny's tutor says . . ."

"It's nice that Donny has a tutor, but you should still be in charge of his
homework. With you, he learned it. Then he passed his tests. With the tutor,
well, it seems the tutor is more of a crutch.[31] 'Donny,' I say, 'a quiz is   175
coming up on Friday. Hadn't you better be listening instead of talking?'
'That's okay, Miss Evans,' he says. 'I have a tutor now.' Like a talisman![32] I
really think you ought to take over,[33] Mrs. Coble."

"I see," said Daisy. "Well, I'll think about that. Thank you for calling."

Hanging up, she felt a rush of anger at Donny. A talisman! For a   180
talisman, she'd given up all luxuries, all that time with her daughter, her
evenings at home!

She dialed Cal's number. He sounded muzzy. "I'm sorry if I woke you,"
she told him, "but Donny's history teacher just called. She says he isn't doing
well."   185

"She should have dealt with me." *Why should she, he is not his parent*

"She wants me to start supervising his homework again. His grades are
slipping."

"Yes," said the tutor, "but you and I both know there's more to it than
agree w/th mere grades, don't we? I care about the *whole* child—his happiness, his self-   190
esteem. The grades will come. Just give them time."

When she hung up, it was Miss Evans she was angry at. What a narrow
woman!

It was Cal this, Cal that, Cal says this, Cal and I did that. Cal lent Donny
an album by the Who. He took Donny and two other pupils to a rock   195
concert. In March, when Donny began to talk endlessly on the phone with a
girl named Miriam, Cal even let Miriam come to one of the tutoring sessions.

---

30. **grill**   question intensely
31. **crutch**   support
32. **talisman**   magic charm
33. **take over**   take control

Daisy was touched that Cal would grow so involved in Donny's life, but she was also a little hurt, because she had offered to have Miriam to dinner and Donny had refused. Now he asked them to drive her to Cal's house without a qualm.[34]

This Miriam was an unappealing girl with blurry lipstick and masses of rough red hair. She wore a short, bulky jacket that would not have been out of place on a motorcycle. During the trip to Cal's she was silent, but coming back, she was more talkative. "What a neat guy,[35] and what a house! All those kids hanging out,[36] like a club. And the stereo playing rock . . . gosh, he's not like a grown-up at all! Married and divorced and everything, but you'd think he was our own age."

"Mr. Beadle was married?" Daisy asked.

"Yeah, to this really controlling lady. She didn't understand him a bit."

"No, I guess not," Daisy said.

Spring came, and the students who hung around at Cal's drifted out to the basketball net above the garage. Sometimes, when Daisy and Matt arrived to pick up Donny, they'd find him there with the others—spiky[37] and excited, jittering on his toes beneath the backboard. It was staying light much longer now, and the neighboring fence cast narrow bars across the bright grass. Loud music would be spilling from Cal's windows. Once it was the Who, which Daisy recognized from the time that Donny had borrowed the album. "*Teenage Wasteland,*" she said aloud, identifying the song, and Matt gave a short, dry laugh. "It certainly is," he said. He'd misunderstood; he thought she was commenting on the scene spread before them. In fact, she might have been. The players looked like hoodlums,[38] even her son. Why, one of Cal's students had recently been knifed in a tavern. One had been shipped off to boarding school in midterm; two had been withdrawn by their parents. On the other hand, Donny had mentioned someone who'd been studying with Cal for five years. "Five years!" said Daisy. "Doesn't anyone ever stop needing him?"

Donny looked at her. Lately, whatever she said about Cal was read as criticism. "You're just feeling competitive," he said. "And controlling."

She bit her lip and said no more.

In April, the principal called to tell her that Donny had been expelled. There had been a locker check, and in Donny's locker they found five cans of beer and half a pack of cigarettes. With Donny's previous record, this offense meant expulsion.

Daisy gripped the receiver tightly and said, "Well, where is he now?"

"We've sent him home," said Mr. Lanham. "He's packed up all his belongings, and he's coming home on foot."

Daisy wondered what she would say to him. She felt him looming[39] closer and closer, bringing this brand-new situation that no one had

---

34. **without a qualm** confidently
35. **a neat guy** a wonderful man (slang)
36. **hanging out** not doing anything in particular (slang)
37. **spiky** sharp and pointy
38. **hoodlums** gangsters
39. **looming** appearing large and threatening

prepared her to handle. What other place would take him? Could they enter   240
him in public school? What were the rules? She stood at the living room
window, waiting for him to show up.⁴⁰ Gradually, she realized that he was
taking too long. She checked the clock. She stared up the street again.

When an hour had passed, she phoned the school. Mr. Lanham's
secretary answered and told her in a grave, sympathetic voice that yes,   245
Donny Coble had most definitely gone home. Daisy called her husband. He
was out of the office. She went back to the window and thought awhile, and
then she called Donny's tutor.

"Donny's been expelled from school," she said, "and now I don't know
where he's gone. I wonder if you've heard from him?"   250

There was a long silence. "Donny's with me, Mrs. Coble," he finally said.

"With you? How'd he get there?"

"He hailed a cab, and I paid the driver."

"Could I speak to him, please?"

There was another silence. "Maybe it'd be better if we had a   255
conference," Cal said.

"I don't *want* a conference. I've been standing at the window picturing
him dead or kidnapped or something, and now you tell me you want a—"

"Donny is very, very upset. Understandably so," said Cal. "Believe me,
Mrs. Coble, this is not what it seems. Have you asked Donny's side of the   260
story?"

"Well, of course not, how could I? He went running off to you instead."

"Because he didn't feel he'd be listened to."

"But I haven't even—"

"Why don't you come out and talk? The three of us," said Cal, "will try to   265
get this thing in perspective."

"Well, all right," Daisy said. But she wasn't as reluctant as she sounded.
Already, she felt soothed by the calm way Cal was taking this.

Cal answered the doorbell at once. He said, "Hi, there," and led her into
the dining room. Donny sat slumped in a chair, chewing the knuckle of one   270
thumb. "Hello, Donny," Daisy said. He flicked his eyes in her direction.

"Sit here, Mrs. Coble," said Cal, placing her opposite Donny. He himself
remained standing, restlessly pacing. "So," he said.

Daisy stole a look at Donny. His lips were swollen, as if he'd been
crying.   275

"You know," Cal told Daisy, "I kind of expected something like this.
That's a very punitive⁴¹ school you've got him in—you realize that. And any
half-decent lawyer will tell you they've violated his civil rights. Locker
checks! Where's their search warrant?"

"But if the rule is—" Daisy said.   280

"Well, anyhow, let him tell you his side."

She looked at Donny. He said, "It wasn't my fault. I promise."

---

40. **show up** appear   41. **punitive** punishing

"They said your locker was full of beer."

"It was a put-up job![42] See, there's this guy that doesn't like me. He put all these beers in my locker and started a rumor going, so Mr. Lanham ordered a locker check."

"What was the boy's name?" Daisy asked.

"Huh?"

"Mrs. Coble, take my word, the situation is not so unusual," Cal said. "You can't imagine how vindictive kids can be sometimes."

"What was the boy's *name*," said Daisy, "so that I can ask Mr. Lanham if that's who suggested he run a locker check."

"You don't believe me," Donny said.

"And how'd this boy get your combination in the first place?"

"Frankly," said Cal, "I wouldn't be surprised to learn the school was in on[43] it. Any kid that marches to a different drummer, why, they'd just love an excuse to get rid of[44] him. The school is where I lay the blame."

"Doesn't *Donny* ever get blamed?"

"Now, Mrs. Coble, you heard what he—"

"Forget it," Donny told Cal. "You can see she doesn't trust me."

Daisy drew in a breath to say that of course she trusted him—a reflex. But she knew that bold-faced, wide-eyed look of Donny's. He had worn that look when he was small, denying some petty misdeed with the evidence plain as day all around him. Still, it was hard for her to accuse him outright. She temporized[45] and said, "The only thing I'm sure of is that they've kicked you out[46] of school, and now I don't know what we're going to do."

"We'll fight it," said Cal.

"We can't. Even you must see we can't."

"I could apply to Brantly," Donny said.

Cal stopped his pacing to beam down at him. "Brantly! Yes. They're really onto where a kid is coming from, at Brantly. Why, *I* could get you into Brantly. I work with a lot of their students."

Daisy had never heard of Brantly, but already she didn't like it. And she didn't like Cal's smile, which struck her now as feverish and avid—a smile of hunger.

On the fifteenth of April, they entered Donny in a public school, and they stopped his tutoring sessions. Donny fought both decisions bitterly. Cal, surprisingly enough, did not object. He admitted he'd made no headway[47] with Donny and said it was because Donny was emotionally disturbed.

Donny went to his new school every morning, plodding[48] off alone with his head down. He did his assignments, and he earned average grades,

---

42. **a put-up job**   an attempt to trap someone secretly (slang)
43. **was in on**   was involved in
44. **get rid of**   be free of
45. **temporized**   compromised
46. **kicked out**   expelled
47. **headway**   progress
48. **plodding**   walking slowly and heavily

but he gathered no friends, joined no clubs. There was something
exhausted and defeated about him.   325

The first week in June, during final exams, Donny vanished. He simply
didn't come home one afternoon, and no one at school remembered seeing
him. The police were reassuring, and for the first few days, they worked
hard. They combed[49] Donny's sad, messy room for clues; they visited
Miriam and Cal. But then they started talking about the number of kids who   330
ran away every year. Hundreds, just in this city. "He'll show up, if he wants
to," they said. "If he doesn't, he won't."

Evidently, Donny didn't want to.

It's been three months now and still no word. Matt and Daisy still look
for him in every crowd of awkward, heartbreaking teenage boys. Every time   335
the phone rings, they imagine it might be Donny. Both parents have aged.
Donny's sister seems to be staying away from home as much as possible.

At night, Daisy lies awake and goes over Donny's life. She is trying to
figure out what went wrong, where they made their first mistake. Often, she
finds herself blaming Cal, although she knows he didn't begin it. Then at   340
other times she excuses him, for without him, Donny might have left earlier.
Who really knows? In the end, she can only sigh and search for a cooler
spot on the pillow. As she falls asleep, she occasionally glimpses something
in the corner of her vision. It's something fleet and round, a ball—a
basketball. It flies up, it sinks through the hoop, descends, lands in a yard   345
littered with last year's leaves and striped with bars of sunlight as white as
bones, bleached[50] and parched and cleanly picked.[51] ◆

---

49. **combed**   searched thoroughly
50. **bleached**   lightened

51. **cleanly picked**   with all the flesh removed

P A R T ◆**1**◆ **F I R S T   R E A D I N G**

A. Thinking about the Story

Did you have the feeling the story would end well or badly? What gave
you that feeling? I think will 346

B. Understanding the Plot

1. Why does the school principal initially request to see Donny's parents?

2. What new information does Daisy receive about Donny in her
   second interview with Mr. Lanham?

3. What is the psychologist's diagnosis of Donny's problems?

4. What is Daisy's state of mind after they return from the psychologist's office?

5. What are Daisy's first impressions of Cal?

6. What does Donny compare his school to?

7. Why is Miss Evans determined to speak to Daisy? Does she succeed in her mission?

8. What information about Cal does Daisy learn from Miriam?

9. Why was Donny expelled from school?

10. How do Cal's and Daisy's reactions to the expulsion differ? What does Donny claim happened?

11. Over what period of time does the story take place?

PART  SECOND READING

A. Exploring Themes

You are now ready to reread "Teenage Wasteland." Try to understand how the weaknesses of the main characters affect their actions, and pay particular attention to the connection between the title and a major theme of the story.

1. How does the description of Donny's changing appearance in paragraph one relate to the story?

2. How do Donny's problems affect his sister Amanda?

3. Is Cal generally successful in helping his students? Explain your answer by giving examples from the story.

4. Does Daisy's personality contribute to Donny's problems? If so, how?

5. What is the role of Donny's father in the story?

6. How does the ending relate to the title of the story?

B. Analyzing the Author's Style

Before you begin to work on this section, turn to the detailed explanation of point of view (page 281) and inference (page 279).

POINT OF VIEW: THIRD-PERSON NARRATION

One of the decisions Anne Tyler has to make in "Teenage Wasteland" is whether her third-person narrator will have *total omniscience* (the narrator is not a participant in the story and has a complete picture of the characters and events) or *limited omniscience* (the narrator can penetrate the thoughts of one or two characters only and provides a subjective view of characters and events).

1. Does the narrator display total or limited omniscience? Explain your answer.
2. Which character's point of view dominates the story?
3. How does this character's point of view affect the way we see Donny?
4. Choose another character and say how the story might be different if it were told from his or her perspective.

INFERENCE

In "Teenage Wasteland" not everything is immediately accessible to the reader. Ann Tyler requires you to **infer**, or deduce, hidden meanings throughout the story.

For example, Tyler writes, *Daisy was often late starting supper.* . . . (line 27), leaving us to infer that because she was spending so much time with Donny, the other family members suffered.

When Tyler describes Cal with hair *as long and stringy as Donny's, and his jeans as faded* (lines 82–83), she is implying that Daisy sees him more like a teenager than an adult.

Later Tyler notes, *Daisy winced at the rock music she had been hearing.* . . . (line 110), suggesting that Daisy probably does not like rock music and disapproves of its being played at the tutor's house.

1. What can you infer about the teenage years from the title of the story?
2. What can you infer about the Cobles' financial situation in lines 45–51?
3. What can you infer about Daisy's thoughts when Donny refers to his father and mother as being "too controlling"(line 134)?
4. The history teacher refers to Cal as "a crutch" (line 175) and "like a talisman" (line 177). What is she implying about Cal's effectiveness as a tutor?

C. Judging for Yourself

Express yourself as personally as you like in your answers to the following questions:

1. Do you agree with the opinion of Donny's psychologist—and later of Cal—that his problem is mainly one of self-esteem?
2. Do you feel that Donny's parents are "too controlling"? If you were Donny's parent, would you give him more freedom? Give reasons for your answer.
3. In your view does Daisy relate to how a teenager feels?
4. Do you agree with the principal's reasons for expelling Donny?

5. In your view is Cal good or bad for Donny?

6. Who do you think is to blame for Donny's problems? Why?

7. Do you think Donny will come home?

D. Making Connections

1. Are the teenage years particularly difficult in your culture?

2. Does your country have a problem with runaway teenagers? If so, what happens to most of them? If not, what do you think the reasons are?

3. If you and your friends faced problems as teenagers, what were they?

4. How do you think parents should deal with their teenage children? Would you handle your teenage child in the same way your parents handled you? Why or why not?

E. Debate

Debate the proposal: Children should have a lot of discipline when growing up.

P A R T **3** **FOCUS ON LANGUAGE**

A. Conditionals

Conditionals, or *if*-clauses, can be divided into two categories—the *real* or *true condition* and the *unreal* or *untrue condition*.

In the **real condition** the main or result clause contains a situation that is likely to happen. When the verb in the conditional clause (cc) is in the present tense or is a present modal (such as *can*), the verb in the main clause (mc) can be in the present or future tense or be a present modal. For example:

$$\text{cc} \qquad\qquad \text{mc}$$
*If Amanda **continues** to stay out late, she **may turn out** like Donny!*

$$\text{cc} \qquad\qquad \text{mc}$$
*If the school rules **are** frequently **broken**, the offending student **will**

be expelled.*

$$\text{cc} \qquad\qquad \text{mc}$$
*If Donny **cannot convince** Daisy to trust him, their relationship **will**

never **improve**!*

When the verb in the conditional clause is in the past tense, the verb in the main clause will be composed of *would/should/could/might* plus the simple verb form. For example:

cc   mc

*If a teacher **had** some complaint,* *she **should phone** Cal.*

(lines 160–161)

An **unreal condition** is unlikely or unable to happen. It suggests that if something were true (but it isn't at the time or can never be), something else would happen.

The verb in the unreal conditional clause (cc) is always in a past tense, while the verb in the main clause (mc) is composed of *would/could/should/might* plus the base form of the verb or *would have/could have/should have/might have* plus the past participle. For example:

cc   mc

*If Daisy **had** her life to live over again,* *she **would** probably **act**

differently toward Donny.* (unreal condition because Daisy cannot

have her life over again)

cc   mc

*If I **were** * Donny,* *I **would** never **have run away** from home.*

(unreal condition because I can never be Donny)

* Note: If you use the verb *to be* in an unreal condition, use *were* for all persons in the conditional clause.

cc   mc

*If Donny **had studied**,* *he **would have passed** his exams.* (unreal

condition because Donny did not study)

Complete the following dialogue with the correct form of the verb in parentheses. If the condition used is real, write *R* above your answer. If the condition is unreal, write *U*.

[R] **PARENT:** If you ~~will not~~ *are* not home by twelve tonight, you *will be punish* (be, punish)

[R] **TEENAGER:** Why are you always so mean to me? Everybody else is allowed to stay out much later. And I know that even if I *get* home early, you *will be* on my back. (get, be)

PARENT: That's not true. And remember, if you *had come* home on time last Saturday, we *would not* . (come, not argue)

argue

be arguing

TEENAGER: You're always looking for an excuse to punish me. If you ___weren't___ so unreasonable, I ___would listen___ to you more. (not be, listen)

PARENT: Perhaps if you ___cooperated___ with us more, you ___would will see___ we aren't so difficult to get along with after all. (cooperate, see)

TEENAGER: This is getting us nowhere. If I ___were___ you, I ___would trust___ my child. You're both jerks! (be, trust)

PARENT: If this conversation ___continues___, we ___will say___ even more hurtful things to each other. (continue, say)

With a partner write a few more sentences to resolve this conflict, also using the conditional. Then act out the dialogue for the class.

B. Building Vocabulary Skills

Complete the sentences with the correct idiom from the list. All the idioms appear in the story and are explained in the accompanying glossary. Be sure to put the verb in the correct person and tense.

get along (line 102)   hang out (line 206)
goof off (line 116)   show up (line 242)
go along (line 145)   be in on (line 296)
take on (line 147)   get rid of (line 297)
take over (line 178)   kick out (line 306)

1. He always ___shows up___ when he needs money.

2. When we were in the army, we relied on our captain to ___take over___ in a difficult situation.

3. As people mature, they tend to ___take on___ more responsibility.

4. If you had ___gone along___ with us when we went to the demonstration, you too might have been arrested.

5. We like to ___hang out___ at our neighborhood club on Saturdays.

6. Will she be ___kicked out___ of the class because of her disruptive behavior?

7. Please reveal to us how you ___got get along___ for so many years without having a single serious quarrel.

8. My husband has great difficulty in ___getting rid of___ his old possessions.

9. Since I was elected to office, I've ___been in on___ all the latest political gossip.

10. How can you expect to pass your exams if you're always ___goof off___?

P A R T **4** **W R I T I N G A C T I V I T I E S**

1. Choose one of the characters in "Teenage Wasteland." Compose diary entries for your character, covering an imaginary week in that troubled year. Try to imagine how your character would think, feel, and act during that week, based on what you have learned about him or her from the story. Try to incorporate examples of real and unreal conditional clauses in some of your entries.

2. In an essay of two to three pages compare and contrast teenagers of your generation with those of your parents' time. You might begin your essay with the sentence: In general, teenagers today have a more difficult/easier time than their parents did. In your supporting paragraphs consider aspects like economic conditions, personal freedom, exposure to harmful substances, peer pressure, and the structure of the family.

3. *The Catcher in the Rye* by J. D. Salinger is a famous American novel about the teenage years. In an essay of one to two pages describe a book or movie you've read or seen that deals with the problems of adolescence. Could you identify with the teens as they were portrayed?

My Oedipus Complex

FRANK O'CONNOR *(1903–1966)*

◆◆◆

BORN IN CORK, Ireland, Frank O'Connor, whose real name was Michael O'Donovan, was the only child of very poor, working-class parents. An Irish nationalist, he joined the Irish Republican Army (IRA) and fought actively for its cause. A prolific writer, O'Connor achieved the most recognition for his short story collections, which include *Guests of the Nation* (1931), *My Oedipus Complex and Other Stories* (1963), and *A Life of Your Own and Other Stories* (1969). He also published a novel, *Dutch Interior* (1940), two autobiographies, several poetry anthologies, four plays, and books of literary criticism.

O'Connor's short stories reflect the realities of Irish life as he knew it. The naturalistic language of his writing seeks to capture the flavor of the Irish tongue, and many of his stories are infused with humor. "My Oedipus Complex" is a semiautobiographical story in which O'Connor depicts his childhood relationship with his parents.

MY OEDIPUS COMPLEX

*A small boy's world is turned upside down when his father
returns home from the war.*

Father was in the army all through the war—the first war, I mean—so, up
to the age of five, I never saw much of him, and what I saw did not worry
me. Sometimes I woke and there was a big figure in khaki[1] peering down at
me in the candlelight. Sometimes in the early morning I heard the slamming
of the front door and the clatter of nailed boots down the cobbles[2] of the   5
lane. These were Father's entrances and exits. Like Santa Claus he came and
went mysteriously.

In fact, I rather liked his visits, though it was an uncomfortable squeeze
between Mother and him when I got into the big bed in the early morning.
He smoked, which gave him a pleasant musty smell,[3] and shaved, an   10
operation of astounding interest. Each time he left a trail of souvenirs—
model tanks and Gurkha[4] knives with handles made of bullet cases, and
German helmets and cap badges and button sticks, and all sorts of military
equipment—carefully stowed away in a long box on top of the wardrobe, in
case they ever came in handy.[5] There was a bit of the magpie[6] about Father;   15
he expected everything to come in handy. When his back was turned,
Mother let me get a chair and rummage through his treasures. She didn't
seem to think so highly of them as he did.

The war was the most peaceful period of my life. The window of my
attic faced southeast. My mother had curtained it, but that had small effect. I   20
always woke with the first light and, with all the responsibilities of the
previous day melted, feeling myself rather like the sun, ready to illumine
and rejoice. Life never seemed so simple and clear and full of possibilities as
then. I put my feet out from under the clothes—I called them Mrs. Left and
Mrs. Right—and invented dramatic situations for them in which they   25
discussed the problems of the day. At least Mrs. Right did; she was very
demonstrative, but I hadn't the same control of Mrs. Left, so she mostly
contented herself with nodding agreement.

They discussed what Mother and I should do during the day, what Santa
Claus should give a fellow for Christmas, and what steps should be taken to   30
brighten the home. There was that little matter of the baby, for instance.
Mother and I could never agree about that. Ours was the only house in the
terrace without a new baby, and Mother said we couldn't afford one till
Father came back from the war because they cost seventeen and six.[7]

1. **khaki** material used for military uniforms
2. **cobbles** cobblestones, round stones for paving streets
3. **musty smell** damp, stale odor
4. **Gurkha** Nepalese who served in the British army
5. **came in handy** were useful
6. **magpie** bird that collects small articles for its nest
7. **seventeen and six** seventeen shillings and six
   pence (British currency)

That showed how simple she was. The Geneys up the road had a baby, and everyone knew they couldn't afford seventeen and six. It was probably a cheap baby, and Mother wanted something really good, but I felt she was too exclusive.[8] The Geney's baby would have done us fine.

Having settled my plans for the day, I got up, put a chair under the attic window, and lifted the frame high enough to stick out my head. The window overlooked the front gardens of the terrace behind ours, and beyond these it looked over a deep valley to the tall, red brick houses terraced up the opposite hillside, which were all still in shadow, while those at our side of the valley were all lit up, though with long strange shadows that made them seem unfamiliar; rigid[9] and painted.

After that I went into Mother's room and climbed into the big bed. She woke and I began to tell her of my schemes. By this time, though I never seemed to have noticed it, I was petrified[10] in my nightshirt, and I thawed as I talked until, the last frost melted, I fell asleep beside her and woke again only when I heard her below in the kitchen, making the breakfast.

After breakfast we went into town; heard Mass at St. Augustine's[11] and said a prayer for Father, and did the shopping. If the afternoon was fine we either went for a walk in the country or a visit to Mother's great friend in the convent, Mother Saint Dominic. Mother had them all praying for Father, and every night, going to bed, I asked God to send him back safe from the war to us. Little, indeed, did I know what I was praying for!

One morning, I got into the big bed, and there, sure enough, was Father in his usual Santa Claus manner, but later, instead of uniform, he put on his best blue suit, and Mother was as pleased as anything. I saw nothing to be pleased about, because, out of uniform, Father was altogether less interesting, but she only beamed, and explained that our prayers had been answered, and off we went to Mass to thank God for having brought Father safely home.

The irony of it! That very day when he came in to dinner he took off his boots and put on his slippers, donned the dirty old cap he wore about the house to save him from colds, crossed his legs, and began to talk gravely to Mother, who looked anxious. Naturally, I disliked her looking anxious, because it destroyed her good looks, so I interrupted him.

"Just a moment, Larry!" she said gently.

This was only what she said when we had boring visitors, so I attached no importance to it and went on talking.

"Do be quiet, Larry!" she said impatiently. "Don't you hear me talking to Daddy?"

This was the first time I heard those ominous[12] words, "talking to Daddy," and I couldn't help feeling that if this was how God answered prayers, he couldn't listen to them very attentively.

---

8. **exclusive** demanding
9. **rigid** stiff
10. **petrified** frozen (unusual use)

11. **heard Mass at St. Augustine's** attended a church service at St. Augustine's
12. **ominous** threatening

"Why are you talking to Daddy?" I asked with as great a show of indifference[13] as I could muster.[14]

"Because Daddy and I have business to discuss. Now, don't interrupt again!"

In the afternoon, at Mother's request, Father took me for a walk. This time we went into town instead of out in the country, and I thought at first, in my usual optimistic way, that it might be an improvement. It was nothing of the sort. Father and I had quite different notions of a walk in town. He had no proper interest in trams, ships, and horses, and the only thing that seemed to divert him was talking to fellows as old as himself. When I wanted to stop he simply went on, dragging me behind him by the hand; when he wanted to stop I had no alternative but to do the same. I noticed that it seemed to be a sign that he wanted to stop for a long time whenever he leaned against a wall. The second time I saw him do it I got wild. He seemed to be settling himself forever. I pulled him by the coat and trousers, but, unlike Mother who, if you were too persistent, got into a wax[15] and said: "Larry, if you don't behave yourself, I'll give you a good slap," Father had an extraordinary capacity for amiable inattention. I sized him up[16] and wondered would I cry, but he seemed to be too remote to be annoyed even by that. Really, it was like going for a walk with a mountain! He either ignored the wrenching[17] and pummeling[18] entirely, or else glanced down with a grin of amusement from his peak. I had never met anyone so absorbed in himself as he seemed.

At teatime, "talking to Daddy" began again, complicated this time by the fact that he had an evening paper, and every few minutes he put it down and told Mother something new out of it. I felt this was foul play.[19] Man for man, I was prepared to compete with him any time for Mother's attention, but when he had it all made up for him by other people it left me no chance. Several times I tried to change the subject without success.

"You must be quiet while Daddy is reading, Larry," Mother said impatiently.

It was clear that she either genuinely liked talking to Father better than talking to me, or else that he had some terrible hold on her[20] which made her afraid to admit the truth.

"Mummy," I said that night when she was tucking me up,[21] "do you think if I prayed hard God would send Daddy back to the war?"

She seemed to think about that for a moment.

"No, dear," she said with a smile. "I don't think He would."

"Why wouldn't He, Mummy?"

---

13. **show of indifference** appearance of not caring
14. **muster** gather
15. **got into a wax** got angry (British slang)
16. **sized him up** judged him
17. **wrenching** strong pulling
18. **pummeling** beating

19. **foul play** not fair
20. **he had some terrible hold on her** he had a frightening control over her
21. **tucking me up** covering me tightly with the bed linen (British)

"Because there isn't a war any longer, dear."

"But, Mummy, couldn't God make another war, if He liked?"

"He wouldn't like to, dear. It's not God who makes wars, but bad people."

"Oh!" I said.

I was disappointed about that. I began to think that God wasn't quite what He was cracked up to be.[22]

Next morning I woke at my usual hour, feeling like a bottle of champagne. I put out my feet and invented a long conversation in which Mrs. Right talked of the trouble she had with her own father till she put him in the Home.[23] I didn't quite know what the Home was but it sounded the right place for Father. Then I got my chair and stuck my head out of the attic window. Dawn was just breaking, with a guilty air that made me feel I had caught it in the act.[24] My head bursting with stories and schemes, I stumbled in next door, and in the half-darkness scrambled into the big bed. There was no room at Mother's side so I had to get between her and Father. For the time being I had forgotten about him, and for several minutes I sat bolt upright,[25] racking my brains[26] to know what I could do with him. He was taking up more than his fair share of the bed, and I couldn't get comfortable, so I gave him several kicks that made him grunt and stretch. He made room all right, though. Mother waked and felt for me. I settled back comfortably in the warmth of the bed with my thumb in my mouth.

"Mummy!" I hummed, loudly and contentedly.

"Sssh! dear," she whispered. "Don't wake Daddy!"

This was a new development, which threatened to be even more serious than "talking to Daddy." Life without my early-morning conferences was unthinkable.

"Why?" I asked severely.

"Because poor Daddy is tired."

This seemed to me a quite inadequate reason, and I was sickened by the sentimentality of her "poor Daddy." I never liked that sort of gush,[27] it always struck me as insincere.

"Oh!" I said lightly. Then in my most winning tone:[28] "Do you know where I want to go with you today, Mummy?"

"No, dear," she sighed.

"I want to go down the Glen and fish for thornybacks with my new net, and then I want to go out to the Fox and Hounds, and —"

"Don't-wake-Daddy!" she hissed angrily, clapping her hand across my mouth.

But it was too late. He was awake, or nearly so. He grunted and reached for the matches. Then he stared incredulously at his watch.

---

22. **God wasn't quite what He was cracked up to be** God didn't live up to His reputation
23. **the Home** an institution for old people
24. **caught it in the act** caught it doing something bad
25. **sat bolt upright** sat very straight
26. **racking my brains** thinking as hard as I could
27. **gush** sentimentality
28. **winning tone** charming voice

"Like a cup of tea, dear?" asked Mother in a meek, hushed voice I had never heard her use before. It sounded almost as though she were afraid.

"Tea?" he exclaimed indignantly. "Do you know what the time is?"

"And after that I want to go up the Rathcooney Road," I said loudly, afraid I'd forget something in all those interruptions.   160

"Go to sleep at once, Larry!" she said sharply.

I began to snivel.[29] I couldn't concentrate, the way that pair went on, and smothering my early-morning schemes was like burying a family from the cradle.   165

Father said nothing, but lit his pipe and sucked it, looking out into the shadows without minding Mother or me. I knew he was mad. Every time I made a remark Mother hushed me irritably. I was mortified.[30] I felt it wasn't fair, there was even something sinister in it. Every time I had pointed out to her the waste of making two beds when we could both sleep in one, she   170 had told me it was healthier like that, and now here was this man, this stranger, sleeping with her without the least regard for her health!

He got up early and made tea, but though he brought Mother a cup he brought none for me.

"Mummy," I shouted, "I want a cup of tea, too."   175

"Yes, dear," she said patiently. "You can drink from Mummy's saucer."

That settled it. Either Father or I would have to leave the house. I didn't want to drink from Mother's saucer; I wanted to be treated as an equal in my own home, so, just to spite her, I drank it all and left none for her. She took that quietly, too.   180

But that night when she was putting me to bed she said gently: "Larry, I want you to promise me something."

"What is it?" I asked.

"Not to come in and disturb poor Daddy in the morning. Promise?"

"Poor Daddy" again! I was becoming suspicious of everything involving   185 that quite impossible man.

"Why?" I asked.

"Because poor Daddy is worried and tired and he doesn't sleep well."

"Why doesn't he, Mummy?"

"Well, you know, don't you, that while he was at the war Mummy got   190 the pennies from the post office?"

"From Miss MacCarthy?"

"That's right. But now, you see, Miss MacCarthy hasn't any more pennies, so Daddy must go out and find us some. You know what would happen if he couldn't?"   195

"No," I said, "tell us."

"Well, I think we might have to go out and beg for them like the poor old woman on Fridays. We wouldn't like that, would we?"

"No," I agreed. "We wouldn't."

"So you'll promise not to come in and wake him?"   200

---

29. **snivel**   whine, complain weakly   30. **mortified**   very embarrassed

"Promise."

Mind you,[31] I meant that. I knew pennies were a serious matter, and I was all against having to go out and beg like the old woman on Fridays. Mother laid out all my toys in a complete ring round the bed so that, whatever way I got out, I was bound to fall over one of them. 205

When I woke I remembered my promise all right. I got up and sat on the floor and played—for hours, it seemed to me. Then I got my chair and looked out the attic window for more hours. I wished it was time for Father to wake; I wished someone would make me a cup of tea. I didn't feel in the least like the sun; instead, I was bored and so very, very cold! I simply 210 longed for the warmth and depth of the big feather bed.

At last I could stand it no longer. I went into the next room. As there was still no room at Mother's side I climbed over her and she woke with a start.

"Larry," she whispered, gripping my arm very tightly, "what did you promise?" 215

"But I did, Mummy," I wailed, caught in the very act. "I was quiet for ever so long."

"Oh, dear, and you're perished!"[32] she said sadly, feeling me all over. "Now, if I let you stay will you promise not to talk?"

"But I want to talk, Mummy," I wailed. 220

"That has nothing to do with it," she said with a firmness that was new to me. "Daddy wants to sleep. Now, do you understand that?"

I understood it only too well. I wanted to talk, he wanted to sleep, whose house was it, anyway?

"Mummy," I said with equal firmness, "I think it would be healthier for 225 Daddy to sleep in his own bed."

That seemed to stagger[33] her, because she said nothing for a while.

"Now, once for all," she went on, "you're to be perfectly quiet or go back to your own bed. Which is it to be?"

The injustice of it got me down.[34] I had convicted her out of her own 230 mouth of inconsistency and unreasonableness, and she hadn't even attempted to reply. Full of spite, I gave Father a kick, which she didn't notice but which made him grunt and open his eyes in alarm.

"What time is it?" he asked in a panic-stricken voice, not looking at mother but at the door, as if he saw someone there. 235

"It's early yet," she replied soothingly. "It's only the child. Go to sleep again. . . . Now, Larry," she added, getting out of bed, "you've wakened Daddy and you must go back."

This time, for all her quiet air, I knew she meant it, and knew that my principal rights and privileges were as good as lost[35] unless I asserted them 240 at once. As she lifted me, I gave a screech, enough to wake the dead, not to mind Father.[36] He groaned.

---

31. **mind you** expression used for emphasis
32. **perished** frozen (unusual use)
33. **stagger** amaze
34. **got me down** depressed me
35. **were as good as lost** were just about lost
36. **not to mind Father** meaning he screeched more than loudly enough to wake Father

"That damn child! Doesn't he ever sleep?"

"It's only a habit, dear," she said quietly, though I could see she was vexed.

"Well, it's time he got out of it," shouted Father, beginning to heave in the bed. He suddenly gathered all the bedclothes about him, turned to the wall, and then looked back over his shoulder with nothing showing only two small, spiteful, dark eyes. The man looked very wicked.

To open the bedroom door, Mother had to let me down, and I broke free and dashed for the farthest corner, screeching. Father sat bolt upright in bed.

"Shut up, you little puppy!" he said in a choking voice.

I was so astonished that I stopped screeching. Never, never had anyone spoken to me in that tone before. I looked at him incredulously and saw his face convulsed with rage. It was only then that I fully realized how God had codded[37] me, listening to my prayers for the safe return of this monster.

"Shut up, you!" I bawled, beside myself.

"What's that you said?" shouted Father, making a wild leap out of the bed.

"Mick, Mick!" cried Mother. "Don't you see the child isn't used to you?"

"I see he's better fed than taught," snarled Father, waving his arms wildly. "He wants his bottom smacked."

All his previous shouting was as nothing to these obscene words referring to my person. They really made my blood boil.

"Smack your own!" I screamed hysterically. "Smack your own! Shut up! Shut up!"

At this he lost his patience and let fly[38] at me. He did it with the lack of conviction you'd expect of a man under Mother's horrified eyes, and it ended up as a mere tap, but the sheer indignity of being struck at all by a stranger, a total stranger who had cajoled[39] his way back from the war into our big bed as a result of my innocent intercession,[40] made me completely dotty. I shrieked and shrieked, and danced in my bare feet, and Father, looking awkward and hairy in nothing but a short gray army shirt, glared down at me like a mountain out for murder. I think it must have been then that I realized he was jealous too. And there stood Mother in her nightdress, looking as if her heart was broken between us. I hoped she felt as she looked. It seemed to me that she deserved it all.

From that morning out my life was a hell. Father and I were enemies, open and avowed. We conducted a series of skirmishes[41] against one another, he trying to steal my time with Mother and I his. When she was sitting on my bed, telling me a story, he took to looking for some pair of old boots which he alleged he had left behind him at the beginning of the war. While he talked to Mother I played loudly with my toys to show my total

---

37. **codded**   played a joke on, tricked (unconventional use)

38. **let fly at**   attacked suddenly

39. **cajoled**   deceived

40. **intercession**   prayer

41. **skirmishes**   small battles

lack of concern. He created a terrible scene one evening when he came in from work and found me at his box, playing with his regimental badges, Gurkha knives and button sticks. Mother got up and took the box from me. 285

"You mustn't play with Daddy's toys unless he lets you, Larry," she said severely. "Daddy doesn't play with yours."

For some reason Father looked at her as if she had struck him and then turned away with a scowl. 290

"Those are not toys," he growled, taking down the box again to see had I lifted[42] anything. "Some of those curios are very rare and valuable."

But as time went on I saw more and more how he managed to alienate[43] Mother and me. What made it worse was that I couldn't grasp his method or see what attraction he had for Mother. In every possible way he 295 was less winning than I. He had a common accent and made noises at his tea. I thought for a while that it might be the newspapers she was interested in, so I made up bits of news of my own to read to her. Then I thought it might be the smoking, which I personally thought attractive, and took his pipes and went round the house dribbling[44] into them till he caught me. I 300 even made noises at my tea, but Mother only told me I was disgusting. It all seemed to hinge round[45] that unhealthy habit of sleeping together, so I made a point of dropping into their bedroom and nosing round, talking to myself, so that they wouldn't know I was watching them, but they were never up to anything that I could see. In the end it beat me. It seemed to 305 depend on being grown-up and giving people rings, and I realized I'd have to wait.

But at the same time I wanted him to see that I was only waiting, not giving up the fight. One evening when he was being particularly obnoxious,[46] chattering away well above my head, I let him have it. 310 "Mummy," I said, "do you know what I'm going to do when I grow up?"

"No, dear," she replied. "What?"

"I'm going to marry you," I said quietly.

Father gave a great guffaw[47] out of him, but he didn't take me in.[48] I knew it must only be pretense. And Mother, in spite of everything, was 315 pleased. I felt she was probably relieved to know that one day Father's hold on her would be broken. "Won't that be nice?" she said with a smile.

"It'll be very nice," I said confidently. "Because we're going to have lots and lots of babies."

"That's right, dear," she said placidly. "I think we'll have one soon, and 320 then you'll have plenty of company."

I was no end pleased about that because it showed that in spite of the way she gave in to Father she still considered my wishes. Besides, it would put the Geneys in their place.

---

42. **lifted**   taken, stolen
43. **alienate**   put a distance between
44. **dribbling**   dropping saliva
45. **hinge round**   depend on
46. **obnoxious**   very unpleasant, offensive
47. **guffaw**   loud laugh
48. **take me in**   deceive me

It didn't turn out like that, though. To begin with, she was very $_{325}$ preoccupied[49]—I supposed about where she would get the seventeen and six—and though Father took to[50] staying out late in the evenings it did me no particular good. She stopped taking me for walks, became as touchy as blazes,[51] and smacked me for nothing at all. Sometimes I wished I'd never mentioned the confounded baby—I seemed to have a genius for bringing $_{330}$ calamity on myself.

And calamity it was! Sonny arrived in the most appalling hullabaloo[52]— even that much he couldn't do without a fuss—and from the first moment I disliked him. He was a difficult child—so far as I was concerned he was always difficult—and demanded far too much attention. $_{335}$

Mother was simply silly about him, and couldn't see when he was only showing off. As company he was worse than useless. He slept all day, and I had to go round the house on tiptoe to avoid waking him. It wasn't any longer a question of not waking Father. The slogan now was "Don't-wake-Sonny!" I couldn't understand why the child wouldn't sleep at the proper $_{340}$ time, so whenever Mother's back was turned I woke him. Sometimes to keep him awake I pinched him as well. Mother caught me at it one day and gave me a most unmerciful flaking.[53]

One evening, when Father was coming in from work, I was playing trains in the front garden. $_{345}$

I let on[54] not to notice him; instead, I pretended to be talking to myself, and said in a loud voice: "If another bloody[55] baby comes into this house, I'm going out."

Father stopped dead and looked at me over his shoulder.

"What's that you said?" he asked sternly. $_{350}$

"I was only talking to myself," I replied, trying to conceal my panic. "It's private."

He turned and went in without a word. Mind you, I intended it as a solemn warning, but its effect was quite different. Father started being quite nice to me. I could understand that, of course. Mother was quite sickening $_{355}$ about Sonny. Even at mealtimes she'd get up and gawk at[56] him in the cradle with an idiotic smile, and tell Father to do the same. He was always polite about it, but he looked so puzzled you could see he didn't know what she was talking about. He complained of the way Sonny cried at night, but she only got cross and said that Sonny never cried except when there was $_{360}$ something up with him—which was a flaming[57] lie, because Sonny never had anything up with him,[58] and only cried for attention. It was really painful to see how simpleminded she was. Father wasn't attractive, but he had a fine intelligence. He saw through Sonny, and now he knew that I saw through him as well. $_{365}$

---

49. **preoccupied**   absorbed, deep in thought
50. **took to**   began to
51. **as touchy as blazes**   quick to lose one's temper
52. **hullabaloo**   confused noise
53. **flaking**   beating (British slang)
54. **let on**   pretended
55. **bloody**   (negative expression—British)
56. **gawk at**   stare stupidly at
57. **flaming**   glaring, obvious
58. **never had anything up with him**   was never ill

One night I woke with a start. There was someone beside me in the bed. For one wild moment I felt sure it must be Mother, having come to her senses and left Father for good, but then I heard Sonny in convulsions in the next room, and Mother saying: "There! There! There!" and I knew it wasn't she. It was Father. He was lying beside me, wide-awake, breathing hard and apparently as mad as hell.   370

After a while it came to me what he was mad about. It was his turn now. After turning me out of the big bed, he had been turned out himself. Mother had no consideration now for anyone but that poisonous pup, Sonny. I couldn't help feeling sorry for Father. I had been through it all myself, and even at that age I was magnanimous.[59] I began to stroke him down and say: "There! There!" He wasn't exactly responsive.   375

"Aren't you asleep either?" he snarled.

"Ah, come on and put your arm around us, can't you?" I said, and he did, in a sort of way. Gingerly,[60] I suppose, is how you'd describe it. He was very bony but better than nothing.   380

At Christmas he went out of his way to[61] buy me a really nice model railway. ◆

---

59. **magnanimous**   generous
60. **gingerly**   carefully

61. **went out of his way to**   went to a lot of trouble

P A R T ◆1◆ **F I R S T R E A D I N G**

A. Thinking about the Story

Were you able to identify with the boy's feelings of displacement? Did you enjoy the warm humor of the piece?

B. Understanding the Plot

1. How does Larry view his father's brief visits home during the war?

2. What is Larry's attitude toward the war?

3. Why does Larry play the imaginary game with his feet?

4. About what time does Larry usually wake up? How do his parents respond to this?

5. What religion does the family practice? How do we know?

6. What prayers are referred to in line 76? Why is Larry disappointed in God's powers? (line 121)

7. Why do Larry's two feet "talk" about putting a parent in a Home?

8. Why isn't Larry's father sleeping well, according to his mother?

9. For how long do you think Larry played alone when he says it seemed "for hours"? (line 207)

10. Why does Larry's father sound panic-stricken about the time? (line 234)

11. How hard does Larry's father hit him? Explain your answer.

12. Why does Larry's father begin to stay out late in the evenings when his wife is pregnant? Where do you think he goes?

13. How does Larry feel about his long-awaited baby brother?

14. What causes Larry's father to become more sympathetic toward him?

P A R T ◆ 2 ◆ **S E C O N D   R E A D I N G**

A. Exploring Themes

You are now ready to reread "My Oedipus Complex." Look carefully at how Frank O'Connor uses humor to lessen the impact of Larry's painful feelings of jealousy and alienation.

1. How are the first and last paragraphs of the story related?

2. In what way does Larry mature and change in the story?

3. How does the jealousy that Larry and his father feel for each other express itself?

4. How does being an only child affect Larry's behavior?

5. How does Larry's mother deal with the conflicting pull on her loyalties?

6. What is the turning point in the relations between Larry and his father? What brings about the change?

B. Analyzing the Author's Style

Before you begin to work on this section, turn to the detailed explanation of humor (page 279).

HUMOROUS EFFECTS

The **humor** in "My Oedipus Complex" arises from several sources. The first one revolves around the oedipal behavior that five-year-old Larry innocently exhibits. The Austrian psychoanalyst Sigmund Freud developed his theory of the Oedipus complex to explain the jealous sexual attachment of a young child for a parent of the opposite sex. For example, when Larry declares to his mother his intention to marry her, he is expressing his desire to take his father's place in her affections and causes the reader to smile at his innocent ignorance.

1. What other examples of oedipal behavior can you find in the text? How do they help create the humor?

The second source of humor arises from the gap between the child's point of view or perception and the adult language he uses to express himself. For example, Larry exhibits his naivete about sex when he accepts his mother's statement that babies may be bought for *seventeen and six,* yet at the same time commenting that his mother was perhaps too *exclusive* (lines 35–38).

2. What other examples can you find of sophisticated language that conflicts with the child's-eye view of the world that is being expressed?

A third area of humor lies in Larry's desperate attempts to be *the man of the house,* while, not surprisingly, he is incapable of filling that role. So, when he announces firmly, *I wanted to be treated as an equal in my own home* (lines 178–179), he follows this up by drinking all the tea his father had made for his mother.

3. Pick out other instances where Larry jealously tries to act, speak, or think like a man but humorously undercuts his own attempts by his childish behavior.

Finally, there is warm humor in the two scenes where father and son are alone with each other and start the process of adapting to each other's existence and slowly identifying with each other.

4. In the first of these scenes (lines 81–99), how are the contrasts between father and son comically magnified in the child's eyes?
5. In the second scene (lines 366–381), what makes the reconciliation between Larry and his father touchingly funny?

C. Judging for Yourself

Express yourself as personally as you like in your answers to the following questions:

1. Do you think Larry's mother handled her son's oedipal behavior wisely?
2. In your view is Larry's mother a good wife? Justify your answer.

3. Do you anticipate that Larry and his father will strengthen their new-found bond in the future?

4. Would you call Larry's strong attachment to his mother unhealthy? Give reasons for your answer.

D. Making Connections

1. Is the Oedipus complex recognized in your culture? Do you feel that it is a valid description and explanation of a young child's relationship with a parent of the opposite sex? Are there other periods in life when children feel closer to one parent than the other?

2. What is the ideal number of children per family in your country? Does religion, economics, or population control play a role in deciding the number?

3. Has your country experienced wars in which men have spent long periods of time away from home? How has this affected their relationship with their families?

4. Is there a particular *hierarchy* (order of importance) in the family in your country? Who is traditionally the most important or influential member of the family? Who is the least important?

E. Debate

Debate the proposal: The saying "Children should be seen but not heard" is a sensible child-rearing philosophy.

PART ◆3◆ **FOCUS ON LANGUAGE**

A. Denotation and Connotation

All words have a **denotation** or specific meaning, which is the dictionary definition of the word. For example, the denotation of *mother* is a female parent. In addition to their denotation, many words have a **connotation**, which is an association suggested by the word and is usually separate from its meaning. Words can have positive and/or negative associations. For example, some positive connotations of *mother* might be love, security, kisses, food, warmth, comforter, bedtime stories, and being spoiled when sick. Some negative connotations of *mother* might include nagging, overanxious, overprotective, arouses guilt feelings, restrictive, and hysterical.

Look at the following list of words from the story.

father (line 1)	mountain (lines 96, 274)
candlelight (line 4)	a bottle of champagne (line 123)
slamming (line 4)	dawn (line 128)
Santa Claus (line 6)	hissed (line 153)
shadow (line 43)	feather bed (line 211)

With the aid of a dictionary write down the denotation of each word from the list. Then look at the listed words again. Write down the connotation(s) that come to mind when you think of these words. Your connotations may be positive or negative or both.

B. Building Vocabulary Skills

Look at this list of idioms from the text. Before doing the exercise that follows, review the context in which each idiom is used in the story. (Some of the verb tenses have been changed.)

come in handy (line 16)	take to (line 281)
size someone up (line 94)	let someone have it (line 310)
foul play (line 102)	take someone in (line 314)
cracked up to be (line 122)	give in to (line 323)
sit bolt upright (line 132)	turn out (lines 325 and 373)—
rack one's brains (line 133)	two different meanings
as good as lost (line 240)	show off (line 337)
let fly (line 267)	

Working with a partner, create a minidialogue relating to each idiom in order to demonstrate that you understand the meaning of the idiom and the correct situation in which it is used. For example:

First Student: That chocolate bar you gave me sure *came in handy* today.
Second Student: Really? In what way?
First Student: I didn't have time for lunch, so I was happy to find it in my pocket.

Use the remaining idioms in similar fashion to complete the exercise.

P A R T ◆4◆ **W R I T I N G A C T I V I T I E S**

1. Compose a short story of three to four pages centering on a conflict between a young child and his or her parents. Tell the story through the child's eyes. Base your story on a real-life conflict you recall. Using Frank O'Connor's narrative technique as a model, try to capture the child's voice in your story without necessarily using childish language.

2. Write two descriptive paragraphs, the first concentrating on words with a positive connotation and the second centering on words with a negative connotation. Begin your first paragraph with: *I woke up with the scent of honey in the air.* . . . Begin your second paragraph with: *The earth began to heave ominously.* . . .

3. Write an essay of two to three pages in which you take a position both for and against the statement that children in single-child families are ultimately disadvantaged. For instance, some people say that such children benefit from the exclusive attention they receive, while other people think that such attention spoils a child. When you have put the case for both sides as well as you can, reread your essay. Then in a concluding paragraph state which side of your argument you were more convinced by.

4. The oedipal theme runs through many novels, plays, and movies. The ancient Greek playwright Sophocles dramatized the Oedipus legend in his famous tragedy *Oedipus Rex*. In modern times D. H. Lawrence's novel *Sons and Lovers* centers on this theme. Similarly, Woody Allen takes up the subject in a humorous vein in his segment of the movie *New York Stories,* entitled "Oedipus Wrecks." Write an essay of two pages in which you briefly describe a work you have read or seen that is dominated by the oedipal theme. Say whether the subject is treated seriously or humorously.

LONELINESS AND ALIENATION

◆◆◆◆◆◆◆◆◆◆◆◆◆◆◆◆◆◆◆◆◆◆◆◆◆

Edvard Munch, *The Lonely One*, 1896

◆◆◆◆◆◆◆◆◆◆◆◆◆◆◆◆◆◆◆◆◆◆◆◆◆

The Model

BERNARD MALAMUD (1914–1986)

◆◆◆

BORN IN BROOKLYN, New York, Bernard Malamud grew up in the Depression years. His parents were Russian Jewish immigrants who worked long hours in their grocery store to make ends meet. Young Bernard began writing in a room at the back of the store when he was still in high school.

Malamud published numerous novels and short stories and received many literary honors. In 1967, he was awarded the Pulitzer Prize for his novel *The Fixer*, and in 1981, the gold medal for fiction from the American Academy and Institute for Arts and Letters. His collection of short stories *The Magic Barrel* was given the National Book Award for fiction in 1959. Two novels—*The Fixer* and *The Natural*—were made into movies, the latter starring Robert Redford.

Most of his writing draws on his and his family's experiences on the Lower East Side of New York City. His work reflects his Jewish consciousness and deals with the struggle of ordinary people to survive in a harsh world.

THE MODEL

An old man asks an agency to send him a model so that he can revive his painting skills, but the sitting does not go as planned.

Early one morning, Ephraim Elihu rang up the Art Students League and asked the woman who answered the phone how he could locate an experienced female model he could paint nude. He told the woman that he wanted someone of about thirty. "Could you possibly help me?"

"I don't recognize your name," said the woman on the telephone. "Have you ever dealt with us before? Some of our students will work as models, but usually only for painters we know." Mr. Elihu said he hadn't. He wanted it understood he was an amateur painter who had once studied at the League.

"Do you have a studio?"

"It's a large living room with lots of light. I'm no youngster," he said, "but after many years I've begun painting again and I'd like to do some nude studies to get back my feeling for form.[1] I'm not a professional painter, but I'm serious about painting. If you want any references as to[2] my character, I can supply them."

He asked her what the going rate[3] for models was, and the woman, after a pause, said, "Six dollars the hour."

Mr. Elihu said that was satisfactory to him. He wanted to talk longer, but she did not encourage him to. She wrote down his name and address and said she thought she could have someone for him the day after tomorrow. He thanked her for her consideration.[4]

That was on Wednesday. The model appeared on Friday morning. She had telephoned the night before, and they had settled on[5] a time for her to come. She rang his bell shortly after nine, and Mr. Elihu went at once to the door. He was a gray-haired man of seventy who lived in a brownstone house near Ninth Avenue, and he was excited by the prospect of painting this young woman.

The model was a plain-looking woman of twenty-seven or so, and the painter decided her best features were her eyes. She was wearing a blue raincoat, though it was a clear spring day. The old painter liked her but kept that to himself. She barely glanced at him as she walked firmly into the room.

"Good day," he said, and she answered, "Good day."

"It's like spring," said the old man. "The foliage[6] is starting up again."

"Where do you want me to change?" asked the model.

Mr. Elihu asked her name, and she responded, "Ms. Perry."

---

1. **form**   shape and structure
2. **as to**   regarding
3. **going rate**   the usual fee
4. **consideration**   thoughtfulness
5. **settled on**   agreed to
6. **foliage**   growth of leaves

"You can change in the bathroom, I would say, Miss Perry, or if you like, my own room—down the hall—is empty, and you can change there also. It's warmer than the bathroom."

The model said it made no difference to her but she thought she would rather change in the bathroom.

"That is as you wish," said the elderly man.

"Is your wife around?" she then asked, glancing into the room.

"No, I happen to be a widower."

He said he had had a daughter once, but she had died in an accident.

The model said she was sorry. "I'll change and be out in a few fast minutes."

"No hurry at all," said Mr. Elihu, glad he was about to[7] paint her.

Ms. Perry entered the bathroom, undressed there, and returned quickly. She slipped off her terry-cloth[8] robe. Her head and shoulders were slender and well formed. She asked the old man how he would like her to pose. He was standing by an enamel-top kitchen table near a large window. On the tabletop he had squeezed out, and was mixing together, the contents of two small tubes of paint. There were three other tubes, which he did not touch. The model, taking a last drag[9] of a cigarette, pressed it out against a coffee-can lid on the kitchen table.

"I hope you don't mind if I take a puff once in a while?"

"I don't mind, if you do it when we take a break."

"That's all I meant."

She was watching him as he slowly mixed his colors.

Mr. Elihu did not immediately look at her nude body but said he would like her to sit in the chair by the window. They were facing a back yard with an ailanthus[10] tree whose leaves had just come out.

"How would you like me to sit, legs crossed or not crossed?"

"However you prefer that. Crossed or uncrossed doesn't make much of a difference to me. Whatever makes you feel comfortable."

The model seemed surprised at that, but she sat down in the yellow chair by the window and crossed one leg over the other. Her figure was good.

"Is this okay for you?"

Mr. Elihu nodded. "Fine," he said. "Very fine."

He dipped his brush into the paint he had mixed on the table-top, and after glancing[11] at the model's nude body, began to paint. He would look at her, then look quickly away, as if he were afraid of affronting[12] her. But his expression was objective. He painted apparently casually, from time to time gazing up at the model. He did not often look at her. She seemed not to be aware of him. Once she turned to observe the ailanthus tree, and he studied her momentarily[13] to see what she might have seen in it.

---

7. **about to**   ready to do something
8. **terry cloth**   cotton material that absorbs water
9. **drag**   a puff on a cigarette
10. **ailanthus**   a tropical tree commonly grown in New York City
11. **glancing**   looking quickly at
12. **affronting**   insulting
13. **momentarily**   quickly and briefly

Then she began to watch the painter with interest. She watched his eyes and she watched his hands. He wondered if he was doing something wrong. At the end of about an hour she rose impatiently from the yellow chair.

"Tired?" he asked.

"It isn't that," she said, "but I would like to know what in the name of Christ you think you are doing? I frankly don't think you know the first thing about painting."

She had astonished him. He quickly covered the canvas with a towel.

After a long moment, Mr. Elihu, breathing shallowly,[14] wet his dry lips and said he was making no claims for himself as a painter.[15] He said he had tried to make that absolutely clear to the woman he talked to at the art school when he called.

Then he said, "I might have made a mistake in asking you to come to this house today. I think I should have tested myself a while longer, just so I wouldn't be wasting anybody's time. I guess I am not ready to do what I would like to do."

"I don't care how long you have tested yourself," said Ms. Perry. "I honestly don't think you have painted me at all. In fact, I felt you weren't interested in painting me. I think you're interested in letting your eyes go over my naked body for certain reasons of your own. I don't know what your personal needs are, but I'm damn well sure that most of them have nothing to do with painting."

"I guess I have made a mistake."

"I guess you have," said the model. She had her robe on now, the belt pulled tight.

"I'm a painter," she said, "and I model because I am broke,[16] but I know a fake[17] when I see one."

"I wouldn't feel so bad," said Mr. Elihu, "if I hadn't gone out of my way to[18] explain the situation to that lady at the Art Students League.

"I'm sorry this happened," Mr. Elihu said hoarsely. "I should have thought it through[19] more than I did. I'm seventy years of age. I have always loved women and felt a sad loss that I have no particular women friends at this time of my life. That's one of the reasons I wanted to paint again, though I make no claims that I was ever greatly talented. Also, I guess I didn't realize how much about painting I have forgotten. Not only about that, but also about the female body. I didn't realize I would be so moved by yours, and, on reflection, about the way my life has gone. I hoped painting again would refresh my feeling for life. I regret that I have inconvenienced and disturbed you."

"I'll be paid for my inconvenience," Ms. Perry said, "but what you can't pay me for is the insult of coming here and submitting myself to your eyes crawling on my body."

---

14. **shallowly**   superficially, not deeply
15. **making no claims for himself as a painter**   not maintaining that he could paint well
16. **am broke**   have no money
17. **a fake**   someone not genuine
18. **gone out of my way to**   taken extra care to
19. **thought it through**   considered it carefully

"I didn't mean it as an insult."

"That's what it feels like to me."

She then asked Mr. Elihu to disrobe. 120

"I?" he said, surprised. "What for?"

"I want to sketch you. Take your pants and shirt off."

He said he had barely got rid of his winter underwear, but she did not smile.

Mr. Elihu disrobed, ashamed of how he must look to her. 125

With quick strokes she sketched his form. He was not a bad-looking man, but felt bad. When she had the sketch, she dipped his brush into a blob[20] of black pigment she had squeezed out of a tube and smeared his features,[21] leaving a black mess.

He watched her hating him, but said nothing. 130

Ms. Perry tossed the brush into a wastebasket and returned to the bathroom for her clothing.

The old man wrote out a check for her for the sum they had agreed on. He was ashamed to sign his name, but he signed it and handed it to her. Ms. Perry slipped the check into her large purse and left. 135

He thought that in her way she was not a bad-looking woman, though she lacked grace.[22] The old man then asked himself, "Is there nothing more to my life than it is now? Is this all that is left to me?"

The answer seemed to be yes, and he wept at how old he had so quickly become. 140

Afterward he removed the towel over his canvas and tried to fill in her face, but he had already forgotten it. ◆

---

20. **blob**   lump
21. **smeared his features**   spread paint across his face

22. **grace**   charm

PART ◆1◆ **FIRST READING**

A. Thinking about the Story

How did you feel when you finished reading the story? Would you have reacted as strongly as the model?

B. Understanding the Plot

1. What information does the woman at the Art Students League request from Mr. Elihu?

2. Why does she question him so closely?

3. Why do you think Mr. Elihu asks for a model around thirty years old?

4. What do we learn about his family situation?

5. What kind of painter is he?

6. List all the things Mr. Elihu does and says that make the model uneasy about him.

7. Why does Ms. Perry choose to undress in the bathroom?

8. What does she accuse Mr. Elihu of?

9. What does she do to revenge herself on Mr. Elihu?

P A R T ◆2◆ **SECOND READING**

A. Exploring Themes

You are now ready to reread "The Model." Look carefully at how the writer lays the basis for the sad misunderstanding that arises between Mr. Elihu and the model.

1. In what season does the story take place? List all the details that support your answer. How does the season relate to a central theme in the story?

2. What are the different expectations of the two characters regarding the modeling session? How do these expectations influence their behavior?

3. How does the tone of Mr. Elihu's greeting differ from the tone of the model's response in lines 31–33?

4. Does Mr. Elihu have another reason for requesting a model than the one he gave the woman at the League?

5. What do you think Mr. Elihu means when he says, "I think I should have tested myself a while longer. . . . "? (line 89)

6. What expression does the model use that describes most vividly her feelings of disgust at Mr. Elihu? Explain the expression fully.

7. What was the model trying to achieve by her act of revenge? Did she succeed?

8. What do you think the ending means?

B. Analyzing the Author's Style

Before you begin to work on this section, turn to the detailed explanation of inference (page 279).

INFERENCE

On several occasions in "The Model," instead of spelling out the details, Bernard Malamud prefers to use **inference**, requiring the reader to discover the inner meaning of a character's thoughts or actions. For example, when the model chooses to change in the bathroom rather than the bedroom, we can infer that she is uncomfortable with the notion of undressing in a strange man's bedroom.

1. What is suggested by the pause the woman from the Art Students League makes before answering Mr. Elihu? (lines 15–16)

2. What can be inferred about the state of mind of Mr. Elihu and the woman from the Art Students League from the sentence, "He wanted to talk longer, but she did not encourage him to"? (lines 17–18)

3. What is implied by the description of the model as "wearing a blue raincoat, though it was a clear spring day"? (lines 28–29)

4. What inference is contained in the reference to the model's robe and belt in lines 99–100? Which word reinforces the inference?

C. Judging for Yourself

Express yourself as personally as you like in your answers to the following questions:

1. Would you agree with the model's view of Mr. Elihu as a dirty old man?

2. What do you think of the model's act of revenge?

3. Do you think Mr. Elihu will ever paint again? Give reasons for your answer.

4. What do you imagine a typical day in Mr. Elihu's life is like?

5. Do you prefer one character over another in this story?

D. Making Connections

1. Are the elderly treated with respect in your country? What have you read and/or observed about the situation of old people in the United States or another foreign country?

2. Are you afraid of growing old?

3. What do you think you could learn from an old person?

4. How is nudity regarded in your culture? Would you agree to model in the nude?

E. Debate

Debate the proposal: Old age is a curse.

PART ◆3◆ **FOCUS ON LANGUAGE**

A. Euphemism

Euphemism is a device by which a writer or speaker softens a word or expression by substituting something pleasant-sounding for something more uncomfortable. For example, in the story when Mr. Elihu says, *I'm no youngster* (line 10), he is really saying, "I'm old." Two other common euphemisms are:

She passed away. (She died.)   He fibbed a lot. (He lied a lot.)

Match the following words in one column with their euphemisms in the other column.

____ 1. ill		a. grease someone's palm
____ 2. die		b. homely
____ 3. poor		c. liquidity crisis
____ 4. bankruptcy		d. let go
____ 5. deaf		e. meet one's maker
____ 6. pregnant		f. hearing impaired
____ 7. fire		g. well-padded
____ 8. bribe		h. under the weather
____ 9. ugly		i. economically disadvantaged
____10. fat		j. expecting

Look at the following sentences with their italicized euphemisms. First guess what they mean in context. Then check your answer with your teacher. Share other euphemisms you know with the class.

1. Now that I am *getting on*, I regret to say my memory is failing.

2. *The happy event* is only six weeks away.

3. Movies in which people *sleep together* often draw large audiences.

4. "Unless you do what I say, you'll *go home in a box*!" he threatened.

5. Would you excuse me while I *powder my nose*?

6. He's had *a glass too many* again.

7. You'd better get some qualifications since you won't be able to rely on *a sugar daddy* all your life.

8. I wasn't at all surprised to hear about their *shotgun marriage*.

9. There's a special class for *late developers* at my son's school.

10. We *put* our old dog *to sleep* yesterday.

B. Building Vocabulary Skills

The word *about* is used in three different ways in the story.

    a. *He told the woman that he wanted someone of* **about** *thirty.*
(line 4)

    b. *"No hurry at all," said Mr. Elihu, glad he was* **about** *to paint her.*
(line 46)

    c. *"Also, I guess I didn't realize how much* **about** *painting I have
forgotten."* (lines 109–110)

1. What does *about* mean in each of these sentences?

2. Make up sentences of your own, using *about* in these three ways.

3. There are many other ways of using *about*. With your dictionary to
help you, try to find out what the following expressions mean.

out and about _____

look about _____

about starved _____

bring about _____

beat about the bush _____

about time _____

Now complete the following sentences with the correct expression from the above list.

1. "You must be _____ ," said the old man, looking at his
watch toward the end of the sitting. "It's past lunch time."

2. The model didn't _____ when she accused Mr. Elihu of
insulting her.

3. Mr. Elihu felt that it was _____ he took steps to try to live
again.

4. The model _____ the room for signs of the old man's
family.

5. The old man failed to _____ the changes in his life that
he'd hoped for.

6. He'd been at home for so long, he desperately longed to go
_____ .

"The Model" has many examples of words and expressions that can be used in more than one way. With the help of your dictionary, explain the difference between the italicized words in the following pairs of sentences. The first sentence of the pair is taken directly from the text, while the second uses the italicized word in an entirely different manner.

1. He thanked her for her *consideration*. (line 20)
   For a small *consideration* I will paint your child's room.

   _____

2. . . . they had *settled on* a time for her to come. (lines 22–23)
   The early pioneers faced many dangers when they *settled on* the land.

   _____

3. The model, taking a last *drag* of a cigarette, pressed it out against a coffee-can lid on the kitchen table. (lines 53–54)
   Most children consider it a *drag* to do household chores.

   _____

4. "I don't mind, if you do it when we take a *break*." (line 56)
   If there's a *break* in relations between the two countries, there's sure to be a war.

   _____

5. They were facing a back yard with an ailanthus tree whose leaves had just *come out*. (lines 60–61)
   My gay nephew recently *came out* and spoke to his parents about his lifestyle.

   _____

6. But his expression was *objective*. (lines 71–72)
   I have been trying hard to discover what your *objective* in life is.

   _____

7. Then she began to watch the painter with *interest*. (line 76)
   Including the *interest*, your loan comes to ten thousand dollars.

   _____

8. Afterward he removed the towel over his canvas and tried to *fill in* her face. . . . (lines 141–142)
   The student teacher was very nervous when he heard there was an emergency and he had to *fill in* for the regular teacher.

   _____

PART ◆4 **WRITING ACTIVITIES**

1. Write an essay of about two pages on what could be done to improve the condition of old people in your country. First describe their condition. Then suggest a number of specific ways to improve it. In your conclusion, say whether you think the authorities would be willing to adopt your proposals.

2. Describe a situation in which you have actually taken revenge on someone or fantasized about doing it. Explain clearly the nature of the situation and the steps you took (or imagined taking) to remedy it.

3. *Driving Miss Daisy* (American) and *Ikuru* (Japanese) are two famous movies in which the main characters are old. Write an essay of one to two pages on any movie you have seen that stars old people. How are they presented in the movie? What does the movie convey about old age?

4. Write three extended paragraphs showing how the time of year in which the story takes place is central to the themes of "The Model," "Dry September" (page 256), and "Story of an Hour" (page 12). Devote one paragraph to each story.

Never

H. E. BATES *(1905–1974)*

◆◆◆

BORN IN NORTHHAMPTONSHIRE, England, Herbert Ernest Bates became one of England's most prolific authors, writing approximately a book a year for fifty years. At the age of twenty, he published his first novel, *The Two Sisters*. This was followed by thirty-five novels and novellas, the best known of which are *The Poacher* and *The Triple Echo*.

During the 1930s, he was recognized as a master short-story writer, frequently exploring the themes of freedom and repression. Over the years eight collections of his stories were published. In the 1940s, while serving in the British Air Force, under the name of "Flying Officer X" he wrote the collections of stories based on his wartime experiences. In addition, over the course of his life, Bates wrote plays, poems, reviews, essays, an autobiography, and a book on literary criticism. In recognition of his contributions to the literary world, he was created Commander of the Order of the British Empire in 1973.

NEVER

*A daughter's attempt to escape from her monotonous
existence with her father proves more difficult than expected.*

It was afternoon: great clouds stumbled[1] across the sky. In the drowsy,[2] half-dark room the young girl sat in a heap near the window, scarcely moving herself, as if she expected a certain timed happening, such as a visit, sunset, a command. Slowly she would draw the fingers of one hand across the back of the other, in the little hollows between the guides, and move her lips in the same sad, vexed[3] way in which her brows came together. And like this too, her eyes would shift about, from the near, shadowed fields, to the west hills, where the sun had dropped a strip of light, and to the woods between, looking like black scars one minute, and like friendly sanctuaries[4] the next. It was all confused. There was the room, too. The white keys of the piano would now and then exercise a fascination over her which would keep her whole body perfectly still for perhaps a minute. But when this passed, full of hesitation, her fingers would recommence the slow exploration of her hands, and the restlessness took her again.

It was all confused. She was going away: already she had said a hundred times during the afternoon—"I am going away, I am going away. I can't stand it any longer." But she had made no attempt to go. In this same position, hour after hour had passed her and all she could think was: "Today I'm going away. I'm tired here. I never do anything. It's dead, rotten."

She said, or thought it all without the slightest trace of exultation[5] and was sometimes even methodical when she began to consider: "What shall I take? The blue dress with the rosette?[6] Yes. What else? what else?" And then it would all begin again: "Today I'm going away. I never do anything."

It was true: she never did anything. In the mornings she got up late, was slow over her breakfast, over everything—her reading, her mending,[7] her eating, her playing the piano, cards in the evening, going to bed. It was all slow—purposely done, to fill up the day. And it was true, day succeeded[8] day and she never did anything different.

But today something was about to happen: no more cards in the evening, every evening the same, with her father declaring: "'I never have a decent hand, I thought the ace of trumps[9] had gone! It's too bad!!" and no more: "Nellie, it's ten o'clock—Bed!" and the slow unimaginative climb of the stairs. Today she was going away: no one knew, but it was so. She was catching the evening train to London.

---

1. **stumbled** moved unsteadily
2. **drowsy** sleepy
3. **vexed** troubled
4. **sanctuaries** safe places
5. **exultation** extreme joy

6. **rosette** decorative ribbon shaped into a rose
7. **mending** repairing of torn clothes
8. **succeeded** followed
9. **the ace of trumps** the best card in a deck of cards

"I'm going away. What shall I take? The blue dress with the rosette? What else?"

She crept upstairs with difficulty, her body stiff after sitting. The years she must have sat, figuratively speaking, and grown stiff! And as if in order to secure some violent reaction against it all she threw herself into the packing of her things with a nervous vigour, throwing in the blue dress first and after it a score[10] of things she had just remembered. She fastened her bag: it was not heavy. She counted her money a dozen times. It was all right! It was all right. She was going away!

She descended into the now dark room for the last time. In the dining-room someone was rattling tea-cups, an unbearable, horribly domestic sound! She wasn't hungry: she would be in London by eight —— eating now meant making her sick. It was easy to wait. The train went at 6.18. She looked it up again: "Elden 6.13, Olde 6.18, London 7.53."

She began to play a waltz. It was a slow, dreamy tune, ta-tum, tum, ta-tum, tum, ta-tum, tum, of which the notes slipped out in mournful,[11] sentimental succession. The room was quite dark, she could scarcely see the keys, and into the tune itself kept insinuating[12] "Elden 6.13, Olde 6.18," impossible to mistake or forget.

As she played on she thought: "I'll never play this waltz again. It has the atmosphere of this room. It's the last time!" The waltz slid dreamily to an end: for a minute she sat in utter silence, the room dark and mysterious, the air[13] of the waltz quite dead, then the tea-cups rattled again and the thought came back to her: "I'm going away!"

She rose and went out quietly. The grass on the roadside moved under the evening wind, sounding like many pairs of hands rubbed softly together. But there was no other sound, her feet were light, no one heard her, and as she went down the road she told herself: "It's going to happen! It's come at last!"

"Elden 6.13. Olde 6.18."

Should she go to Elden or Olde? At the crossroads she stood to consider, thinking that if she went to Elden no one would know her. But at Olde someone would doubtless notice her and prattle[14] about it. To Elden, then, not that it mattered. Nothing mattered now. She was going, was as good as gone![15]

Her breast, tremulously[16] warm, began to rise and fall as her excitement increased. She tried to run over[17] the things in her bag and could remember only "the blue dress with the rosette," which she had thrown in first and had since covered over. But it didn't matter. Her money was safe, everything was safe, and with that thought she dropped into a strange quietness, deepening as she went on, in which she had a hundred emotions and convictions. She was never going to strum[18] that waltz again, she had played cards for the

---

10. **a score** a large number
11. **mournful** sad, grieving
12. **insinuating** suggesting indirectly
13. **air** tune
14. **prattle** talk meaninglessly

15. **She was as good as gone!** It was as if she had already departed.
16. **tremulously** fearfully
17. **run over** go over, repeat
18. **strum** play a stringed instrument carelessly

last, horrible time, the loneliness, the slowness, the oppression were ended, all ended.

"I'm going away!"

She felt warm, her body tingled[19] with a light delicious thrill that was like the caress[20] of a soft night-wind. There were no fears now. A certain indignation, approaching fury even, sprang up instead, as she thought: "No one will believe I've gone. But it's true—I'm going at last."

Her bag grew heavy. Setting it down in the grass she sat on it for a brief while, in something like her attitude in the dark room during the afternoon, and indeed actually began to rub her gloved fingers over the backs of her hands. A phrase or two of the waltz came back to her. . . .That silly piano! Its bottom G was flat, had always been flat! How ridiculous! She tried to conjure up[21] some sort of vision of London, but it was difficult and in the end she gave way again to the old cry: "I'm going away." And she was pleased more than ever deeply.

On the station a single lamp burned, radiating a fitful[22] yellowness that only increased the gloom.[23] And worse, she saw no one and in the cold emptiness traced and retraced her footsteps without the friendly assurance of another sound. In the black distance all the signals showed hard circles of red, looking as if they could never change. But she nevertheless told herself over and over again: "I'm going away—I'm going away." And later: "I hate everyone. I've changed until I hardly know myself."

Impatiently she looked for the train. It was strange. For the first time it occurred to her to know the time and she pulled back the sleeve of her coat. Nearly six-thirty! She felt cold. Up the line every signal displayed its red ring, mocking[24] her. "Six-thirty, of course, of course." She tried to be careless. "Of course, it's late, the train is late," but the coldness, in reality her fear, increased rapidly, until she could no longer believe those words. . . .

Great clouds, lower and more than ever depressing, floated above her head as she walked back. The wind had a deep note that was sad too. These things had not troubled her before, now they, also, spoke failure and foretold misery and dejection. She had no spirit, it was cold, and she was too tired even to shudder.[25]

In the absolutely dark, drowsy room she sat down, telling herself: "This isn't the only day. Some day I shall go. Some day."

She was silent. In the next room they were playing cards and her father suddenly moaned: "I thought the ace had gone." Somebody laughed. Her father's voice came again: "I never have a decent hand! I never have a decent hand! Never!"

It was too horrible! She couldn't stand it! She must do something to stop it! It was too much. She began to play the waltz again and the dreamy, sentimental arrangement made her cry.

---

19. **tingled**   lightly stung with a pleasant sensation
20. **caress**   a loving touch
21. **conjure up**   imagine
22. **fitful**   irregular

23. **gloom**   darkness, sadness
24. **mocking**   laughing at (negatively)
25. **shudder**   shake uncontrollably

"This isn't the only day," she reassured herself. "I shall go. Some day!"

And again and again as she played the waltz, bent her head and cried, she would tell herself that same thing:

"Some day! Some day!" ◆

120

P A R T ◆**1** **F I R S T   R E A D I N G**

A. Thinking about the Story

Were you oppressed by the atmosphere of the story? Did you believe that the girl would succeed in her attempt to escape? Did you want her to?

B. Understanding the Plot

1. What is Nellie's state of mind as the story opens? Give details to substantiate your answer.
2. What noun does the pronoun *it* refer to in line 19?
3. What is Nellie's daily routine?
4. Why does Nellie count her money "a dozen times"? (line 42)
5. Why doesn't Nellie like the waltz music she plays?
6. What does Nellie plan to do at Elden? Where is her ultimate destination?
7. At what point in the story does Nellie's mood change significantly? How are her feelings expressed?
8. Did Nellie always feel so unhappy? Support your answer.
9. Is it likely Nellie will try to escape again? Say why or why not.

P A R T ◆**2** **S E C O N D   R E A D I N G**

A. Exploring Themes

You are now ready to reread "Never." Be sensitive to the atmosphere of the story, and ask yourself whether Nellie ever really had a chance to catch the train to freedom.

1. How does Nellie's view of the woods in paragraph one sum up her state of mind at that moment?
2. What imagery dominates lines 79–80? How does this imagery reflect her new feelings?
   Note: For information on imagery, see page 279.

3. Why does Nellie's bag change from feeling "not heavy" (line 42) to "heavy" (line 83)?

4. What can you infer about Nellie's relationship with her father?

5. Why did Nellie not succeed in catching the train? Examine the psychological obstacles to her doing so.

6. How does the weather reflect what is happening in the story?

B. Analyzing the Author's Style

Before you begin to work on this section, turn to the detailed explanation of repetition (page 282) and personification (page 280).

REPETITION

H. E. Bates uses **repetition** throughout "Never" to explore how Nellie's personality is formed and imprisoned by the repressive monotony of her surroundings and routine. It takes the form of repetitive vocabulary and circular thoughts and actions. For example, in her desperate efforts to convince herself to act, Nellie's repeated *I'm going away* runs like a refrain through the story. When she thinks of her father before leaving, she hears him exclaiming, *I never have a decent hand, I thought the ace of trumps had gone!* (lines 30–31) Later as she re-enters her house, she hears her father complaining, *I thought the ace had gone. . . . I never have a decent hand!* (lines 112–113)

1. What actions does Nellie repeat in the story? What is their thematic significance?

2. Which of Nellie's thoughts are repeated? What do they reveal about her?

3. Which aspects of the room in which Nellie sits are described again later in the story? How do they reinforce the atmosphere?

4. What adjective describes how Nellie's body feels after hours of idle sitting? What is the effect of immediately repeating the adjective as a metaphor? How, by contrast, is her body described when she believes she is successfully escaping?

5. What earlier setting does the description of the scene at the station remind us of? Which words in particular link the two scenes?

PERSONIFICATION

"Never" is sprinkled with **personification**, a figure of speech by which H. E. Bates gives human characteristics to nonhuman things. The story opens with the description, *It was afternoon: great clouds stumbled across the sky.* Here the clouds are likened to people who fall or trip while walking carelessly. Just as Nellie will later figuratively stumble and fall in her attempt to flee her home, so the clouds are doing that already.

1. In what way is the "drowsy, half-dark room" in lines 1–2 a personification?
2. How are the woods in line 8 personified?
3. Find an example of personification in lines 29–34 and explain it.
4. Explain the personification contained in "the waltz slid dreamily to an end." (lines 55–56)
5. In what way is the night-wind in line 80 personified?
6. Find an example of personification in lines 98–103 and explain it.
7. Make up an example of personification and use it in a sentence relating to the story.

C. Judging for Yourself

Express yourself as personally as you like in your answers to the following questions:

1. How old do you think Nellie is?
2. In your view is Nellie to blame at all for the unhappy situation she is in?
3. Where do you imagine Nellie's mother is?
4. Why do you suppose Nellie did not openly rebel against her father? Would it have helped her situation?
5. What do you imagine could have happened to Nellie if she had caught the train to London?

D. Making Connections

1. In your culture is a daughter expected to stay home and look after her father if her mother dies or leaves the house? Would a son be likely to find himself in this position?
2. In your country what might a typical day be of a woman who does not work outside the house? How is such a woman viewed by society?
3. Is it common for young adults to rebel against their father's wishes in your culture? What are some of the consequences of doing that?
4. What happens to young women with no professional training or independent means who run away from home in your country?

E. Debate

Debate the proposal: Children should be expected to make sacrifices for their parents.

PART ◆3◆ **FOCUS ON LANGUAGE**

A. Practice with Prepositions

Complete the following sentences with the correct preposition. All of the expressions appear in the text. Try to complete the exercise without looking back at the story.

1. Great clouds stumbled _____ the sky.
2. The white keys of the piano would now and then exercise a fascination _____ her.
3. Her fingers would recommence the slow exploration _____ her hands, and the restlessness took her again.
4. She said it all _____ the slightest trace of exultation.
5. And, as if in order to secure some violent reaction _____ it all, she threw herself into the packing of her things with a nervous vigour.
6. She descended _____ the dark room for the last time.
7. For a minute she sat _____ utter silence, the room dark and mysterious.
8. Her body tingled _____ a light delicious thrill that was like the caress _____ a soft night-wind.
9. She began to rub her gloved fingers _____ the backs of her hands.
10. And worse, she saw no one and in the cold emptiness traced and retraced her footsteps _____ the friendly assurance of another sound.

B. Building Vocabulary Skills

Look at the following words and expressions from the story:

succeeded (line 27)

threw herself into (line 39)

rattled (line 57)

as good as (line 67)

run over (line 70)

dropped into (line 73)

setting (line 83)

conjure up (line 88)

gave way to (line 89)

pulled back (line 99)

Each of the above words or expressions has at least two meanings, which are reflected in the following pairs of sentences. Explain how the meaning differs in each pair of sentences. Mark with an asterisk (*) the sentence that uses the word or expression in the same way as the story.

1. The year that succeeded the abolition of slavery was very difficult.
   The year that the abolition of slavery succeeded was very difficult.
2. My children quickly threw themselves into learning to swim in a pool.
   My children quickly threw themselves into the pool when learning to swim.
3. The wind against the panes rattled her as she tried to get to sleep.
   The wind rattled against the panes as she tried to get to sleep.
4. The athlete had as good as won when she tripped and broke her ankle.
   She was as good as the athlete who won, when she tripped and broke her ankle.
5. The witness ran over the details of the accident for the policeman.
   The witness ran over the policeman after giving him details of the accident.
6. On hearing that war had broken out, our guests from abroad dropped into a state of shock.
   Our guests from abroad who dropped in to visit us were in a state of shock on hearing that war had broken out.
7. Setting the traps to catch the foxes was unexpectedly hard work, so the boy rested a while.
   Setting down the traps to catch the foxes, the boy rested a while after his unexpectedly hard work.
8. The magician conjured up a rabbit from his hat as I watched his act.
   The magician conjured up thoughts of rabbits in hats as I watched his act.
9. I noticed that in England drivers gave way to pedestrians more often than at home.
   I noticed that in England drivers gave way to honking at pedestrians more often than at home.
10. The general pulled back at the last minute from sending his troops to battle.
    At the last minute the general pulled back his cloak to reveal his military rank before sending his troops to battle.

P A R T ◆4◆ **WRITING ACTIVITIES**

1. Write a two-page essay examining the responsibilities parents and children have toward each other. Say whether you think families in general in your country live up to your requirements, and if not, analyze what could be done to change the situation.

2. Write your own version of "Never" in a short story beginning with, "As Nellie sank down on the platform, she heard the whistle of the train." In your story use repetition of vocabulary and theme as H. E. Bates does to reinforce aspects of Nellie's life and personality. Try to include some examples of personification in your descriptive scenes.

3. The situation of a young woman tyrannized by a parent has been portrayed in books, opera, fairy tales, and movies. In *Dubliners,* James Joyce's story "Eveline," with its emphasis on how an authoritarian father rules his daughter's life and destroys her spirit, closely resembles the theme of "Never." More recently, the Mexican writer Laura Esquivel's book *Like Water for Chocolate* (also made into a movie) centers on a powerful mother who ruthlessly controls the life of her younger daughter. Write an essay discussing the plot of a work you have seen, heard, or read that reflects an unequal parent-child power struggle. Describe the reasons for the parent's authoritarian behavior, say how the story ended, and consider whether the child was in any way responsible for his or her predicament.

4. Write an essay in which you compare and contrast the characters and situations of Nellie and Miss Brill (page 178). Say which character you sympathize with more, and why.

Disappearing

MONICA WOOD *(b. 1953)*

◆◆◆

BORN IN MAINE, the American writer Monica Wood grew
up listening to her mother and father tell wonderful stories in the
tradition of their homeland, Prince Edward Island, Canada. Wood
lives in Portland, Maine, and works as a free-lance copy editor and
part-time writing instructor for the University of Southern Maine.
She is also a regular instructor at the Stonecoast Writer's
Conference.

Wood's short stories have appeared in *Redbook, The North
American Review, Yankee, Fiction Network, Manoa,* and the
anthology *Sudden Fiction International.* Her short stories have
been nominated for the National Magazine Awards, and in 1991
she received a special mention from the Pushcart Prize. Her first
novel, *Secret Language,* was published in 1993. She has also
edited *Short Takes: 15 Contemporary Stories* and has written a
fiction-writing handbook, *Description.* A recurring theme in her
work is the sense of loss and retrieval felt by her characters.

DISAPPEARING

*Her obsession with swimming radically changes the life of a
grossly overweight woman.*

When he starts in, I don't look anymore, I know what it looks like, what he
looks like, tobacco on his teeth. I just lie in the deep sheets and shut my
eyes. I make noises that make it go faster and when he's done he's as far
from me as he gets. He could be dead he's so far away.

Lettie says leave then stupid but who would want me. Three hundred   5
pounds anyway but I never check. Skin like tapioca pudding,[1] I wouldn't
show anyone. A man.

So we go to the pool at the junior high, swimming lessons. First it's blow
bubbles and breathe, blow and breathe. Awful, hot nosefuls of chlorine.[2]
My eyes stinging red and patches on my skin. I look worse. We'll get caps   10
and goggles[3] and earplugs and body cream Lettie says. It's better.

There are girls there, what bodies. Looking at me and Lettie out the side
of their eyes. Gold hair, skin like milk, chlorine or no.

They thought when I first lowered into the pool, that fat one parting the
Red Sea.[4] I didn't care. Something happened when I floated. Good said the   15
little instructor. A little redhead in an emerald suit, no stomach, a depression
almost, and white wet skin. Good she said you float just great. Now we're
getting somewhere. The whistle around her neck blinded my eyes. And the
water under the fluorescent lights. I got scared and couldn't float again. The
bottom of the pool was scarred, drops of gray shadow rippling.[5] Without   20
the water I would crack open my head, my dry flesh would sound like a
splash on the tiles.

At home I ate a cake and a bottle of milk. No wonder you look like that
he said. How can you stand yourself. You're no Cary Grant[6] I told him and
he laughed and laughed until I threw up.   25

When this happens I want to throw up again and again until my heart
flops[7] out wet and writhing[8] on the kitchen floor. Then he would know I
have one and it moves.

So I went back. And floated again. My arms came around and the groan
of the water made the tight blondes smirk[9] but I heard Good that's the crawl   30
that's it in fragments[10] from the redhead when I lifted my face. Through the

---

1. **tapioca pudding**   dessert made from a grainy
   starch (has a lumpy look)
2. **chlorine**   chemical used to purify swimming pool
   water
3. **goggles**   protective glasses for underwater swimming
4. **parting the Red Sea**   a Biblical reference to the
   parting of the Red Sea by God to enable the Israelites
   to cross from Egypt to Palestine
5. **rippling**   flowing in small waves
6. **Cary Grant**   a movie star famous for his good
   looks and charm
7. **flops**   drops down in a heavy or clumsy way
8. **writhing**   twisting in pain
9. **smirk**   a silly smile
10. **fragments**   little pieces

earplugs I heard her skinny[11] voice. She was happy that I was floating and moving too.

Lettie stopped the lessons and read to me things out of magazines. You have to swim a lot to lose weight. You have to stop eating too. Forget cake and ice cream. Doritos[12] are out.[13] I'm not doing it for that I told her but she wouldn't believe me. She couldn't imagine.

Looking down that shaft[14] of water I know I won't fall. The water shimmers and eases up and down, the heft[15] of me doesn't matter I float anyway.

He says it makes no difference I look the same. But I'm not the same. I can hold myself up in deep water. I can move my arms and feet and the water goes behind me, the wall comes closer. I can look down twelve feet to a cold slab of tile and not be afraid. It makes a difference I tell him. Better believe it mister.

Then this other part happens. Other men interest me. I look at them, real ones, not the ones on TV that's something else entirely. These are real. The one with the white milkweed[16] hair who delivers the mail. The meter man from the light company, heavy thick feet in boots. A smile. Teeth. I drop something out of the cart in the supermarket to see who will pick it up. Sometimes a man. One had yellow short hair and called me ma'am. Young. Thin legs and an accent. One was older. Looked me in the eyes. Heavy, but not like me. My eyes are nice. I color the lids. In the pool it runs off in blue tears. When I come out my face is naked.

The lessons are over, I'm certified. A little certificate signed by the redhead. She says I can swim and I can. I'd do better with her body, thin calves hard as granite.[17]

I get a lane to myself, no one shares. The blondes ignore me now that I don't splash the water, know how to lower myself silently. And when I swim I cut the water cleanly.

For one hour every day I am thin, thin as water, transparent, invisible, steam or smoke.

The redhead is gone, they put her at a different pool and I miss the glare of the whistle dangling[18] between her emerald breasts. Lettie won't come over at all now that she is fatter than me. You're so uppity[19] she says. All this talk about water and who do you think you are.

He says I'm looking all right, so at night it is worse but sometimes now when he starts in I say no. On Sundays the pool is closed I can't say no. I haven't been invisible. Even on days when I don't say no it's all right, he's better.

One night he says it won't last, what about the freezer full of low-cal dinners[20] and that machine in the basement. I'm not doing it for that and he

11. **skinny** very thin	16. **milkweed** plant with milky sap
12. **Doritos** spicy corn chips	17. **granite** hard rock
13. **are out** are not allowed	18. **dangling** hanging loosely
14. **shaft** column	19. **uppity** snobbish
15. **heft** weight	20. **low-cal dinners** low-calorie dinners

doesn't believe me either. But this time there is another part. There are other men in the water I tell him. Fish he says. Fish in the sea. Good luck.

Ma you've lost says my daughter-in-law, the one who didn't want me in the wedding pictures. One with the whole family, she couldn't help that. I learned how to swim I tell her. You should try it, it might help your ugly disposition.[21]

75

They closed the pool for two weeks and I went crazy. Repairing the tiles. I went there anyway, drove by in the car. I drank water all day.

80

Then they opened again and I went every day, sometimes four times until the green paint and new stripes looked familiar as a face. At first the water was heavy as blood but I kept on until it was thinner and thinner, just enough to hold me up. That was when I stopped with the goggles and cap and plugs, things that kept the water out of me.

85

There was a time I went the day before a holiday and no one was there. It was echoey silence just me and the soundless empty pool and a lifeguard behind the glass. I lowered myself so slow it hurt every muscle but not a blip[22] of water not a ripple not one sound and I was under in that other quiet, so quiet some tears got out, I saw their blue trail swirling.

90

The redhead is back and nods, she has seen me somewhere. I tell her I took lessons and she still doesn't remember.

This has gone too far he says I'm putting you in the hospital. He calls them at the pool and they pay no attention. He doesn't touch me and I smile into my pillow, a secret smile in my own square of the dark.

95

Oh my God Lettie says what the hell are you doing what the hell do you think you're doing. I'm disappearing I tell her and what can you do about it not a blessed thing.

For a long time in the middle of it people looked at me. Men. And I thought about it. Believe it, I thought. And now they don't look at me again. And it's better.

100

I'm almost there. Almost water.

The redhead taught me how to dive, how to tuck my head[23] and vanish like a needle into skin, and every time it happens, my feet leaving the board, I think, this will be the time. ◆

105

---

21. **disposition**   temper, personality
22. **blip**   interruption

23. **tuck my head**   bend my neck, drawing my head to my chest

PART ◆1◆ FIRST READING

A. Thinking about the Story

Did your attitude toward the narrator change as the story progressed?
Did you feel optimistic or pessimistic at the end of the story?

B. Understanding the Plot

1. Who is the man referred to in the first paragraph?

2. What activity is being described in the opening paragraph? How do the participants feel about it?

3. Who is Lettie? What advice does she give the narrator regarding her marriage?

4. Why is the narrator's entry into the pool compared with the parting of the Red Sea? (lines 14–15) Is this description still accurate at the end of the story? Explain your answer.

5. What details give you an idea about the quantity of food the narrator consumes?

6. Why did Lettie stop swimming?

7. What do the men in lines 47–53 have in common?

8. What day of the week is the most difficult for the narrator? Explain why.

9. What does the narrator's husband predict about her weight loss? What is the basis for his prediction?

10. What is the relationship between the narrator and her daughter-in-law? Why is it like this?

11. How does the narrator react when the pool is closed?

12. Why does the narrator's husband threaten to put her in the hospital? (line 93)

13. What does "in the middle of it" (line 99) refer to? What did the narrator consider doing then?

14. What word in the conclusion is a synonym for "disappear"?

P A R T ◆2◆ **SECOND READING**

A. Exploring Themes

You are now ready to reread "Disappearing." Try to decide what the connection is between the nature of the narrator's personal relationships and her obsession with swimming.

1. How does swimming change the narrator's relationship with her husband? Give examples from the story.

2. Why is the narrator unable to follow through on the new interest in her shown by other men? Give some psychological reasons that you can infer from the story.

3. What do you think the ending means? What imagery in the story reinforces your answer?

4. What are the probable roots of the narrator's obsession with disappearing?

5. Discuss the symbolic nature of water in the story.
   Note: For information on symbolism, see page 283.

B. Analyzing the Author's Style

Before you begin to work on this section, turn to the detailed explanation of ellipsis (page 277) and imagery (page 279).

ELLIPSIS

In "Disappearing" Monica Wood uses a narrative style in which the language is for the most part informal and crisp. She relies on **ellipsis**, in which parts of sentences—in particular, verbs—are left out but are nevertheless easily understood or inferred. For example, when the narrator compares herself unfavorably with the thin swimmers around her, she describes them as *Gold hair, skin like milk, chlorine or no.* (line 13) Here the absence of verbs makes the visual impact stronger and reminds us of her less flattering description of herself as *skin like tapioca pudding.* (line 6)

Supply what has been left out but implied in these sentences and phrases from the story. You need to refer back to the text each time before answering.

1. When he starts in   (line 1)
2. Three hundred pounds anyway   (lines 5–6)
3. A man.   (line 7)
4. And the water under the fluorescent lights. (lines 18–19)
5. You're no Cary Grant.   (line 24)
6. She couldn't imagine.   (line 37)
7. Fish in the sea.   (line 74)
8. Ma you've lost   (line 75)
9. Believe it, I thought.   (line 100)

IMAGERY

There are moments when the narrator's voice in "Disappearing" becomes less colloquial and more poetic and we feel keenly the pathos underlying her situation. This change is accomplished through the employment of powerful **imagery**, or pictures that appeal to our visual (sight), auditory (hearing), and tactile (touch) senses. For example, *the groan of water* (lines 29–30) encourages one to hear the water's strained sounds as the very fat woman labors through it.

Look at the following images from the story. Say whether they are visual, auditory, or tactile, and explain the effect of each image as fully as possible.

1. my dry flesh would sound like a splash on the tiles   (line 21)
2. my heart flops out wet and writhing on the kitchen floor   (line 26)
3. tight blondes   (line 30)
4. skinny voice   (line 32)
5. a cold slab of tile   (line 44)
6. it runs off in blue tears   (line 53)
7. thin calves hard as granite   (line 57)
8. thin as water   (line 61)
9. emerald breasts   (line 64)
10. the water was heavy as blood   (line 83)
11. my own square of the dark   (line 95)
12. vanish like a needle into the skin   (line 104)

C. Judging for Yourself

Express yourself as personally as you like in your answers to the following questions:

1. In your view was Lettie a good friend?
2. Is it fair to blame the husband for his wife's problems?
3. Should the wife have followed Lettie's advice and left her husband?
4. Would it have made a great difference to her life if she had encouraged one of the men who began to look at her as her figure and her morale improved?
5. Do you think the wife is being courageous or cowardly in her quest to disappear? Support your answer.

D. Making Connections

1. What is your society's attitude toward fat people?
2. Would you say that fat people are discriminated against in your culture? Give examples to substantiate your answer.

3. Are eating disorders common in your society? What do you think causes people deliberately to overeat or starve themselves?

4. Does the concept of marital rape exist in your country? Do you think a man is raping his wife if he insists on having sex with her against her wishes? Should he be punished?

E. Debate

Debate the proposal: A person's weight is a reflection of his or her willpower.

PART ◆3◆ FOCUS ON LANGUAGE

A. Building Vocabulary Skills

Complete the following sentences with appropriate glossed words from the text. You may need to change the form or tense of some verbs. First try to do the exercise by referring to the story alone without looking at the definitions of the words.

1. Monuments are frequently made of _____ because it is a material that lasts.

2. I have never met anyone as popular as my sister. Everybody is attracted to her because of her sunny _____.

3. They did not feel comfortable with the new people in the neighborhood who were very _____ and didn't want to mix with the residents.

4. Because of his illness he _____ into bed straight after dinner every evening.

5. When you stir your tea, you will see the liquid _____.

6. If you want to avoid burning your eyes under water, always wear _____.

7. The athlete _____ in agony from a broken ankle when I rushed up to help her.

8. My cousin always looked unpleasant in his school photos as he gazed out _____ at the unseen face of the photographer.

9. It was a terrifying sight to see a leg _____ out of the car after the accident.

10. As a result of the concussion she suffered, only _____ of her memory returned.

PART ◆4◆ **WRITING ACTIVITIES**

1. Imagine that you have woken up one morning one hundred pounds (forty-five kilos) heavier or lighter than your usual weight.
   Using the informal narrative voice in "Disappearing" as a guideline, write a monologue in which you express your immediate thoughts and feelings about this extraordinary event.

2. Have you or has anybody you know been obsessed with something? Write an essay of two to three pages in which you first outline the nature and source of the obsession. Next consider its effect on the obsessed person as well as on the people around this individual. In your conclusion, say whether you think the person can be "cured" of this obsession and if so, how.

3. In *Hedda Gabler,* a play by the Norwegian playwright Henrik Ibsen, the heroine shoots herself at the end as a way out of an unhappy marriage that she feels is killing her. Outline the plot of a book or movie you know in which a character feels forced to take drastic action to escape from an unloved spouse. In your discussion of the plot, try to convey the desperation of the character. Then give your opinion of the action the character took.

4. Both "The Rocking-Horse Winner" (page 80) and "Disappearing" are centered on an obsession and its drastic repercussions for the characters concerned. In a two-page essay briefly describe the main characters of both stories, as well as their obsessions. Consider which story was more disturbing to you, and analyze the reasons for your response. Say whether you empathized more with one character than the other.

Miss Brill

KATHERINE MANSFIELD *(1888–1923)*

◆◆◆

BORN IN WELLINGTON, New Zealand, Katherine Mansfield was the daughter of a wealthy businessman and a cold, sickly mother. In 1908, determined to become a writer, she left for London, where she relished its intellectual stimulation. She was at the height of her literary powers when she was diagnosed with tuberculosis in 1917.

Mansfield worked tirelessly to refine the technique of impressionist writing. Ironically, she was to find almost all the material she needed for her stories in her early life with her family in New Zealand. She drew on her past for many of her themes, especially those which highlighted the price paid by a woman in marriage and the plight of a woman on her own in an unfriendly world.

Her volumes of short stories include *In a German Pension* (1911), *Prelude* (1918), *Bliss and Other Stories* (1923), and *Stories by Katherine Mansfield* (1930).

MISS BRILL

A lonely woman enjoys her Sunday afternoon outings to the park until her encounter with a thoughtless young couple.

Although it was so brilliantly fine—the blue sky powdered with gold and great spots of light like white wine splashed over the Jardins Publics[1]—Miss Brill was glad that she had decided on her fur. The air was motionless, but when you opened your mouth there was just a faint chill, like a chill from a glass of iced water before you sip, and now and again a leaf came drifting[2]—from nowhere, from the sky. Miss Brill put up her hand and touched her fur. Dear little thing! It was nice to feel it again. She had taken it out of its box that afternoon, shaken out the moth-powder, given it a good brush, and rubbed the life back into the dim little eyes. "What has been happening to me?" said the sad little eyes. Oh, how sweet it was to see them snap at her again from the red eiderdown![3] . . . But the nose, which was of some black composition, wasn't at all firm. It must have had a knock, somehow. Never mind—a little dab of black sealing-wax[4] when the time came—when it was absolutely necessary. . . . Little rogue![5] Yes, she really felt like that about it. Little rogue biting its tail just by her left ear. She could have taken it off and laid it on her lap and stroked it. She felt a tingling[6] in her hands and arms, but that came from walking, she supposed. And when she breathed, something light and sad—no, not sad, exactly—something gentle seemed to move in her bosom.

There were a number of people out this afternoon, far more than last Sunday. And the band sounded louder and gayer.[7] That was because the Season had begun. For although the band played all the year round on Sundays, out of season[8] it was never the same. It was like some one playing with only the family to listen; it didn't care how it played if there weren't any strangers present. Wasn't the conductor wearing a new coat, too? She was sure it was new. He scraped with his foot and flapped his arms like a rooster about to crow,[9] and the bandsmen sitting in the green rotunda[10] blew out their cheeks and glared at the music. Now there came a little "flutey"[11] bit— very pretty!—a little chain of bright drops. She was sure it would be repeated. It was; she lifted her head and smiled.

Only two people shared her "special" seat: a fine old man in a velvet coat, his hands clasped over a huge carved walking-stick, and a big old woman, sitting upright, with a roll of knitting on her embroidered apron.

---

1. **Jardins Publics**   Public Gardens (French)
2. **drifting**   floating down
3. **eiderdown**   a warm bed cover
4. **dab of black sealing-wax**   a tiny amount of black patching material
5. **rogue**   a mischievous person
6. **tingling**   a prickly sensation
7. **gayer**   happier
8. **out of season**   during the less important months
9. **about to crow**   getting ready to make a rooster's cry
10. **rotunda**   a round building covered by a dome
11. **"flutey"**   like a flute (usually spelled *fluty*)

They did not speak. This was disappointing, for Miss Brill always looked forward to the conversation. She had become really quite expert, she thought, at listening as though she didn't listen, at sitting in other people's lives just for a minute while they talked round her. 35

She glanced, sideways, at the old couple. Perhaps they would go soon. Last Sunday, too, hadn't been as interesting as usual. An Englishman and his wife, he wearing a dreadful Panama hat[12] and she button boots. And she'd 40 gone on[13] the whole time about how she ought to wear spectacles; she knew she needed them; but that it was no good getting any; they'd be sure to break and they'd never keep on. And he'd been so patient. He'd suggested everything—gold rims, the kind that curved round your ears, little pads inside the bridge. No, nothing would please her. "They'll always be 45 sliding down my nose!" Miss Brill had wanted to shake her.

The old people sat on the bench, still as statues. Never mind, there was always the crowd to watch. To and fro,[14] in front of the flower-beds and the band rotunda, the couples and groups paraded, stopped to talk, to greet, to buy a handful of flowers from the old beggar who had his tray fixed to the 50 railings. Little children ran among them, swooping[15] and laughing; little boys with big white silk bows under their chins, little girls, little French dolls, dressed up in velvet and lace. And sometimes a tiny staggerer came suddenly rocking into the open from under the trees, stopped, stared, as suddenly sat down "flop," until its small high-stepping mother, like a young 55 hen, rushed scolding[16] to its rescue. Other people sat on the benches and green chairs, but they were nearly always the same, Sunday after Sunday, and—Miss Brill had often noticed—there was something funny about nearly all of them. They were odd, silent, nearly all old, and from the way they stared they looked as though they'd just come from dark little rooms or 60 even—even cupboards![17]

Behind the rotunda the slender trees with yellow leaves down drooping, and through them just a line of sea, and beyond the blue sky with gold-veined clouds.

Tum-tum-tum tiddle-um! tiddle-um! tum tiddley-um tum ta! blew the 65 band.

Two young girls in red came by and two young soldiers in blue met them, and they laughed and paired and went off arm-in-arm. Two peasant women with funny straw hats passed, gravely, leading beautiful smoke-coloured donkeys. A cold, pale nun hurried by. A beautiful woman came 70 along and dropped her bunch of violets, and a little boy ran after to hand them to her, and she took them and threw them away as if they'd been poisoned. Dear me! Miss Brill didn't know whether to admire that or not! And now an ermine toque[18] and a gentleman in grey met just in front of her. He was tall, stiff, dignified, and she was wearing the ermine toque she'd 75

---

12. **Panama hat** a lightweight straw hat
13. **gone on** talked endlessly
14. **to and fro** forward and backward
15. **swooping** moving downward quickly
16. **scolding** expressing disapproval
17. **cupboards** small closets
18. **ermine toque** a close-fitting, small woman's hat made of the fur of an ermine

bought when her hair was yellow. Now everything, her hair, her face, even her eyes, was the same colour as the shabby[19] ermine, and her hand, in its cleaned glove, lifted to dab her lips, was a tiny yellowish paw. Oh, she was so pleased to see him—delighted! She rather thought they were going to meet that afternoon. She described where she'd been—everywhere, here, there, along by the sea. The day was so charming—didn't he agree? And wouldn't he, perhaps? . . .But he shook his head, lighted a cigarette, slowly breathed a great deep puff into her face, and, even while she was still talking and laughing, flicked the match away and walked on. The ermine toque was alone; she smiled more brightly than ever. But even the band seemed to know what she was feeling and played more softly, played tenderly, and the drum beat, "The Brute! The Brute!" over and over. What would she do? What was going to happen now? But as Miss Brill wondered, the ermine toque turned, raised her hand as though she'd seen some one else, much nicer, just over there, and pattered[20] away. And the band changed again and played more quickly, more gaily than ever, and the old couple on Miss Brill's seat got up and marched away, and such a funny old man with long whiskers[21] hobbled[22] along in time to the music and was nearly knocked over by four girls walking abreast.[23]

Oh, how fascinating it was! How she enjoyed it! How she loved sitting here, watching it all! It was like a play. It was exactly like a play. Who could believe the sky at the back wasn't painted? But it wasn't till a little brown dog trotted on solemn and then slowly trotted off, like a little "theatre" dog, a little dog that had been drugged, that Miss Brill discovered what it was that made it so exciting. They were all on the stage. They weren't only the audience, not only looking on; they were acting. Even she had a part and came every Sunday. No doubt somebody would have noticed if she hadn't been there; she was part of the performance after all. How strange she'd never thought of it like that before! And yet it explained why she made such a point of[24] starting from home at just the same time each week—so as not to be late for the performance—and it also explained why she had quite a queer, shy feeling at telling her English pupils how she spent her Sunday afternoons. No wonder! Miss Brill nearly laughed out loud. She was on the stage. She thought of the old invalid[25] gentleman to whom she read the newspaper four afternoons a week while he slept in the garden. She had got quite used to the frail head on the cotton pillow, the hollowed eyes, the open mouth and the high pinched[26] nose. If he'd been dead she mightn't have noticed for weeks; she wouldn't have minded. But suddenly he knew he was having the paper read to him by an actress! "An actress!" The old head lifted; two points of light quivered in the old eyes. "An actress—are ye?" And Miss Brill smoothed the newspaper as though it were the manuscript of her part and said gently: "Yes, I have been an actress for a long time."

---

19. **shabby**   much worn, old-looking
20. **pattered**   ran with light, quick steps
21. **whiskers**   a beard or sometimes a mustache
22. **hobbled**   walked with great difficulty
23. **walking abreast**   walking side by side
24. **made such a point of**   insisted on
25. **invalid**   sickly person
26. **pinched**   narrow

The band had been having a rest. Now they started again. And what they played was warm, sunny, yet there was just a faint chill—a something, what was it?—not sadness—no, not sadness—a something that made you want to sing. The tune lifted, lifted, the light shone; and it seemed to Miss Brill that in another moment all of them, all the whole company, would begin singing. The young ones, the laughing ones who were moving together, they would begin, and the men's voices, very resolute and brave, would join them. And then she too, she too, and the others on the benches—they would come in with a kind of accompaniment—something low, that scarcely rose or fell, something so beautiful—moving. . . . And Miss Brill's eyes filled with tears and she looked smiling at all the other members of the company. Yes, we understand, we understand, she thought—though what they understood she didn't know.

Just at that moment a boy and girl came and sat down where the old couple had been. They were beautifully dressed; they were in love. The hero and heroine, of course, just arrived from his father's yacht.[27] And still soundlessly singing, still with that trembling smile, Miss Brill prepared to listen.

"No, not now," said the girl. "Not here, I can't."

"But why? Because of that stupid old thing at the end there?" asked the boy. "Why does she come here at all—who wants her? Why doesn't she keep her silly old mug[28] at home?"

"It's her fu-fur which is so funny," giggled the girl. "It's exactly like a fried whiting."[29]

"Ah, be off with you!" said the boy in an angry whisper. Then: "Tell me, ma petite chérie—"[30]

"No, not here," said the girl. "Not *yet*."

On her way home she usually bought a slice of honey-cake at the baker's. It was her Sunday treat. Sometimes there was an almond[31] in her slice, sometimes not. It made a great difference. If there was an almond it was like carrying home a tiny present—a surprise—something that might very well not have been there. She hurried on the almond Sundays and struck the match for the kettle[32] in quite a dashing way.

But to-day she passed the baker's by, climbed the stairs, went into the little dark room—her room like a cupboard—and sat down on the red eiderdown. She sat there for a long time. The box that the fur came out of was on the bed. She unclasped the necklet quickly; quickly, without looking, laid it inside. But when she put the lid on she thought she heard something crying.◆

---

27. **yacht**   small sailing ship, a cruise boat
28. **mug**   ugly face (slang)
29. **whiting**   a kind of fish
30. **ma petite chérie**   my little darling (French)
31. **almond**   a type of small nut
32. **struck the match for the kettle**   lit her stove to boil water for tea

P A R T ◆1◆ **F I R S T R E A D I N G**

A. Thinking about the Story

Did you feel the sadness that lay beneath the story, even when Miss Brill seemed at her happiest? Were you moved by the ending?

B. Understanding the Plot

1. In what season does the story take place? How do you know?

2. What is unusual about the way Miss Brill regards her fox fur?

3. How long is it since Miss Brill has last worn her fur?

4. What is special about the band that Sunday afternoon?

5. Why is Miss Brill disappointed in the old man and woman who are sharing the bench? With whom does she compare them?

6. What word would you use to describe what the gentleman in grey does to the woman in the ermine toque?

7. With what does Miss Brill compare the Sunday afternoon scenes she witnesses? How does she see herself? How does she initially see the young couple?

8. How often does Miss Brill go to the park?

9. How does she earn her living?

10. What is different for Miss Brill about this Sunday afternoon's return from the park?

11. What is Miss Brill's financial situation? Give details to support your answer.

P A R T ◆2◆ **S E C O N D R E A D I N G**

A. Exploring Themes

You are now ready to reread "Miss Brill." Note how Katherine Mansfield unfolds in painstaking detail the scenes Miss Brill witnesses until everything is as vivid as it would be in a movie, a play, or a complex painting. Be sensitive to the gently sad atmosphere that pervades the story.

1. What role does the season play in the story?

2. What does the fox fur symbolize in the story? Be as detailed as possible in your answer. Note: For information on symbol, see page 283.

3. What does the thrill Miss Brill gets from *eavesdropping* (listening in to other people's conversations) tell us about the kind of life she leads?

4. What is ironic about the way Miss Brill sees the silent old people who frequent the park? (lines 56–61)
   Note: For information on irony, see page 280.

5. What later scene does the incident with the "ermine toque" foreshadow? (lines 74–90) Explain the parallels.

6. Discuss the implications of the ending.

B. Analyzing the Author's Style

Before you begin to work on this section, turn to the detailed explanation of synecdoche (page 283) and simile (page 282).

SYNECDOCHE

Katherine Mansfield makes interesting use of **synecdoche**, a figure of speech in which a part is used to describe a whole. For example, Miss Brill continually refers to the woman she sees and pities as an *ermine toque*. (line 74) In this example the woman's fur hat both represents her person and also draws attention to the symbolic parallels between her fur hat and Miss Brill's fur wrap.

Work with a partner to decide what the following sentences mean. Point out the synecdoche in each sentence, and explain the whole that the part stands for.

1. The rancher who owns fifty thousand head of cattle was arrested last week.

2. Their brother had the reputation of being the heart and soul of any party he attended.

3. Since I have to earn my bread, I cannot afford to take a vacation.

4. The orchestra's strong point is its strings.

5. Our neighbor recently won an important award for his rhyme.

6. Let me introduce you to the brains behind this project.

7. The captain yelled for all hands on deck during the storm.

8. In spite of all our misfortunes, we still have a roof over our head.

What other examples of synecdoche can you think of?

SIMILE

"Miss Brill" resonates with **similes** (explicit comparisons that use *like* or *as* to unite the two elements). For example, the story opens with a description of a blue sky with *great spots of light like white wine.* Here, the two elements compared are light and wine, and the effect is an image of crisp, sparkling afternoon light.

1. What other simile may be found in the first paragraph? What two elements are being compared?
2. As Miss Brill observes the passing parade, she often registers what the people are doing in terms of similes. How many such similes can you find? Name them. How do these similes add color to the descriptions?
3. What does the young girl compare Miss Brill's fox fur to? What does this simile suggest about the appearance of the fur? How does it contradict Miss Brill's own image of her fur?
4. What simile is used to describe Miss Brill's room? What is the full effect of using this simile?

C. Judging for Yourself

Express yourself as personally as you like in your answers to the following questions:

1. Do you think Miss Brill will return to the park on the following Sunday? Justify your answer.
2. In your view was she wrong to eavesdrop? Should eavesdroppers always be prepared to hear something hurtful about themselves?
3. Do you feel that Miss Brill will ever take her fox fur out of the box again? Explain your answer.
4. What do you imagine a regular weekday to be like for Miss Brill?
5. Did you sympathize with Miss Brill's need for fantasy?

D. Making Connections

1. Who are the loneliest segments of the population in your country? Explain why they are so lonely.
2. What facilities are there in your home town for people to get together and socialize? Have you made use of any of these facilities?
3. Is there a correlation between age, gender, and poverty in your country?
4. Have you ever witnessed anybody being humiliated or been in that situation yourself? Describe what happened.

E. Debate

Debate the proposal: Lonely people have only themselves to blame.

PART ◆3◆ **FOCUS ON LANGUAGE**

A. Verbs of Movement

Katherine Mansfield employs a variety of verbs to describe the leg, arm, and hand movements of her characters.

Look at the following list of verbs taken from the text, although not necessarily in the same form or tense.

stroke (line 16)	dab (line 78)
flap (line 26)	flick (line 84)
clasp (line 32)	patter (line 90)
parade (line 49)	hobble (line 93)
stagger (line 53)	trot (line 98)

Make two columns, one for leg movements and one for hand/arm movements and put each word listed above into its appropriate column.

Complete the following paragraph with the appropriate verb. Make sure you use the correct form and tense of the verb.

Miss Brill _____ her forehead with her handkerchief as she
                        1.

sat watching the scene unfold in front of her. As the people

_____ before her in twos and threes, she _____
          2.   3.

her fox fur absentmindedly. She felt sorry for the old man who came

_____ forward, _____ his cane tightly. She
          4.   5.

watched as a puppy _____ up to the playing children and
                                6.

wagged its tail. An anxious mother rushed up, _____ her
                                                                7.

arms wildly to shoo it away, but the puppy, unafraid, went on lightly

_____ after them. Miss Brill smiled when a toddler began
          8.

_____ uncertainly toward her, then gasped as she witnessed
          9.

the man in grey _____ the cigarette ash off his jacket while
                              10.

he brutally turned his back on the lady in the ermine toque.

B. Building Vocabulary Skills

Look at the following adjectives from the story:

embroidered (line 33)   frail (line 111)

slender (line 62)   resolute (line 124)

drooping (line 63)   trembling (line 134)

dignified (line 75)   dashing (line 150)

queer (line 106)

1. With the help of your dictionary, find a synonym for each adjective.

2. Write a paragraph using each of the adjectives in a context that illustrates its meaning.

PART 4 **WRITING ACTIVITIES**

1. Write an essay of two to three pages examining the situation of older single women in your culture. Begin your essay with the statement: In general, my culture extends/does not extend the same respect to an older single woman as it gives to an older married woman. Go on to explain the reasons for this and show the economic and social consequences. Conclude your essay with a comment on whether the present situation is likely to change and why.

2. Select a place where you can watch a parade of people. Note carefully what they are doing, saying, and wearing. Then, using the lively pictorial writing in lines 31–94 of "Miss Brill" as a model, write three paragraphs on what you have observed. Try to include original similes in your piece.

3. The aging single woman is frequently treated as a lonely, tragic figure in literature, as epitomized by the fading beauty Blanche DuBois in Tennessee Williams' play *A Streetcar Named Desire*. Write an essay of one to two pages about a play, book, or movie you are familiar with in which an older unmarried woman plays a central role. Briefly describe that role and say whether the woman is presented in a positive or negative light.

16

The Swimmer

JOHN CHEEVER (1912–1982)

◆◆◆

BORN IN MASSACHUSETTS, John Cheever used the New
England world he knew intimately as the setting for many of his
stories. In 1935, he published a story in *The New Yorker,*
beginning a connection with the magazine that lasted until his
death. *The Enormous Radio and Other Stories* (1953) firmly
established his reputation as one of America's finest short-story
writers.

Most of Cheever's stories are set in the affluent middle-class
suburbs of Westchester County, New York, and Connecticut,
where he examines the troubled and morally empty lives of their
privileged inhabitants. Because of his clear eye, his compassion,
and his superb control of the short fiction form, he has been
compared to the Russian master Anton Chekhov. In 1958, he
received the National Book Award for his novel *The Wapshot
Chronicle,* and his anthology *The Stories of John Cheever* (1978)
won the Pulitzer Prize and the National Book Critics Circle Award
in 1979 and the American Book Award in 1981.

THE SWIMMER

*An aging man lightly embarks on an unusual journey that
quickly assumes serious overtones.*

It was one of those midsummer Sundays when everyone sits around saying,
"I *drank* too much last night." You might have heard it whispered by the
parishioners leaving church, heard it from the lips of the priest himself,
struggling with his cassock[1] in the *vestiarium,* heard it from the golf links
and the tennis courts, heard it from the wild-life preserve where the leader   5
of the Audubon group[2] was suffering from a terrible hangover.[3] "I *drank*
too much," said Donald Westerhazy. "We all *drank* too much," said Lucinda
Merrill. "It must have been the wine," said Helen Westerhazy. "I *drank* too
much of that claret."

This was the edge of the Westerhazys' pool. The pool, fed by an artesian   10
well[4] with a high iron content, was a pale shade of green. It was a fine day.
In the west there was a massive stand of cumulus cloud so like a city seen
from a distance—from the bow of an approaching ship—that it might have
had a name. Lisbon. Hackensack. The sun was hot. Neddy Merrill sat by the
green water, one hand in it, one around a glass of gin. He was a slender   15
man—he seemed to have the especial slenderness of youth—and while he
was far from young he had slid down his banister[5] that morning and given
the bronze backside of Aphrodite[6] on the hall table a smack, as he jogged
toward the smell of coffee in his dining room. He might have been
compared to a summer's day, particularly the last hours of one, and while   20
he lacked a tennis racket or a sail bag the impression was definitely one of
youth, sport, and clement[7] weather. He had been swimming and now he
was breathing deeply, stertorously[8] as if he could gulp into his lungs the
components of that moment, the heat of the sun, the intenseness of his
pleasure. It all seemed to flow into his chest. His own house stood in Bullet   25
Park, eight miles to the south, where his four beautiful daughters would
have had their lunch and might be playing tennis. Then it occurred to him
that by taking a dogleg[9] to the southwest he could reach his home by water.

His life was not confining and the delight he took in this observation
could not be explained by its suggestion of escape. He seemed to see, with   30
a cartographer's[10] eye, that string of swimming pools, that quasi-subterranean

---

1. **cassock** an ankle-length religious garment
2. **the Audubon group** a society devoted to the
   conservation of wildlife
3. **hangover** disagreeable feeling after drinking too
   much alcohol
4. **artesian well** well made by digging deep into the
   earth

5. **banister** handrail along a staircase
6. **Aphrodite** Greek goddess of love and beauty
7. **clement** mild
8. **stertorously** a harsh snoring or gasping sound
9. **dogleg** sharp bend
10. **cartographer's** map maker's

stream that curved across the county. He had made a discovery, a contribution to modern geography; he would name the stream Lucinda after his wife. He was not a practical joker nor was he a fool but he was determinedly original and had a vague and modest idea of himself as a legendary figure. The day was beautiful and it seemed to him that a long swim might enlarge and celebrate its beauty.

He took off a sweater that was hung over his shoulders and dove in. He had an inexplicable contempt for men who did not hurl themselves into pools. He swam a choppy[11] crawl,[12] breathing either with every stroke or every fourth stroke and counting somewhere well in the back of his mind the one-two one-two of a flutter kick. It was not a serviceable stroke for long distances but the domestication of swimming had saddled[13] the sport with some customs and in his part of the world a crawl was customary. To be embraced and sustained by the light green water was less a pleasure, it seemed, than the resumption of a natural condition, and he would have liked to swim without trunks, but this was not possible, considering his project. He hoisted[14] himself up on the far curb—he never used the ladder—and started across the lawn. When Lucinda asked where he was going he said he was going to swim home.

The only maps and charts he had to go by were remembered or imaginary but these were clear enough. First there were the Grahams, the Hammers, the Lears, the Howlands, and the Crosscups. He would cross Ditmar Street to the Bunkers and come, after a short portage,[15] to the Levys, the Welchers, and the public pool in Lancaster. Then there were the Hallorans, the Sachses, the Biswangers, Shirley Adams, the Gilmartins, and the Clydes. The day was lovely, and that he lived in a world so generously supplied with water seemed like a clemency, a beneficence.[16] His heart was high and he ran across the grass. Making his way home by an uncommon route gave him the feeling that he was a pilgrim, an explorer, a man with a destiny,[17] and he knew that he would find friends all along the way; friends would line the banks of the Lucinda River.

He went through a hedge that separated the Westerhazys' land from the Grahams', walked under some flowering apple trees, passed the shed that housed their pump and filter, and came out at the Grahams' pool. "Why, Neddy," Mrs. Graham said, "what a marvelous surprise. I've been trying to get you on the phone all morning. Here, let me get you a drink." He saw then, like any explorer, that the hospitable customs and traditions of the natives would have to be handled with diplomacy if he was ever going to reach his destination. He did not want to mystify or seem rude to the Grahams nor did he have the time to linger there. He swam the length of their pool and joined them in the sun and was rescued, a few minutes later, by the arrival of two carloads of friends from Connecticut. During the

35

40

45

50

55

60

65

70

---

11. **choppy** not smooth
12. **crawl** swimming stroke
13. **saddled** burdened
14. **hoisted** lifted

15. **portage** the carrying of a boat and its load overland to the next waterway
16. **beneficence** kindness, good deed
17. **destiny** a particular fate

uproarious[18] reunions he was able to slip away. He went down by the front
of the Grahams' house, stepped over a thorny hedge, and crossed a vacant   75
lot to the Hammers'. Mrs. Hammer, looking up from her roses, saw him
swim by although she wasn't quite sure who it was. The Lears heard him
splashing past the open windows of their living room. The Howlands and
the Crosscups were away. After leaving the Howlands' he crossed Ditmar
Street and started for the Bunkers', where he could hear, even at that   80
distance, the noise of a party.

The water refracted[19] the sound of voices and laughter and seemed to
suspend it in midair. The Bunkers' pool was on a rise and he climbed some
stairs to a terrace where twenty-five or thirty men and women were
drinking. The only person in the water was Rusty Towers, who floated there   85
on a rubber raft. Oh, how bonny and lush were the banks of the Lucinda
River! Prosperous[20] men and women gathered by the sapphire-colored
waters while caterer's men in white coats passed them cold gin. Overhead a
red de Haviland trainer[21] was circling around and around and around in the
sky with something like the glee of a child in a swing. Ned felt a passing   90
affection for the scene, a tenderness for the gathering, as if it was something
he might touch. In the distance he heard thunder. As soon as Enid Bunker
saw him she began to scream: "Oh, look who's here! What a marvelous
surprise! When Lucinda said you couldn't come I thought I'd *die*." She made
her way to him through the crowd, and when they had finished kissing she   95
led him to the bar, a progress that was slowed by the fact that he stopped to
kiss eight or ten other women and shake the hands of as many men. A
smiling bartender he had seen at a hundred parties gave him a gin and tonic
and he stood by the bar for a moment, anxious not to get stuck in any
conversation that would delay his voyage. When he seemed about to be   100
surrounded he dove in and swam close to the side to avoid colliding with
Rusty's raft. At the far end of the pool he bypassed the Tomlinsons with a
broad smile and jogged up the garden path. The gravel cut his feet but this
was the only unpleasantness. The party was confined to the pool, and as he
went toward the house he heard the brilliant, watery sound of voices fade,   105
heard the noise of a radio from the Bunkers' kitchen, where someone was
listening to a ball game. Sunday afternoon. He made his way through the
parked cars and down the grassy border of their driveway to Alewives Lane.
He did not want to be seen on the road in his bathing trunks but there was
no traffic and he made the short distance to the Levys' driveway, marked   110
with a PRIVATE PROPERTY sign and a green tube for *The New York Times*. All
the doors and windows of the big house were open but there were no signs
of life; not even a dog barked. He went around the side of the house to the
pool and saw that the Levys had only recently left. Glasses and bottles and
dishes of nuts were on a table at the deep end, where there was a   115

---

18. **uproarious**   very noisy
19. **refracted**   broke up
20. **prosperous**   rich

21. **de Haviland trainer**   single-engined biplane used
for training pilots

bathhouse or gazebo,[22] hung with Japanese lanterns. After swimming the pool he got himself a glass and poured a drink. It was his fourth or fifth drink and he had swum nearly half the length of the Lucinda River. He felt tired, clean, and pleased at that moment to be alone; pleased with everything.

It would storm. The stand of cumulus cloud—that city—had risen and darkened, and while he sat there he heard the percussiveness[23] of thunder again. The de Haviland trainer was still circling overhead and it seemed to Ned that he could almost hear the pilot laugh with pleasure in the afternoon; but when there was another peal of thunder he took off for home. A train whistle blew and he wondered what time it had gotten to be. Four? Five? He thought of the provincial station at that hour, where a waiter, his tuxedo concealed by a raincoat, a dwarf with some flowers wrapped in newspaper, and a woman who had been crying would be waiting for the local. It was suddenly growing dark; it was that moment when the pin-headed birds seemed to organize their song into some acute and knowledgeable recognition of the storm's approach. Then there was a fine noise of rushing water from the crown of an oak at his back, as if a spigot[24] there had been turned. Then the noise of fountains came from the crowns of all the tall trees. Why did he love storms, what was the meaning of his excitement when the door sprang open and the rain wind fled rudely up the stairs, why had the simple task of shutting the windows of an old house seemed fitting and urgent, why did the first watery notes of a storm wind have for him the unmistakable sound of good news, cheer, glad tidings? Then there was an explosion, a smell of cordite,[25] and rain lashed the Japanese lanterns that Mrs. Levy had bought in Kyoto the year before last, or was it the year before that?

He stayed in the Levys' gazebo until the storm had passed. The rain had cooled the air and he shivered. The force of the wind had stripped a maple of its red and yellow leaves and scattered them over the grass and the water. Since it was midsummer the tree must be blighted,[26] and yet he felt a peculiar sadness at this sign of autumn. He braced his shoulders,[27] emptied his glass, and started for the Welchers' pool. This meant crossing the Lindleys' riding ring and he was surprised to find it overgrown with grass and all the jumps[28] dismantled.[29] He wondered if the Lindleys had sold their horses or gone away for the summer and put them out to board.[30] He seemed to remember having heard something about the Lindleys and their horses but the memory was unclear. On he went, barefoot through the wet grass, to the Welchers', where he found their pool was dry.

---

22. **gazebo**   small roofed structure usually open on the sides, found in gardens
23. **percussiveness**   loud noise (usually made by striking percussion instruments, such as a drum)
24. **spigot**   faucet, tap
25. **cordite**   a smokeless explosive
26. **blighted**   diseased

27. **braced his shoulders**   firmly pulled his shoulders back
28. **jumps**   obstacles for horses to jump over
29. **dismantled**   taken to pieces
30. **put them out to board**   sent them temporarily to other stables

This breach[31] in his chain of water disappointed him absurdly, and he   155
felt like some explorer who seeks a torrential headwater[32] and finds a dead
stream. He was disappointed and mystified. It was common enough to go
away for the summer but no one ever drained his pool. The Welchers had
definitely gone away. The pool furniture was folded, stacked, and covered
with a tarpaulin.[33] The bathhouse was locked. All the windows of the house   160
were shut, and when he went around to the driveway in front he saw a FOR
SALE sign nailed to a tree. When had he last heard from the Welchers—when,
that is, had he and Lucinda last regretted an invitation to dine with them? It
seemed only a week or so ago. Was his memory failing or had he so
disciplined it in the repression of unpleasant facts that he had damaged his   165
sense of the truth? Then in the distance he heard the sound of a tennis
game. This cheered him, cleared away all his apprehensions[34] and let him
regard the overcast sky and the cold air with indifference.[35] This was the
day that Neddy Merrill swam across the county. That was the day! He started
off then for his most difficult portage.   170

   Had you gone for a Sunday afternoon ride that day you might have seen
him, close to naked, standing on the shoulders of Route 424, waiting for a
chance to cross. You might have wondered if he was the victim of foul
play,[36] had his car broken down, or was he merely a fool. Standing barefoot
in the deposits of the highway—beer cans, rags, and blowout patches[37]—   175
exposed to all kinds of ridicule, he seemed pitiful. He had known when he
started that this was a part of his journey—it had been on his maps—but
confronted with the lines of traffic, worming through the summery light, he
found himself unprepared. He was laughed at, jeered at, a beer can was
thrown at him, and he had no dignity or humor to bring to the situation. He   180
could have gone back, back to the Westerhazys', where Lucinda would still
be sitting in the sun. He had signed nothing, vowed nothing, pledged
nothing, not even to himself. Why, believing as he did, that all human
obduracy[38] was susceptible[39] to common sense, was he unable to turn
back? Why was he determined to complete his journey even if it meant   185
putting his life in danger? At what point had this prank, this joke, this piece
of horseplay become serious? He could not go back, he could not even
recall with any clearness the green water at the Westerhazys', the sense of
inhaling the day's components, the friendly and relaxed voices saying that
they had *drunk* too much. In the space of an hour, more or less, he had   190
covered a distance that made his return impossible.
   An old man, tooling[40] down the highway at fifteen miles an hour, let
him get to the middle of the road, where there was a grass divider. Here he

---

31. **breach** break
32. **torrential headwater** rapidly flowing water at the
    source or beginning of a stream
33. **tarpaulin** waterproof material, like canvas
34. **apprehensions** anxieties
35. **indifference** lack of concern

36. **foul play** violence
37. **blowout patches** remains of tires
38. **obduracy** stubbornness
39. **susceptible** open, vulnerable
40. **tooling** driving

was exposed to the ridicule of the northbound traffic, but after ten or fifteen minutes he was able to cross. From here he had only a short walk to the Recreation Center at the edge of the village of Lancaster, where there were some handball courts and a public pool.

The effect of the water on voices, the illusion of brilliance and suspense, was the same here as it had been at the Bunkers' but the sounds here were louder, harsher, and more shrill, and as soon as he entered the crowded enclosure he was confronted with regimentation.[41] "ALL SWIMMERS MUST TAKE A SHOWER BEFORE USING THE POOL. ALL SWIMMERS MUST USE THE FOOTBATH. ALL SWIMMERS MUST WEAR THEIR IDENTIFICATION DISKS." He took a shower, washed his feet in a cloudy and bitter solution, and made his way to the edge of the water. It stank of chlorine and looked to him like a sink. A pair of lifeguards in a pair of towers blew police whistles at what seemed to be regular intervals and abused the swimmers through a public address system. Neddy remembered the sapphire water at the Bunkers' with longing and thought that he might contaminate[42] himself—damage his own prosperousness and charm—by swimming in this murk,[43] but he reminded himself that he was an explorer, a pilgrim, and that this was merely a stagnant[44] bend in the Lucinda River. He dove, scowling with distaste, into the chlorine and had to swim with his head above water to avoid collisions, but even so he was bumped into, splashed, and jostled. When he got to the shallow end both lifeguards were shouting at him: "Hey, you, you without the identification disk, get outa the water." He did, but they had no way of pursuing him and he went through the reek[45] of suntan oil and chlorine out through the hurricane fence and passed the handball courts. By crossing the road he entered the wooded part of the Halloran estate. The woods were not cleared and the footing was treacherous and difficult until he reached the lawn and the clipped beech hedge that encircled their pool.

The Hallorans were friends, an elderly couple of enormous wealth who seemed to bask[46] in the suspicion that they might be Communists. They were zealous reformers but they were not Communists, and yet when they were accused, as they sometimes were, of subversion, it seemed to gratify and excite them. Their beech hedge was yellow and he guessed this had been blighted like the Levys' maple. He called hullo, hullo, to warn the Hallorans of his approach, to palliate[47] his invasion of their privacy. The Hallorans, for reasons that had never been explained to him, did not wear bathing suits. No explanations were in order,[48] really, Their nakedness was a detail in their uncompromising zeal for reform and he stepped politely out of his trunks before he went through the opening in the hedge.

Mrs. Halloran, a stout woman with white hair and a serene face, was reading the *Times*. Mr. Halloran was taking beech leaves out of the water

---

41. **regimentation**   strict rules
42. **contaminate**   pollute
43. **murk**   dark
44. **stagnant**   still water

45. **reek**   strong disagreeable smell
46. **bask**   take pleasure in
47. **palliate**   lessen
48. **were in order**   were needed or appropriate

with a scoop. They seemed not surprised or displeased to see him. Their   235
pool was perhaps the oldest in the country, a fieldstone rectangle, fed by a
brook. It had no filter or pump and its waters were the opaque gold of the
stream.

"I'm swimming across the county," Ned said.

"Why, I didn't know one could," exclaimed Mrs. Halloran.   240

"Well, I've made it from the Westerhazys'," Ned said. "That must be
about four miles."

He left his trunks at the deep end, walked to the shallow end, and swam
this stretch. As he was pulling himself out of the water he heard Mrs.
Halloran say, "We've been *terribly* sorry to hear about all your misfortunes,   245
Neddy."

"My misfortunes?" Ned asked. "I don't know what you mean."

"Why we heard that you'd sold the house and that your poor children. . . ."

"I don't recall having sold the house," Ned said, "and the girls are at
home."   250

"Yes," Mrs. Halloran sighed. "Yes. . . ." Her voice filled the air with an
unseasonable melancholy and Ned spoke briskly. "Thank you for the
swim."

"Well, have a nice trip," said Mrs. Halloran.

Beyond the hedge he pulled on his trunks and fastened them. They   255
were loose and he wondered if, during the space of an afternoon, he could
have lost some weight. He was cold and he was tired and the naked
Hallorans and their dark water had depressed him. The swim was too much
for his strength but how could he have guessed this, sliding down the
banister that morning and sitting in the Westerhazys' sun? His arms were   260
lame. His legs felt rubbery and ached at the joints. The worst of it was the
cold in his bones and the feeling that he might never be warm again. Leaves
were falling down around him and he smelled wood smoke on the wind.
Who would be burning wood at this time of the year?

He needed a drink. Whiskey would warm him, pick him up,[49] carry him   265
through the last of his journey, refresh his feeling that it was original and
valorous to swim across the county. Channel swimmers took brandy. He
needed a stimulant. He crossed the lawn in front of the Hallorans' house
and went down a little path to where they had built a house for their only
daughter, Helen, and her husband, Eric Sachs. The Sachses' pool was small   270
and he found Helen and her husband there.

"Oh, *Neddy*," Helen said. "Did you lunch at Mother's?"

"Not *really*," Ned said. "I *did* stop to see your parents." This seemed to
be explanation enough. "I'm terribly sorry to break in on[50] you like this but
I've taken a chill and I wonder if you'd give me a drink."   275

"Why, I'd *love* to," Helen said, "but there hasn't been anything in this
house to drink since Eric's operation. That was three years ago."

Was he losing his memory, had his gift for concealing painful facts let
him forget that he had sold his house, that his children were in trouble, and

---

49. **pick him up** revive him, refresh him   50. **break in on** interrupt, intrude

that his friend had been ill? His eyes slipped from Eric's face to his abdomen, where he saw three pale, sutured[51] scars, two of them at least a foot long. Gone was his navel, and what, Neddy thought, would the roving hand, bed-checking one's gifts at 3 A.M., make of a belly with no navel, no link to birth, this breach in the succession?

"I'm sure you can get a drink at the Biswangers'," Helen said. "They're having an enormous do.[52] You can hear it from here. Listen!"

She raised her head and from across the road, the lawns, the gardens, the woods, the fields, he heard again the brilliant noise of voices over water. "Well, I'll get wet," he said, still feeling that he had no freedom of choice about his means of travel. He dove into the Sachses' cold water, and gasping, close to drowning, made his way from one end of the pool to the other. "Lucinda and I want *terribly* to see you," he said over his shoulder, his face set toward the Biswangers'. "We're sorry it's been so long and we'll call you *very* soon."

He crossed some fields to the Biswangers' and the sounds of revelry[53] there. They would be honored to give him a drink, they would be happy to give him a drink. The Biswangers invited him and Lucinda for dinner four times a year, six weeks in advance. They were always rebuffed[54] and yet they continued to send out their invitations, unwilling to comprehend the rigid and undemocratic realities of their society. They were the sort of people who discussed the price of things at cocktails, exchanged market tips during dinner, and after dinner told dirty stories to mixed company.[55] They did not belong to Neddy's set—they were not even on Lucinda's Christmas card list. He went toward their pool with feelings of indifference, charity, and some unease, since it seemed to be getting dark and these were the longest days of the year. The party when he joined it was noisy and large. Grace Biswanger was the kind of hostess who asked the optometrist, the veterinarian, the real-estate dealer, and the dentist. No one was swimming and the twilight, reflected on the water of the pool, had a wintry gleam. There was a bar and he started for this. When Grace Biswanger saw him she came toward him, not affectionately as he had every right to expect, but bellicosely.[56]

"Why, this party has everything," she said loudly, "including a gate crasher."[57]

She could not deal him a social blow—there was no question about this and he did not flinch. "As a gate crasher," he asked politely, "do I rate a drink?"

"Suit yourself," she said. "You don't seem to pay much attention to invitations."

She turned her back on him and joined some guests, and he went to the bar and ordered a whiskey. The bartender served him but he served him

---

51. **sutured** surgically closed
52. **do** party
53. **revelry** noisy partying
54. **rebuffed** refused sharply

55. **mixed company** a gathering of men and women
56. **bellicosely** aggressively
57. **gate crasher** uninvited guest

rudely. His was a world in which the caterer's men kept the social score, and to be rebuffed by a part-time barkeep meant that he had suffered some loss of social esteem. Or perhaps the man was new and uninformed. Then he heard Grace at his back say: "They went for broke overnight[58]—nothing but income—and he showed up drunk one Sunday and asked us to loan him five thousand dollars. . . ." She was always talking about money. It was worse than eating your peas off a knife. He dove into the pool, swam its length and went away. 325

The next pool on his list, the last but two, belonged to his old mistress, Shirley Adams. If he had suffered any injuries at the Biswangers' they would be cured here. Love—sexual roughhouse in fact—was the supreme elixir,[59] the pain killer, the brightly colored pill that would put the spring back into his step, the joy of life in his heart. They had had an affair last week, last month, last year. He couldn't remember. It was he who had broken it off, his was the upper hand, and he stepped through the gate of the wall that surrounded her pool with nothing so considered as self-confidence. It seemed in a way to be his pool, as the lover, particularly the illicit[60] lover, enjoys the possessions of his mistress with an authority unknown to holy matrimony. She was there, her hair the color of brass, but her figure, at the edge of the lighted, cerulean[61] water, excited in him no profound memories. It had been, he thought, a lighthearted affair, although she had wept when he broke it off. She seemed confused to see him and he wondered if she was still wounded. Would she, God forbid, weep again? 330 335 340

"What do you want?" she asked. 345

"I'm swimming across the county."

"Good Christ. Will you ever grow up?"

"What's the matter?"

"If you've come here for money," she said, "I won't give you another cent."

"You could give me a drink." 350

"I could but I won't. I'm not alone."

"Well, I'm on my way."

He dove in and swam the pool, but when he tried to haul himself up onto the curb he found that the strength in his arms and shoulders had gone, and he paddled to the ladder and climbed out. Looking over his shoulder he saw, in the lighted bathhouse, a young man. Going out onto the dark lawn he smelled chrysanthemums or marigolds—some stubborn autumnal fragrance—on the night air, strong as gas. Looking overhead he saw that the stars had come out, but why should he seem to see Andromeda, Cepheus, and Cassiopeia?[62] What had become of the constellations of midsummer? He began to cry. 355 360

It was probably the first time in his adult life that he had ever cried, certainly the first time in his life that he had ever felt so miserable, cold,

---

58. **They went for broke overnight.** They suddenly lost all their money.
59. **elixir** substance capable of curing anything
60. **illicit** unlawful

61. **cerulean** resembling the blue of the sky
62. **Andromeda, Cepheus, and Cassiopeia** constellations of stars that are seen in the fall

tired, and bewildered. He could not understand the rudeness of the caterer's barkeep or the rudeness of a mistress who had come to him on her knees and showered his trousers with tears. He had swum too long, he had been immersed too long, and his nose and his throat were sore from the water. What he needed then was a drink, some company, and some clean, dry clothes, and while he could have cut directly across the road to his home he went on to the Gilmartins' pool. Here, for the first time in his life, he did not dive but went down the steps into the icy water and swam a hobbled sidestroke[63] that he might have learned as a youth. He staggered with fatigue on his way to the Clydes' and paddled the length of their pool, stopping again and again with his hand on the curb to rest. He climbed up the ladder and wondered if he had the strength to get home. He had done what he wanted, he had swum the county, but he was so stupefied with exhaustion that his triumph seemed vague. Stooped, holding on to the gateposts for support, he turned up the driveway of his own house.

The place was dark. Was it so late that they had all gone to bed? Had Lucinda stayed at the Westerhazys' for supper? Had the girls joined her there or gone someplace else? Hadn't they agreed, as they usually did on Sunday, to regret all their invitations and stay at home? He tried the garage doors to see what cars were in but the doors were locked and rust came off the handles onto his hands. Going toward the house, he saw the force of the thunderstorm had knocked one of the rain gutters[64] loose. It hung down over the front door like an umbrella rib, but it could be fixed in the morning. The house was locked, and he thought that the stupid cook or the stupid maid must have locked the place up until he remembered that it had been some time since they had employed a maid or cook. He shouted, pounded on the door, tried to force it with his shoulder, and then, looking in at the windows, saw that the place was empty. ◆

---

63. **hobbled sidestroke** a normally easy swimming stroke done with difficulty

64. **gutters** channels on the roof to catch and carry off rain water

P A R T ◆**1**◆ **F I R S T R E A D I N G**

A. Thinking about the Story

How long did it take you to realize that Neddy Merrill's swim had a deeper significance than at first seemed the case? Were you able to follow the twists and turns of Neddy's mind, particularly regarding his dislocation in time?

B. Understanding the Plot

1. What season of the year does Neddy Merrill think it is? Why does he begin to doubt that he is right?

2. What social class does Neddy belong to? How do you know?

3. What are some typical activities engaged in by Neddy and his neighbors? List as many as possible.

4. What kind of swimming stroke does Neddy favor? Does he sustain that stroke throughout his journey? Explain your answer.

5. What does the explosion and smell of cordite (line 140) refer to?

6. When does Neddy start to feel uneasy about his memory? What causes his unease?

7. How does the first half of Neddy's journey differ from the second half?

8. What does Neddy learn during his visit to the Hallorans'? How does he react to this information?

9. Why couldn't Neddy get a drink at the Sachses'?

10. How does Neddy account for his memory loss?

11. How does Neddy expect to be treated at the Biswangers'? Are his expectations fulfilled? Explain your answer.

12. Why was Neddy so confident that Shirley Adams would receive him warmly? Was his confidence justified?

13. What discovery does Neddy make when he reaches home?

P A R T 2 **S E C O N D   R E A D I N G**

A. Exploring Themes

You are now ready to reread "The Swimmer." Look carefully at how John Cheever depicts Neddy's painful growing awareness that his situation is not what it seems to be.

1. How does Neddy's confusion of the seasons relate to the theme of the story?

2. Discuss the reasons that Neddy's social peers turned against him. Was he an innocent victim of a heartless society? Explain your answer.

3. What is the effect of the brief, abrupt switch in narration from the third-person narrative to one directly addressing the reader in lines 171–176?
   Note: For information on point of view, see page 281.

4. What is the significance of the scenes in which Neddy crosses a public highway and swims in a public pool?

5. What is the role of the two bartenders in the story?

6. Does the ending give you any cause for optimism? Explain your answer.

7. What is the symbolic significance of Neddy's making his way through water?

B. Analyzing the Author's Style

Before you begin to work on this section, turn to the detailed explanation of setting (page 282).

SETTING

"The Swimmer" takes place on a Sunday afternoon in modern times, with the scenes primarily confined to the luxurious poolsides of wealthy, upper-middle-class American suburbanites. However, at the same time, Cheever also manages to imbue "The Swimmer" with a timeless mythical framework by having his central character, Neddy Merrill, initially see himself as a hero of epic proportions, a Ulysses who embarks on a dangerous journey by water, facing with courage the mounting obstacles he encounters on his way.

1. Describe the various private pool settings. What do they reveal about the people around them? What comment does Cheever seem to be making about this society's values?

2. List the different settings in the story. (The private pools count as one setting.) Explain why there are several settings and show the relation of each to the theme.

3. In line 35, Neddy Merrill thinks of himself as "a legendary figure." What details relating to the setting contribute to Neddy's image of himself as a modern-day Ulysses? Give as many examples as possible.

4. Is there anything in the setting to indicate that Neddy's journey might be a dream? If that were so, would it make any difference to the themes Cheever explores in the story?

C. Judging for Yourself

Express yourself as personally as you like in your answers to the following questions:

1. Do you believe it is possible to repress memories of unpleasant facts as Neddy did?

2. What do you think Neddy does after he sees his closed-up house?

3. Do you get the feeling that Neddy's wife Lucinda and his daughters have stood by him during his financial troubles?

4. Do you think anybody behaved well in the story? Justify your answer.

5. Did you feel sorry for Neddy? Why or why not?

D. Making Connections

1. In your country does wealth, birth, fame, or education determine your place in society? If not, what does?

2. Names like the Howlands, the Crosscups, the Gilmartins, the Clydes, and the Westerhazys evoke the upper middle class in the United States. Do names in your country point to your social status?

3. Is it common in your country for rich people to spend their weekend drinking and socializing around a swimming pool? If not, explain what such people usually do in their leisure time.

4. How is bankruptcy viewed in your culture? Do bankrupt people lose their social status and their friends?

E. Debate

Debate the proposition: The rich have different values from those of the rest of society.

P A R T **3** **F O C U S   O N   L A N G U A G E**

A. Adjective Clauses

An **adjective clause** is a subordinate or dependent clause introduced by the following relative pronouns: *who, whom, whose, which,* or *that,* as well as by the relative adverbs *when* and *where.* As a clause it must have its own subject and verb, and as a dependent clause it cannot stand alone but must be in a sentence with an independent (main) clause. Adjective clauses modify (describe) nouns or pronouns just as adjectives do.

Note: For information on and practice with main clauses see "Dry September" (page 269).

1. The relative pronouns *who, that, whose,* and *whom* are used to refer to people. In the following examples, the pronouns *who* and *that* may be used interchangeably; so may the pronouns *whom* and *that.*

   *Grace Biswanger was the kind of hostess **who [that] asked the optometrist, the veterinarian, the real estate dealer, and the dentist.*** (lines 307–308)

   The relative pronoun *who* or *that* acts as the subject of the verb *asked.* The **antecedent** (the noun the pronoun refers to) is *hostess.*

   *Everybody admired the Hallorans, **whose swimming pool was perhaps the oldest in the country.***

   The antecedent is *Hallorans.*

   *The Biswangers were neighbors **whom [that] he hadn't seen for a long time.***

   The relative pronoun *whom* or *that* is the object of the verb *hadn't seen.* The antecedent is *neighbors.* (In informal English, *who* is frequently used instead of *whom.*)

   *The Biswangers were neighbors **he hadn't seen for a long time.***

   The relative pronoun *whom* or *that* may be omitted when it functions as the object in the relative clause.

   *A smiling bartender, **to whom he had given a generous tip,** passed him a gin and tonic.*

   Always use *whom* after a preposition because pronouns that follow prepositions are in the object form. The antecedent is *bartender.*

2. The relative pronouns *which, that,* and *whose* are used to refer to animals or things. In the following examples, the pronouns *which* and *that* may be used interchangeably.

> *. . . and rain lashed the Japanese lanterns that [which] Mrs. Levy* **had bought in Kyoto the year before last. . . .** (lines 140–141)

The relative pronoun is the object of the verb *had bought.* The antecedent is *lanterns.*

> *Rain lashed the Japanese lanterns* **Mrs. Levy had bought in Kyoto the year before last.**

The relative pronoun *which* or *that* may be omitted when it functions as the object.

> *His was a world* **in which the caterer's men kept the social score. . . .** (line 322)

The antecedent is *world.*

> *Neddy looked at the trees* **whose leaves were turning red.**

The antecedent is *trees.*

3. The relative adverb *when* modifies nouns of time.

> *. . . it was that moment* **when the pin-headed birds seemed to organize their song into some acute and knowledgeable recognition of the storm's approach.** (lines 130–132)

The antecedent is *moment.*

Note: *When* may also introduce adverbial and noun clauses. For information on and practice with adverbial clauses, see page 221, and for noun clauses, see page 250.

The relative adverb *where* modifies nouns of place.

> *An old man, tooling down the highway at 15 miles an hour, let him get to the middle of the road,* **where there was a grass divider.** (lines 192–193)

The antecedent is *road.*

Note: *Where* may also introduce noun clauses, see page 251.

4. If an adjective clause is linked to another clause by *and, but,* or *or,* the second clause will also be an adjective clause.

> *. . . he felt like some explorer **who seeks a torrential headwater** **and [who] finds a dead stream.*** (lines 155–157)

The antecedent for both clauses is *explorer.*

PUNCTUATION: RESTRICTIVE AND NONRESTRICTIVE CLAUSES

Adjective clauses are divided into *restrictive* and *nonrestrictive* clauses.

The **restrictive clause** identifies and limits the noun it modifies. It cannot be omitted without changing the meaning of the sentence. Since it is essential to the noun it modifies, it is not set off by commas from its antecedent. In a restrictive clause, *who* and *that* are interchangeable, and *which* and *that* are interchangeable.

> *He had an inexplicable contempt for men **who [that] did not hurl** **themselves into pools.*** (lines 38–40)

The antecedent is *men.* In this sentence, his contempt is restricted to a certain class of men (those who did not hurl themselves into pools) and does not refer to all men.

> *The gazebo **which [that] the Levys had recently built** was Neddy's favorite shelter.*

The antecedent is *gazebo.* In this sentence, Neddy's favorite shelter is restricted to the gazebo built by the Levys and does not refer to any other shelter.

The **nonrestrictive clause** is not essential to the meaning of the sentence. It does not limit the noun it modifies but gives additional details or information. It is set off by commas from its antecedent. In nonrestrictive clauses, always use *who* when referring to people, and *which* when referring to things. Never use the relative pronoun *that.*

> *Neddy, **who had drunk too much,** openly showed his contempt for the cautious swimmers in the pool.*

The antecedent is *Neddy.*

> *He stayed in the Levy's gazebo, **which provided him with shelter,** until the storm had passed.*

The antecendent is *gazebo.*

Look at lines 82–120 in "The Swimmer."

1. Underline all the adjective clauses with a single line. Put a double line under the relative pronoun or relative adverb that begins the clause. Circle its antecedent.

2. How many adjective clauses did you find?

3. Do any of the adjective clauses begin with a relative adverb? If so, which one(s)?

4. Are any adjective clauses joined by the conjunctions *and, but,* or *or?* If so, which one(s)?

5. Give an example of a restrictive and a nonrestrictive adjective clause in this paragraph.

6. In which adjective clause is the relative pronoun omitted but understood? Name the omitted pronoun. Is the relative pronoun the subject or the object of the verb?

7. Is the clause *when they had finished kissing* (line 95) an adjective clause? Explain your answer.

8. Is the clause *that the Levys had only recently left* (line 114) an adjective clause? Explain your answer.

Complete the following sentences with the correct relative pronoun. Punctuate each sentence according to whether the relative clause is restrictive or nonrestrictive.

1. Neddy Merrill _____ had drunk too much began to feel drowsy that Sunday afternoon.

2. Neddy saw himself as an explorer to _____ the world owed respect.

3. He left the pool _____ water had glistened so enticingly.

4. He picked up his towel from the bench _____ he had left it.

5. Helen looked at the scar _____ ran across Eric's abdomen and sighed.

6. The wine _____ the bartender served was chilled just right.

7. He decided to leave the Biswangers' _____ he had been so insulted.

8. The neighbors on _____ he most relied let him down.

9. His bathing suit _____ was now too loose on him felt extremely uncomfortable.

10. The moment _____ he arrived home was the most shocking experience of his life.

Write five more sentences relating to the story, using an adjective clause in each one. Include different relative pronouns in each sentence. Incorporate at least one example of a restrictive and a nonrestrictive adjective clause.

B. Building Vocabulary Skills

With a partner look at the following sets of words. All the words appear in one form or another in "The Swimmer." Each set has two words with the same meaning. Circle the word that does not match the other two. Take turns with your partner to explain the reason for your choice.

cartographer	explorer	pilgrim
conditions	customs	traditions
cerulean	light green	sapphire-colored
cheer	clemency	glee
glad tidings	good news	uproarious reunions
concealment	disappointment	repression
jeered	laughed at	lingered
blighted	pledged	vowed
louder	ruder	shriller
choppy	cloudy	murky
bumped	flinched	jostled
fragrance	reek	stink
lush	prosperous	wealthy
bathing suits	sweaters	trunks
recall	refract	remember
abdomen	belly	shoulder
do	party	set
haul	hoist	slide
affection	tenderness	slenderness

PART ◆ **WRITING ACTIVITIES**

1. Look at the editorial page of a large daily newspaper. Read the editorials carefully, paying special attention to their format and style. Take a position on a controversial topic, such as whether or not to raise taxes significantly on the wealthy to help society's less fortunate members. Write an editorial to persuade the reader of the soundness of your point of view. Think up an apt heading for your piece.

2. In an essay of two to three pages, write a personal account of a journey you took that fundamentally changed your life. This could be an actual or a symbolic journey. Describe the preparations for the trip, and explain what happened and why it had such a profound effect on you.

3. Using lines 171–221 from "The Swimmer" as a model, write an extended description of an acutely uncomfortable and humiliating sequence of events as seen through the eyes of its central participant. From your description the reader should be vividly aware of what this person sees, hears, feels, tastes, or smells, as well as what he or she thinks. Frame your scene within a particular setting. If appropriate, use adjective clauses in your writing to help flesh out the details and bring the scene to life.

4. The lifestyle of the rich has fascinated many writers. F. Scott Fitzgerald in his classic novel *The Great Gatsby* dissected the opulent world of his mysterious central character, Gatsby. More recently, novelist Tom Wolfe in *The Bonfire of the Vanities* and playwright John Guare in *Six Degrees of Separation* have satirized the lives of ultrawealthy New Yorkers. These books have all been made into movies. Write an essay of two pages on a work you have seen or read that centers on the world of the wealthy. Describe the society depicted, and say whether the dominant tone of the piece is satirical, ironic, admiring, humorous, or serious. In your conclusion, say whether you enjoyed the work and why.

SOCIAL CHANGE AND INJUSTICE

Jacob Lawrence, *The Migration Series*, (1940–1941) Panel No. 15, Another cause was lynching.

Like a Winding Sheet

ANN PETRY *(b. 1911)*

◆◆◆

BORN INTO AN AFRICAN-AMERICAN family, Ann Petry
grew up in the mainly white community of Old Saybrook,
Connecticut. Although the family was middle class and reasonably
well off, Petry was exposed to racism from an early age and has
recalled many of those incidents in her writing. In 1938, Petry
married and went to live in Harlem in New York City, and while
working as a journalist there, she learned at close hand about the
struggle for survival of urban blacks.

Petry has written three novels: *The Street* (1946), *Country
Place* (1947), and *The Narrows* (1953), a collection of short stories
Miss Muriel and Other Stories (1971), as well as children's books
and historical biographies. Her writing focuses on the troubled
relationships between blacks and whites. Her story "Like a
Winding Sheet" received critical acclaim and was included in
Martha Foley's *Best American Short Stories of 1946*.

LIKE A WINDING SHEET

*The accumulated stress of living in a racist society finally
causes a factory worker to explode.*

He had planned to get up before Mae did and surprise her by fixing
breakfast.[1] Instead he went back to sleep and she got out of bed so quietly
he didn't know she wasn't there beside him until he woke up and heard the
queer soft gurgle[2] of water running out of the sink in the bathroom.

He knew he ought to get up but instead he put his arms across his   5
forehead to shut the afternoon sunlight out of his eyes, pulled his legs up
close to his body, testing them to see if the ache was still in them.

Mae had finished in the bathroom. He could tell because she never
closed the door when she was in there and now the sweet smell of talcum
powder was drifting down the hall and into the bedroom. Then he heard   10
her coming down the hall.

"Hi, babe," she said affectionately.

"Hum," he grunted, and moved his arms away from his head, opened
one eye.

"It's a nice morning."   15

"Yeah." He rolled over and the sheet twisted around him, outlining his
thighs, his chest. "You mean afternoon, don't ya?"

Mae looked at the twisted sheet and giggled. "Looks like a winding
sheet,"[3] she said. "A shroud—" Laughter tangled with her words and she
had to pause for a moment before she could continue. "You look like a   20
huckleberry[4]—in a winding sheet—"

"That's no way to talk. Early in the day like this," he protested.

He looked at his arms silhouetted against the white of the sheets. They
were inky black by contrast and he had to smile in spite of himself and he
lay there smiling and savoring[5] the sweet sound of Mae's giggling.[6]   25

"Early?" She pointed a finger at the alarm clock on the table near the bed
and giggled again. "It's almost four o'clock. And if you don't spring up out
of there, you're going to be late again."

"What do you mean 'again'?"

"Twice last week. Three times the week before. And once the week   30
before and—"

"I can't get used to sleeping in the daytime," he said fretfully. He pushed
his legs out from under the covers experimentally. Some of the ache had
gone out of them but they weren't really rested yet. "It's too light for good
sleeping. And all that standing beats the hell out of my legs."[7]   35

---

1. **fixing breakfast**   making breakfast
2. **gurgle**   pleasant sound of running water
3. **winding sheet**   sheet in which a dead body is
   wrapped
4. **huckleberry**   a dark blue-black berry
5. **savoring**   enjoying
6. **giggling**   little broken laughs
7. **beats the hell out of my legs**   hurts my legs badly

"After two years you oughta be used to it," Mae said.

He watched her as she fixed her hair, powdered her face, slipped into a pair of blue denim overalls. She moved quickly and yet she didn't seem to hurry.

"You look like you'd had plenty of sleep," he said lazily. He had to get up but he kept putting the moment off, not wanting to move, yet he didn't dare let his legs go completely limp[8] because if he did he'd go back to sleep. It was getting later and later but the thought of putting his weight on his legs kept him lying there.

When he finally got up he had to hurry, and he gulped his breakfast so fast that he wondered if his stomach could possibly use food thrown at it at such a rate of speed. He was still wondering about it as he and Mae were putting their coats on in the hall.

Mae paused to look at the calendar. "It's the thirteenth," she said. Then a faint excitement in her voice, "Why, it's Friday the thirteenth." She had one arm in her coat sleeve and she held it there while she stared at the calendar. "I oughta stay home," she said. "I shouldn't go outa the house."

"Aw, don't be a fool," he said. "Today's payday. And payday is a good luck day everywhere, any way you look at it." And as she stood hesitating he said, "Aw, come on."

And he was late for work again because they spent fifteen minutes arguing before he could convince her she ought to go to work just the same. He had to talk persuasively, urging her gently, and it took time. But he couldn't bring himself to talk to her roughly or threaten to strike her like a lot of men might have done. He wasn't made that way.

So when he reached the plant he was late and he had to wait to punch the time clock[9] because the day-shift workers were streaming out in long lines, in groups and bunches that impeded his progress.

Even now just starting his workday his legs ached. He had to force himself to struggle past the outgoing workers, punch the time clock, and get the little cart he pushed around all night, because he kept toying with[10] the idea of going home and getting back in bed.

He pushed the cart out on the concrete floor, thinking that if this was his plant he'd make a lot of changes in it. There were too many standing-up jobs for one thing. He'd figure out some way most of 'em could be done sitting down and he'd put a lot more benches around. And this job he had— this job that forced him to walk ten hours a night, pushing this little cart, well, he'd turn it into a sitting-down job. One of those little trucks they used around railroad stations would be good for a job like this. Guys sat on a seat and the thing moved easily, taking up little room and turning in hardly any space at all, like on a dime.[11]

He pushed the cart near the foreman. He never could remember to refer to her as the forelady even in his mind. It was funny to have a white woman for a boss in a plant like this one.

8. **go limp** lose all strength
9. **punch the time clock** register on a special clock one's time of arrival and departure
10. **toying with** considering (but not seriously)
11. **turning on a dime** turning accurately in a very small space

She was sore about something.[12] He could tell by the way her face was red and her eyes were half-shut until they were slits.[13] Probably been out late and didn't get enough sleep. He avoided looking at her and hurried a little, head down, as he passed her though he couldn't resist stealing a glance at her out of the corner of his eye. He saw the edge of the light-colored slacks she wore and the tip end of a big tan shoe.

"Hey, Johnson!" the woman said.

The machines had started full blast.[14] The whirr and the grinding[15] made the building shake, made it impossible to hear conversations. The men and women at the machines talked to each other but looking at them from just a little distance away, they appeared to be simply moving their lips because you couldn't hear what they were saying. Yet the woman's voice cut across the machine sounds—harsh, angry.

He turned his head slowly. "Good evenin', Mrs. Scott," he said, and waited.

"You're late again."

"That's right. My legs were bothering me."

The woman's face grew redder, angrier looking. "Half this shift comes in late," she said. "And you're the worst one of all. You're always late. Whatsa matter with ya?"

"It's my legs," he said. "Somehow they don't ever get rested. I don't seem to get used to sleeping days. And I just can't get started."

"Excuses. You guys always got excuses," her anger grew and spread. "Every guy comes in here late always has an excuse. His wife's sick or his grandmother died or somebody in the family had to go to the hospital," she paused, drew a deep breath. "And the niggers[16] is the worse. I don't care what's wrong with your legs. You get in here on time. I'm sick of you niggers—"

"You got the right to get mad," he interrupted softly. "You got the right to cuss me four ways to Sunday[17] but I ain't letting nobody call me a nigger."

He stepped closer to her. His fists were doubled. His lips were drawn back in a thin narrow line. A vein in his forehead stood out swollen, thick.

And the woman backed away from him, not hurriedly but slowly—two, three steps back.

"Aw, forget it," she said. "I didn't mean nothing by it. It slipped out.[18] It was an accident." The red of her face deepened until the small blood vessels in her cheeks were purple. "Go on and get to work," she urged. And she took three more slow backward steps.

He stood motionless for a moment and then turned away from the sight of the red lipstick on her mouth that made him remember that the foreman was a woman. And he couldn't bring himself to hit a woman.[19] He felt a

---

12. **sore about** angry about (colloquialism)
13. **slits** narrow openings
14. **full blast** at full speed
15. **whirr and grinding** noises made by a machine
16. **niggers** insulting reference to black people

17. **cuss me four ways to Sunday** curse me every possible way (slang)
18. **slipped out** came out suddenly
19. **he couldn't bring himself to hit a woman** he was unable to persuade himself to hit a woman

curious tingling[20] in his fingers and he looked down at his hands. They were clenched[21] tight, hard, ready to smash some of those small purple veins in her face.

He pushed the cart ahead of him, walking slowly. When he turned his head, she was staring in his direction, mopping[22] her forehead with a dark blue handkerchief. Their eyes met and then they both looked away.

He didn't glance in her direction again but moved past the long work benches, carefully collecting the finished parts, going slowly and steadily up and down, and back and forth the length of the building, and as he walked he forced himself to swallow his anger, get rid of it.

And he succeeded so that he was able to think about what had happened without getting upset about it. An hour went by but the tension stayed in his hands. They were clenched and knotted on the handles of the cart as though ready to aim a blow.

And he thought he should have hit her anyway, smacked her hard in the face, felt the soft flesh of her face give under the hardness of his hands. He tried to make his hands relax by offering them a description of what it would have been like to strike her because he had the queer feeling that his hands were not exactly a part of him anymore—they had developed a separate life of their own over which he had no control. So he dwelt on[23] the pleasure his hands would have felt—both of them cracking at her, first one and then the other. If he had done that his hands would have felt good now—relaxed, rested.

And he decided that even if he'd lost his job for it, he should have let her have it[24] and it would have been a long time, maybe the rest of her life, before she called anybody else a nigger.

The only trouble was he couldn't hit a woman. A woman couldn't hit back the same way a man did. But it would have been a deeply satisfying thing to have cracked her narrow lips wide open with just one blow, beautifully timed and with all his weight in back of it. That way he would have gotten rid of all the energy and tension his anger had created in him. He kept remembering how his heart had started pumping blood so fast he had felt it tingle even in the tips of his fingers.

With the approach of night, fatigue[25] nibbled[26] at him. The corners of his mouth drooped,[27] the frown between his eyes deepened, his shoulders sagged; but his hands stayed tight and tense. As the hours dragged by[28] he noticed that the women workers had started to snap and snarl[29] at each other. He couldn't hear what they said because of the sound of machines but he could see the quick lip movements that sent words tumbling from the

---

20. **tingling**   a prickly sensation
21. **clenched**   tightly closed
22. **mopping**   wiping
23. **dwelt on**   concentrated on
24. **he should have let her have it**   he should have hit her (slang)
25. **fatigue**   tiredness
26. **nibbled**   took little bites
27. **drooped**   turned down
28. **dragged by**   passed very slowly
29. **snarl**   speak angrily

sides of their mouths. They gestured irritably with their hands and scowled[30] as their mouths moved.

Their violent jerky motions told him that it was getting close on to   160
quitting time but somehow he felt that the night still stretched ahead of him,
composed of endless hours of steady walking on his aching legs. When the
whistle finally blew he went on pushing the cart, unable to believe that it
had sounded. The whirring of the machines died away to a murmur and he
knew then that he'd really heard the whistle. He stood still for a moment,   165
filled with a relief that made him sigh.

Then he moved briskly, putting the cart in the storeroom, hurrying to
take his place in the line forming before the paymaster. That was another
thing he'd change, he thought. He'd have the pay envelopes handed to the
people right at their benches so there wouldn't be ten or fifteen minutes lost   170
waiting for the pay. He always got home about fifteen minutes late on
payday. They did it better in the plant where Mae worked, brought the
money right to them at their benches.

He stuck his pay envelope in his pants' pocket and followed the line of
workers heading for the subway in a slow-moving stream. He glanced up at   175
the sky. It was a nice night, the sky looked packed full to running over with
stars. And he thought if he and Mae would go right to bed when they got
home from work they'd catch a few hours of darkness for sleeping. But they
never did. They fooled around[31]—cooking and eating and listening to the
radio and he always stayed in a big chair in the living room and went almost   180
but not quite to sleep and when they finally got to bed it was five or six in
the morning and daylight was already seeping around the edges of the sky.

He walked slowly, putting off the moment when he would have to
plunge into the crowd hurrying toward the subway. It was a long ride to
Harlem and tonight the thought of it appalled[32] him. He paused outside an   185
all-night restaurant to kill time,[33] so that some of the first rush of workers
would be gone when he reached the subway.

The lights in the restaurant were brilliant, enticing.[34] There was life and
motion inside. And as he looked through the window he thought that
everything within range of his eyes gleamed—the long imitation marble   190
counter, the tall stools, the white porcelain-topped tables and especially the
big metal coffee urn right near the window. Steam issued from its top and a
gas flame flickered under it—a lively, dancing, blue flame.

A lot of the workers from his shift—men and women—were lining up
near the coffee urn. He watched them walk to the porcelain-topped tables   195
carrying steaming cups of coffee and he saw that just the smell of the coffee
lessened the fatigue lines in their faces. After the first sip their faces
softened, they smiled, they began to talk and laugh.

On a sudden impulse he shoved the door open and joined the line in
front of the coffee urn. The line moved slowly. And as he stood there the   200

---

30. **scowled**   made an angry facial expression
31. **fooled around**   wasted time
32. **appalled**   shocked

33. **kill time**   spend time doing nothing in particular
34. **enticing**   inviting

smell of the coffee, the sound of the laughter and of the voices, helped dull the sharp ache in his legs.

He didn't pay any attention to the white girl who was serving the coffee at the urn. He kept looking at the cups in the hands of the men who had been ahead of him. Each time a man stepped out of the line with one of the thick white cups the fragrant steam got in his nostrils. He saw that they walked carefully so as not to spill a single drop. There was a froth[35] of bubbles at the top of each cup and he thought about how he would let the bubbles break against his lips before he actually took a big deep swallow.

Then it was his turn. "A cup of coffee," he said, just as he had heard the others say.

The white girl looked past him, put her hands up to her head and gently lifted her hair away from the back of her neck, tossing her head back a little.

"No more coffee for a while," she said.

He wasn't certain he'd heard her correctly and he said "What?" blankly.

"No more coffee for a while," she repeated.

There was silence behind him and then uneasy movement. He thought someone would say something, ask why or protest, but there was only silence and then a faint shuffling sound as though the men standing behind him had simultaneously shifted their weight from one foot to the other.

He looked at the girl without saying anything. He felt his hands begin to tingle and the tingling went all the way down to his finger tips so that he glanced down at them. They were clenched tight, hard, into fists. Then he looked at the girl again. What he wanted to do was to hit her so hard that the scarlet lipstick on her mouth would smear and spread over her nose, her chin, out toward her cheeks, so hard that she would never toss her head again and refuse a man a cup of coffee because he was black.

He estimated the distance across the counter and reached forward, balancing his weight on the balls of his feet, ready to let the blow go. And then his hands fell back down to his sides because he forced himself to lower them, to unclench them and make them dangle[36] loose. The effort took his breath away because his hands fought against him. But he couldn't hit her. He couldn't even now bring himself to hit a woman, not even this one, who had refused him a cup of coffee with a toss of her head. He kept seeing the gesture with which she had lifted the length of her blond hair from the back of her neck as expressive of her contempt for him.

When he went out the door he didn't look back. If he had he would have seen the flickering blue flame under the shiny coffee urn being extinguished.[37] The line of men who had stood behind him lingered[38] a moment to watch the people drinking coffee at the tables and then they left just as he had without having had the coffee they wanted so badly. The girl behind the counter poured water in the urn and swabbed it out[39] and as she waited for the water to run out, she lifted her hair gently from

---

35. **froth** bubbles on a liquid
36. **dangle** hang loosely
37. **extinguished** put out
38. **lingered** stayed behind
39. **swabbed it out** cleaned it out

the back of her neck and tossed her head before she began making a fresh lot of coffee. 245

But he had walked away without a backward look, his head down, his hands in his pockets, raging at himself and whatever it was inside of him that had forced him to stand quiet and still when he wanted to strike out.

The subway was crowded and he had to stand. He tried grasping an overhead strap and his hands were too tense to grip it. So he moved near the 250 train door and stood there swaying[40] back and forth with the rocking of the train. The roar of the train beat inside his head, making it ache and throb, and the pain in his legs clawed up into his groin so that he seemed to be bursting with pain and he told himself that it was due to all that anger-born energy that had piled up in him and not been used and so it had spread 255 through him like a poison—from his feet and legs all the way up to his head.

Mae was in the house before he was. He knew she was home before he put the key in the door of the apartment. The radio was going. She had it turned up loud and she was singing along with it.

"Hello, babe," she called out, as soon as he opened the door. 260

He tried to say "hello" and it came out half grunt and half sigh.

"You sure sound cheerful," she said.

She was in the bedroom and he went and leaned against the doorjamb. The denim overalls she wore to work were carefully draped over the back of a chair by the bed. She was standing in front of the dresser, tying the sash 265 of a yellow housecoat around her waist and chewing gum vigorously as she admired her reflection in the mirror over the dresser.

"Whatsa matter?" she said. "You get bawled out[41] by the boss or somep'n?"

"Just tired," he said slowly. "For God's sake, do you have to crack that 270 gum like that?"

"You don't have to lissen to me," she said complacently.[42] She patted a curl in place near the side of her head and then lifted her hair away from the back of her neck, ducking her head forward and then back.

He winced[43] away from the gesture. "What you got to be always fooling 275 with your hair for?" he protested.

"Say, what's the matter with you anyway?" She turned away from the mirror to face him, put her hands on her hips. "You ain't been in the house two minutes and you're picking on me."[44]

He didn't answer her because her eyes were angry and he didn't want to 280 quarrel with her. They'd been married too long and got along too well and so he walked all the way into the room and sat down in the chair by the bed and stretched his legs out in front of him, putting his weight on the heels of his shoes, leaning way back in the chair, not saying anything.

---

40. **swaying**   moving unsteadily
41. **get bawled out**   be severely criticized (slang)
42. **complacently**   with self-satisfaction
43. **winced**   made a quick facial movement of pain
44. **picking on me**   criticizing me

"Lissen," she said sharply. "I've got to wear those overalls again 285 tomorrow. You're going to get them all wrinkled up[45] leaning against them like that."

He didn't move. He was too tired and his legs were throbbing[46] now that he had sat down. Beside the overalls were already wrinkled and dirty, he thought. They couldn't help but be[47] for she'd worn them all week. He 290 leaned farther back in the chair.

"Come on, get up," she ordered.

"Oh, what the hell," he said wearily, and got up from the chair. "I'd as soon live in a subway.[48] There'd be just as much place to sit down."

He saw that her sense of humor was struggling with her anger. But her 295 sense of humor won because she giggled.

"Aw, come on and eat," she said. There was a coaxing[49] note in her voice. "You're nothing but an old hungry nigger trying to act tough and—" she paused to giggle and then continued, "You—"

He had always found her giggling pleasant and deliberately said things 300 that might amuse her and then waited, listening for the delicate sound to emerge from her throat. This time he didn't even hear the giggle. He didn't let her finish what she was saying. She was standing close to him and that funny tingling started in his finger tips, went fast up his arms and sent his fist shooting straight for her face. 305

There was the smacking sound of soft flesh being struck by a hard object and it wasn't until she screamed that he realized he had hit her in the mouth——so hard that the dark red lipstick had blurred and spread over her full lips, reaching up toward the tip of her nose, down toward her chin, out toward her cheeks. 310

The knowledge that he had struck her seeped through him slowly and he was appalled but he couldn't drag his hands away from her face. He kept striking her and he thought with horror that something inside him was holding him, binding him to this act, wrapping and twisting about him so that he had to continue it. He had lost all control over his hands. And he 315 groped for[50] a phrase, a word, something to describe what this thing was like that was happening to him and he thought it was like being enmeshed[51] in a winding sheet—that was it—like a winding sheet. And even as the thought formed in his mind, his hands reached for her face again and yet again. ◆ 320

---

45. **wrinkled up**   unironed
46. **throbbing**   beating with pain
47. **They couldn't help but be**   They would have to be
48. **I'd just as soon live in a subway**   I'd willingly live in a subway
49. **coaxing**   pleading
50. **groped for**   searched for
51. **enmeshed**   trapped

P A R T ◆**1**◆ **FIRST READING**

A. Thinking about the Story

Could you feel the rage that was building up in Mr. Johnson, and were you able to sympathize with him at the end? Did you predict that the story would end so badly? What made you think that?

B. Understanding the Plot

1. What kind of relationship do Mae and her husband have at the start of the story? Illustrate your answer with concrete examples.

2. What does Mr. Johnson look like when he is lying in bed? Explain the comparison.

3. How does Mr. Johnson feel about working the night shift?

4. Is Mae superstitious?

5. What aspect of his job is most stressful to Mr. Johnson?

6. What was offensive about the forewoman's behavior to Mr. Johnson? Give examples.

7. Why didn't Mr. Johnson hit the forewoman as he desperately wanted to do?

8. What part of Mr. Johnson's body continually suggests the suppressed rage he feels?

9. Why does Mr. Johnson delay going home?

10. Where do he and Mae live?

11. Why doesn't the girl serve coffee to Mr. Johnson? What does he think the reason is?

12. What is the final act of the day, which causes Mr. Johnson to snap and beat up Mae?

P A R T ◆**2**◆ **SECOND READING**

A. Exploring Themes

You are now ready to reread "Like a Winding Sheet." Look at Mr. Johnson's swelling rage and frustration, and consider how the day's events are connected.

1. What is the significance of the title to the central theme of the story?

2. How does the story serve as a critique of factory working conditions?

3. Examine closely what links the three women in the story. What is the importance of these connections?

4. Is Mr. Johnson naturally violent? Explain your answer.

5. Whose point of view dominates the story? How is this character's point of view crucial to an understanding of what happened in the cafeteria? Note: For information on point of view, see page 281.

6. Explain how the reference to Mr. Johnson's anger being "like a poison" (line 256) contributes to our understanding of his actions.

B. Analyzing the Author's Style

Before you begin to work on this section, turn to the detailed explanation of colloquialism (page 275), dialect (page 276), and imagery (page 279).

COLLOQUIALISM AND DIALECT

The dialogue in "Like a Winding Sheet" is very **colloquial**, or informal, and makes liberal use of New York working-class **dialect**, in which words are often changed, left out, or elided (joined together). By using language in this way, Petry reinforces the authenticity of her characters and effectively establishes their social class, as well as their prejudices. For example, when Mr. Johnson remarks that the forewoman was *sore about something* (line 79), it could be more formally rephrased as she was *angry about something.* Later the forewoman snaps, *"Whatsa matter with ya?"* (lines 97–98), which can be rewritten in standard English as *What's the matter with you?* and then she adds in a racist aside, *"I'm sick of you niggers—"* (line 105).

Look at the following expressions from the text and rewrite them in more formal English, correcting any grammatical errors you see.

1. "After two years you oughta be used to it," Mae said. (line 36)

2. "I shouldn't go outa the house." (line 51)

3. "Every guy comes in here late always has an excuse." (line 102)

4. "And the niggers is the worse." (line 104)

5. "You got the right to cuss me four ways to Sunday but I ain't letting nobody call me a nigger." (lines 106–107)

6. "Aw, forget it," she said. "I didn't mean nothing by it." (line 112)

Can you find at least three more examples of colloquial language in the story?

Runple
metaphore

IMAGERY

The cafeteria scene (lines 188–209) in "Like a Winding Sheet" is packed full of distinctive **images**, or verbal pictures, that engage the senses (taste, touch, sight, hearing, and smell), sometimes more than one at the same time. For example:

> *He watched them walk to the porcelain-topped tables carrying steaming cups of coffee . . .* (lines 195–196)

In this one sentence Petry conveys the image of the man taking in the cool shining table tops while feeling the heat from the steaming cups that people were carrying, as if he were already carrying one himself, and then, in his imagination, gratefully tasting the hot liquid.

Read lines 188–209 carefully; then analyze how the following sentences appeal to the senses:

1. The lights in the restaurant were brilliant, enticing. (line 188)

2. Steam issued from its top and a gas flame flickered under it—a lively, dancing, blue flame. (lines 192–193)

3. And as he stood there the smell of coffee, the sound of the laughter and of the voices, helped dull the sharp ache in his legs. (lines 200–202)

4. Each time a man stepped out of the line with one of the thick white cups the fragrant steam got in his nostrils. (lines 205–206)

5. There was a froth of bubbles at the top of each cup and he thought about how he would let the bubbles break against his lips before he actually took a big deep swallow. (lines 207–209)

C. Judging for Yourself

Express yourself as personally as you like in your answers to the following questions:

1. Why do you think Mae's husband hit her instead of one of the other two women?

2. Do you blame Mr. Johnson for finally boiling over? Should he have exercised more self-control? What other options were open to him to release his anger?

3. What kinds of racial insults do you imagine Mr. Johnson encountered daily?

4. Do you suppose that Mr. Johnson is likely to be violent again?

5. In your view can Mae ever forgive her husband?

D. Making Connections

1. Is there a tendency in your country to solve disputes by violence?

2. Are many women beaten by their husbands, fathers, or boyfriends in your country? How does the society at large view such acts? Are there shelters women can go to in order to escape such violence?

3. What are factory conditions like where you live? Is there an attempt to humanize life for the workers?

4. Which groups of people are discriminated against in your society? What is the discrimination based on—race, gender, caste, religion, other categories?

E. Debate

Debate the proposal: Violence can be a more effective tool than reason when dealing with prejudiced people.

P A R T ◆3◆ **F O C U S   O N   L A N G U A G E**

A. Adverbial Clauses

An **adverbial clause** is a subordinate, or dependent, clause introduced by a subordinating conjunction such as *when, after, because, in order that, if,* and *although.* As a clause it must have its own subject and verb, and as a dependent clause it cannot stand alone but must be in a sentence with an independent (main) clause. Adverbial clauses may be grouped into categories of time, reason, result, condition, and concession.

Note: For information on and practice with main clauses see "Dry September" (page 269).

1. An **adverbial clause of time** may start with words such as *before, after, when, as, until,* and *as soon as.* For example:

   He had planned to get up ***before Mae did*** *and surprise her by fixing breakfast.* (lines 1–2)

   As the hours dragged by *he noticed that the women workers had started to snap and snarl at each other.* (lines 154–156)

2. An **adverbial clause of reason** may start with words such as *because, since,* and *as.* For example:

   . . . they appeared to be simply moving their lips ***because you couldn't hear*** *what they were saying.* (lines 89–90)

3. An **adverbial clause of result** starts with *so that, so. . . that,* and *such. . . that.* For example:

The roar of the train beat inside his head, making it ache and throb, and the pain in his legs clawed up into his groin **so that he seemed to be bursting with pain. . . .** (lines 252–254)

The above sentence could be rewritten as:

The pain in his legs was **so great that he seemed to be bursting with pain.**

4. An **adverbial clause of condition** starts with words such as *if, provided that, unless,* and *whether or not.* For example:

"And **if you don't spring up out of there,** *you're going to be late again."* (lines 27–28)

If you use the verb *to be* in an unreal condition, use *were* for all persons in the conditional clause. For example:

"If I were you, *I'd get up quickly or you'll be late."*

5. An **adverbial clause of concession** starts with words such as *although, though,* and *whereas.* For example:

He avoided looking at her and hurried a little, head down, as he passed her **though he couldn't resist stealing a glance at her out of the corner of his eye.** (lines 81–83)

Note: If one adverbial clause is linked to another clause by *and, but,* or *or,* the second clause will also be an adverbial clause. For example:

He didn't answer her **because her eyes were angry** *and* **he didn't want to quarrel with her.** (lines 280–281)

PUNCTUATION OF ADVERBIAL CLAUSES

If the adverbial clause comes after the independent clause, no commas are used to set it off from that clause. For example:

Mae was in the house **before he was.** *(line 257)*

If the adverbial clause precedes the independent clause, a comma is used to set it off from that clause. For example:

Before he reached home, *Mae had already arrived and was preparing dinner.*

Note: These punctuation rules are frequently *not* followed in "Like a Winding Sheet" since authors often bend punctuation rules to fit in with their individual writing styles. However, it is good practice to follow the rules in your own writing.

In the following sentences relating to the story, underline the adverbial clause and write what kind of adverbial clause it is (time, reason, result, condition, or concession) on the line provided.

1. If he had done that, his hands would have felt good now—relaxed, rested. (lines 140–141) __if__

2. . . . yet he didn't dare let his legs go completely limp because if he did he'd go back to sleep. (lines 40–41) ___Reason___ or ___condition___

3. What he wanted to do was hit her so hard that the scarlet lipstick ~result~ on her mouth would smear and spread over her nose. . . . (lines 224–225) _____

4. "Hello, babe," she called out, as soon as he opened the door. (line 260) ___Time___

5. Although Mae was exhausted at the end of the day, she always C folded her clothes neatly over the chair. _____ ___Concession or contrast___

The following sentences are all related to the plot of "Like a Winding Sheet." Complete them with adverbial clauses that would be appropriate to the story. Use a different kind of adverbial clause in each sentence.

1. ___Although___, he was unable to hit the two women.

2. He managed to control his explosive anger ___because he was believe in not hitting woman___.

3. _____, he would reform many of the working conditions in the factory.

4. He felt so insulted by the women ___because he was called a niggle___ and ___and his condition was ignor___.

5. Mae was annoyed with him ___because he snapped her rumple___.

Write five sentences of your own using an adverbial clause from each category. In one sentence join two adverbial clauses with *and, but,* or *or.* Relate your sentences to the story.

B. Building Vocabulary Skills

Look at the following sentences and complete each one with a suitable synonym from the list below. Both the italicized word and its synonym appear in the story. You may need to change the tense or form of the word. Try to do this exercise first without referring back to the story.

bunch	strike	sag	snarl
rock	froth	twist	knot

1. He stood *swaying* and _____ in the subway train as it rushed toward Harlem.

2. She was so tired after a hard day's work that her shoulders *drooped* and _____ as she collapsed into the chair.

3. The workers in the factory would *snap* and _____ at each other toward the end of the day.

4. He saw the people in the cafeteria standing in *groups* or _____ as they waited for the coffee to be poured.

5. He could feel his poisonous anger *wrapping* and _____ round him as he struggled to control himself.

6. His hands were *clenched* and _____ after the forewoman insulted him.

7. The coffee looked so enticing with the steaming *bubbles* and _____.

8. He felt himself *smack* and _____ her over and over, but he could do nothing about it.

P A R T ◆4◆ **WRITING ACTIVITIES**

1. Write a two-page essay discussing domestic violence in your country. Consider what forms the violence takes; for example, violence can include verbal insults as well as physical blows. Explain who the chief victims are and who mainly inflicts the violence. Analyze the reasons for such behavior. In your conclusion, say whether the victims are treated sympathetically by society.

2. Imagine you are extremely hungry and for some reason you cannot satisfy your craving to eat. Write two to three paragraphs in which you either see or imagine the food you desperately want. Use the story's cafeteria scene, with its intensely evocative imagery, as a model to convey your situation, as well as your feelings at the time. Make clear in your writing why you are unable to eat immediately.

3. Write a dialogue between Mae and her husband five hours after the beating takes place. Have them speak frankly to each other about what happened and the reasons for it. According to the way the dialogue is constructed, convey whether their relationship can be saved or not.

4. Novels such as *The Color Purple* by Alice Walker and *The Joy Luck Club* by Amy Tan both deal with, among other themes, the anguish of domestic violence. Write an essay of one or two pages on a book you have read or a movie you have seen in which a woman or child is subject to violence from a husband or father. Describe the relationship and analyze the reasons for this situation. Does the victim try to do anything about this abuse? Say what happens.

18

Is There Nowhere Else Where We Can Meet?

NADINE GORDIMER *(b. 1923)*

◆◆◆

BORN IN SOUTH AFRICA, Nadine Gordimer has over the years established herself as the conscience of white South Africa. In her many novels and short stories she consistently portrays the tragic consequences of *apartheid,* or racial separation, as they affect both blacks and whites. Unlike many of her white literary compatriots, Gordimer has chosen to remain in South Africa.

Gordimer's novels include *The Lying Days* (1953), *A World of Strangers* (1958), *Occasion for Loving* (1963), *A Guest of Honour* (1970), *The Conservationist* (1974), *Burger's Daughter* (1979), *July's People* (1981), and *A Sport of Nature* (1987). In addition, she has written several volumes of short stories, among which are *The Soft Voice of the Serpent* (1952), *Six Feet of the Country* (1956), *Livingstone's Companions* (1971), and *Crimes of Conscience* (1991).

She has been showered with literary awards, receiving America's James Tait Black Memorial Prize in 1972, England's Booker Prize in 1974, and the Nobel Prize for Literature in 1991.

IS THERE NOWHERE ELSE WHERE WE CAN MEET?

A white woman is walking along a lonely country path in South Africa when a black man suddenly appears. Their encounter disturbs and changes the woman in a surprising way.

➤ To appreciate "Is There Nowhere Else Where We Can Meet?" it is important to understand that until recently apartheid, or complete segregation of the races, was written into South African law. This meant that blacks and whites were kept apart in every sphere of life—residential areas, schools, restaurants, movie theaters, transportation, and so on, and it was virtually impossible to cross barriers.

It was a cool grey morning and the air was like smoke. In that reversal of the elements that sometimes takes place, the grey, soft, muffled[1] sky moved like the sea on a silent day.

The coat collar pressed rough against her neck and her cheeks were softly cold as if they had been washed in ice water. She breathed gently with the air; on the left a strip of veld[2] fire curled silently, flameless. Overhead a dove purred. She went on over the flat straw grass, following the trees, now on, now off the path. Away ahead, over the scribble of twigs,[3] the sloping lines of black and platinum grass—all merging, tones but no colour, like an etching—was the horizon, the shore at which cloud lapped.[4]

Damp burnt grass puffed black, faint dust from beneath her feet. She could hear herself swallow.

A long way off she saw a figure with something red on its head, and she drew from it the sense of balance she had felt at the particular placing of the dot of a figure in a picture. She was here; someone was over there . . .Then the red dot was gone, lost in the curve of the trees. She changed her bag and parcel from one arm to the other and felt the morning, palpable,[5] deeply cold and clinging against her eyes.

She came to the end of a direct stretch of path and turned with it round a dark-fringed pine and a shrub, now delicately boned, that she remembered hung with bunches of white flowers like crystals in the summer. There was a native[6] in a red woollen cap standing at the next clump of trees, where the path crossed a ditch and was bordered by white-splashed stones. She had pulled a little sheath of pine needles,[7] three in a

5

10

15

20

---

1. **muffled**   covered
2. **veld**   a grassy plain in southern Africa
3. **scribble of twigs**   small branches arranged like careless handwriting
4. **lapped**   moved in small waves

5. **palpable**   able to be touched or felt
6. **a native**   insulting reference to a black South African
7. **sheath of pine needles**   bunch of needlelike leaves from the pine tree

twist of thin brown tissue, and as she walked she ran them against her   25
thumb. Down; smooth and stiff. Up; catching in gentle resistance as the
minute serrations snagged at the skin.[8] He was standing with his back
towards her, looking along the way he had come; she pricked the ball of her
thumb with the needle-ends. His one trouser leg was torn off above the
knee, and the back of the naked leg and half-turned heel showed the   30
peculiarly dead, powdery black of cold. She was nearer to him now, but she
knew he did not hear her coming over the damp dust of the path. She was
level with[9] him, passing him; and he turned slowly and looked beyond
her, without a flicker of interest as a cow sees you go.

 The eyes were red, as if he had not slept for a long time, and the strong   35
smell of old sweat burned at her nostrils. Once past, she wanted to cough, but a
pang of guilt at the red weary eyes stopped her. And he had only a filthy
rag—part of an old shirt?—without sleeves and frayed away[10] into a great
gap[11] from underarm to waist. It lifted in the currents of cold as she passed.
She had dropped the neat trio of pine needles somewhere, she did not   40
know at what moment, so now, remembering something from childhood,
she lifted her hand to her face and sniffed: yes, it was as she remembered,
not as chemists pretend it in the bath salts, but a dusty green scent,
vegetable rather than flower. It was clean, unhuman. Slightly sticky too;
tacky[12] on her fingers. She must wash them as soon as she got there. Unless   45
her hands were quite clean, she could not lose consciousness of them, they
obtruded upon her.[13]

 She felt a thudding through the ground like the sound of a hare running
in fear and she was going to turn around and then he was there in front of
her, so startling, so utterly unexpected, panting right into her face. He stood   50
dead still and she stood dead still.[14] Every vestige[15] of control, of sense, of
thought, went out of her as a room plunges into dark at the failure of power
and she found herself whimpering[16] like an idiot or a child. Animal sounds
came out of her throat. She gibbered.[17] For a moment it was Fear itself that
had her by the arms, the legs, the throat; not fear of the man, of any single   55
menace[18] he might present, but Fear, absolute, abstract. If the earth had
opened up in fire at her feet, if a wild beast had opened its terrible mouth to
receive her, she could not have been reduced to less than she was now.

 There was a chest heaving[19] through the tear in front of her; a face
panting; beneath the red hairy woollen cap the yellowish-red eyes holding   60
her in distrust. One foot, cracked from exposure until it looked like broken
wood, moved, only to restore balance in the dizziness that follows running,

---

 8. **minute serrations snagged at the skin** very small,
  sharp points caught at and tore the skin
 9. **she was level with** she was parallel with
10. **frayed away** worn away
11. **gap** hole, space
12. **tacky** sticky
13. **they obtruded upon her** they made her
  uncomfortably aware of them

14. **dead still** without moving
15. **vestige** last remaining bit
16. **whimpering** making a weak cry
17. **gibbered** made nonsense sounds
18. **menace** threat
19. **heaving** rising and falling

but any move seemed towards her and she tried to scream, and the awfulness of dreams came true and nothing would come out. She wanted to throw the handbag and the parcel at him, and as she fumbled[20] crazily for them she heard him draw a deep, hoarse breath and he grabbed out at her and—ah! It came. His hand clutched her shoulder.

Now she fought with him and she trembled with strength as they struggled. The dust puffed round her shoes and his scuffling[21] toes. The smell of him choked her—It was an old pyjama jacket, not a shirt—His face was sullen[22] and there was a pink place where the skin had been grazed off.[23] He sniffed desperately, out of breath. Her teeth chattered,[24] wildly she battered him with her head, broke away, but he snatched at the skirt of her coat and jerked her back. Her face swung up and she saw the waves of a grey sky and a crane[25] breasting them, beautiful as the figurehead of a ship. She staggered for balance and the handbag and parcel fell. At once he was upon them, and she wheeled about;[26] but as she was about to fall on her knees to get there first, a sudden relief, like a rush of tears, came to her and, instead, she ran. She ran and ran, stumbling wildly off through the stalks of dead grass, turning over her heels against hard winter tussocks,[27] blundering[28] through trees and bushes. The young mimosas[29] closed in, lowering a thicket of twigs right to the ground, but she tore herself through, feeling the dust in her eyes and the scaly twigs hooking at her hair. There was a ditch, knee-high in blackjacks;[30] like pins responding to a magnet they fastened along her legs, but on the other side there was a fence and then the road . . . She clawed[31] at the fence—her hands were capable of nothing—and tried to drag herself between the wires, but her coat got caught on a barb,[32] and she was imprisoned there, bent in half, while waves of terror swept over her in heat and trembling. At last the wire tore through its hold on the cloth; wobbling,[33] frantic, she climbed over the fence.

And she was out. She was out on the road. A little way on there were houses, with gardens, postboxes, a child's swing. A small dog sat at a gate. She could hear a faint hum, as of life, of talk somewhere, or perhaps telephone wires.

She was trembling so that she could not stand. She had to keep on walking, quickly, down the road. It was quiet and grey, like the morning. And cool. Now she could feel the cold air round her mouth and between her brows, where the skin stood out in sweat. And in the cold wetness that soaked down beneath her armpits and between her buttocks. Her heart thumped slowly and stiffly. Yes, the wind was cold; she was suddenly cold,

---

20. **fumbled**   reached awkwardly
21. **scuffling**   moving as in a struggle
22. **sullen**   moody, bad-tempered
23. **the skin had been grazed off**   the skin had been scraped off
24. **her teeth chattered**   her teeth knocked together rapidly (from fright)
25. **a crane**   a wading bird
26. **she wheeled about**   she turned around rapidly
27. **tussocks**   clumps of grass
28. **blundering**   moving wildly
29. **mimosas**   flowering trees
30. **blackjacks**   small black thorns
31. **clawed**   scratched wildly
32. **a barb**   a sharp point
33. **wobbling**   with a swaying, unsteady movement

damp-cold, all through. She raised her hand, still fluttering[34] uncontrollably, and smoothed her hair; it was wet at the hairline. She guided her hand into her pocket and found a handkerchief to blow her nose.

There was the gate of the first house, before her.

She thought of the woman coming to the door, of the explanations, of the woman's face, and the police. Why did I fight, she thought suddenly. What did I fight for? Why didn't I give him the money and let him go? His red eyes, and the smell and those cracks in his feet, fissures,[35] erosion.[36] She shuddered. The cold of the morning flowed into her.

She turned away from the gate and went down the road slowly, like an invalid,[37] beginning to pick the blackjacks from her stockings. ◆

---

34. **fluttering**   shaking
35. **fissures**   cracks

36. **erosion**   a slow wearing away
37. **invalid**   a sick person

P A R T   ◆**1**   **FIRST READING**

A. Thinking about the Story

Were you surprised by the man's attack on the woman? Did you hope she would successfully repel his assault, or were you more sympathetic toward the man?

B. Understanding the Plot

1. How does the woman feel at the opening of the story? Pick out the expressions that describe her appearance and emotions.

2. Where does the story take place? Describe the woman's surroundings.

3. When she first sees the figure, how does the woman react?

4. Which senses of the woman are most affected by the man's appearance? Give examples to illustrate your answer.

5. What does the woman do with the pine needles? What do the pine needles remind her of? Why does she feel the need to wash her hands?

6. At what point and in what way does the woman's mood change?

7. Why does the man attack her?

8. How is her fear portrayed?

9. Does the woman seek help when she can?

P A R T ◆2◆ **S E C O N D   R E A D I N G**

A. Exploring Themes

You are now ready to reread "Is There Nowhere Else Where We Can Meet?" Try to follow the complex psychological responses of the woman, who cannot separate herself from the guilty consequences of being born white in a society where the color of a person's skin determines the level of privileges he or she can enjoy. Look too at how Gordimer uses a dense mix of imagery to create the atmosphere, setting, characters, and themes of the story.

Note: For an explanation of how imagery works, you might want to read the section on simile and metaphor in this chapter on page 233 before reading the story again.

1. What are the underlying reasons that the woman does not immediately give up her parcel and handbag to her attacker? What, in your view, makes her unexpectedly decide to give up the fight?

2. By the end of the story, how has the woman changed?

3. What parallels does Gordimer draw between the woman and her attacker? What language conveys these parallels? What point do you think Gordimer is making by linking the characters so closely?

4. What does the veld represent? What is it contrasted with at the end of the story?

5. Why do you think the characters never speak to each other?

6. What is the political theme of the story?

7. How does the title relate to the political framework in which the story is set? How does the title help explain the ending?

8. The scene with the pine needles in lines 40–47 is symbolic. To understand the symbolism first look at the sentence:

   Unless her hands were quite clean, she could not lose consciousness of them, they obtruded upon her. (lines 45–47)

   In this sentence Gordimer suggests a double meaning of clean hands. Explain the double meaning. What do the pine needles and their lingering scent symbolize? How does this symbol relate to the story's political theme?

Note: For more information on symbol, see page 283.

B. Analyzing the Author's Style

Before you begin to work on this section, turn to the detailed explanation of imagery (page 279), simile (page 282), and metaphor (page 280).

IMAGERY: SIMILE AND METAPHOR

Nadine Gordimer's writing abounds in **imagery**, and she makes full and imaginative use of **similes** (direct comparisons) and **metaphors** (implied comparisons) to enrich her many descriptions. She opens her story with two similes using *like* to unite the two elements of the comparison:

> *It was a cool grey morning and the air was like smoke. . . . the grey, soft, muffled sky moved like the sea on a silent day.*

With these two similes she has created a picture of a gentle, quiet morning where the sky with its smokelike color and texture seems to be moving up and down like a calm sea. The overwhelming impression is one of peacefulness.

In sharp contrast is her description of the panic the woman feels when overcome by terror:

> *Every vestige of control, of sense, of thought, went out of her as a room plunges into dark at the failure of power. . . .*(lines 51–52)

In the above example *as* unites the two elements of the comparison.

The Gordimer story also contains a great many metaphors. In lines 74–75 Gordimer writes:

> *. . . she saw the waves of a grey sky and a crane breasting them, . . .*

Here, with great economy, we have two linking metaphors. The first is *the waves of the grey sky*, in which the sky is described in terms of the sea. (Remember how Gordimer used a simile to make the same comparison in the opening paragraph.) The second is *a crane breasting them*, in which she continues the image of the sky as the sea and describes the bird flying through the air in terms of a swimmer going over the top of a wave.

1. With what animal is the man first compared? What images come to mind from this comparison? The man is later compared to another animal. Which one is it? How does the new animal comparison reflect the change in the atmosphere of the story?

2. What similes convey the woman's terror in lines 48–58?

3. What sense does the simile in the following sentence appeal to?

   There was a ditch, knee-high in blackjacks; like pins responding to a magnet they fastened along her legs, . . . (lines 83–85)

   Explain how the simile expresses the woman's condition.

4. Pick out and explain three more similes in the story that strike you as unusual or powerful.

5. What is the dove described as in line 7? Explain what the two elements of the metaphor convey.

6. What noun does the metaphor *the shore at which cloud lapped* refer to? (line 10) Explain the metaphor.

7. What metaphor is used that involves the woman's sense of smell in lines 35–46? Explain the two elements of the metaphor.

8. Find a metaphor in lines 48–58 that conveys the sense of touch. Explain how it works.

9. Pick out and explain three other metaphors in the story that strike you as unusual or powerful.

C. Judging for Yourself

Express yourself as personally as you like in your answers to the following questions:

1. If you had been in the woman's place, would you have fought fiercely for your property if someone tried to steal it from you? Explain your answer.

2. Do you think the man had any justification for attacking the woman?

3. Was the woman wrong not to report the incident to the police? Do you think she may change her mind about not going to the police?

4. Do you blame either of the characters for what happened? Give reasons for your answer.

D. Making Connections

1. Do you have distinct divisions in your country based on social, economic, racial, religious, or caste differences? Analyze carefully the reasons for these, and say whether the situation is changing at all.

2. What is the attitude toward property in your country? Does its possession confer status? Is property considered important enough to fight over and even die for? Is the accumulation of wealth more prized than the development of the spirit?

3. How do you feel when you meet a street person who is panhandling? Do you give him or her money? What suggestions do you have for solving the homeless problem?

4. What do you know about the historic changes that have taken place in South Africa? What has helped bring about those changes?

E. Debate

Debate the proposal: It is impossible for people of different races and/or religions to live together peacefully.

PART ◆3◆ FOCUS ON LANGUAGE

A. Practice with Similes and Metaphors

Make up your own similes to complete the following sentences.

1. Her heart thumped as loudly as _____.

2. Fearing for her life, she ran like _____.

3. As he came closer, he looked like _____.

4. The path twisted and turned like _____.

5. Her throat was as dry as _____.

6. The trees closed in on her like _____.

7. When he attacked her, she fought as _____ as _____.

8. He grabbed her arm fiercely _____.

9. After she had escaped, she felt _____.

10. It was as _____ as _____ that she would not report the matter to the police.

Underline the metaphors in the following sentences, and explain what two elements are being compared.

1. The clouds sailed slowly across the sky.

2. His scarecrow figure terrified her as he approached rapidly.

3. The claws of fear fastened around her throat when she tried to scream.

4. Relief flooded through her when she realized he had gone.

5. When it was over, her strength bled out of her and she fluttered to the ground.

B. Building Vocabulary Skills

In the left-hand column is a list of adjectives from the story. In the right-hand column is a list of situations that the adjectives might appropriately refer to. Match each adjective to its situation. The first one is done for you as an example.

ADJECTIVE	SITUATION
_g_ 1. filthy (line 37)	a. first steps of a baby
____ 2. muffled (line 2)	b. heart beats while waiting for exam results
____ 3. frayed (line 38)	c. sound under a pillow
____ 4. sticky (line 44)	d. carpet after many years of hard use
____ 5. startling (line 50)	e. attempt to call the police in an emergency
____ 6. heaving (line 59)	f. lips after eating honey
____ 7. hoarse (line 66)	g. clothes after a long dusty trip
____ 8. sullen (line 71)	h. response to an unexpected noise
____ 9. wobbling (line 90)	i. expression of a child who is denied a request
____ 10. frantic (line 90)	j. shoulders after a fast run
____ 11. fluttering (line 101)	k. voice during a cold

Make up sentences using each adjective with its corresponding situation. For example:

My clothes were absolutely **filthy** after I had been three weeks in the desert without washing them.

P A R T ◆4◆ **WRITING ACTIVITIES**

1. Write an essay of two or three pages in which you analyze the people who are poor in your country. First define and describe the different groups of poor and examine the reasons for their poverty. Next include a description of measures being taken by the government to deal with their situation. In conclusion, say what solutions you would suggest if you had the power to implement them.

2. Write two or three paragraphs describing an occasion in which you felt great fear. Give as many sensory details as possible to convey the experience. Include a description of when it happened, where you were, what occurred, and how you felt.

3. *Cry, the Beloved Country* by Alan Paton, *Burger's Daughter* by Nadine Gordimer, and *The Blood Knot* by Athol Fugard are powerful literary works by South African writers that deal with the tragic effects of apartheid. In an essay write about a novelist, poet, or playwright in your country who consistently speaks out against social or political injustice in his or her work. Discuss the particular concerns of the writer, and show how he or she develops them in his or her work. Comment on what makes their books memorable and distinguished.

The Catbird Seat

JAMES THURBER *(1894–1961)*

◆◆◆

BORN IN COLUMBUS, Ohio, James Thurber used his hometown as the setting for many of his humorous writings. His mild-tempered father and dominant mother served as the prototypes for his many explorations of the war between the sexes. After Thurber began working for *The New Yorker* magazine in 1927 his career took off as he became widely known for his humorous essays, stories, cartoons, and illustrations.

Today Thurber is considered by many to be the greatest American humorist since Mark Twain. Beneath the humor of his work lies a concern with the consequences of marital humiliations, the destructive effects of technology, and the dangers of fascism. Thurber always admired the instinctive wisdom of animals and used them prominently in his work.

His large body of work, for which he won numerous awards, includes *My Life and Hard Times* (1933), *The Middle-Aged Man on the Flying Trapeze* (1935), *Further Fables for Our Time* (1940), *The Thurber Carnival* (1945), and *Thurber's Dogs* (1955).

THE CATBIRD SEAT

*A head filing clerk whose job is threatened takes drastic and
ingenious measures to protect himself.*

[handwritten: Mr. Martin, Mrs Barrows, Mr. Fitweiler]

Mr. Martin bought the pack of Camels on Monday night in the most
crowded cigar store on Broadway. It was theatre time and seven or eight
men were buying cigarettes. The clerk didn't even glance at Mr. Martin, who
put the pack in his overcoat pocket and went out. If any of the staff at F & S
had seen him buy the cigarettes, they would have been astonished, for it   5
was generally known that Mr. Martin did not smoke, and never had. No one
saw him.

It was just a week to the day since Mr. Martin had decided to rub out
Mrs. Ulgine Barrows. The term "rub out" pleased him because it suggested
nothing more than the correction of an error—in this case an error of Mr.   10
Fitweiler. Mr. Martin had spent each night of the past week working out his
plan and examining it. As he walked home now he went over it again. For
the hundredth time he resented the element of imprecision, the margin of
guesswork[1] that entered into the business. The project as he had worked it
out was casual and bold, the risks were considerable. Something might go   15
wrong anywhere along the line. And therein lay the cunning of his scheme.
No one would ever see in it the cautious, painstaking hand of Erwin Martin,
head of the filing department at F & S, of whom Mr. Fitweiler had once said,
"Man is fallible but Martin isn't."[2] No one would see his hand, that is, unless
it were caught in the act.   20

Sitting in his apartment, drinking a glass of milk, Mr. Martin reviewed his
case against Mrs. Ulgine Barrows, as he had every night for seven nights. He
began at the beginning. Her quacking voice and braying laugh had first
profaned[3] the halls of F & S on March 7, 1941 (Mr. Martin had a head for dates).
Old Roberts, the personnel chief, had introduced her as the newly appointed   25
special adviser to the president of the firm, Mr. Fitweiler. The woman had
appalled Mr. Martin instantly, but he hadn't shown it. He had given her his dry
hand, a look of studious concentration, and a faint smile. "Well," she had said,
looking at the papers on his desk, "are you lifting the oxcart out of the ditch?"[4]
As Mr. Martin recalled that moment, over his milk, he squirmed[5] slightly. He   30
must keep his mind on her crimes as a special adviser, not on her peccadillos[6]
as a personality. This he found difficult to do, in spite of entering an objection

---

1. **he resented the element of imprecision, the margin of guesswork** He did not like the fact that the tiniest detail could cause the plan to go wrong.
2. **"Man is fallible, but Martin isn't"** A humorous reference to the notion that usually only God cannot make a mistake.
3. **profaned** treated something sacred with vulgarity
4. **"Are you lifting the oxcart out of the ditch?"** Are you attempting the impossible?
5. **squirmed** moved uncomfortably
6. **peccadillos** slight offenses

and sustaining it.[7] The faults of the woman as a woman kept chattering on in
his mind like an unruly witness. She had, for almost two years now, baited
him. In the halls, in the elevator, even in his own office, into which she romped   35
now and then like a circus horse, she was constantly shouting these silly
questions at him. "Are you lifting the oxcart out of the ditch? Are you tearing up
the pea patch? Are you hollering[8] down the rain barrel? Are you scraping the
bottom of the pickle barrel? Are you sitting in the catbird seat?"[9]

It was Joey Hart, one of Mr. Martin's two assistants, who had explained   40
what the gibberish[10] meant. "She must be a Dodger fan," he had said. "Red
Barber[11] announces the Dodger games over the radio and he uses those
expressions—picked 'em up down South." Joey had gone on to explain one
or two. "Tearing up the pea patch" meant going on a rampage;[12] "sitting in
the catbird seat" meant sitting pretty,[13] like a batter with three balls and no   45
strikes on him.[14] Mr. Martin dismissed all this with an effort. It had been
annoying, it had driven him near to distraction, but he was too solid a man
to be moved to murder by anything so childish. It was fortunate, he
reflected as he passed on to the important charges against Mrs. Barrows, that
he had stood up under it so well.[15] He had maintained always an outward   50
appearance of polite tolerance. "Why, I even believe you like the woman,"
Miss Paird, his other assistant, had once said to him. He had simply smiled.

A gavel[16] rapped in Mr. Martin's mind and the case proper was resumed.
Mrs. Ulgine Barrows stood charged with willful,[17] blatant,[18] and persistent
attempts to destroy the efficiency and system of F & S. It was competent,   55
material, and relevant to review her advent and rise to power. Mr. Martin had
got the story from Miss Paird, who seemed always able to find things out.
According to her, Mrs. Barrows had met Mr. Fitweiler at a party, where she
had rescued him from the embraces of a powerfully built drunken man who
had mistaken the president of F & S for a famous retired Middle Western   60
football coach. She had led him to a sofa and somehow worked upon him a
monstrous magic. The aging gentleman had jumped to the conclusion there
and then that this was a woman of singular attainments,[19] equipped to bring
out the best in him and in the firm. A week later he had introduced her into
F & S as his special adviser. On that day confusion got its foot in the door.   65
After Miss Tyson, Mr. Brundage, and Mr. Bartlett had been fired and Mr.
Munson had taken his hat and stalked out,[20] mailing in his resignation later,

---

7. **entering an objection and sustaining it**   In a court
   of law an attorney may object to a line of questioning
   by his opponent and the judge may sustain (agree
   with) the objection or overrule (disagree with) it
8. **hollering**   shouting
9. **sitting in the catbird seat**   enjoying an
   advantageous position
10. **gibberish**   meaningless language
11. **Red Barber**   a sports broadcaster, born in
    Mississippi, who covered the Brooklyn Dodgers
12. **going on a rampage**   getting violently out of
    control

13. **sitting pretty**   in an advantageous position
14. **like a batter with three balls and no strikes on him**
    In baseball, a situation where a batter is likely to do
    well
15. **had stood up under it so well**   had successfully
    endured it
16. **gavel**   small hammer a judge uses in the
    courtroom
17. **willful**   deliberate
18. **blatant**   offensively noticeable
19. **singular attainments**   unusual achievements
20. **stalked out**   walked out proudly

old Roberts had been emboldened to speak Mr. Fitweiler. He mentioned that Mr. Munson's department had been "a little disrupted" and hadn't they perhaps better resume the old system there? Mr. Fitweiler had said certainly not. He had the greatest faith in Mrs. Barrows' ideas. "They require a little seasoning, a little seasoning, is all," he had added. Mr. Roberts had given it up. Mr. Martin reviewed in detail all the changes wrought by Mrs. Barrows. She had begun chipping at the cornices of the firm's edifice and now she was swinging at the foundation stones with a pickaxe.[21]

Mr. Martin came now, in his summing up, to the afternoon of Monday, November 2, 1942—just one week ago. On that day, at 3 P.M., Mrs. Barrows had bounced into his office. "Boo!" she had yelled. "Are you scraping around the bottom of the pickle barrel?" Mr. Martin had looked at her from under his green eyeshade, saying nothing. She had begun to wander about the office, taking it in with her great popping eyes. "Do you really need *all* these filing cabinets?" she had demanded suddenly. Mr. Martin's heart had jumped. "Each of these files," he had said, keeping his voice even, "plays an indispensable part in the system of F & S." She had brayed at him, "Well, don't tear up the pea patch!" and gone to the door. From there she had bawled, "But you sure have got a lot of fine scrap[22] in here!" Mr. Martin could no longer doubt that the finger was on his beloved department. Her pickaxe was on the upswing, poised for the first blow. It had not come yet; he had received no blue memo from the enchanted Mr. Fitweiler bearing nonsensical instructions deriving from the obscene[23] woman. But there was no doubt in Mr. Martin's mind that one would be forthcoming. He must act quickly. Already a precious week had gone by. Mr. Martin stood up in his living room, still holding his milk glass. "Gentlemen of the jury," he said to himself, "I demand the death penalty for this horrible person."

The next day Mr. Martin followed his routine, as usual. He polished his glasses more often and once sharpened an already sharp pencil, but not even Miss Paird noticed. Only once did he catch sight of his victim; she swept past him in the hall with a patronizing "Hi!" At five-thirty he walked home, as usual, and had a glass of milk, as usual. He had never drunk anything stronger in his life—unless you could count ginger ale. The late Sam Schlosser, the S of F & S, had praised Mr. Martin at a staff meeting several years before for his temperate[24] habits. "Our most efficient worker neither drinks nor smokes," he had said. "The results speak for themselves." Mr. Fitweiler had sat by, nodding approval.

Mr. Martin was still thinking about that red-letter day[25] as he walked over to the Schrafft's on Fifth Avenue near Forty-sixth Street. He got there, as he always did, at eight o'clock. He finished his dinner and the financial page of the *Sun* at a quarter to nine, as he always did. It was his custom after

---

21. **She had begun chipping at the cornices of the firm's edifice and now she was swinging at the foundation stones with a pickaxe** Mrs. Barrows had started by slowly changing some aspects of the business and was now revolutionizing everything

22. **scrap** useless material
23. **obscene** vulgar, indecent
24. **temperate** moderate
25. **red-letter day** excitingly memorable day

[margin notes: emboldened, wrought, cornices, edifice]

dinner to take a walk. This time he walked down Fifth Avenue at a casual pace. His gloved hands felt moist and warm, his forehead cold. He transferred the Camels from his overcoat to a jacket pocket. He wondered, as he did so, if they did not represent an unnecessary note of strain. Mrs. Barrows smoked only Luckies. It was his idea to puff a few puffs on a Camel (after the rubbing-out), stub it out in the ashtray holding her lipstick-stained Luckies, and thus drag a small red herring[26] across the trail. Perhaps it was not a good idea. It would take time. He might even choke, too loudly.

Mr. Martin had never seen the house on West Twelfth Street where Mrs. Barrows lived, but he had a clear enough picture of it. Fortunately, she had bragged to everybody about her ducky[27] first-floor apartment in the perfectly darling three-story red-brick. There would be no doorman or other attendants; just the tenants of the second and third floors. As he walked along, Mr. Martin realized that he would get there before nine-thirty. He had considered walking north on Fifth Avenue from Schrafft's to a point from which it would take him until ten o'clock to reach the house. At that hour people were less likely to be coming in or going out. But the procedure would have made an awkward loop in the straight thread of his casualness, and he had abandoned it. It was impossible to figure when people would be entering or leaving the house, anyway. There was a great risk at any hour. If he ran into anybody, he would simply have to place the rubbing-out of Ulgine Barrows in the inactive file forever. The same thing would hold true if there were someone in her apartment. In that case he would just say that he had been passing by, recognized her charming house, and thought to drop in.[28]

It was eighteen minutes after nine when Mr. Martin turned into Twelfth Street. A man passed him, and a man and a woman, talking. There was no one within fifty paces when he came to the house, half-way down the block. He was up the steps and in the small vestibule[29] in no time, pressing the bell under the card that said "Mrs. Ulgine Barrows." When the clicking in the lock started, he jumped forward against the door. He got inside fast, closing the door behind him. A bulb in a lantern hung from the hall ceiling on a chain seemed to give a monstrously bright light. There was nobody on the stair, which went up ahead of him along the left wall. A door opened down the hall in the wall on the right. He went toward it swiftly, on tiptoe.

"Well, for God's sake, look who's here!" bawled Mrs. Barrows, and her braying laugh rang out like the report of a shotgun. He rushed past her like a football tackle, bumping her. "Hey, quit shoving!" she said, closing the door behind them. They were in her living room, which seemed to Mr. Martin to be lighted by a hundred lamps. "What's after you?" she said. "You're as jumpy[30] as a goat." He found he was unable to speak. His heart was wheezing in his throat. "I—yes," he finally brought out. She was jabbering and laughing as she started to help him off with his coat. "No, no", he said. "I'll put it here." He took it off and put it on a chair near the door.

---

26. **red herring**   deliberately false clue
27. **ducky**   cute (slang)
28. **drop in**   visit unexpectedly

29. **vestibule**   entrance hall of a building
30. **jumpy**   nervous

"Your hat and gloves, too," she said. "You're in a lady's house." He put his hat on top of the coat. Mrs. Barrows seemed larger than he had thought. He kept his gloves on. "I was passing by," he said. "I recognized—is there anyone here"? She laughed louder than ever. "No," she said, "we're all alone. You're as white as a sheet, you funny man. Whatever *has* come over you? I'll mix you a toddy."[31] She started toward a door across the room. "Scotch-and soda be all right? But say, you don't drink, do you?" She turned and gave him her amused look. Mr. Martin pulled himself together.[32] "Scotch-and-soda will be all right," he heard himself say. He could hear her laughing in the kitchen.

Mr. Martin looked quickly around the living room for the weapon. He had counted on finding one there. There were andirons[33] and a poker[34] and something in a corner that looked like an Indian club. None of them would do.[35] It couldn't be that way. He began to pace around. He came to a desk. On it lay a metal paper knife with an ornate handle. Would it be sharp enough? He reached for it and knocked over a small brass jar. Stamps spilled out of it and it fell to the floor with a clatter. "Hey," Mrs. Barrows yelled from the kitchen, "are you tearing up the pea patch?" Mr. Martin gave a strange laugh. Picking up the knife, he tried its point against his left wrist. It was blunt.[36] It wouldn't do.

When Mrs. Barrows reappeared, carrying two highballs, Mr. Martin, standing there with his gloves on, became acutely conscious of the fantasy he had wrought. Cigarettes in his pocket, a drink prepared for him—it was all too grossly improbable. It was more than that; it was impossible. Somewhere in the back of his mind a vague idea stirred, sprouted.[37] "For heaven's sake, take off those gloves," said Mrs. Barrows. "I always wear them in the house," said Mr. Martin. The idea began to bloom, strange and wonderful. She put the glasses on a coffee table in front of a sofa and sat on the sofa. "Come over here, you odd little man," she said. Mr. Martin went over and sat beside her. It was difficult getting a cigarette out of the pack of Camels, but he managed it. She held a match for him, laughing. "Well," she said, handing him his drink, "this is perfectly marvellous. You with a drink and a cigarette."

Mr. Martin puffed, not too awkwardly, and took a gulp of the highball. "I drink and smoke all the time," he said. He clinked his glass against hers. "Here's nuts to that old windbag, Fitweiler,"[38] he said, and gulped again. The stuff tasted awful, but he made no grimace. "Really, Mr. Martin," she said, her voice and posture changing, "you are insulting our employer." Mrs. Barrows was now all special adviser to the president. "I am preparing a bomb," said Mr. Martin, "which will blow the old goat higher than hell." He had only had a little of the drink, which was not strong. It couldn't be

---

31. **toddy**   a hot, alcoholic drink
32. **pulled himself together**   got control of himself
33. **andirons**   a pair of metal supports for firewood
34. **poker**   a metal rod for stirring a fire
35. **would do**   were acceptable
36. **blunt**   not sharp
37. **sprouted**   began to grow
38. **"Here's nuts to that old windbag, Fitweiler"**   a disrespectful expression suggesting that his boss talks too much

that. "Do you take dope or something?" Mrs. Barrows asked coldly. "Heroin," said Mr. Martin. "I'll be coked to the gills[39] when I bump that old buzzard off."[40] "Mr. Martin!" she shouted, getting to her feet. "That will be all of that. You must go at once." Mr. Martin took another swallow of his drink. He tapped his cigarette out in the ashtray and put the pack of Camels on the coffee table. Then he got up. She stood glaring at him. He walked over and put on his hat and coat. "Not a word about this," he said, and laid an index finger against his lips. All Mrs. Barrows could bring out was "Really!" Mr. Martin put his hand on the doorknob. "I'm sitting in the catbird seat," he said. He stuck his tongue out at her and left. Nobody saw him go.

Mr. Martin got to his apartment, walking, well before eleven. No one saw him go in. He had two glasses of milk after brushing his teeth, and he felt elated. It wasn't tipsiness,[41] because he hadn't been tipsy. Anyway, the walk had worn off all effects of the whiskey. He got in bed and read a magazine for a while. He was asleep before midnight.

Mr. Martin got to the office at eight-thirty the next morning, as usual. At a quarter to nine, Ulgine Barrows, who had never before arrived at work before ten, swept into his office. "I'm reporting to Mr. Fitweiler now!" she shouted. "If he turns you over to the police, it's no more than you deserve!" Mr. Martin gave her a look of shocked surprise. "I beg your pardon?" he said. Mrs. Barrows snorted and bounced out of the room, leaving Miss Paird and Joey Hart staring after her. "What's the matter with that old devil now?" asked Miss Paird. "I have no idea," said Mr. Martin, resuming his work. The other two looked at him and then at each other. Miss Paird got up and went out. She walked slowly past the closed door of Mr. Fitweiler's office. Mrs. Barrows was yelling inside, but she was not braying. Miss Paird could not hear what the woman was saying. She went back to her desk.

Forty-five minutes later, Mrs. Barrows left the president's office and went into her own, shutting the door. It wasn't until half an hour later that Mr. Fitweiler sent for Mr. Martin. The head of the filing department, neat, quiet, attentive, stood in front of the old man's desk. Mr. Fitweiler was pale and nervous. He took his glasses off and twiddled them. He made a small, bruffing sound in his throat. "Martin," he said, "you have been with us more than twenty years." "Twenty-two, sir," said Mr. Martin. "In that time," pursued the president, "your work and your–uh–manner have been exemplary." "I trust so, sir," said Mr. Martin. "I have understood, Martin," said Mr. Fitweiler, "that you have never taken a drink or smoked." "That is correct, sir," said Mr. Martin. "Ah, yes." Mr. Fitweiler polished his glasses. "You may describe what you did after leaving the office yesterday, Martin," he said. Mr. Martin allowed less than a second for his bewildered pause. "Certainly, sir," he said, "I walked home. Then I went to Schrafft's for dinner. Afterward I walked home again. I went to bed early, sir, and read a magazine for a while. I was asleep before

---

39. **coked to the gills** filled with drugs (slang)
40. **bump that old buzzard off** kill that horrible man

41. **tipsiness** slight drunkenness

eleven." "Ah, yes," said Mr. Fitweiler again. He was silent for a moment, 235
searching for the proper words to say to the head of the filing department.
"Mrs. Barrows," he said finally, "Mrs. Barrows has worked hard, Martin, very
hard. It grieves me to report that she has suffered a severe breakdown. It has
taken the form of a persecution complex accompanied by distressing
hallucinations."[42] "I am very sorry, sir," said Mr. Martin. "Mrs. Barrows is under 240
the delusion,"[43] continued Mr. Fitweiler, "that you visited her last evening and
behaved yourself in an–uh–unseemly[44] manner." He raised his hand to
silence Mr. Martin's little pained outcry. "It is the nature of these psychological
diseases," Mr. Fitweiler said, "to fix upon the least likely and most innocent
party as the–uh–source of persecution. These matters are not for the lay[45] 245
mind to grasp, Martin. I've just had my psychiatrist, Dr. Fitch, on the phone.
He would not, of course, commit himself, but he made enough
generalizations to substantiate my suspicions. I suggested to Mrs. Barrows,
when she had completed her–uh–story to me this morning, that she visit Dr.
Fitch, for I suspected a condition at once. She flew, I regret to say, into a rage, 250
and demanded–uh–requested that I call you on the carpet.[46] You may not
know, Martin, but Mrs. Barrows had planned a reorganization of your
department–subject to my approval, of course, subject to my approval. This
brought you, rather than anyone else, to her mind–but again that is a
phenomenon for Dr. Fitch and not for us. So, Martin, I am afraid Mrs. Barrows' 255
usefulness here is at an end." "I am dreadfully sorry, sir," said Mr. Martin.

It was at this point that the door to the office blew open with the
suddenness of a gas-main explosion and Mrs. Barrows catapulted through
it. "Is the little rat denying it?" she screamed. "He can't get away with that!"
Mr. Martin got up and moved discreetly to a point beside Mr. Fitweiler's 260
chair. "You drank and smoked at my apartment," she bawled at Mr. Martin,
"and you know it! You called Mr. Fitweiler an old windbag and said you
were going to blow him up when you got coked to the gills on your
heroin!" She stopped yelling to catch her breath and a new glint came into
her popping eyes. "If you weren't such a drab, ordinary little man," she 265
said, "I'd think you'd planned it all. Sticking your tongue out, saying you
were sitting in the catbird seat, because you thought no one would believe
me when I told it! My God, it's really too perfect!" She brayed loudly and
hysterically, and the fury was on her again. She glared at Mr. Fitweiler.
"Can't you see how he has tricked us, you old fool? Can't you see his little 270
game?" But Mr. Fitweiler had been surreptitiously[47] pressing all the buttons
under the top of his desk and employees of F & S began pouring into the
room. "Stockton," said Mr. Fitweiler, "you and Fishbein will take Mrs.
Barrows to her home. Mrs. Powell, you will go with them." Stockton, who
had played a little football in high school, blocked Mrs. Barrows as she 275
made for[48] Mr. Martin. It took him and Fishbein together to force her out of

---

42. **hallucinations** fantastic images
43. **is under the delusion** falsely believes
44. **unseemly** improper
45. **lay** amateur, not professional

46. **call you on the carpet** criticize you severely
    (slang)
47. **surreptitiously** secretly
48. **made for** attempted to attack

the door into the hall, crowded with stenographers and office boys. She was still screaming imprecations at Mr. Martin, tangled and contradictory imprecations. The hubbub finally died out down the corridor.

"I regret that this has happened," said Mr. Fitweiler. "I shall ask you to 280 dismiss it from your mind, Martin." "Yes, sir," said Mr. Martin, anticipating his chief's "That will be all" by moving to the door. "I will dismiss it." He went out and shut the door, and his step was light and quick in the hall. When he entered his department he had slowed down to his customary gait, and he walked quietly across the room to the W20 file, wearing a look of studious 285 concentration. ◆

PART ◆ 1 ◆ FIRST READING

A. Thinking about the Story

Did you sympathize with Mr. Martin's murderous impulses? Were you hoping that he'd succeed in his plan to "rub out" Mrs. Barrows?

B. Understanding the Plot

1. What is Mr. Martin planning to do when he buys his unaccustomed pack of cigarettes?

2. What does Mr. Fitweiler's reference to Mr. Martin—"Man is fallible, but Martin isn't"—tell us about Mr. Martin's character? (line 19)

3. What animals does Mr. Martin compare Mrs. Barrows to? What do these animals have in common?

4. What is the situation of a baseball player who is "sitting in the catbird seat"? How does the comparison that he is "like a batter with three balls and no strikes on him" (lines 45–46) help reinforce your answer?

5. Why is it important to the success of Mr. Martin's plan that he has "maintained always an outward appearance of polite tolerance" toward Mrs. Barrows? (lines 50–51)

6. What exactly does he accuse Mrs. Barrows of doing?

7. How did Mrs. Barrows initially come to the attention of Mr. Fitweiler?

8. When did Mr. Martin decide to take action against Mrs. Barrows?

9. Why is it important for Mr. Martin to follow his routine on the day he plans to "rub out" Mrs. Barrows?

10. What is the "red herring" he drags across the trail? (line 115) Why does he need these red herrings?

11. Why do the lights in Mrs. Barrows' apartment building make Mr. Martin uncomfortable?

12. Why does he keep his gloves on but take his hat and coat off?

13. What goes wrong with Mr. Martin's scheme?

14. What idea "sprouted" and then began "to bloom" in Mr. Martin's mind? (lines 176–178) How does he implement this idea?

15. What does Mr. Fitweiler decide to do about Mrs. Barrows? How did he come to that decision?

PART ◆2◆ **SECOND READING**

A. Exploring Themes

You are now ready to reread "The Catbird Seat." Look at how Thurber draws Mr. Martin with minute descriptive details and sets him against Mrs. Barrows in an archetypal battle of the sexes.

1. When Mr. Martin reviews his case against Mrs. Barrows (lines 21–94), what role does he adopt for himself in his imagination, and in what setting does he see himself playing this role? What particular words and expressions does he use to help him sustain this imaginary role?

2. What kind of relationship between men and women is Thurber poking fun at in the story?

3. What makes this story funny? Give examples from the story, and explain the different elements Thurber uses to create the humor.

4. From reading "The Catbird Seat," what can you infer about Thurber's attitude to modernization? Justify your answer.

5. What parallels does Thurber draw between the characters of Mr. Fitweiler and Mr. Martin?

B. Analyzing the Author's Style

Before you begin to work on this section, turn to the detailed explanation of understatement (page 284).

UNDERSTATEMENT AND HUMOR

In creating Mr. Martin, James Thurber has his character constantly understate, or de-emphasize, his position in order to create humor through the contrast between what he says and the actual dramatic situation he is describing. This **understatement** also serves to reinforce the aspects of Mr. Martin's personality crucial to his makeup. In fact, the males in general are given to understatement in this story, a trait that unites them in comic brotherhood against the loud, exaggerated ranting of Mrs. Barrows.

For example, when we first encounter Mr. Martin, he is thinking about his decision to *rub out* Mrs. Barrows. (lines 8–9) Taken literally, *rub out* means to erase a mistake as a clerk might erase a wrong entry in a file. Although Mr. Martin is planning to kill Mrs. Barrows, he cannot bring himself to use violent language.

1. In what way is "project" an understatement? (line 14) What word could be substituted?

2. Mr. Martin describes the immediate consequences of Mrs. Barrows's appointment as "confusion got its foot in the door." (line 65) What confusion is he referring to here? What more direct phrase could he have used?

3. Explain Mr. Roberts's understated comment to Mr. Fitweiler, and say what he really meant to convey. (line 69) What does Mr. Fitweiler reply? Convey his answer in more forceful language.

4. In a deliberate and humorous reversal, Mr. Martin unexpectedly sheds his naturally understated speech and talks very plainly in the style of Mrs. Barrows when he says:

   a. "Here's nuts to that old windbag, Fitweiler." (line 187)

   b. "I'll be coked to the gills when I bump that old buzzard off." (lines 194–195)

   c. "I'm sitting in the catbird seat." (lines 201–202)

   How might he have phrased these three sentences in his naturally understated manner?

5. When Mr. Fitweiler tells Mr. Martin that Mrs. Barrows had accused him of behaving in an "unseemly manner" (line 242) and demanded that he be "called on the carpet" (line 251), what do you think she really said?

C. Judging for Yourself

Express yourself as personally as you like in your answers to the following questions:

1. Do you think that Thurber was fair to Mrs. Barrows in the way he portrayed her? Justify your answer.

2. In your view, did F & S appear to need some restructuring? How would you characterize the business?

3. Were you confident that Mr. Martin would triumph over Mrs. Barrows? Explain your answer.

4. Did you feel that Mr. Martin acted ethically toward Mrs. Barrows at the end?

5. What do you think life at F & S will be like in the future?

D. Making Connections

1. How is progress viewed in your culture? Do you think that all progress is automatically good?

2. If a woman has a dominant personality, how is she viewed in your country? Are the same standards applied to an aggressive man?

3. Have you ever been fired from a job? Discuss what led up to the firing and how you handled it.

4. Have sporting terms influenced your language? In what way?

E. Debate

Debate the proposal: The end justifies the means.

PART ◆3◆ **FOCUS ON LANGUAGE**

A. Noun Clauses

A **noun clause** is a dependent clause that functions as a noun. It can act as either the subject of a clause or as the object of a transitive verb or a preposition. As a clause it must have its own subject and verb, and as a dependent clause it cannot stand alone but must be in a sentence with an independent (main) clause.

Note: For information on and practice with main clauses see "Dry September" page 269.

> He mentioned **that Mr. Munson's department had been "a little disrupted"** . . . . (lines 68–69)

The noun clause is the object of the transitive verb *mentioned*.

> **That Mr. Munson's department had been "a little disrupted"** *came as no surprise to the staff at F & S.*

The noun clause is the subject of the verb *came*.

A noun clause may also come after a clause beginning with the neutral *it*.

> . . . *it was generally known* **that Mr. Martin did not smoke.** . . . (lines 5–6)

This sentence could also be written in the following way:

> ***That Mr. Martin did not smoke*** *was generally known.*

Look at the following examples from "The Catbird Seat," which indicate other ways noun clauses may be used.

1. Noun clauses are most commonly introduced by the word **that**, which may sometimes be omitted.

> *"You called Mr. Fitweiler an old windbag and said **you were going to blow him up when you got coked to the gills on your heroin!** "* (lines 262–264)

The noun clause is the object of the verb *said*. It also includes the dependent adverbial clause *when you got coked to the gills on your heroin.*

2. Noun clauses may also be introduced by the following words: *whether, if, where, when, why, how, who, whom, whose, what,* and *which.*

> *"Can't you see **how he has tricked us, you old fool?"*** (line 270)

The noun clause is the object of the verb *see.*

Note: The above list of words may also introduce adjectival and adverbial clauses. For information on and practice with adjectival clauses see page 201, and for adverbial clauses see page 221.

3. If one noun clause is linked to another clause by *and, but,* or *or,* the second clause will also be a noun clause.

> *Mr. Barrows said **that Mr. Martin had visited her last evening** and **had behaved himself in an unseemly manner.***

The two noun clauses are the object of the verb *said.*

Answer the questions concerning the following sentences from the story:

1. It was fortunate, he reflected as he passed on to the important charges against Mrs. Barrows, that he had stood up under it so well. ~~main clause~~ (lines 48–50)
   a. Underline the noun clause.
   b. Which clause does it relate to?
   c. Rewrite the sentence, placing the noun clause at the beginning.

2. "Why I even believe you like the woman," Miss Paird, his other assistant, had once said to him. (lines 51–52)

   a. Underline the noun clause.

   b. What word is missing from the noun clause but is implied?

   c. Which clause is the noun clause dependent on?

   d. Is it the subject or the object of the verb in that clause?

3. It was at this point that the door to the office blew open with the suddenness of a gas-main explosion and Mrs. Barrows catapulted through it. (lines 257–259)

   a. How many noun clauses are in this sentence? Underline them.

   b. What word is omitted, but understood? Where would you place it?

   c. Which clause do the noun clauses relate to?

4. "You may describe what you did, after leaving the office yesterday, Martin," he said. (lines 230–231)

   a. Underline the noun clause.

   b. Which clause does it relate to?

   c. Is it the subject or the object of the clause?

5. It was his idea to puff a few puffs on a Camel (after the rubbing-out), stub it out in the ashtray holding her lipstick-stained Luckies, and thus drag a small red herring across the trail. (lines 113-115)

   a. Are there any noun clauses in this sentence?

   b. If your answer is yes, underline them/it. If your answer is no, explain why not.

6. Make up five noun clauses of your own relating to the story, using the above examples as models. Start your noun clauses with the following words: *that, who, where, why,* and *how.* At least one noun clause should be the subject of the main clause and one the object, and one should come after the neutral *it.* One sentence should contain two noun clauses.

B. Building Vocabulary Skills

The following two-word verbs appear in "The Catbird Seat":

went over (line 12)

worked out (line 14)

stood up (line 50)

ran into (line 129)

turn (you) over (line 211)

The above verbs have at least two meanings. Find the verbs in the story and in your dictionary. Then complete the following sentences with the correct expression from the list. Each expression will be used twice: once as it is found in the story and once with an alternate meaning. On the line at the end of each sentence, write a (synonym) for the expression to show you understand it.

1. She often _Works out_ at her gym in her lunch break.
   exercise exercise

2. He _ran into_ his teacher when he least expected to see her.
   saw

3. If I catch you shoplifting again, I'm going to _turn you over_ to the police. _take you (report)_

4. The employee _worked out went over_ her proposal at least twice before submitting it to her boss. _look through_

5. After drinking too many beers at the party, the driver _ran ran into_ a parked car. _hit_

6. No matter how many times I tried to introduce my friend to eligible partners, it never _work out be accepted_

7. When my mother was a child, all the children _stood up_ when the teacher entered the room. _arse from their sit_

8. In order to prevent you from getting sores, I must _turn you over_ in your bed every two hours. _chang position_

9. This house _stood up_ in spite of the two hurricanes that have battered it this season. _stay in good shap_

10. When the play _went over_ with the first-night audience, the producers knew they had a hit on their hands. _performed_

Thurber makes use of two expressions in "The Catbird Seat" that contain the color red. Mr Martin fondly remembers a special occasion as a *red-letter day*. (line 105) He also thinks it would be a good idea to drag a *red herring* along the trail and so divert the police's suspicions from himself. (line 115)

Use your dictionary to find out the meaning of the following expressions. Then write sentences using each expression appropriately.

red-blooded _有朝气, 精力充沛的_   ✓ a green thumb
✓ a blue streak _no stopping for talking_   yellow journalism
in the black _for money finacial_   white-collar

Can you add any expressions of your own?

P A R T ◆4◆ **WRITING ACTIVITIES**

1. Have you ever been the victim of a domineering personality? Perhaps it was at work, at school, or in the family. Write an essay of two pages outlining your relationship to the person, and say what he or she did to you. Describe how you felt and what measures you took to deal with the situation.

2. "Like attracts like" or "Opposites attract." Which of these is true for you? Write a two-page essay considering the advantages or disadvantages of your choice when it comes to the work place. State whether you think the advantages outweigh the disadvantages or vice versa. Try to include various types of noun clauses in your piece.

3. Many books, movies, plays, and cartoons deal with the war between the sexes. For example, the Spencer Tracy/Katharine Hepburn screen battles have become American movie classics, as has the film version of Edward Albee's play *Who's Afraid of Virginia Woolf?* starring Richard Burton and Elizabeth Taylor. Write an essay of two pages analyzing how men and women are presented in a work you have seen or read regarding the gender war. Say whether you think a war of the sexes is the natural outcome of the society we live in.

4. In both "The Boarding House" (page 98) and "The Catbird Seat" a trap is set that is crucial to the success of a central character's scheme. In an essay compare and contrast the two stories and their main characters, bringing out as much as possible their similarities and differences.

Dry September

WILLIAM FAULKNER *(1897–1962)*

◆◆◆

BORN IN MISSISSIPPI, William Faulkner spent most of his life in that state and set his fiction there. He is recognized as one of America's greatest writers of the twentieth century. His work reflects his preoccupation with the South, the historical and social changes it had endured, the connection of the past to the present, and the complex moral issues arising out of the relationships between whites and blacks. His writing is characterized by the use of the different dialects spoken by the people of Mississippi.

Faulkner's novels include *The Sound and the Fury* (1929), *As I Lay Dying* (1930), *Sanctuary* (1931), and, *Absalom, Absalom!* (1936). Among his volumes of short stories are *Go Down, Moses* (1942) and *Collected Short Stories of William Faulkner* (1950).

In 1949 Faulkner was awarded the Nobel Prize for Literature. He also received the National Book Award for *Collected Short Stories*, the Legion of Honor Award from France, and the Pulitzer Prize in 1955 for his novel *A Fable*.

(margin notes, handwritten):
men/man
pen/pan
left/laughed
said/sad
dead/Dad

DRY SEPTEMBER

*A middle-aged white woman in the Deep South accuses a black
man of sexual assault, setting off a violent train of events.*

➤ Up to the 1960s, lynchings were common in the Deep South. Blacks were often forcibly removed from their homes or public places by a mob of white men and brutally killed on the pretext of having committed a crime. The Ku Klux Klan was the most notorious group involved in this vicious behavior.

I

Through the bloody September twilight, aftermath of sixty-two rainless days, it had gone like a fire in dry grass—the rumor, the story, whatever it was. Something about Miss Minnie Cooper and a Negro. Attacked, insulted, frightened: none of them, gathered in the barber shop on that Saturday evening where the ceiling fan stirred, without freshening it, the vitiated[1] air, 5 sending back upon them, in recurrent surges of stale pomade[2] and lotion, their own stale breath and odors, knew exactly what had happened.

"Except it wasn't Will Mayes," a barber said. He was a man of middle age; a thin, sand-colored man with a mild face, who was shaving a client. "I know Will Mayes. He's a good nigger.[3] And I know Miss Minnie Cooper, too." 10

"What do you know about her?" a second barber said.

"Who is she?" the client said. "A young girl?"

"No," the barber said. "She's about forty, I reckon. She ain't married. That's why I don't believe—"

"Believe, hell!" a hulking[4] youth in a sweat-stained silk shirt said. "Won't 15 you take a white woman's word before a nigger's?"

"I don't believe Will Mayes did it," the barber said. "I know Will Mayes."

"Maybe you know who did it, then. Maybe you already got him out of town, you damn niggerlover."

"I don't believe anybody did anything. I don't believe anything 20 happened. I leave it to you fellows if them ladies that get old without getting married don't have notions that a man can't—"

"Then you are a hell of a white man," the client said. He moved under the cloth. The youth had sprung to his feet.

"You don't?" he said. "Do you accuse a white woman of lying?" 25

The barber held the razor poised above the half-risen client. He did not look around.

"It's this durn[5] weather," another said. "It's enough to make a man do anything. Even to her."

---

1. **vitiated** weakened and polluted
2. **pomade** hair cream
3. **nigger** insulting reference to an African-American
4. **hulking** big and clumsy
5. **durn** a regional word for *darn*, which is a euphemism for *damn*, a mild swear word

Nobody laughed. The barber said in his mild, stubborn tone: "I ain't   30
accusing nobody of nothing.[6] I just know and you fellows know how a
woman that never—"

"You damn niggerlover!" the youth said.

"Shut up, Butch," another said. "We'll get the facts in plenty of time to
act."   35

"Who is? Who's getting them?" the youth said. "Facts, hell! I—"

"You're a fine white man," the client said. "Ain't you?" In his frothy beard
he looked like a desert rat[7] in the moving pictures. "You tell them, Jack," he
said to the youth. "If there ain't any white men in this town, you can count
on me, even if I ain't only a drummer[8] and a stranger."   40

"That's right, boys," the barber said. "Find out the truth first. I know Will
Mayes."

"Well, by God!" the youth shouted. "To think that a white man in this
town—"

"Shut up, Butch," the second speaker said. "We got plenty of time."   45

The client sat up. He looked at the speaker. "Do you claim that anything
excuses a nigger attacking a white woman? Do you mean to tell me you are
a white man and you'll stand for[9] it? You better go back North where you
came from. The South don't want your kind here."

"North what?" the second said. "I was born and raised in this town."   50

"Well, by God!" the youth said. He looked about with a strained,
baffled[10] gaze, as if he was trying to remember what it was he wanted to say
or to do. He drew his sleeve across his sweating face. "Damn if I'm going to
let a white woman—"

"You tell them, Jack," the drummer said. "By God, if they—"   55

The screen door crashed open. A man stood in the floor, his feet apart
and his heavy-set body poised easily. His white shirt was open at the throat;
he wore a felt hat. His hot, bold glance swept the group. His name was
McLendon. He had commanded troops at the front in France and had been
decorated for valor.   60

"Well," he said, "are you going to sit there and let a black son rape a
white woman on the streets of Jefferson?"

Butch sprang up again. The silk of his shirt clung flat to his heavy
shoulders. At each armpit was a dark half moon. "That's what I been telling
them! That's what I—"   65

"Did it really happen?" a third said. "This ain't the first man scare she
ever had, like Hawkshaw says. Wasn't there something about a man on the
kitchen roof, watching her undress, about a year ago?"

---

6. **I ain't accusing nobody of nothing**   I am not
   accusing anybody of anything (dialect)
7. **desert rat**   person who likes to live in the desert,
   especially an old, gray-bearded seeker of gold and
   other minerals
8. **drummer**   traveling salesman
9. **stand for**   endure
10. **baffled**   confused

"What?" the client said. "What's that?" The barber had been slowly forcing him back into the chair; he arrested himself[11] reclining, his head lifted, the barber still pressing him down. 70

McLendon whirled on the third speaker. "Happen? What the hell difference does it make? Are you going to let the black sons get away with it until one really does it?"

"That's what I'm telling them!" Butch shouted. He cursed, long and steady, pointless. 75

"Here, here," a fourth said. "Not so loud. Don't talk so loud."

"Sure," McLendon said; "no talking necessary at all. I've done my talking. Who's with me?" He poised on the balls of his feet, roving his gaze.[12]

The barber held the drummer's face down, the razor poised. "Find the facts first, boys. I know Willy Mayes. It wasn't him. Let's get the sheriff and do this thing right." 80

McLendon whirled upon him his furious, rigid face. The barber did not look away. They looked like men of different races. The other barbers had ceased also above their prone[13] clients. "You mean to tell me," McLendon said, "that you'd take a nigger's word before a white woman's? Why, you damn niggerloving—" 85

The third speaker rose and grasped McLendon's arm; he too had been a soldier. "Now, now. Let's figure this thing out. Who knows anything about what really happened?" 90

"Figure out hell!" McLendon jerked his arm free. "All that're with me get up from there. The ones that ain't—" He roved his gaze, dragging his sleeve across his face.

Three men rose. The drummer in the chair sat up. "Here," he said, jerking at the cloth about his neck; "get this rag off me. I'm with him. I don't live here, but by God, if our mothers and wives and sisters—" He smeared the cloth over his face and flung it to the floor. McLendon stood in the floor and cursed the others. Another rose and moved toward him. The remainder sat uncomfortable, not looking at one another, then one by one they rose and joined him. 95

100

The barber picked the cloth from the floor. He began to fold it neatly. "Boys, don't do that. Will Mayes never done it. I know."

"Come on," McLendon said. He whirled. From his hip pocket protruded the butt[14] of a heavy automatic pistol. They went out. The screen door crashed behind them reverberant[15] in the dead air. 105

The barber wiped the razor carefully and swiftly, and put it away, and ran to the rear, and took his hat from the wall. "I'll be back as soon as I can," he said to the other barbers. "I can't let—" He went out, running. The two other barbers followed him to the door and caught it on the rebound,[16]

---

11. **he arrested himself**   he stopped himself
12. **roving his gaze**   looking all around
13. **prone**   lying down, reclining
14. **the butt of a pistol**   the handle of a pistol
15. **reverberant**   echoing
16. **caught it on the rebound**   caught it as it swung open again

leaning out and looking up the street after him. The air was flat and dead. It   110
had a metallic taste at the base of the tongue.

"What can he do?" the first said. The second one was saying "Jees Christ,
Jees Christ" under his breath. "I'd just as lief be Will Mayes as Hawk,[17] if he
gets McLendon riled."

"Jees Christ, Jees Christ," the second whispered.   115

"You reckon he really done it to her?" the first said.

II

She was thirty-eight or thirty-nine. She lived in a small frame house with
her invalid mother and a thin, sallow, unflagging[18] aunt, where each
morning between ten and eleven she would appear on the porch in a lace-
trimmed boudoir cap, to sit swinging in the porch swing until noon. After   120
dinner she lay down for a while, until the afternoon began to cool. Then, in
one of the three or four new voile[19] dresses which she had each summer,
she would go downtown to spend the afternoon in the stores with the other
ladies, where they would handle the goods and haggle[20] over the prices in
cold, immediate voices, without any intention of buying.   125

She was of comfortable people—not the best in Jefferson, but good
people enough—and she was still on the slender side of ordinary looking,
with a bright, faintly haggard manner and dress. When she was young she
had had a slender, nervous body and a sort of hard vivacity which had
enabled her for a time to ride upon the crest of the town's social life[21] as   130
exemplified by the high school party and church social[22] period of her
contemporaries while still children enough to be unclassconscious.

She was the last to realize that she was losing ground[23]; that those
among whom she had been a little brighter and louder flame than any other
were beginning to learn the pleasure of snobbery—male—and   135
retaliation[24]—female. That was when her face began to wear that bright,
haggard look. She still carried it to parties on shadowy porticoes and summer
lawns, like a mask or a flag, with that bafflement of furious repudiation of
truth[25] in her eyes. One evening at a party she heard a boy and two girls, all
schoolmates, talking. She never accepted another invitation.   140

She watched the girls with whom she had grown up as they married and
got homes and children, but no man ever called on[26] her steadily until the
children of the other girls had been calling her "aunty" for several years, the
while their mothers told them in bright voices about how popular Aunt
Minnie had been as a girl. Then the town began to see her driving on   145
Sunday afternoons with the cashier in the bank. He was a widower of about

---

17. **I'd just as lief be Will Mayes as Hawk**   The
    customer is implying that Hawk will be in the same
    bad situation as Will Mayes
18. **unflagging**   untiring
19. **voile**   thin, sheer fabric
20. **haggle**   argue or bargain

21. **to ride upon the crest of the town's social life**
    to be very popular
22. **church social**   party held by a church
23. **losing ground**   failing to keep one's position
24. **retaliation**   revenge
25. **repudiation of truth**   rejection of truth
26. **called on**   visited

forty—a high-colored man, smelling always faintly of the barber shop or of whisky. He owned the first automobile in town, a red runabout; Minnie had the first motoring bonnet and veil the town ever saw. Then the town began to say: "Poor Minnie." "But she is old enough to take care of herself," others said. That was when she began to ask her old schoolmates that their children call her "cousin" instead of "aunty."

It was twelve years now since she had been relegated into adultery by public opinion, and eight years since the cashier had gone to a Memphis bank, returning for one day each Christmas, which he spent at an annual bachelors' party at the hunting club on the river. From behind their curtains the neighbors would see the party pass, and during the over-the-way Christmas day visiting[27] they would tell her about him, about how well he looked, and how they heard that he was prospering[28] in the city, watching with bright, secret eyes her haggard, bright face. Usually by that hour there would be the scent of whisky on her breath. It was supplied her by a youth, a clerk at the soda fountain: "Sure; I buy it for the old gal. I reckon[29] she's entitled to a little fun."

Her mother kept to her room[30] altogether now; the gaunt aunt ran the house. Against that background Minnie's bright dresses, her idle and empty days, had a quality of furious unreality. She went out in the evenings only with women now, neighbors, to the moving pictures. Each afternoon she dressed in one of the new dresses and went downtown alone, where her young "cousins" were already strolling in the late afternoons with their delicate, silken heads and thin, awkward arms and conscious hips, clinging to one another or shrieking and giggling with paired boys in the soda fountain when she passed and went on along the serried[31] store fronts, in the doors of which the sitting and lounging men did not even follow her with their eyes any more.

III

The barber went swiftly up the street where the sparse lights, insect-swirled, glared in rigid and violent suspension in the lifeless air. The day had died in a pall[32] of dust; above the darkened square, shrouded[33] by the spent dust, the sky was as clear as the inside of a brass bell. Below the east was a rumor of the twice-waxed moon.[34]

When he overtook them McLendon and three others were getting into a car parked in an alley. McLendon stooped his thick head, peering out beneath the top. "Changed your mind, did you?" he said. "Damn good thing; by God, tomorrow when this town hears about how you talked tonight—"

"Now, now," the other ex-soldier said. "Hawkshaw's all right. Come on, Hawk; jump in."

---

27. **over-the-way Christmas day visiting**   visiting neighbors on Christmas day
28. **prospering**   doing well financially
29. **reckon**   think (dialect)
30. **kept to her room**   stayed in her room
31. **serried**   pressed close together
32. **pall**   covering
33. **shrouded**   concealed or hidden *is always related to death*
34. **twice-waxed moon**   suggestion of a very large, bright moon (poetic)

"Will Mayes never done it, boys," the barber said. "If anybody done it.   185
Why, you all know well as I do there ain't any town where they got better
niggers than us. And you know how a lady will kind of think things about
men when there ain't any reason to, and Miss Minnie anyway—"

"Sure, sure," the soldier said. "We're just going to talk to him a little;   190
that's all."

"Talk, hell!" Butch said. "When we're through with the—"

"Shut up, for God's sake!" the soldier said. "Do you want everybody in
town—"

"Tell them, by God!" McLendon said. "Tell every one of the sons that'll
let a white woman—"   195

"Let's go; let's go: here's the other car." The second car slid squealing
out of a cloud of dust at the alley mouth. McLendon started his car and took
the lead. Dust lay like fog in the street. The street lights hung nimbused[35] as
in water. They drove on out of town.

A rutted lane turned at right angles. Dust hung above it too, and above   200
all the land. The dark bulk of the ice plant, where the Negro Mayes was
night watchman, rose against the sky. "Better stop here, hadn't we?" the
soldier said. McLendon did not reply. He hurled the car up and slammed to
a stop, the headlights glaring on the blank wall.

"Listen here, boys," the barber said; "if he's here, don't that prove he   205
never done it? Don't it? If it was him, he would run. Don't you see he
would?" The second car came up and stopped. McLendon got down; Butch
sprang down beside him. "Listen, boys," the barber said.

"Cut the lights off!" McLendon said. The breathless dark rushed down.
There was no sound in it save[36] their lungs as they sought air in the parched   210
dust in which for two months they had lived; then the diminishing crunch of
McLendon's and Butch's feet, and a moment later McLendon's voice:

"Will! . . . Will!"

Below the east the wan hemorrhage[37] of the moon increased. It heaved
above the ridge, silvering the air, the dust, so that they seemed to breathe,   215
live, in a bowl of molten lead. There was no sound of nightbird nor insect, no
sound save their breathing and a faint ticking of contracting metal about the
cars. Where their bodies touched one another they seemed to sweat dryly, for
no more moisture came. "Christ!" a voice said; "let's get out of here."

But they didn't move until vague noises began to grow out of the darkness   220
ahead; then they got out and waited tensely in the breathless dark. There was
another sound: a blow, a hissing expulsion of breath and McLendon cursing in
undertone. They stood a moment longer, then they ran forward. They ran in a
stumbling clump, as though they were fleeing something. "Kill him, kill the
son," a voice whispered. McLendon flung them back.   225

"Not here," he said. "Get him into the car." "Kill him, kill the black son!"
the voice murmured. They dragged the Negro to the car. The barber had

---

35. **nimbused**   like a shining circle of light   37. **wan hemorrhage**   pale bleeding
36. **save**   except

waited beside the car. He could feel himself sweating and he knew he was
going to be sick at the stomach.

"What is it, captains?" the Negro said. "I ain't done nothing. 'Fore God, 230
Mr John." Someone produced handcuffs. They worked busily about the
Negro as though he were a post, quiet, intent, getting in one another's way.
He submitted to the handcuffs, looking swiftly and constantly from dim face
to dim face. "Who's here, captains?" he said, leaning to peer into the faces
until they could feel his breath and smell his sweaty reek. He spoke a name 235
or two. "What you all say I done, Mr John?"

McLendon jerked the car door open. "Get in!" he said.

The Negro did not move. "What you all going to do with me, Mr John? I
ain't done nothing. White folks, captains, I ain't done nothing: I swear 'fore
God." He called another name. 240

"Get in!" McLendon said. He struck the Negro. The others expelled their
breath in a dry hissing and struck him with random blows and he whirled
and cursed them, and swept his manacled[38] hands across their faces and
slashed the barber upon the mouth, and the barber struck him also. "Get
him in there," McLendon said. They pushed at him. He ceased struggling 245
and got in and sat quietly as the others took their places. He sat between the
barber and the soldier, drawing his limbs in so as not to touch them, his
eyes going swiftly and constantly from face to face. Butch clung to the
running board.[39] The car moved on. The barber nursed his mouth with his
handkerchief. 250

"What's the matter, Hawk?" the soldier said.

"Nothing," the barber said. They regained the high road and turned
away from town. The second car dropped back out of the dust. They went
on, gaining speed; the final fringe of houses dropped behind.

"Goddamn, he stinks!" the soldier said. 255

"We'll fix that," the drummer in the front beside McLendon said. On the
running board Butch cursed into the hot rush of air. The barber leaned
suddenly forward and touched McLendon's arm.

"Let me out, John," he said.

"Jump out, niggerlover," McLendon said without turning his head. He 260
drove swiftly. Behind them the sourceless lights of the second car glared in
the dust. Presently McLendon turned into a narrow road. It was rutted with
disuse. It led back to an abandoned brick kiln[40]—a series of reddish
mounds and weed- and vine-choked vats[41] without bottom. It had been
used for pasture once, until one day the owner missed one of his mules. 265
Although he prodded carefully in the vats with a long pole, he could not
even find the bottom of them.

"John," the barber said.

"Jump out, then," McLendon said, hurling the car along the ruts. Beside
the barber the Negro spoke: 270

---

38. **manacled** handcuffed
39. **running board** a ledge on the side of an
automobile which a passenger could step on

40. **kiln** a furnace used for baking, burning, or drying
41. **vats** large containers for holding liquids

"Mr Henry."

The barber sat forward. The narrow tunnel of the road rushed up and past. Their motion was like an extinct furnace blast: cooler, but utterly dead. The car bounded from rut to rut.

"Mr Henry," the Negro said.   275

The barber began to tug furiously at the door. "Look out, there!" the soldier said, but the barber had already kicked the door open and swung onto the running board. The soldier leaned across the Negro and grasped at him, but he had already jumped. The car went on without checking speed.

The impetus hurled him crashing through dust-sheathed weeds, into the   280
ditch. Dust puffed about him, and in a thin, vicious crackling of sapless stems he lay choking and retching until the second car passed and died away. Then he rose and limped on until he reached the high road and turned toward town, brushing at his clothes with his hands. The moon was higher, riding high and clear of the dust at last, and after a while the town began to glare   285
beneath the dust. He went on, limping. Presently he heard cars and the glow of them grew in the dust behind him and he left the road and crouched⁴²
again in the weeds until they passed. McLendon's car came last now. There were four people in it and Butch was not on the running board.

They went on; the dust swallowed them; the glare and the sound died   290
away. The dust of them hung for a while, but soon the eternal dust absorbed it again. The barber climbed back onto the road and limped on toward town.

IV

As she dressed for supper on that Saturday evening, her own flesh felt like fever. Her hands trembled among the hooks and eyes, and her eyes had   295
a feverish look, and her hair swirled crisp and crackling under the comb. While she was still dressing the friends called for her and sat while she donned her sheerest underthings and stockings and a new voile dress. "Do you feel strong enough to go out?" they said, their eyes bright too, with a dark glitter. "When you have had time to get over the shock, you must tell   300
us what happened. What he said and did; everything."

In the leafed darkness, as they walked toward the square, she began to breathe deeply, something like a swimmer preparing to dive, until she ceased trembling, the four of them walking slowly because of the terrible heat and out of solicitude⁴³ for her. But as they neared the square she began   305
to tremble again, walking with her head up, her hands clenched at her sides, their voices about her murmurous, also with that feverish, glittering quality of their eyes. They entered the square, she in the center of the group, fragile in her fresh dress. She was trembling worse. She walked slower and slower, as children eat ice cream, her head up and her eyes bright in the haggard   310
banner of her face, passing the hotel and the coatless drummers in chairs along the curb looking around at her: "That's the one: see? The one in pink

---

42. **crouched** bent low   43. **solicitude** attentive care

in the middle." "Is that her? What did they do with the nigger? Did they—?" "Sure. He's all right." "All right, is he?" "Sure. He went on a little trip." Then the drug store, where even the young men lounging in the doorway tipped their hats and followed with their eyes the motion of her hips and legs when she passed. 315

They went on, passing the lifted hats of the gentlemen, the suddenly ceased voices, deferent, protective. "Do you see?" the friends said. Their voices sounded like long, hovering sighs of hissing exultation.[44] "There's not a Negro on the square. Not one." 320

They reached the picture show. It was like a miniature fairyland with its lighted lobby and colored lithographs of life caught in its terrible and beautiful mutations. Her lips began to tingle. In the dark, when the picture began, it would be all right; she could hold back the laughing so it would not waste away so fast and so soon. So she hurried on before the turning faces, the undertones of low astonishment, and they took their accustomed places where she could see the aisle against the silver glare and the young men and girls coming in two and two against it. 325

The lights flicked away; the screen glowed silver, and soon life began to unfold, beautiful and passionate and sad, while still the young men and girls entered, scented and sibilant[45] in the half dark, their paired backs in silhouette delicate and sleek, their slim, quick bodies awkward, divinely young, while beyond them the silver dream accumulated, inevitably on and on. She began to laugh. In trying to suppress it, it made more noise than ever; heads began to turn. Still laughing, her friends raised her and led her out, and she stood at the curb, laughing on a high, sustained note, until the taxi came up and they helped her in. 330 335

They removed the pink voile and the sheer underthings and the stockings, and put her to bed, and cracked ice for her temples, and sent for the doctor. He was hard to locate, so they ministered to her[46] with hushed ejaculations, renewing the ice and fanning her. While the ice was fresh and cold she stopped laughing and lay still for a time, moaning only a little. But soon the laughing welled again and her voice rose screaming. 340

"Shhhhhhhhhhh! Shhhhhhhhhhhhhhh!" they said, freshening the icepack, smoothing her hair, examining it for gray; "poor girl!" Then to one another: "Do you suppose anything really happened?" their eyes darkly aglitter, secret and passionate. "Shhhhhhhhhh! Poor girl! Poor Minnie!" 345

V

It was midnight when McLendon drove up to his neat new house. It was trim and fresh as a birdcage and almost as small, with its clean, green-and-white paint. He locked the car and mounted the porch and entered. His wife rose from a chair beside the reading lamp. McLendon stopped in the floor and stared at her until she looked down. 350

---

44. **exultation** great joy
45. **sibilant** hissing

46. **ministered to her** helped her

"Look at that clock," he said, lifting his arm, pointing. She stood before   355
him, her face lowered, a magazine in her hands. Her face was pale, strained,
and weary-looking. "Haven't I told you about sitting up like this, waiting to
see when I come in?"

"John," she said. She laid the magazine down. Poised on the balls of his
feet, he glared at her with his hot eyes, his sweating face.   360

"Didn't I tell you?" He went toward her. She looked up then. He caught
her shoulder. She stood passive, looking at him.

"Don't, John. I couldn't sleep. . . . The heat; something. Please, John.
You're hurting me."

"Didn't I tell you?" He released her and half struck, half flung her across   365
the chair, and she lay there and watched him quietly as he left the room.
He went on through the house, ripping off his shirt, and on the dark,
screened porch at the rear he stood and mopped his head and shoulders
with the shirt and flung it away. He took the pistol from his hip and laid it
on the table beside the bed, and sat on the bed and removed his shoes, and   370
rose and slipped his trousers off. He was sweating again already, and he
stooped and hunted furiously for the shirt. At last he found it and wiped his
body again, and, with his body pressed against the dusty screen, he stood
panting. There was no movement, no sound, not even an insect. The dark
world seemed to lie stricken[47] beneath the cold moon and the lidless stars. ◆   375

---

47. **stricken** overcome by disease or sorrow

PART **1** **FIRST READING**

A. Thinking about the Story

Were you frightened and appalled by the atmosphere of violence in this
story? Consider the barber's actions, and think how you might react
under similar pressure.

B. Understanding the Plot

The following questions are grouped into sections matching those in the
story:

SECTION I

1. What is the accusation against Will Mayes? Is there concrete proof to
   support this accusation?

2. Why does the barber refuse to believe the accusation? Analyze his
   reasons carefully.

racail bigot

3. Why are the men—and especially McLendon—so unwilling to consider the possibility of Mayes's innocence?

4. Why does the barber decide to go with the mob?

SECTION II

1. What kind of life is Minnie leading at the time of the accusation?

2. What do we learn about her younger life?

3. Explain the sentence: "She was the last to realize she was losing ground." (line 133) What "truth" was she repudiating? (line 139)

4. Why do the townspeople say "Poor Minnie" after she is seen in the frequent company of the widower?

5. What happened to Minnie after her relationship with the widower ended?

SECTION III

1. Why does McLendon stop the men from killing Mayes immediately? What does he plan to do with Will's body?

2. How does the barber behave toward Will in the car?

3. Why won't McLendon allow the barber to leave the car voluntarily?

4. Does the barber fear for his life? Explain your answer.

SECTION IV

1. Why are Minnie's friends paying her so much attention?

2. What is different for Minnie about her walk to the movie theater that evening?

3. What are her friends compared to in lines 319–320? Do you think the comparison is an apt one?

4. What does Minnie's wild laughter tell us about her frame of mind?

SECTION V

1. Why is McLendon angry at his wife for waiting up for him?

2. Does he behave differently at home from the way he acts outside?

3. What is the dominant image in the concluding sentence to the story?

P A R T ◆2◆ **S E C O N D   R E A D I N G**

A. Exploring Themes

You are now ready to reread "Dry September." Try to analyze the complex motives of the characters, which spring from psychological and racist sources. Be sensitive to the atmosphere created by the constant references to the intense heat and dust in which the characters move.

1. What attitudes toward women prevail in the society of "Dry September"?
2. How is social class an issue in the story?
3. What concepts of justice are raised in "Dry September"?
4. Do Minnie's friends help her or harm her? Explain your answer.
5. What is the role of the heat and dust in the story? Explain the significance of the title.
6. What is the importance of the relationship of the past to the present in the story?

B. Analyzing the Author's Style

Before you begin to work on this section, turn to the detailed explanation of atmosphere (page 274) and setting (page 282).

ATMOSPHERE AND SETTING

The **atmosphere** in "Dry September" is a compelling element of the story and is frequently heightened by Faulkner's detailed description of the **setting**. For example, in the first paragraph the immediate setting—the barber shop—is filled with an atmosphere of violence and dangerous excitement emanating from both inside and outside the shop. Faulkner instantly achieves this in his opening sentence with his reference to the *bloody September twilight,* which describes a sunset, but also connotes an evening of injury or death. He continues the image of destruction with mention of a rumor that has spread *like a fire in dry grass.* Similarly, inside, the air is so stale and the odors so strong that we feel the suffocation of the characters and their corresponding inability to think clearly.

1. How does the entrance of McLendon intensify the atmosphere in the first section?
2. What expressions in lines 106–111 of Section I reinforce the atmosphere? Explain how the language does this.

3. What kind of atmosphere dominates the opening paragraph of Section II? How does it differ from that in Section I? How does the setting contribute to this atmosphere?

4. In Section II, lines 153–162, Faulkner evokes more atmosphere. What is it and what words reinforce it?

5. Look carefully at the imagery in the opening paragraph of Section III. How do the metaphors create the atmosphere?
   Note: For information on metaphor, see page 280.

6. How does the setting where the murder of Will Mayes is committed reinforce the horror of the event?

7. The verbs used in connection with McLendon throughout the story have something in common. What is it? Explain how these verbs contribute to the atmosphere of the story.

C. Judging for Yourself

Express yourself as personally as you like in your answers to the following questions:

1. What do you think happened to the barber afterward?

2. Do you think any of the men were ever officially accused of the murder of Will Mayes?

3. In your opinion did Minnie mean to have Mayes killed as a result of her accusation?

4. What do you imagine Minnie's life will be like after the excitement dies down?

5. In your view could anyone have prevented the tragedy? Give reasons for your answer.

D. Making Connections

1. Have you ever been the victim of a racist attack or known anyone who has?

2. What is the climate like in your country? To what extent do you think the weather can influence people's actions in general?

3. What do you know about the Ku Klux Klan? Is there or has there been a similar organization in your country?

4. Is it considered improper in your culture for a woman to have an affair but all right for a man to do so?

5. How common is sexual harassment in your society? What is the attitude toward rape?

E. Debate

Debate the proposal: It is sometimes permissible to take the law into one's own hands.

P A R T ◈ **F O C U S O N L A N G U A G E**

A. Main Clauses

Faulkner's writing is characterized by long, leisurely sentences in which clause follows clause to create a dramatic effect.

A **clause** is a group of words with a subject and a verb. Every sentence contains at least one **main clause**, which is an independent clause that stands on its own and does not depend on any other clause for its existence.

A sentence that contains more than one clause may be a *compound* or a *complex* sentence.

A COMPOUND SENTENCE

A **compound sentence** consists of two or more main clauses only. The clauses are linked to each other within the sentence by the conjunctions *and, but, or, nor, for, yet,* or *so.* For example:

> *The screen door **crashed** open. A man **stood** in the floor, his feet apart. . . . His name **was** McLendon. He **had commanded** troops at the front in France and [he] **had been decorated** for valor.* (lines 56–60)

This paragraph is easy to read and understand. It is composed solely of main clauses; each verb is part of an independent clause. The last sentence, with its two clauses linked by *and,* is a compound sentence.

A COMPLEX SENTENCE

A **complex sentence** consists of one main clause and one or more subordinate clauses. **Subordinate clauses** are not independent clauses, but instead rely on other clauses for their existence. They may be noun, adjectival, or adverbial. For specific information on and practice with noun clauses see "The Catbird Seat" (page 250); for adjectival clauses see "The Swimmer" (page 201); and for adverbial clauses see "Like a Winding Sheet" (page 221).

To better understand Faulkner's sentences—and the complex syntax of authors like Katherine Mansfield, Nadine Gordimer, and James Thurber—it is helpful to break down the sentences into their separate components.

Reread lines 367–375 in Section V. Answer the following questions:

1. How many main clauses can you find in this paragraph? Write each one down and underline its verb.
2. Is "ripping off his shirt" a clause? Explain your answer.

   is a phrase.

3. How many compound sentences are in the paragraph?

It is not always easy to find the main clauses in "Dry September." Look at the sentence below. It is long and tricky, but when we find the main clause it becomes easier to understand the structure of the sentence and, therefore, its meaning too.

> *Attacked, insulted, frightened: none of them, gathered in the barber shop on that Saturday evening where the ceiling fan stirred without freshening it, the vitiated air, sending back upon them in recurrent surges of stale pomade and lotion, their own stale breath and odors, knew exactly what had happened.* (lines 3–7)

1. What is the main clause? Write it down in its entirety.
2. What is the subordinate clause? Write it down.
3. Why isn't "attacked, insulted, frightened" a clause? Are there any other parts of the sentence that look like clauses, but aren't? Name them and say why they aren't clauses.
4. Apply this same principle of breaking down a complex sentence into its main and subordinate clauses to any other difficult passage in the story. Does it make it easier to understand the writing?

B. Building Vocabulary Skills

"Dry September" has many examples of words and expressions that can be used in more than one way. The first sentence of the pairs that follow is taken directly from the text, while the second uses the italicized word or expression in an entirely different manner. With the help of your dictionary explain the difference between the pairs of italicized words.

1. "Do you mean to tell me you're a white man and you'll *stand for* it?" (lines 47–48)

   The political party I join will have to *stand for* racial equality.

2. He *arrested* himself reclining, his head lifted, the barber still pressing him down. (lines 70–71)

   He was such an honest policeman he would have *arrested* his mother if he'd had to.

3. She was of *comfortable* people—not the best in Jefferson, but good people enough. . . . (lines 126–127)

   She tried to find a *comfortable* position, but her painful leg prevented this.

4. Her mother *kept to* her room altogether now. (line 163)

   She *kept to* herself the news that she was pregnant.

5. The car went on without *checking* speed. (line 279)

   Police officers use radar for *checking* the speed of vehicles on the roads.

Faulkner uses the following verbs to express motion:

spring (line 24)	stumble (line 224)
fling (line 97)	bound (line 274)
stroll (line 168)	limp (line 283)
hurl (line 203)	swirl (line 296)
heave (line 214)	lounge (line 315)

Some of these verbs suggest quick movement and others suggest slow movement. Put these verbs into two columns, one for the first category of movement and the other for the second category.

Add five more appropriate verbs of your own to each column. Write sentences to illustrate their correct use.

PART ◆4◆ **WRITING ACTIVITIES**

1. Imagine you are one of the following characters from "Dry September": Minnie, Will Mayes, the barber, McLendon, or Mrs. McLendon. Write a monologue in which you express what is going on in your character's head at one dramatic moment in the story. Try to remain true to what you know about the character regarding the way he or she thinks, speaks, and acts.

2. Write a fictional account in which an act of violence is committed. Try to include complex sentences as Faulkner does in "Dry September" to help create the setting and atmosphere.

3. *To Kill a Mockingbird* by Harper Lee, *Beloved* by Toni Morrison, and *Go Tell It on the Mountain* by James Baldwin are three novels that confront the racism in American society. Write a two-page essay describing a book or short story you have read that deals with discrimination and that has impressed you deeply. Outline the nature of the discrimination and say who the victims are. Explain why you were so affected. In your conclusion, analyze what actions you can take as an individual to help fight discrimination.

4. Nadine Gordimer in "Is There Nowhere Else Where We Can Meet?" (page 228) and William Faulkner in "Dry September" deal with the harsh consequences of racism in very different ways. In a two-page essay compare the central act of violence in each story, and discuss the different approaches of the two authors to the topic. Say which story you prefer and why.

EXPLANATION OF LITERARY TERMS

◆◆

ONE of the keys to appreciating literature is an awareness of the literary devices writers use to enrich their language and create complexity within a story. In order to understand the *plot* (the elements of character, time, place, and action in a story) and the *themes* (the underlying connections that reveal the inner truths of the story), you should be familiar with such stylistic devices as *metaphor, simile, symbol,* and *point of view.* As you read the short stories in this book, you will be directed to the following explanations of literary terms:

Alliteration 起頭押韻 *alliterate (vt, vi)* *alliterative (a)* *alliteratively (ad)*

In alliteration a consonant—usually the first one in a word—is repeated in succeeding words to produce a certain effect. Poets most frequently use alliteration; the full effect of the sounds is heard when the verse is read aloud.

In "Dry September" (page 256), William Faulkner creates the excited, whispering undercurrent amongst an audience in a movie theater with the repetition of the **s** consonant in this description:

> . . . the **s**creen glowed **s**ilver, and **s**oon life began to unfold, beautiful and passionate and **s**ad, while **s**till the young men and girls entered, **c**entered and **s**ibilant in the half dark, their paired backs in **s**ilhouette delicate and **s**leek, their **s**lim, quick bodies awkward, divinely young. . . . (lines 330–334)

Katherine Mansfield in the following sentence from "Miss Brill" (page 178) repeats the short, sharp **st** sound to reinforce the jerky, uncertain movements of a small child in the park, as well as the agitated walk of its mother:

> And sometimes a tiny **st**aggerer came suddenly rocking into the open from the trees, **st**opped, **st**ared, as suddenly sat down "flop" until its small high-**st**epping mother, like a young hen, rushed scolding to its rescue. (lines 53–56)

For practice with alliteration see "Snow" (page 25).

Anachronism

Anachronism refers to a situation in which people say, do, or see something that is inconsistent with the time they live in. For example, if a boy were to play with World War II mementos in a story set in 1914, this would constitute an anachronism. Similarly, teenagers in the 1990s could not use 1940s slang without being thoroughly inconsistent with their time. And if a character in a novel set in the nineteenth century were to look up and spot an airplane, this too would indicate an anachronism.

For practice with anachronism see "The Kugelmass Episode" (page 53).

Atmosphere

Atmosphere refers to a dominant *feeling* in a story. It points to the mental and moral environment of the story and is different from the *setting*, which describes the physical environment in which the characters operate. Frequently the setting helps create the atmosphere.

Nadine Gordimer opens her story "Is There Nowhere Else Where We Can Meet?" (page 228) with a description that immediately creates an atmosphere of tranquillity:

> *It was a cool grey morning and the air was like smoke. . . . The coat collar pressed rough against her neck and her cheeks were softly cold as if they had been washed in ice water. She breathed gently with the air. . . . Overhead a dove purred.* (lines 1–7)

By the end of the story the atmosphere has become charged with fear:

> *The young mimosas closed in, lowering a thicket of twigs right to the ground, but she tore herself through, feeling the dust in her eyes and the scaly twigs hooking at her hair.* (lines 81–83)

Ann Petry in "Like a Winding Sheet" (page 210) evokes the tension in a factory with her description of the unbearable noise that the workers must endure every day:

> *The machines had started full blast. The whirr and the grinding made the building shake, made it impossible to hear conversations. The men and women at the machines talked to each other but looking at them from just a little distance away, they appeared to be simply moving their lips because you couldn't hear what they were saying.* (lines 86–90)

For practice with atmosphere see "Dry September" (page 267).

Characterization: Round and Flat Characters

The English novelist and critic E. M. Forster divided characters into categories of round and flat. Round characters are fully formed, complex people who may act unpredictably and who in the course of the story, struggle and change, finally achieving a greater self-knowledge. Flat characters, in contrast, are one-dimensional, predictable people who do not change or in any way increase their self-awareness by the end of the story.

"The Rocking-Horse Winner" (page 80) and "The Catbird Seat" (page 240) contain examples of flat characters. In the first story, D. H. Lawrence presents the gardener in a static fashion. His conversation is limited to respectful references to his social superiors and never reveals his thoughts or feelings. At no time does he demonstrate awareness of his possible role in a boy's tragedy. In the second story, James Thurber portrays a woman whose behavior never varies: she expresses herself in a high-pitched, hysterical fashion in every situation and never stops to contemplate the human consequences of her actions.

By contrast, the young narrator in "My Oedipus Complex" (page 128) is an example of a round character. As the story progresses, we learn much about his inner thoughts and feelings and accompany him on his journey of growth, sharing with him his painfully gained independence and self-knowledge.

For practice with characterization see "The Kugelmass Episode" (page 53).

Colloquialism

Colloquial English is informal or conversational language. It echoes the natural, unforced speech rhythms and vocabulary of everyday speech. Such language is frequently livened with slang. The sentences are short and often bend the rules of grammar. In several of the stories colloquialisms go hand in hand with *dialect*. (See Dialect below.)

The characters in "The Kugelmass Episode" (page 42) express themselves very informally all the time. In the examples below the original dialogue is given first, followed by a more formal version in brackets. At his first meeting with the magician Persky, Kugelmass immediately asks him, *"What's your scam?"* (line 60) ["What are you scheming?"] Persky later assures Kugelmass, *"You could carry on all you like with a real winner. Then when you've had enough you give a yell, and I'll see you back here in a split second."* (lines 75–77) ["You could have as much sex as you like with your dream woman. Then when you've had enough, call me, and I'll bring you back immediately."]

Daphne Kugelmass is no less informal when she confronts her husband with, *"Where the hell do you go all the time? . . . You got a chippie stashed somewhere?"* (lines 204–206) ["Where in the world do you go all the time? Have you got another woman hidden away somewhere?"] Even Emma Bovary catches the mood of informality when she complains about her husband to her lover: *"Oh, Kugelmass,"* Emma sighed. *"What I have to put up with. Last night at dinner, Mr. Personality dropped off to sleep in the middle of the dessert course. I'm pouring my heart out about Maxim's and the ballet, and out of the blue I hear snoring."* (lines 176–179) ["Oh, Kugelmass, I have to endure so much. Last night at dinner, my boring husband fell asleep in the middle of the dessert course. I was explaining how I really felt about Maxim's and the ballet when suddenly I heard him snoring."]

For practice with colloquialisms see "Like a Winding Sheet" (page 219).

Dialect

Dialect is a variety of speech different from the standard language of the culture. It usually corresponds to such differences among population groups as geographical location, social class, or age. Writers use dialect to make their characters seem authentic. In the examples below the original dialogue is given first, followed by a more formal version in brackets. The characters in "Like a Winding Sheet" (page 210) speak with a distinctive black working-class voice. When a wife senses that something is wrong, she asks her husband, *"Whatsa matter? . . . You get bawled out by the boss or somep'n?"* (lines 268–269) ["What's the matter? Did your boss get angry and yell at you or did something else happen?"] He replies irritably, *"What you got to be always fooling with your hair for?"* (lines 275–276) ["Why are you always arranging your hair?"]

William Faulkner's stories are rich in the dialect of his native Mississippi, where the action takes place. In "Dry September" (page 256) black and white characters alike speak in their native idiom. A white client in the barber shop questions the truthfulness of a woman's claim to have been assaulted. *"Did it really happen? . . . This ain't the first man scare she ever had, like Hawkshaw says."* (lines 66–67) ["According to Hawkshaw, this isn't the first time she's claimed to have been frightened by a man."] The barber agrees, *"Boys, don't do that. Will Mayes never done it. I know."* (line 102) ["I'm certain that Will Mayes didn't do it."] Later, Will Mayes fearfully asks the leader of the lynch group, *"What you all going to do with me, Mr John? I ain't done nothing. White folks, captains, I ain't done nothing: I swear 'fore God."* (lines 238–240) ["What are all of you going to do with me, Mr. John? I haven't done anything. I swear before God."]

For practice with dialect see "Like a Winding Sheet" (page 219).

Dialogue

Stories vary widely in the amount and type of dialogue, or conversation, that is present. A story like "Teenage Wasteland" (page 112) has a great deal of dialogue, which reflects the characters and their situations and which helps push the plot along rapidly. At the other end of the spectrum is "The Swimmer" (page 188), in which the action moves at a leisurely pace and the dialogue, echoing the story's upper-class characters, is kept to a minimum. In "Dry September" (page 256) William Faulkner splits the story into scenes where the *dialect*-filled dialogue of the men propels the action and scenes where lengthy descriptions prevail and the central character, Minnie, maintains an eerie silence. (See Dialect above.) Then, in stories like "Disappearing" (page 168) and "Snow" (page 22) the narrator carries on an interior conversation; in "Disappearing" the natural cadences of everyday speech are reproduced, whereas in "Snow" the conversation is much more literary.

For practice with dialogue, see "The Kugelmass Episode" (page 52).

Ellipsis

Ellipsis means that parts of sentences or words are left out but can nevertheless be understood or inferred. A writer may use ellipsis to give the reader the impression of being in direct, unfiltered contact with the thoughts or feelings of a character or narrator. For example, in "The Kugelmass Episode" (page 42) when a wife reminds her husband of her father's forthcoming birthday, she says, *"My whole family will be there. We can see the twins. And Cousin Hamish. You should be more polite to Cousin Hamish—he likes you."* (lines 213–214) The sentence "And Cousin Hamish" is elliptical; the words *will be there* are omitted but understood. In turn, her husband's elliptical reply, *"Right, the twins"* (line 215), contains a wealth of unspoken hostility toward his wife and her family and a clear lack of interest in what she is saying.

   In "The Swimmer" (page 188) a woman is reluctant to spell out what she knows about her neighbor's situation. She remarks, *"Why we heard that you'd sold the house and that your poor children. . . ."* (line 248) Although her sentence is elliptical, it is clear that she stopped herself before saying something more about the unfortunate state of his children.

For practice with ellipsis see "Disappearing" (page 172).

Epiphany

Epiphany is a literary device in which a character experiences an unexpected flash of understanding about the true nature of a person or situation, deeply altering his or her perception of that individual or event. James Joyce, in particular, refined the use of epiphany, and this device is closely associated with him.

An example of epiphany occurs in "My Oedipus Complex" (page 136) when the narrator's father, on overhearing his son muttering to himself about the new baby, realizes in a moment of sudden intuition that he and his son share the same feelings toward the baby. This recognition helps forge a close new relationship between them.

For practice with epiphany see "Story of an Hour" (page 15).

Fable

A fable is a short story, often with animals in it, that is told to illustrate a moral. The moral is the lesson to be drawn from the story and is usually stated clearly at the end. Famous fabulists include Aesop, La Fontaine, and more recently, James Thurber.

For practice with fable see "The Rocking-Horse Winner" (page 93).

Flashback

The flashback is a narrative technique in which a narrator or character interrupts the present time and returns to the past. Through this device, some aspect of the character or incident is illuminated. Movie directors commonly employ flashbacks in order to condense the story and highlight the significance of certain events. Barbra Streisand does this most effectively in *Prince of Tides,* where the central character played by Nick Nolte is forced to relive a childhood rape, a reenactment that is crucial to his recovery as an adult. The movie *Fried Green Tomatoes* is narrated almost entirely in flashback as the elderly Jessica Tandy character, encouraged by a younger companion, recounts a series of dramatic events from her youth.

Virginia Woolf manipulates time in "The Legacy" (page 30), when a husband, on reading his wife's diary after her death, relives past events as if they were occurring in the present. In one such example he reenacts a political dinner at which he and his wife were present many years ago. *He could see her now sitting next to old Sir Edward; and making a conquest of that formidable old man, his chief.* (lines 118–119)

For practice with flashback see "Mother" (page 72).

Humor

Humor takes many forms. It ranges from the exaggerated situations, snappy lines, and parody (comical imitation) in "The Kugelmass Episode," through the sharp *irony* of "The Boarding House" and the gentle irony of "My Oedipus Complex," to the comic characterizations and ingeniously funny plot of "The Catbird Seat." (See Irony below.)

For practice with humor, see "The Kugelmass Episode" (page 53), "The Boarding House" (page 105), "My Oedipus Complex" (page 138), and "The Catbird Seat" (page 248).

Imagery

Imagery is used by writers to create vivid pictures that our senses (sight, touch, smell, hearing, and taste) respond to. The most effective writing contains striking and fresh images and avoids commonly used comparisons. Adjectival or descriptive writing is a dominant element of imagery. Often the language is figurative (not literal) and takes the form of *metaphors* and *similes*. (See Metaphor and Simile below.)
Almost every scene in "Dry September" (page 256) is filled with memorable imagery. The young people in a town parade visibly, audibly, and tangibly before us in the following lines:

> *Each afternoon she dressed in one of the new dresses and went downtown alone, where her young "cousins" were already strolling in the late afternoons with their delicate, silken heads and thin, awkward arms and conscious hips, clinging to one another or shrieking and giggling with paired boys in the soda fountain when she passed. . . .* (lines 166–171)

For practice with imagery see "The Boarding House" (page 106), "Disappearing" (page 172), and "Like a Winding Sheet" (page 220).

Inference

Frequently writers are interested in suggesting rather than explaining a theme or detail. This enables the writer to be subtle or indirect, leaving the reader to infer, or deduce, the writer's meaning. For example, in "My Oedipus Complex" (page 135, lines 284–288), when a wife refers to her husband's precious war memorabilia as "toys," she is suggesting that these are childish pleasures. Similarly, when the central character in "Miss Brill" (page 178, lines 7–9) takes out her fox fur, shakes out the moth-powder, and rubs the life back into its eyes, the reader is left to infer that she has not worn the fur cape for a long time.

For practice with inference see "Teenage Wasteland" (page 122) and "The Model" (page 150).

Irony

Irony occurs when a person says one thing but really means something else. It also exists when a person does something that has the opposite effect from what he or she intended. It can be used to convey both the seriousness and humor of situations. For example, when a woman in "Story of an Hour" (page 12) begs her sister to open the door, saying, "You will make yourself ill" (line 67), the irony lies in her ignorance of the fact that her sister has indeed never been happier in her life. Another example of irony is found in "My Oedipus Complex" (page 129, lines 54–56, and page 30, lines 108–122) when a small boy's prayers regarding his father's safe return from the war are answered, yet he finds himself in a worse position as a result of his father's presence.

For practice with irony see "Can-Can" (page 7) and "The Boarding House" (page 105).

Metaphor

A metaphor is an implied comparison in which one element is described in terms of another to create a connection. Unlike a *simile*, in which the two parts of the comparison are united by *like* or *as*, a metaphor is more indirect, and the reader has to work at understanding the two elements involved. (See Simile below.) For example, it is said of a character in "The Rocking-Horse Winner" (page 85) that *his eyes were blue fire.* (lines 208–209) In this instance, the two elements being compared are the boy's eyes and fire. The image is further compounded by the addition of the color blue to both parts of the comparison. There is a sustained metaphor in "The Swimmer" (page 190) in which all the swimming pools in the area are combined to form a river in the main character's imagination and the green grass surrounding them is referred to as the fertile river banks: *Oh, how bonny and lush were the banks of the Lucinda River!* (lines 86–87)

For practice with metaphor see "Story of an Hour" (page 16), "A Short Digest of a Long Novel" (page 64), and "Is There Nowhere Else Where We Can Meet?" (page 233).

Personification

Personification is a figure of speech in which animals or things are given human characteristics. Like *metaphors* and *similes*, personification heightens our imaginative response to what is being described. (See Metaphor above and Simile below.) For example, in "My Oedipus Complex" (page 131), the narrator observes, *Dawn was just breaking, with a guilty air.* (line 128) Here dawn, a natural phenomenon, is characterized as displaying the behavior of someone who has done something wrong.

Personification pervades the following scene in "The Rocking-Horse Winner" (page 86) in the form of the whispering house, which torments its residents and which stands for the parents who are never satisfied with what they have:

> *"But what are you going to do with your money?" asked the uncle.*
> *"Of course," said the boy, "I started it for mother. She said she had no luck, because father is unlucky, so I thought if **I** was lucky, it might stop whispering."*
> *"What might stop whispering?"*
> *"Our house. I **hate** our house for whispering."* (lines 285–290)

For practice with personification see "Story of an Hour" (page 16) and "Never" (page 162).

Point of View

Point of view refers to the specific character or narrator through whose eyes all or part of the story unfolds. What the narrator or character knows or is ignorant of will affect his or her view of the action. When reading a story, it is important to be alert to the narrator's prejudices, which will certainly influence the way he or she perceives the action and thus the telling of the story.

Stories are usually narrated in the first or third person. A story narrated in the first person means that it is told by a participating character using the pronoun *I.* In first-person narration the point of view of the narrator is necessarily subjective and incomplete, since he or she is not granted a full view of the action and does not have access to other characters' thoughts. "My Oedipus Complex" (page 128), which is filtered through the limited vision of a five-year-old boy, is narrated in the first person.

A story narrated in the third person is told by a narrator using the pronouns *he, she,* and *they.* A third-person narrator may have either *total omniscience* (the narrator is not a participant in the story and has a complete view of the characters and events) or *limited omniscience* (the narrator can penetrate the thoughts of one or two characters only and provides a subjective view of characters and events). An omniscient narrator relentlessly unfolds the tragic events in "Dry September" (page 256), and a narrator with limited omniscience presents "The Catbird Seat" primarily through the perspective of its main character (page 240).

Very rarely are stories narrated in the second person using the pronoun *you* as a direct address to the reader. One such example occurs when John Cheever unexpectedly and briefly shifts the point of view in

"The Swimmer" (page 192) by abruptly drawing the reader into the story: *Had you gone for a Sunday afternoon ride that day you might have seen him, close to naked, standing on the shoulders of Route 424, waiting for a chance to cross.* (lines 171–173)

For practice with point of view, see "Snow" (page 25), "The Legacy" (page 37), and "Teenage Wasteland" (page 121).

Repetition

Repetition can be a most effective way of creating atmosphere or of pointing to a theme in a story. It can take the form of repetitive language as in the insistent, sinister refrain of "There must be more money" in "The Rocking-Horse Winner" (page 80, lines 33–42); or of the striking alliterative repetition of consonants in "A Short Digest of a Long Novel" (page 60) when a father suggests his daughter's hair is like "ma*ple po*lished to a *go*l*d*en *g*rain" (lines 6–7); or of repeated events as in the parallel walks a small boy takes with his father and mother in "My Oedipus Complex" (page 129, lines 51–56, and page 130, lines 81–99), which highlight the different ways the boy relates to each parent.

For practice with repetition see "Never" (page 162).

Setting

The setting of a story refers to the time and place in which the action unfolds. It can also include the society being depicted, as well as its values. The setting helps us understand the characters and themes of a story. For example, the descriptions of the dreary house in which a woman is trapped in "Never" (page 159) are an essential element in our understanding of her psychological damage. Likewise, the raw depiction of factory life in "Like a Winding Sheet" (page 213) is integral to the theme of the brutalization of a man. And, in "Miss Brill" (page 178), Katherine Mansfield devotes most of the story to the main character's view of scenes in a park. This focus heightens our awareness of the character's role as a lonely observer.

For practice with setting see "The Swimmer" (page 199) and "Dry September" (page 267).

Simile

A simile is an explicit comparison that contains the words *like* or *as*. This usually makes it quite easy to identify the two elements of the comparison. For example, in "Dry September" (page 261) William Faulkner writes, *Dust lay like fog in the street.* (line 198) In this comparison we can see the dust lying thick on the ground in the same way that fog covers the earth. In the same story a house is described as being *trim and fresh as a birdcage and almost as small, with its clean, green-and-white paint.* (page 264, lines 351–352) The comparison of the house to a birdcage is particularly effective since the house may also be seen as an extension of the small, fragile woman inside, who in turn is as helpless as a tiny bird against her husband's brutality. Another example of a simile is found in "My Oedipus Complex" (page 131), when the narrator wakes up feeling *like a bottle of champagne* (lines 123–124), which suggests that his mood is as bright and bubbly as the celebratory drink.

For practice with similes see "Story of an Hour" (page 16), "A Short Digest of a Long Novel" (page 64), "Miss Brill" (page 183), and "Is There Nowhere Else Where We Can Meet?" (page 233).

Symbol

A symbol may be a person, an object, or an action that represents something else because of its association with it. It is frequently a visible sign of something invisible. For example, newly fallen snow is recognized as a symbol of purity. Symbols may be general—the lion is a symbol of courage and strength, an olive branch is a symbol for peace, a cross represents Christianity, and a red rose stands for romantic love— or they may be particular, arising out of the story itself, and connected to a central theme. In "The Legacy" (page 31) a black coat is a generally accepted emblem of mourning, whereas the symbolism of the pine needle scene in "Is There Nowhere Else Where We Can Meet?" (pages 228–229) and the symbol of the fox fur in "Miss Brill" (page 178) are peculiar to these stories only and have no wider reference.

For practice with symbol see "Can-Can" (page 7) and "The Rocking-Horse Winner" (page 93).

Synecdoche （以部分表示全体，以特殊表示一般的叙述法，有时也有相反的情形。）

Synecdoche is a figure of speech in which a part is used to describe the whole or the whole is used for a part; the special is used for the general or the general for the special. Writers often employ synecdoche as a dramatic shorthand to focus sharply on an element of the story, as well as to express something in a striking fashion. For example, in "Mother" (page 70) Grace Paley writes: *She'd just quit the shop for the kitchen.* (lines 26–27) Here, the kitchen represents the house, so in a condensed way we learn that a mother gave up her job as a shop assistant for a life as a homemaker. On the other hand, a policeman might refer to himself as *the law*, a generalized expression standing for a special representative.

For practice with synecdoche see "Miss Brill" (page 183).

Tone

The tone of a story refers to the attitude of the writer or that of one of the characters in the story. For example, the tone may be humorous, sarcastic, ironic, cheerful, pessimistic, angry, unfeeling, or satirical. A story in which humor is the prevailing tone is "My Oedipus Complex" (page 128), while pessimism dominates "The Model" (page 146), anger pervades "Dry September" (page 256), and a tone of sad regret fills "Mother" (page 70).

For practice with tone see "The Boarding House" (page 105).

Understatement

Understatement occurs when a writer deliberately de-emphasizes the dialogue or action. There may be diverse reasons for doing this. In "Snow" (page 22) the narrator seems determined to keep her feelings under control, so she minimizes the drama of the breakup of her relationship and the death of a friend. In contrast, James Thurber in "The Catbird Seat" (page 240) uses understatement to heighten the comedy of the story's plot and its characters.

For practice with understatement see "The Catbird Seat" (page 248).

TEXT CREDITS

◆◆

Woody Allen. "The Kugelmass Episode" from *Side Effects* by Woody Allen. Copyright © 1975, 1976, 1977, 1979, 1980 by Woody Allen. Reprinted by permission of Random House, Inc.

H. E. Bates. "Never" from *Day's End* by H. E. Bates. Copyright © 1928 by H. E. Bates. Reprinted by permission of the Estate of H. E. Bates as represented by Lawrence Pollinger Ltd.

Ann Beattie. "Snow" from *Where You'll Find Me* by Ann Beattie. Originally appeared in *Vanity Fair*. Copyright © 1983 and 1986 by Irony & Pity, Inc. Reprinted by permission of Simon & Schuster, Inc. and International Creative Management, Inc.

John Cheever. "The Swimmer" from *The Stories of John Cheever* by John Cheever. Copyright © 1964 by John Cheever. Reprinted by permission of Alfred A. Knopf, Inc. and Wylie, Aitken & Stone, Inc.

Kate Chopin. "The Story of an Hour." First published in *Vogue, IV* (December 1894).

William Faulkner. "Dry September" from *Collected Stories of William Faulkner* by William Faulkner. Copyright © 1930 and renewed 1958 by William Faulkner. Reprinted by permission of Random House, Inc. and Curtis Brown London.

Nadine Gordimer. "Is There Nowhere Else Where We Can Meet?" from *The Soft Voice of the Serpent* and *Selected Stories* by Nadine Gordimer. Copyright © 1951 by Nadine Gordimer. Reprinted by permission of Viking Penguin, a division of Penguin Books USA Inc. and Random Century Group, London.

James Joyce. "The Boarding House" from *Dubliners* by James Joyce. Copyright © 1916 by B. W. Heubsch. Definitive text copyright 1967 by the Estate of James Joyce. Reprinted by permission of Viking Penguin, a division of Penguin Books USA Inc., and the Estate of James Joyce.

D. H. Lawrence. "The Rocking-Horse Winner" from *Complete Short Stories of D. H. Lawrence* by D. H. Lawrence. Copyright © 1933 by the Estate of D. H. Lawrence, renewed 1961 by Angelo Ravagli and C. M. Weekley, Executors of the Estate of Frieda Lawrence. Reprinted by permission of Viking Penguin, a division of Penguin Books USA Inc. and Lawrence Pollinger Ltd., London.

PHOTO CREDITS

◆◆

Shu-hua Luo
Oct 26, 00